I0582276

REAPER'S GRACE · BOOK ONE

THE REAPER'S GAMBIT

JANET OPPEDISANO

The Reaper's Gambit
ISBN Digital: 978-1-7386998-2-7
ISBN Paperback: 978-1-7386998-3-4

Copyright © 2023
Cover Art Copyright © 2023

Cover Artist: Joy Author Design Studio

This is a work of fiction. Names, characters, places, and events are from the author's imagination or are used fictitiously. Any resemblance to actual persons, living or dead, business, companies, events, or places, is purely coincidental.

All rights reserved. No part of this publication may be used or reproduced in any form, whether by printing, photocopying, scanning, or otherwise without the written permission of the author, except for the use of brief quotations in a book review.

Ellis's List of the Best Things

1. Go for a walk in the park
2. Listen to music
3. Enjoy laughter
4. Have a birthday party
5. Eat a delicious meal
6. Go dancing
7. See a beautiful sunset
8. Do a good deed
9. Fall in love

Chapter 1

Danielle

An unnaturally frigid breeze swirled around me, far colder than normal for Central Park in mid-June. I pulled my thin cardigan tighter and focused on my book. Weeks ago, the pergola above me was covered in brilliant purple wisteria blossoms, but the flowers had died. As everything did. Now all the vine-laden structure did was shade me from the sun.

"Are you playing or just borrowing the table?" The man's voice was deep, soothing, tugging at something in the back of my brain. But its owner had ignored my book—my obvious message to the outside world saying, *Leave me alone. Find an empty seat.*

Keeping my eyes on the text, I said, "I'm waiting for my partner."

"Mind if I sit until they arrive?"

I tucked a finger in the book and closed it, looking up with a practiced glare. Late twenties or early thirties, like me, but with dark eyes more suited to one of the older men who frequented the Chess House. As though he'd already faced a lifetime of love and loss. He leaned on the park bench opposite me and smiled, radiating a kindness that pulled at my heart even more than his voice had.

His faded jeans were slim, showing off muscular legs, and his light-gray T-shirt stretched across his broad chest. Dark ivy league-cut hair, artfully messed, paired with an immaculate five o'clock shadow.

No way he was here for chess.

I'd set up my board the same way I did every Saturday—three and a half turns into the last game Dad and I had played, right down to the way he'd left his c6-knight facing b6. The stranger stretched for the board, his graceful fingers barely touching the black knight, swiveling it to face white.

"Stop!" My hand shot out, sending the book tumbling to the ground.

His brow creased, and he returned the piece to its original orientation, his hand retreating faster than I'd reacted. "You're very particular about your board."

I slumped against the wooden slats of the bench, breath rough, stroking the scar on the inside of my right palm. That was my father's knight. *Take it easy, Dani. No need to freak out.* But the intruder said nothing more about my ridiculous outburst. Instead, he knelt and picked up my book.

"*The Count of Monte Cristo*?" He smiled, and my lungs calmed, as though he fed serenity directly into them. Thumbing through the book, he stopped two-thirds through and read. "'There are two ways of seeing: with the body and with the soul. The body's sight can sometimes forget, but the soul remembers forever.' That's one of my favorite lines."

He placed the book on the side of the table, his long fingers lingering on it. I stared at his elegant hands—odd on such an athletic body—as my breathing slowed. If only the soul *could* forget. If only the soul could let go of the moment two years ago that the body couldn't remember. The moment that lived only in my nightmares.

"I set the pieces up..." I tore my gaze away from the book, back to his smile and the comfort it gave. "Then I read a little. When the mood strikes, I analyze the board."

He slid onto the bench. A move others had received a verbal beating for. Why wasn't I chasing him away? He folded his arms and rested them on the stone table, a subtle scent of cinnamon wafting off him. "You were here by yourself the last two Saturdays as well."

The hair at the nape of my neck rose and my pulse quickened. Was that a warning or excitement? There was something familiar about him, as if we'd met before. But where? When? "That's creepy."

A smile tugged at the corner of his mouth. "Just came off my shift at the hospital. Same shift the last two weeks. I peruse the open games on my way through the park and consider joining, but I'm usually too tired. Can't help but notice the rather intense brunette intentionally not playing, hogging a table."

"Lots of people come here and wait for an opponent."

"True." He raised an eyebrow, drawing my gaze to his dark eyes. Strangest thing. They were shot with flecks of gray, like stars glittering in an inky sky. "But you don't set up a game-in-progress and wait for a stranger to join you. Maybe an e4, but not Evans Gambit."

My heart gave a traitorous flutter. Not only did he know chess, but he knew the opening. "What do you do at the hospital?"

"Trauma unit." He leaned his chin on his hand. "Name's Ellis, by the way."

"Danielle." I didn't offer a hand to shake, but neither did he. Worked at the hospital, seemed nice enough, outrageously handsome. And all sorts of not-what-I-needed. "Alright, Ellis. Either you're an aggressive player and you'd take the offered pawn, or you're defensive and you'd move your bishop out of harm's way. You interrupting my book tells me it's probably the former."

"That's confidence." He winked at me. "Not aggression."

Arrogance could have been a better word. "Some might say the two go hand-in-hand."

"Some might." He studied the board. "However, there's no denying this opening is one of the most aggressive white has. So, while *my* personality's up for debate, yours isn't."

My intentional frown broke for a fraction of a second, until I forced it back into place. His charm didn't belong at my table.

"My guess is you want your opponent to take the pawn as a distraction while you claim the middle of the board and lay waste to them."

"Or I'm ready for anything, whether they accept or decline the gambit."

"Not surprised." Leaving his head on his hand, he extended his free arm, fingers hovering over the black bishop. The corner of his lips twitched. "May I touch your pieces now?"

I swallowed hard, an almost-forgotten heat flushing through my cheeks. Who was this guy? Why did he choose my table? And was that a pickup line?

He smirked but didn't touch without permission. "I bet you're a formidable opponent."

A challenge. I hadn't had a real one in two years. My frown faltered again, and I inclined my head toward the board. "The turn is yours."

His face lit up, and he moved his bishop to d4, declining my pawn, claiming the center. "Let's see what you do with that."

"Empty threat." I moved my pawn to c3, prepared to take his bishop without giving up my knight.

"My threats are never empty." He moved the bishop back to where he should have on his first turn, and we fell into a rhythm. Attack, counterattack, and defense. He was a smart player, making few mistakes, taking minor risks. But he was too cautious, and I dominated the game.

The longer we played, the more pronounced his peculiar accent became. There was a hint of British or Irish, but I couldn't put my finger on it.

"Funny story." I smiled, unable to maintain the frown any longer. "The man who taught me had a thick accent, and I grew up thinking it was called Heaven's Gambit."

He chuckled as I took his queen, and he repaid the favor by claiming the rook I'd sacrificed. "Do you believe in Heaven?"

My stomach lurched, and I knocked over one of his pawns by my queen.

He didn't flinch, but righted the pawn before I could. "Too personal?"

Yes! Especially from the gorgeous trauma guy who was good at chess and possibly flirting with me. The answer was a gaping wound in my chest, and all I could do was close my fingers over the scar on my palm while my throat went dry. But when I looked up, our eyes locked, and the calm came over me again. As though all was right with the world.

How did he do that?

I shook my head. "I don't know. Do you? With your job, you must confront that question every day?"

A cool breeze blew past us, and I shivered. I should have sat in the sunshine.

"I can't tell you what comes next, but I believe our words create our reality. And if that's true, it means each soul has the opportunity to determine whether their afterlife is a good one or not." He kept his eyes on mine, brows drawing together as he leaned forward slightly. "Every day you wake up—still on this side of mortality—is another day you can earn paradise. I've seen hundreds of people this week alone who'd give anything to be in your position right now."

But they didn't know the life I lived. The emptiness. The loneliness. How my soul cried out every day, demanding I find the people responsible. *Stop thinking about it.*

I made my final move. "Checkmate. We're done."

He stared at the board and nodded, not speaking for a moment.

Not leaving, either.

My throat was thick, but I swallowed it down. I'd built the barrier around me so high, so strong, but it was like he pulled one brick out and the whole thing tumbled down on top of me. "That means you can leave."

His eyes remained downcast as he spoke quietly. "What drew me to your table is the sadness which emanates from you."

A cloud passed over the sun, and the light dimmed, but I couldn't rip my gaze off him—off the way the shadow seemed darker around him than anything else. My fingers remained on the scar, the smooth skin a reminder of better times. Worse times. God, just different times.

He leaned forward, looking up at me. "I see it day-in and day-out and thought it might help to remind you of the good things you have in life. Because I can tell you've forgotten."

My breath caught, pain stabbing at the backs of my eyes. Good things? What did *he* know about good things in *my* life? I couldn't manage anything louder than a whisper. "You don't know me. You don't know what I do and don't have."

"I know more than you think I do." He picked up his king and folded it in his fist, clenching tight. "And I'm here with a warning, Danielle Cristina Edmonds."

I launched from the bench, eyes wide, heart thundering. "How do you—"

A darkness came over his features as he stood, sending goose bumps up my arms and legs. "Give up your hunt, or you'll never escape the hell you've built for yourself."

"Give that piece back." I held out my hand, unable to stop it from shaking. Was he in on it? Did that mean I was getting close? "And if you ever come near me again, I'm calling the cops."

He dropped the king into my palm. It was so cold I yelped, yanking my hand away. Covered in a thick layer of frost, the piece tumbled to the ground, shattering on the stones at my feet.

No! No! No! Dad's king.

Gone.

And so was Ellis.

CHAPTER 2

ELLIS

I strode through Central Park until I arrived at West 59th, searching faces as I moved, looking for answers. Why did seeing Danielle cause so much conflict inside of me? She made me feel... what?

Things I wasn't supposed to.

My kind learned long ago that human emotions were best kept behind a wall, like a dam holding back the swell of a mighty river. But like any dam, the floodgates needed to open when storms raged else the waters rise too high and crash over the top.

For us, the floodgate was a two-week hiatus every century, full of emotions which tore through us with the power of a tidal wave.

My dam cracked the night I met Danielle. Instead of immediately starting my vacation as I should have, I postponed, hoping in vain I'd been mistaken about what happened. Two years later, and feelings I shouldn't have been capable of continued to seep through.

As I walked, no one returned my gaze. Given my power to determine when humans saw me, this was normal.

But Danielle's light-brown eyes, which glittered like topaz when the sun hit them right? They pierced the barrier surrounding me, and she actually *saw* me. Whether I was invisible or in any number of forms—a woman holding a door open, a tall man retrieving a bottle from a high shelf, a boy on a train—every time I was near, her eyes found mine.

Perhaps I shouldn't have sought her out so often, but from that first night, there was something that drew me toward Danielle. And her toward me. She felt it, for sure, the way she calmed when I smiled. How her frown gradually—

Tires squealed, followed by the rumble of crumpling metal, dragging my thoughts to the present.

Two shock waves hit me in quick succession.

Every person stopped and turned to a collision on the road. A black SUV had run a red light, careening onto the sidewalk and into the low stone wall at the park's border, hitting a pedestrian in its path. Screams erupted from the crowd, but the weight of quiet inside the vehicle and in its wake pulled at me as the shock waves collapsed back on themselves.

Two deaths. Two shock waves. Two contracts to be doled out.

I held up a hand, searching within the ether for one of the contracts, but they were already assigned to others. Fewer and fewer came to me over the last year, leaving me bored and wandering the city—a subtle hint from my boss, Azrael, to take my vacation and straighten my head out.

People ran to the crash, yelling at each other to call 9-1-1. Asking if there were any doctors.

I remained on the sidewalk, observing. A man next to me merely glanced at the scene, scurrying along whatever path he thought more important than the end of two lives. What insignificant moment held greater sway over him?

Dark smoke gathered on the street, swirling upward, gradually revealing a figure clad all in black. He wore a tattered cloak which billowed in an unearthly wind, absorbing all the light, transforming sunshine into shadow. He towered over the surrounding people, moving through them with effortless grace. Each person he touched jolted, looking about frantically for the invisible source of the disturbance. The cold.

I knew that reaction too well. Even Danielle had burrowed deep in her little sweater the moment I approached her. I'd been visible, though, and she shouldn't have felt it.

The cloak flared, instilling a discomfort around the figure, causing the crowd to separate while he worked. He lifted an arm toward the SUV. The tip of one bony finger extended from the sleeve, pointing to the driver. His other arm raised to the side, skeletal hand outstretched, and an immense scythe of gnarled wood and black metal coalesced out of the darkness which emanated from him.

Nothing happened. The creature took a step forward, stretching his hand toward the vehicle. A blast of cold erupted off him, agitating the crowd.

"Let go!" The thundering voice echoed off the buildings and vehicles, beyond mortal ears. He planted his feet and swung the scythe with both hands, slicing unseen through those who were not his target, slamming into the soul hiding inside the vehicle.

He wrenched the weapon back, severing the soul's link to its body, and hauled it through the windshield.

The driver flailed his arms, as though that trivial action could fend off inevitability. He landed on his knees, staring through the golden wisps of his limbs at the monstrous figure.

A parchment appeared above the giant's hand, and he rasped out the words, "I am here to deliver you to the afterlife. Your judgment has not been a favorable one."

At the figure's feet, the pavement shimmered, gradually shifting into a red light which expanded and deepened until it arrived at the soul. Clawed, demonic hands reached from it, the screams of the damned shrieking for the next victim to join them. The stench of sulfur, ash, and decay invaded my nostrils.

The Pit.

No matter how many times I watched its sinister maw gape in front of those who'd earned it, it never ceased to impress.

The soul of the driver howled as the figure lifted him above the horror, taunting him, until it abandoned him into damnation. The light vanished, and the figure turned toward me, its face hidden in the shadows of its voluminous hood.

The next instant, it stood beside me.

"Hello, Reg." I held out a fist to bump. "What happened there?"

The figure bumped with me. "Heart attack. Just came from his doctor's office and a lecture on taking better care of himself."

"Humans." I shook my head, scanning the height of him. "Have you gotten taller? What are you now, ten feet?"

"Only nine. I added a few inches last month."

Ambulance and police sirens compounded the chaos on the road, many drivers honking their horns to signal their irritation over the holdup. Two souls being reaped, and these temporal creatures were upset over a few minutes' delay.

"I was six feet when I recruited you!" He held one bony hand to measure the old height, then waved it away. "The whole cloak and skeleton thing used to be enough, but it doesn't scare them anymore. I blame the video games."

Black smoke swirled on the sidewalk where the pedestrian lay, growing until two cloaked figures—no taller than those in the crowd—arrived. Their hoods were down, dark hair dancing about them, kind smiles on their serene faces. They held their arms wide, as though offering an embrace, an invitation toward the soul. A Grim Pair, bonded for eternity, their connection conferring a strength unequaled by any half dozen unbonded Reapers.

"They don't even need scythes, Reg," I sighed.

The colossal figure shrugged, clattering bones echoing underneath his cloak, which never stopped swirling about him. "Those two rarely deal with souls who resist. Even if they did, they'd just hug it out."

I held the chuckle in as best I could but sensed Reg's glower.

The radiant soul of the pedestrian rose from the sidewalk until it faced the Reapers. A parchment materialized in front of the Grim Pair, and a bright-white doorway formed, revealing a gleaming staircase.

Most souls I collected passed through the gateway to paradise, so I knew their words well. 'We are here to deliver you to the afterlife. Your judgment has been a favorable one.'

They spoke for a few moments, the spirit glanced around as it came to accept its fate, and it nodded. But it didn't move toward the door, which closed and vanished. This soul was not destined for the afterlife.

The Pair turned to Reg and me, stood to either side of the soul, and all three appeared next to us. The Pair spoke as one. "Sorry we missed your delivery, Reg."

They'd chosen female bodies with black hair, light-brown skin and eyes. Practically twins, they were never apart and rarely let go of each other's hand. They'd been the ones to escort Danielle's mother and brother to the White Stairs that night.

"Not an exciting reaping today, I'm afraid. A few screams, some howling from the Pit. Same old, same old. Although he resisted, so that was fun. I'll play it up next time." He nodded to the soul standing between them, little more than shimmering light in a vaguely human shape. "New recruit?"

The Pair held up the pedestrian's contract, which stated her Reaper status. "We're taking her to see Azrael now."

"Any idea who'll be mentoring—" Reg cut off as time stretched.

The humans around us slowed, gradually coming to a halt. The vehicles, leaves in the trees, the birds flying overhead all stopped. Each of us groaned.

"Great," muttered Reg.

"Stay quiet until he's gone," I whispered to the soul.

A streak of white and gold plummeted from the heavens. The ground trembled as an angel slammed into the sidewalk to my left, none of us having to guess who it would be. His sickly sweet scent and annoyingly glorious aura were all we needed.

Raguel, Archangel of Justice, landed with knees bent, head down. As always, his glimmering golden wings extended at his sides, ready to strike. Before he straightened, I checked Reg, who'd already shortened to match my six-foot-two height.

The angel wore gold armor over an ivory robe, short strawberry-blond hair swept up and away from his face. His piercing blue eyes evaluated each of us, squared jaw flexing. "Why are you not working, collectors?"

Reg, the most senior among our group, was the first who dared speak. "No contracts pending."

"Then you should be training."

Those of us reaping for paradise or the undetermined did our best to connect with humans as we reaped them. A Reaper with an appreciation for their small lives—their hobbies, habits, culture—eased the transition to the next stage, helping ensure they didn't resist. For the last several years, I'd spent my training hours at a hospice, laying the groundwork for what was to come.

I clasped my hands in front of me, pushing back the tide of emotion the angel evoked. "The Pair and Reg just finished—"

Raguel turned his glower on me. His judgmental glare, as though he were cataloging everything I'd ever done wrong. "Was I speaking to you, golden boy?"

Golden boy? That was new. "No, archangel."

"You were lazing about with a human today." His eyes narrowed, one wing closing in on me. "Does Azrael allow that?"

Of course, she did, and he knew that. Bloody archangel. And it was hardly *lazing*.

"As long as I'm not shirking my duties." I shifted my gaze to the ground, as we all did, avoiding his Glory. His irritating-as-the-Pit Glory. This was so much easier when he sent one of his Furies to harass us. We could converse with his immortal employees, discuss our jobs, and get back to work. But, when he came himself, it was eyes on the ground.

"Duties?" The wing curled around me, tilting my chin so I faced him. "It seems to me one of your duties is to take your vacation, isn't it? I can tell from your scent you're shirking that particular responsibility. Perhaps we should tack on a few more weeks, to help remind you of why you do it?"

A shock wave ran through me—another death somewhere nearby. Each Reaper lifted a hand, searching for the death contract and a way out of this confrontation.

Please let it be assigned to me.

The Pair took advantage of the momentary distraction. "We need to get our soul to Azrael for induction." They smiled at Raguel, resulting in a rumble inside the angel's throat, and vanished into a swirl of blackness with New York City's newest Reaper before anyone could speak.

The contract hadn't been assigned to either Reg or to me, leaving us no escape from the archangel with an attitude problem.

"Pathetic." Raguel's lip curled as he forced me to look at him again.

The emotions swirling just below my surface beat at my brain, begging for release, the waters ready to crash over top of the dam and flood everything in their path. I worked hard, focusing on keeping the energy inside me down to Reaper levels—to unfeeling, uncaring levels.

"There is a balance to all things, little collector. You're a strain on that balance. So, either do what you're supposed to—take care of your *duties*—or your services will no longer be required. Stop playing with that human and take your vacation." Raguel's other wing pressed against my chest, where a heart once beat. "Azrael may grant you latitude, but I won't be so kind if you continue to unbalance the Order of Nature."

Before I could decide how or even whether to respond or not, he released me, giving one mighty flap of his wings, and ascended in a blur. Reg and I stared into the sky together as time began ticking forward. The people and vehicles moved, the noise closed around us, and the birds flew.

Visiting Danielle was not against the rules. I never ignored a contract in favor of time near her, nor had I ever revealed my true nature. Although freezing that king was pushing the limits.

The growl which had been building in my throat escaped. I hated that angel. That smug, all-important, rule-twisting angel.

No, wait. Reapers didn't hate. *Calm down, Ellis.*

Reg nudged me. "He was talking about that woman, wasn't he? You saw her again?"

I exhaled my revulsion at having his wings on me and let my mind wander back to her shoulder-length brown hair dancing in the breeze which followed me. The way she tucked it behind her ear after each move. How she stroked the scar on her palm, tugging at my essence. Did she remember how she got it? "We played a game of chess."

Reg smacked a hand to his forehead, jostling his hood free so I could see him clearly. Today, he'd chosen dull bone, white pinpricks of light gleaming in his eye sockets. When he'd taken the driver, those eyes would have been crimson flames, the skull covered in filth and worms. He'd always been a master at terrifying the damned.

I scratched the light stubble on my cheek, trying to hide the smile creeping across my face. "And she was really good."

"Bloody Pit, Ellis, you're a mess!" Reg slammed the end of his scythe against the sidewalk, and the weapon vanished. Someone walked through us, pulling their arms closer for warmth. "You swore you wouldn't interact with her after the last time I caught you helping her with some ridiculously mundane task! You're liable to start making promises you can't keep!"

"You should be proud. I received her contract early this morning, and I waited nine whole hours before I went to see her." Her contract was a special one. Most were assigned at the time of death, but I'd placed a claim on her soul two years ago. So, when the Fates drew up her contract, they sent it to Azrael for final determination, but they delivered a copy to me as well. From that moment, Danielle had fifteen days at the most. Depending on the schedule of whichever Fate would clip her life thread, it could be less. Fortunately, they were usually on time. "We still have two weeks to fix things."

"Don't you dare say 'we' again!" Reg's white pinprick eyes flared briefly, erupting into white flames. Perhaps he was going to need a vacation soon too. "*She* can't change that much in two weeks."

"You're right, you're right, but I have to try." I plucked Danielle's contract out of the ether and showed it to him. The words looped across the page one at a time, their golden ink flashing in the sunshine, until it reached the final, inescapable word: *Damned*. "I did this to her."

Reg shook his head, meeting a finger and thumb where his nose would have been. "No, you didn't. That's your guilt talking."

"Reapers don't feel guilt, you know that."

"Reapers who take their vacations when they're supposed to don't." Reg nudged my shoulder. "By my estimation, you're at least two years overdue. How you're still standing is a mystery to me."

"I've been too busy. This city's a hectic assignment."

"There are hundreds of Reapers in New York. You'd barely be missed." He laid a hand on my shoulder, the touch of a friend. "Transfer the contract to me. Spend your vacation somewhere far away from here, and I'll take care of her."

"Not a chance." I couldn't abandon her to that fate when I was responsible for it.

Reg pointed a skeletal finger at me. "Don't tell me you're going to—"

I swatted at the finger, cutting him off. "Yes, I'm going to visit her a few more times and see what I can do. And before you say it... No, I don't know what I'm getting myself into."

"What is it about her?"

"Powers that be, we've been trying to figure that out since I met her!" I read the parchment again, as though I had any power over the decision. How could she be damned? It simply wasn't right. "But the way I feel when she smiles at me—"

"Stop throwing the F-word around so casually." He shuddered, bones rattling from head to toe. "You're giving me the creeps."

"I don't understand it." From the night we met in the car, when I felt the first stirrings of emotions that I shouldn't have been capable of, I hadn't been able to stop thinking about her. Why? Why was I compelled to seek her out? "But in fifteen more days, it won't matter, anyway."

I closed my hand and the parchment vanished. Danielle's soul was damned, unless she turned her life around.

And I had precious little time left to ensure she did.

CHAPTER 3

DANIELLE

"How'd the hustle go today, Dani?" Abby Beckett called to me from the steps of her parents' brownstone, which adjoined mine. Petite and fair, with a short blond bob, she'd been my neighbor and best friend since I was a baby.

I sidestepped through the small opening in the stone wall separating my minuscule front yard from the sidewalk, narrowly avoiding a pair of power-walking mothers with strollers. I grew up half a block from Prospect Park in Brooklyn, in the house my grandparents had passed on to Dad before it came to me. Five stories of dull gray limestone, seven bedrooms, and just me.

How many real estate agents had come knocking on my door before my family's bodies were even in the ground?

"I don't hustle people. I just like playing." One more scan of the street and over my shoulder for Mr. Creepy Trauma Guy before climbing the stone steps. *He's not following you. It's okay.* I stopped at the first landing where the steps took a right turn up to the door and sank onto the broad railing next to the acorn-shaped newel.

Chris Beckett, Abby's father and my godfather, hollered through the open living room window of his house. "Your father used to!"

"You keep telling me that, Chris, but I still don't believe you!" I laid my bag on the ground at my feet, the chess pieces rattling inside. Maybe I could fix Dad's old king.

Abby laughed and hopped off the side of her steps into my yard. The block was alive with activity. Cars of all sizes edged down the one-way street, thick with parked vehicles. Trees heavy with leaves lined the sidewalk and yards, almost enough to make a person forget where they were.

The tiny space in front of the Becketts' house was packed with greenery, including three perfectly round globe bushes. In stark contrast, the front of mine had a single tree and one flowerpot. The woman who cleaned for me took care of the flowers, otherwise they wouldn't have lasted a week.

Abby climbed the stairs and sat next to me. "A bunch of us are heading to a movie tonight. Want to come?"

Yes! I kept my eyes on my backpack. "No, you know how Byte gets when I go out at night."

"Mom and Dad can take him. They used to all the—"

I shook my head, pulling the bag onto my lap. Sitting to talk was a bad idea. Time to get going.

"You still seeing that cute blond guy?"

"He's a private investigator." I stood, slinging the bag over my shoulder and checking the street again. "I wasn't seeing him; it was business."

"He didn't find anything out about the accident though?"

I balled my right hand, stroking the scar. Was this the hunt that guy had been talking about? Creepy what's-his-name? A shiver ran the length of my spine. His strange eyes, calming smile, what he did to the king after I won... Surely, it was a trick, some sleight of hand? But how did he know my name? Maybe *he* was a PI?

He said he worked in the trauma unit. Why didn't I ask which hospital to verify? Was there a chance he was working when I came in after the crash?

Deep breath, Dani. "He's coming over this afternoon for an update."

Chris came out his front door. His pale, lined face was soft, with that same old look in his eyes. That *poor thing* look everyone gave me. All that was missing was the head pat. "Dani, honey, how many PIs have you hired over the last two years?"

Not enough. I started up the steps to the wrought-iron front door. I put my hand on it but turned around instead of opening it. "It wasn't an accident. I know it. Something deep inside me just knows."

Abby stood and climbed the steps until she was next to me. "The police said it was."

"I know. The police, the media, the insurance company, the car company..." I could have leaned in and accepted the hug I knew Abby wanted to give me. That's what best friends did for each other. It was too late with everyone else, but it wouldn't have been with her.

"Dani!" called a man from down the street.

Abby peered over my shoulder, looking in the voice's direction. "Speak of the cute PI."

I turned, and Alex Shepherd held up a hand to wave.

She was right—he was easy to look at with his close-cropped strawberry-blond hair, blue eyes, and perfect smile. He wore faded black denim and a light-blue button-front which highlighted his broad chest, made more casual by having the top buttons undone and sleeves rolled up. He was exactly the kind of man I needed in my life. Serious. Focused. Intent on tracking down the people behind my family's deaths.

"I know I'm early, but I had a cancellation." He stopped on the sidewalk at the front of my house and nodded at my best friend and her father. "I can come back later if you're busy?"

"Now's good." I looked at Abby, who offered me the poor thing look. The stinging hit the back of my eyes for the fiftieth time since I woke up. *Keep moving forward. Keep searching for answers.* "Maybe I'll stop by tomorrow or something?"

"Yes." Abby grasped my upper arms, eyes wide. "I'd love that."

With a forced smile, I shrugged out of her grip and unlocked the front door. "Let's see what you've got, Alex."

"Tomorrow. It's a date." Abby squeezed my arm before heading down the stairs.

"I really can come back later," said Alex as I held the door open for him.

"Your timing's perfect, actually." Before the outer door settled behind us, a blur of brown and black moved frantically on the other side of the frosted inner door. My heart skipped, and a genuine smile tugged at my lips with the sound of his excited yips. "I warn you—he barks at pretty much every man on the planet."

Alex shifted his messenger bag from crossbody to one shoulder. "Dogs love me."

"Don't be so sure of that." I pushed open the door, and my little Yorkshire Terrier, Byte, leaped up for me to catch him. He was what I had left. He was my sunshine.

But instead of the welcome-home face bath Byte normally gave me, he growled at the obvious intruder.

"This is why I always lock him in my room when visitors come by."

Alex held a hand to my furious protector's nose, but the growling continued. "Got any treats I can give him? I guarantee I can win him over before I leave."

"In the kitchen." I carried Byte into the bright white and gold living room and plucked a remote from the glass coffee table in front of the long couch. The wall-mounted television played a nature show about monkeys in Gibraltar, which I flicked off since Byte didn't need the company anymore. "You said you had something for me?"

"I do. Want to review at the dining room table?"

"Kitchen first." I dropped the remote onto the table, and we made our way through the parlor with its upright piano, through the soft-yellow wallpapered dining room with its tiled fireplace, and finally into the pale-blue country kitchen at the back of the house. I gestured to a black ceramic container on the counter. "Treats are in there."

Alex dropped his bag onto the large butcher's block island and opened the container.

Byte began squirming, practically leaping out of my arms.

"He loves these, doesn't he?" Alex knelt and held the small piece of dehydrated liver out.

Dad used to hide them around the house and take Byte hunting through each room until he found them. 'Who needs the Beagle Brigade when you've got Byte?' he'd say.

The growling continued, even though Alex tossed him two pieces and Byte ate the third from Alex's hand.

"He's a tough nut to crack."

"About whatever you found though?"

"I have an idea." He held up one finger and withdrew another treat. "Yorkies are quite intelligent and like to work." He put his hand up and said, "Stay."

Byte twisted his head, his collar tag jingling.

Alex backed away slowly, keeping his eyes on Byte, while mine shifted to the bag with the information I wanted. He crouched behind the island, then stood and snapped his fingers. "Go find it!"

Exactly how Dad started training him.

Without a growl or a yip, Byte darted toward Alex, slowing to sniff the floor as he got closer. The hiding place must not have been a difficult one because he found it immediately.

"Good boy." Alex leaned down to ruffle Byte's hair and was rewarded with a paw on his foot and a quick yip for more.

I tapped the messenger bag on the island. "I hope you're not charging me by the hour for playing with my dog?"

"Has he always been that protective?" He flipped open the top of his bag and pulled out a large manila envelope.

"No." It had gotten much worse over the past two years—when I became his whole world—except for the times

Abby's family watched him for me. "Although it only took you, what, four treats?"

"I'm almost as good at reading animals as I am at reading people." He smiled as he opened the envelope. "You didn't mention your father's car went in for work the day before the crash."

"What?" There was no way. "The four of us were in Boston visiting friends of the family that weekend."

"In your father's car?"

"No. We borrowed our neighbor's SUV. It fit the four of us better." Like most people in our area, we usually took the train everywhere, so we didn't have to worry about parking. The night of the crash was one of the few times we'd jammed ourselves into the sedan, trying to relive the road trip spirit.

"This tells a different story." Alex handed a photograph to me. He was my age but claimed he didn't trust technology—printouts rather than emails, in-person meetings rather than video calls. In his line of business, privacy was important, and nothing digital was fully secure.

The photo was of a work order from a mechanic's shop in Jersey, with Dad's name and signature on it. The date was the day before the crash. We drove back that night. "The car was here when we got home that day."

He shrugged. "Is that your father's signature?"

"Yeah." I pulled it closer. Something was off. But what? "Hold on."

"I was talking to your lawyer yesterday, by the way."

"Why?" I stared at the work order, scrolling through memories, searching for what was niggling my brain.

"He and your Uncle Mike are drawing up the final paper-work for your memorial scholarship. There's some background checks they asked me to take care of before appointing the administrator."

Neil had been my dad's lawyer and friend. He'd swept in and helped with so much after the crash. If I hadn't had him, I likely wouldn't have gotten a fraction of the settlements I did.

"The settlements." That was it! "Come with me!"

CHAPTER 4

DANIELLE

I dashed down two flights of stairs, past the garden floor, into the cellar. Underground, where my parents had converted the tiny dirt space into a furnished sixth floor three years ago. Gym equipment, media room, and bathroom.

More importantly, my evidence board, safe from prying eyes.

Ten photographs at the bottom, five along the side. Names, dates, questions. And at the center, the two key facts I hadn't been able to reconcile in my brain: the life insurance policy and the bank records.

Alex scanned everything. "No changes since the last time you brought me down here?"

How many hours had I spent staring at this board? Writing questions and suspicions, erasing things, adding photographs and taking them away. The only constants were those two items.

Six months before the car accident that claimed my father, mother, and brother: My father had taken out a five-million-dollar life insurance policy. What did a retired software programmer and part-time professor need with that much life insurance? The house alone was worth more than that, if any-one needed the money in the event he died.

One month before the accident: A strange pair of trans-actions into an account of my father's that I'd been the sole surviving beneficiary on. Four hundred thousand in, then one hundred and fifty thousand out.

My parents had always said they shared their finances, so the mere existence of that account surprised me. Years ago, Dad's brother Mike had told them it was wiser to have separate ac-counts. From the way my aunt had reacted to that conversation, I was sure it was one of the many sore spots in their failed marriage.

I'd tried to get the details from the bank, but the digital image was corrupted, and the canceled check itself was nowhere to be found.

After every official investigation into the crash closed six months ago, I'd hired a few PIs to dig into what had happened. It wasn't an accident. I couldn't put my finger on how I knew that, but I knew. And it had finally paid off.

I grabbed a magnet and secured Alex's printout to the board, then pulled the life insurance policy down. I flipped to the back page and held it up beside the garage receipt. "Notice anything?"

"Well done." Alex folded his arms. "These signatures aren't the same. Close, but not a match. The E is wrong"

The insurance and money transfers were conjecture, but the car being in the shop? *This* was something. This was proof.

"What's your next move?" asked Alex. "Want me to get more information? See if I can find some video footage that's still around from two years ago?"

"How did you find this when no one else did? Neil hired a PI during the initial investigation. I'd assumed that was you?"

Alex barely shrugged one shoulder, instead focusing on the pictures at the side, showing the wreckage. "I'm better than the PI he hired for that job."

"Picked the wrong guy, I guess." How would this have changed things if he'd discovered it two years ago?

"He did." Alex tapped the work order. "What do you want me to do?"

What I wanted was to forget about all of it. I wanted the whole thing behind me. Wanted to know the truth about what happened. Wanted the sick feeling inside my stomach every time I looked at this board to go away.

More than anything, I wanted my family back. But that was the one thing I couldn't have.

"See if you can find out who brought the car in. Maybe it wasn't even his car and the work order's a cover for something else."

Byte hopped up in the big chair next to the board and let out a small growl.

"Guess I need more treats." Alex checked his watch. "I should get going—see where this takes me."

I walked upstairs with him, Byte's collar jingling behind us. "Do you think the police would open the case again?"

"Possible." He paused at the inner door. "Listen, your Uncle Mike told me what you used to do for a living. Can you check if there's anything on their computer systems?"

It wouldn't be the first time I used what Dad had taught me to gain more information than I should have been able to access. "I can do that."

"And once we find out the truth, any chance you want a job? I could use someone with your skills."

"I test security systems for a living." At least, I used to. "I don't do it maliciously."

"The pursuit of truth is hardly malicious."

"Depends on how the truth is used."

"Good answer." He put a hand on the outer door's handle, but said over his shoulder before he left, "We'll get these scales balanced again, Dani. Trust me."

After he was gone, I locked the door and set the alarm. I grabbed another treat for Byte before pulling a bottle of vodka and a glass off the counter, then made my way back to the cellar.

I poured myself a shot and downed it before dropping into my chair in front of the board. Elbows on my knees, I opened my hand, stroking the only scar I had from the accident. An inch-long strip of smooth skin which resembled something between butterfly wings and an hourglass.

Three of them dead, and all my cuts and bruises had healed like I hadn't even been there with them. Except that one. No memories of the event, just nightmares. Mostly of sitting in the car and looking over to see my brother—

My breath caught, and I sank back into the plush chair, pulling my knees against my chest as my lungs slowly constricted and my throat thickened.

Alex's visit had been a distraction. Maybe I could still go out with Abby and distract myself longer. But that would require changing, hair, makeup. Socializing. Mental energy. I let out a long sigh.

Byte's collar jingled as he jumped from his chair and hopped up next to me.

I pulled him into my lap, and he whimpered, nestling his head on my shoulder. "How am I supposed to let this go? Someone killed our family and no one's trying to find out who, except me."

'Give up your hunt,' Creepy Trauma Guy had said. How did he know? Maybe whoever was behind it hired him to deliver a message. *I did set the alarm, right? Yeah, definitely. Always.*

I squeezed my eyes closed, tears threatening to overwhelm me, the permanent pit in my stomach widening.

When would it stop? The need to be held, smiled at, laughed with. Then cringing when any of them were offered. Every day felt like drowning, reaching for a hand that wasn't there, gasping for breath that became progressively harder to find.

'Or you'll never escape the hell you've built for yourself,' he'd said.

I opened my eyes and looked at Byte, at his tan face and black ears. "You know what the worst thing was?"

He twisted his head to the side, and I matched him.

"I liked him, Byte. No matter how weird the whole thing ended up, every time he smiled..." I blinked away the few tears which had collected on my bottom lids and stared at the board again. Playing chess with him—talking, joking, flirting—felt like life before the crash. Like maybe I really could put all this behind me. But then he said my name—a name he shouldn't have known.

And the frozen king.

Goose bumps crawled up my arms.

Byte licked my nose suddenly, and I laughed despite myself.

"Everyone thinks I should stop looking for the truth, Byte. Other than Alex, who I'm paying, so he hardly counts. What do you think?"

He lay his head on my shoulder again, and I scratched up and down his sides. He wiggled his body back and forth on my chest, nestling in for a nap. Before he could sleep, I filled the glass and rested my cheek against his silky hair.

This board was everything. I'd left my job, abandoned my friends, poured so much money into the investigation. And what had it gained me?

Nothing.

I took a swallow from the glass, the liquid barely touching my tongue on its way to smother the memories. All alone in the cellar of a six-story house with nothing more than my dog—another swallow—and a bottle of vodka for company.

CHAPTER 5

ELLIS

In the wee hours of Sunday morning, Jessica Madden—Jessica Grimm now—and I stood side-by-side next to a large, plush bed. A thick navy comforter enveloped a frail man who slept on the side closest to us. His wisp of white hair and paper-thin flesh full of wrinkles and age spots must have held hundreds of stories. The photos on his bedstand and on the wall told the most important story: He'd been loved. I scanned the images of a younger him with a stunning woman who smiled in every photo, surrounded by children, by adults, by friends. He'd traveled the world with her and then alone. He'd led a good life.

"Most contracts you receive will have one of three judgments: Damned, Blessed, or Undetermined."

Jessica wore hazel eyes and dark-blond hair which brushed her shoulders. Like many Reapers, she'd chosen to look as she had in life. I hadn't seen her before yesterday's incident, so I didn't know how true to form she was. She could've added or lost pounds, removed scars or kept them, or changed coloration.

The familiarity was a comfort for a new Reaper, so it was all likely close to original. The more experience she had, the more she might modify her appearance.

"We call the Pit to Hell for the first, the Stairs to Heaven for the second, and the Gray Hallway for those who wait."

"Wait?" Her voice was quiet, gaze darting around the room, intentionally avoiding me.

The man's breathing slowed. But still, his body clung to life.

"Some wait until they're ready to decide. The longer the soul is apart from its body, the more it realizes its true purpose. It understands what it needs before it can be placed in a new body. Heaven for those who lived a good life and simply need to rest. Hell for those who must be cleansed of what they did in life, so they have a better chance in the next lifetime."

"Chance at what?"

The ultimate prize. What every soul, once freed of their earthly desires, wanted. "To find their missing Pair."

"Pair of what?"

Someday, Azrael needed to create a welcome handbook. The questions were always the same. "Your Pair is what you might have called a soulmate while you were alive."

"I thought my boyfriend was my soulmate?"

"Yes, I hear that often." Temporal creatures were so short-sighted. "Every soul is free to love, but through all your lifetimes, you'll only Bond with your true Pair once, then you can retire."

Before Jessica could ask another question, the man's breath stopped, and the death wave shot out from him, buffeting us with its full force. She stumbled back, not realizing the strength of her new being. "What was that?"

If I hadn't been answering so many questions, I could've warned her. "There are three types of waves. That one signaled that the Fates have snipped the thread of his life."

"I didn't see that."

"You and I can't see them." I gestured vaguely around the bed. "We'll discuss hierarchy later."

"If you can't see them, how do you know they—"

"I need you to focus right now. We don't have a great deal of time once the soul is released." I reached into the ether, the space beyond sight, beyond perception, to the area where I kept my few possessions. I pulled out my scythe—dark wooden handle with a pale metal blade, a ragged hamon decorating its surface—and rested it against my shoulder. With it, my cloak formed all around me, billowing in the unseen breeze which followed each Reaper as we worked.

Jessica nodded and finally didn't ask a question. She was a particularly curious thing, more so than the last few Reapers I'd trained. The first half hour we'd stood there, she'd asked approximately fifty. How are Reapers created? How could she move from place to place on her own? When would she get a scythe?

Maybe *I* should have written the handbook so I could distribute them at each induction.

"The death wave is strongest at the point of origin. That's why we don't feel the deaths of everyone across the world. It's a proximity thing. There's also the training wave, which told me where to find this gentleman. The Fates provide it when we have a trainee and they've dispatched one of their own with the shears."

The body shimmered, light emanating from his head and his chest, through the covers over top of him.

"It's so sad." Jessica's hand covered her mouth and her eyes glistened. "He died alone."

It would take her many reapings before she could handle the emotions. First would come the easy ones—natural deaths at the end of a long life, for souls deemed worthy of the White Stairs. The better control she found, the more challenging the assignments. Gradually, she'd find a rhythm and work whatever contracts Azrael allocated to her.

"It's not sad. It's the way of things." I nudged her hand upward. "His soul is emerging. I need you to watch him. Focus on the way the tingles spread up your arm as a pure soul approaches. Use that feeling to reach into the nothingness around you and find his contract."

Her chest heaved as though she were still breathing, and released slowly. "Reach into nothing and pull out something?"

"It'll make more sense once you've done it. And it gets easier the more times you do." All of it got easier. Until you encountered someone like Danielle and your emotions started spiraling out of control.

Jessica extended her hand and closed her eyes, contorting her face as though in concentration. This wasn't how you watched a soul. "What did mine say?"

"Your what?" I placed my hand underneath hers to help, while keeping my eye on our target as the soul sat up and peered around the room.

"My contract. What did it say? They said my judgment was a favorable one. The white door, was that—"

"Reap now, questions later." I took over, plucking the contract out of the ether and revealing it to her. "If the soul gets too far without us having the contract, sometimes they run."

She spun toward me, eyes widened. "Run? What does that mean?"

"It means you need to focus."

The stunning parchment hung in the air, the letters appearing one at a time, as though the Fate who designed it were standing between us. Azrael's final decision scrawled across the bottom in her elegant hand: *Paired*.

That suited the photographs.

"You said it would be Damned, Blessed, or Undetermined?"

"Most are one of those three, not all. It means he Bonded with his Pair during this life and they'll be reunited once he makes his way up the Stairs."

The soul turned toward us, swinging his legs over the edge of the bed as though he were still in his body. It always took them time before they realized what had happened. He whispered in a voice as ethereal as his transparent limbs, "Who are you?"

"My name is Ellis. This is Jessica. And we're here to guide you to the afterlife."

CHAPTER 6

DANIELLE

I choked through the smoke, gasping for breath. There wasn't enough oxygen to fill my lungs, and each pull brought more of the metallic taste down my throat instead of air. The eyes were there, all I could see through the tears and the haze. John's eyes. The pain. The blood. He was right next to me, leaned back against his headrest, eyes wide and full of terror.

He knew.

I knew.

My body refused to reach for him, no matter how much I told it to. I was pinned, paralyzed, something.

He blinked slowly, his lids not opening all the way before they stopped. My stomach plummeted, and what little air I'd found rushed out of my body. My brother was gone.

"John!" I screamed, willing my arms to move. When they finally did, I grabbed for him, to shake him, wake him up.

But he wasn't there.

My focus sharpened.

Just a dream.

But I wasn't in bed, either. *Where am I? Did I fall asleep in the cellar?*

A door closed, almost soundless. A low, deep voice rumbled upstairs, "What the fuck was that?"

An icy fist wrapped around my heart. Someone was in my house.

No barking.

Where was Byte?

"I thought you said she'd be asleep?" came the deep voice, followed by hurried footsteps on the stairs.

I jumped out of the chair—too fast. The room spun around me, and I crashed into the wall.

"She should've been upstairs," said a different voice. A hoarse whisper.

The space was open. The bathroom was too close to the stairs. No windows anywhere down here. There was nowhere to go. I tore over to the media area to hide behind one of the chairs, but the footsteps overcame me, and someone grabbed a fistful of my hair. They jerked me back, and I fell hard to the ground.

Pain exploded through my head and my vision blurred. *Oh, god.* I didn't see the person, just the thick handle of a flashlight hurtling toward my face.

And darkness.

· · • • • • • • • · ·

"There's got to be something in here," hissed one of the men. They were right there, moving around the space.

I lay on a smooth surface. Hardwood floor? A slab? Not cold like concrete. Opening my eyes a sliver took immense effort. It let in the light, catapulting pain through my throbbing head, so I closed them again. Did they think I was dead? If I moved, would I give myself away?

"She'll know."

"I doubt it."

A soft tap on my cheek jarred my head enough to sting. "Wake up."

I raised a hand to shield my eyes from the light, but they both lifted, crossed and bound with duct tape. My heart beat in double-time, lungs taking in shallow sips of air. I was in a small office—desk, cabinets, powered-up laptop, and two monitors—with two men in dark clothes and covered faces. "What the—"

The man at the desk launched at me, his open hand connecting with the side of my face. Bright lights flooded my vision when my head bounced off the floor, a stabbing sensation that traveled from my back to my forehead and echoed through every inch of my upper body.

What am I going to do?

The smaller of the two pushed the larger back against the desk, away from me. There was a door beside them. The light from the office spilled out enough to illuminate... my cellar? How was this my cellar when I was in a room I'd never seen before?

Where was Byte? Was he okay?

Why wasn't the alarm going?

How did they get in?

What did they want?

The intruders split again, the smaller one sitting in front of the laptop, the larger one kneeling in front of me. I inched away, trying to disappear into the floor, overwhelmed by his body odor and stale cigarette breath. Another rumble deep in his chest, and he grabbed my bound hands, pressing them against me. "Where's the program, bitch?"

"What program?"

"Your father's fucking program." His foul breath flowed over me through his face covering, and I turned my head, pain streaking through it again.

My chin quivered, and the tears started. How was I going to get out of this? "I don't know what you're talking about."

He wrapped a meaty fist around my left pinky finger. His eyes narrowed, and my body reacted.

I whimpered.

He snapped the finger back so forcefully I heard it crack.

Agony shot through my hand, through my entire palm and up my arm. I screamed.

"What are you doing?" rasped the man at the laptop.

"Advanced interrogation methods." He grabbed my ring finger and broke it with no more effort than breaking a turkey's wishbone. I screamed again, black spots clouding the sides of my vision. My muscles slacked, but he slapped my cheek and kept me conscious.

"Doesn't look advanced to me." The smaller man slammed the laptop shut, grabbed a notebook, and stood. He kept his voice down the entire time, as though afraid someone else was in the house. "I can't do this here. Especially with all that noise. She doesn't know anything."

The man wrapped his hand around another of my fingers. His skin was tanned, eyes and brows dark, the rest of his face covered by a balaclava which didn't reveal his mouth. But underneath, from the way his eyes crinkled at the corners, I knew he was smiling. His partner shoved him with a foot, and he let go of me to catch himself from falling.

"Stop toying with her." The smaller man leaned to the side, peering around his partner, who turned to face him. His eyes were shadowed in the pale light, so I couldn't make anything out under his face covering. He was in charge. Maybe he was my way out of this.

"Please—" My voice broke, unable to get anything else out.

The larger man backhanded me. Blood sprayed out of my mouth, splattering the wall, but I whipped my face back to plead with the one calling the shots.

"I won't call the cops. Just let me go?" *Please, please.*

The smaller man's shoulders sagged, and he looked at the floor. He made his way out of the office with the laptop and notebook, pausing briefly at the door. "Make sure she doesn't talk."

The larger man, still crouched over me, waggled his eyebrows. "Just you and me now, babe."

He stood slowly and took a few steps toward the door. His back turned to me as he closed it, a gun tucked in his waistband.

Oh god, I'm dead.

I inched back again, and my head met the wall. One eye was already swelling shut, and the taste of iron coated my busted lips. I scanned the room, searching for an out. For something, anything.

And there it was, in the narrow space under the bookcase next to me.

A box cutter, covered in dust and cobwebs. *Thank you.*

I swallowed hard, biting back the pain as I stretched my bound hands into the small space, careful not to hit my broken fingers on anything. *Don't make any noise.* Once it was in my grasp, I planted my elbow on the floor and with a grunt I shot up to lunge for the intruder.

He spun toward me, laughing. His fist headed for my face again, but I swiped at him, his knuckles striking the blade instead of me. "Fucking bitch!"

It barely slowed him. He grabbed for his gun, arms swinging to his front to cock it. As he did, as the click sounded, I drove at him, at the exposed flesh at his neck. Blood poured out of the wound.

I did it! I was going to escape!

But it didn't matter.

The crack was so much louder than I would have expected. And the scent of the gunpowder hit me almost as fast as the bullet searing through my gut. The ringing in my ears blocked all the other noises out, except for the constant high-pitched hum. He dropped the gun and grabbed his throat. My vision became hazy, but there was no mistaking the bright red gushing through his fingers, causing his dark shirt to glisten with the moisture.

While his lifeblood drained away, I fell to my knees, my good hand clenched over the gunshot wound in my stomach.

The pain in my head and fingers faded as pins and needles settled in, followed by a sense of familiarity. Like my nightmares every night when I sat paralyzed in the car. I could still see my limbs, but all sensation drained out of them. As though someone else was controlling me, easing me to the floor.

We were behind a closed door in a below-grade cellar in the middle of the night. But the houses were close. And he'd fired a gun.

How long did I have? Did anyone hear it? Would an ambulance find the right house in time?

Was this what shock felt like?

I lay back, head swimming. The intruder stopped moving, facedown on the floor. What had they been looking for?

It was tiring, so much activity. My body begged for sleep. I inched away from the dead man, far enough I propped my head against the wall.

This was my house, right?

My breathing slowed, and the grip on my stomach weakened. How was I going to stop the bleeding if I couldn't keep any pressure on it?

Mr. Hot Trauma Guy would have known what to do. He'd warned me, hadn't he?

I'd wanted to listen to his advice. His bizarre freezing-my-black-king advice.

'Give up the hunt,' he'd said. Didn't even get a chance to, did I?

My eyes fluttered closed.

So tired.

Time to sleep.

The intruders were searching for some program my father wrote. A clue? Something worth breaking into my house for. And apparently worth killing over.

'Do you believe in Heaven?' Trauma Guy had asked.

Ellis. His name was Ellis. Like the island. How could I forget that?

Didn't matter anymore, did it?

Chapter 7

Ellis

The soul nodded slowly. "My wife died five years ago. You're saying I'll see her again?"

"Yes. You'll meet her once you've climbed the Stairs." I'd never been through the portals to the afterlife myself, so it could have been a lie for all I knew. If nothing else, all Reapers were instructed to tell the same story.

"And the rest of my family?"

Jessica looked at me, her eyebrows drawing down in that way they did before each question. They were both too close to their mortality to understand the cyclic nature of existence.

"The rest of your earthly family—" A wave pulsed through me, nearly knocking me over. The death wave never hit Reapers while we were collecting a contract, and it certainly was not a training wave, since I was already training.

No, the third type of wave was sharper, stronger, so it would never be missed. Only a single Reaper ever felt it, when someone we'd marked was close to the end, to ensure we arrived on time.

"Are you okay?" asked Jessica.

I had to go. I didn't have time for this. For training, for the man's soul, for the contract. I flung a hand out, and the white door appeared, searing light behind it illuminating the room. The door swung open, and the man's soul raised an incorporeal arm, as if to shield his eyes from the radiance. I slammed my scythe against the floor and shouted, "Reg!"

The soul cocked his head. "I didn't have any family members named Reg."

Jessica remained still, no scythe in her hand, no cloak—because I was failing in my job.

But there was something far more important for me to do. I had two outstanding claims and had only received a contract for one of them. Danielle. Something had happened to her, and I had to hurry. "Reg!"

"What?" came the bellowing growl before a swirl of black smoke spun around the floor and Reg appeared.

Jessica jolted back, as though she were about to hide behind me.

"New Reaper." I pointed at Jessica, then at the soul. "Show her how to send him through the door. Don't forget, she can still choose the Stairs if she doesn't want to stay a Reaper."

Reg towered over me, his eyes flaring with red flames. "I don't reap for—"

"Gotta go!" I waved a hand to fling open the door to the Stairs—less grace than the portal to paradise deserved—and I left.

The wave collapsed in on itself, and I followed it—back to Danielle. If I didn't arrive before her body died, another Reaper might have to contain her. As my mentor, and a specialist in damned souls, Reg was a possibility, but hopefully I'd delayed him. He was the last thing I wanted anywhere near her, especially in the mood I'd left him in. Her transition needed to be as peaceful as possible, despite its horrendous outcome.

Chapter 8

Ellis

The room was small, an office space belowground with no windows. And there was Danielle Edmonds, head propped against the wall, in a pool of blood. A man by the closed door, facedown, made a barely audible noise. He must have done this to her. She had a broken nose and possibly cheekbone and eye socket, broken fingers, bloodied and swollen face. Her hands lay limp at her sides, next to the wound in her stomach.

Her breathing was slow and shallow. Less than twelve hours since my warning—which she obviously hadn't listened to—and I was already having to deal with the consequences. While I could talk a soul out of the Gray Hallway, the Pit gave no quarter.

I wasn't about to let her go without a fight. "If there are any Fates in this room, please come back at the end of her contract."

As I did two years ago, I placed a hand on her and closed my eyes, reversing time for her body. The seconds ticked backward into minutes, the blood pool receding slightly, but only enough that she could speak. This time, she had to agree first.

Strands of hair thick with blood clung to her face, and I brushed them behind her ears, the same way she did when her shoulder-length brown locks were caught in a breeze. Her face was a pulpy mess. Why did humans do this to each other?

"Danielle," I whispered.

She didn't budge.

I grasped her right hand—the left, taped to it, had been ruined—and tried again with a more familiar name. "Dani, I need you to wake up."

A shock wave nearly bowled me over from behind, signaling the end of the other man. I froze. Someone had clipped his thread. That meant a Fate was in the room with us. If they were going to end Dani, there was nothing I could do to stop it.

Her eyes cracked open, and she whimpered, attempting feebly to wrest her hand from my grip.

"You!" Her voice was little more than a rasp.

I'd ceased the passage of time in her stomach, but the pain must have been excruciating.

A familiar presence coalesced behind me, followed by the distinctive crack of a Reaper's cloak billowing in the wind. Danielle's eyes snapped to the figure, and she trembled. She saw *him* as well? She didn't only see me?

"Make it quick, Reg." I moved between Danielle and him, so she couldn't see. Laying a hand on an undamaged portion of her cheek, I shushed her and smiled. "Focus on me, Dani. Keep your eyes on me. I need to speak with you."

She stopped writhing, but her lungs heaved.

Please give her until the end of her contract. Maybe if I thought the words enough times, someone would listen.

The Pit opened in the center of the room, the red light undulating with shadows from the hands reaching out of it. I didn't turn to watch Reg work but knew his process well enough. The scent of smoke and sulfur clogged the air, and a thousand voices, the damned moaning and screaming, overcame us.

Danielle tried in vain to move and look past me, but I stayed in the way. "What is that?"

"You've sustained some serious injuries, and you're about to die."

She choked, a shudder wracking her body. "I knew you were trouble."

I gave her my most reassuring smile. That trick had worked perfectly in the park, but it didn't temper her panic at this moment. No, she cringed and attempted to turn away from me.

The voice behind me boomed out, shaking everything not nailed down. "I am here to—"

"What's going on?" Her tear-filled eyes flitted back and forth, terror in their bloodshot depths.

"Reg!" I hissed. What was he doing? Had he shrunk to fit into the room or was he crouched over, playing up his size? Not that I was about to check. "Keep it down!"

"Oh, seriously!" He shoved the butt of his scythe into my back and finished in clipped tones. "Fine. You. Damned."

The soul of the man who'd hurt her wailed for the briefest instant before being swallowed by the Pit. The red light remained, the voices growing more insistent, demanding another soul. Demanding Danielle.

I moved closer, blocking out as much of the horror behind me as I could. "I have a deal for you."

She winced as she pressed her head against the wall, trying to create distance between us. "I don't know anything about the program, I swear."

"I can either deliver you to the afterlife, which won't be a pleasant one—"

Her gaze flew over my shoulder, and she attempted to cradle her broken hand against her chest. "What are you?"

"We're Grim Reapers."

"That—that's not real."

"It is." I sat on the floor and removed her binding, squeezing her good hand.

Her lids eased closed, face softening.

"I'll be on vacation for the next two weeks. If you agree to be my guide, I can grant you an extension."

Confusion washed away some of her fright, and she wrinkled her nose as she opened her eyes a crack. "A what?"

"I have a list of things to do, but I need a human's help to do them." This was a stupid idea, but I didn't have time to figure something else out. If I convinced her she had to spend time with me and limit her experiences to good ones, maybe that would fix things.

She moaned, rolling her head from side to side slowly. "This is the worst dream I've ever had."

"Accept my offer. I won't save you without permission. Tell me you'll be my guide in exchange for two more weeks of life." *Please, Danielle. Please say yes.*

Her hand in mine grew heavy. There was a wound somewhere I hadn't accounted for; she was slipping away. "Yeah, whatever. I accept."

"If there are any Fates in this room…" I released her hand and touched her abdomen, bright light flowing around us. "Please come back at the end of her contract."

I focused on turning back her time, soaking up the pool of blood, removing the bullet, repairing her mangled hand. Curing the trauma to her head, the concussion and fractured orbital bone. They all healed, save the black eyes, broken nose, and the blood splatters. The police would retrieve the would-be killer's body, and she would need those injuries when she spoke to them.

As I worked, the room grew silent. The Pit closed over with no soul to claim, and the scents switched to human. The man she'd killed stank. Urine, feces, and body odor.

When I finished, she was far more like her usual self, serene and beautiful, despite her marred face. She deserved better than what that man had done to her.

Her eyes drifted open and settled on mine. Her physical pain would be almost gone, but she'd be exhausted after this. "Now pinch me, so I wake up."

"When the cops arrive."

"Sure." She yawned and curled up on the floor, nestling her head on my lap.

My hands flew up, away from her. That was unexpected. What now? Tentatively, I brushed the side of her head, and she sighed. So peaceful. The contact felt… Powers that be, it felt good and warm, and a flutter burst in my chest.

Wait. That wasn't right.

Reapers didn't have flutters.

"Ellis!"

I craned my neck around to Reg, whose dirt-covered skull scraped the ceiling. He smashed his scythe against the floor and it vanished, causing the dancing crimson flames in his eye sockets to flare. He folded his arms, bones rattling against each other.

"Did you ask him why he hurt Danielle before you—"

"Are you kidding?" He flung his arms out, pacing across the small room. "You revealed yourself to a human and offered her more life! And that's all you have to say for yourself?"

"I thought—"

"You can't leave her alone now, you know that, right? You can't risk her telling anyone!"

Exactly.

Reg stopped pacing, a worm crawling out of a hole in his jawbone. "I'm calling Azrael about this!"

"Don't, please." I lay my hand on Danielle's cheek, and her sleeping form—infinitely fragile—tucked a hand under my leg, nestling close. "If I start now, I can finish my vacation just before the contract comes due and I can reap her soul like I promised I would."

"This is the most absurd, short-sighted, asinine decision you've ever made!"

"Is it? That's what you said the first time I healed her."

"But her contract wasn't due that time, you fool."

"If the Fates come for her before I'm done with my vacation, then I want you to take her contract. But go easy on her?"

"I don't go easy on anyone."

"Please, Reg."

"You left me with that initiate and the bloody White Stairs, and now you're asking for favors? You know I don't reap those do-gooders."

"I'm sorry. I panicked when I felt Danielle's warning."

"Reapers don't feel panic."

"You were right. I should have taken my vacation two years ago. I can't go on any longer without it."

"Fine." His bones creaked as he knelt next to me, the edge coming off his tone. "This vacation is going to be the hardest one you've endured. Swear to me you'll never delay it again?"

"I promise. Now start my time."

He shook his skull, the dirt and worm vanishing, eye sockets reverting to white flickers. "Not here. Not with her." He pointed to the door. "We're going out there."

"I'm not leaving her."

Reg slammed a hand against his forehead. "You don't need to make it more difficult."

"I do. This is what I deserve." I pulled her right hand into mine and traced the mark on her palm. "I've got two weeks to resolve this."

She'd rubbed the mark twice in the park, and countless times before that. Each one tugged at me. To her eyes, it was nothing but a scar. To a Reaper, it revealed the claim I'd put on her soul.

Once I finished the outline, the hourglass glowed with a golden light. "What's this?"

Reg grunted, almost sounding surprised. "Looks like they heard you."

The grains of sand in the full top began falling across her palm.

"I've seen this twice before. Visible to any immortal and to the human sporting it." Reg pulled her hand toward himself. "The Fates have let you know she has time left."

"And when the grains run out?"

"No more second chances." He placed her hand on her stomach. "Are you sure about this?"

I nodded. "I have to do it, eventually."

"Alright, but I warned you." He shifted to the other side of Danielle's resting body and placed both hands on me, one on my forehead and one on my chest. "May that which is unseen be seen, that which is unfelt be felt. Take these two weeks and remember what you once were."

The floodgates of my dam burst open, a torrent of emotion crashing down on me. My heart pummeled the inside of my chest cavity and my lungs burned with each breath. How did they deal with all this every single day? The stabbing pain behind my eyes was the only warning before the tears came and my body convulsed. I clasped her hand, my lifeline, squeezing hard enough Reg had to pry it open.

"No! Danielle, no! I'm sorry!" I pulled her sleeping body into my lap and wrapped my arms around her. "Powers that be, I'd take it back if I could."

I rocked with her, unable to stop the shaking. Or the tears. Or the guilt. I destroyed her life. It was my fault she was heading to the Pit. I had to fix this. I had to redeem her soul.

"Ellis." Reg gripped my shoulder.

I could barely open my eyes, but I could hold her. Surely, the contact would mend the hole inside of me. My streaming tears fell to her hair, mingling with the remaining blood. "I left you all alone in the world. I'm sorry I took him from you! I'm so sorry."

A rough but fleshy hand tilted my chin up, and I blinked, the tears blurring my vision. Reg wore his old form. The kind man with the short blond beard and blue eyes who'd taught me our ways.

"I may as well have killed her myself." The words were too much for me, and I choked out, "I'm a monster, just like Catherine said!"

"That was seven hundred years ago. She was as wrong then as she is now." He shook his head slowly. "You're part of the natural order, Ellis. We both are."

"They're so much stronger than they've ever been before." I cradled Danielle's head to my chest, resting a cheek on her matted hair. But it wasn't enough. All I could do was ride the crest and wait for the transition to pass.

Reg whispered as he stroked my arm, "You've done it before, and you'll get through it again. This part only lasts a few minutes."

"You were right—" I swallowed hard, everything lodging in my throat. I gasped, trying to pull in the air I suddenly needed. Tried to clear the disgusting saliva. "I shouldn't have put it off."

He smirked at me. "I'll remind you of that if you try this again."

The warmth gradually returned to her body, and the initial onslaught of my emotions abated. My heart continued to hammer in my chest, but I took deep breaths, adjusting to the changes in my temporary shell. All the emotions.

And I was already starving for human food.

"You alright?"

Sirens sounded outside, piercing the quiet in the little office.

I nodded, placing Danielle on the ground against the back wall. The blood from her stomach wound was gone, but the other man's injury was a different matter. It would take a lot of effort to clean.

"You're a disaster, Ellis."

"Just as well. It'll help me convince the police." I knelt in front of Danielle and shook her gently. "I need you awake."

She stirred, moaning, and put a hand to her head. "I need more sleep."

"I know. The police are here. Where's the front door?"

Her hand flew to my arm, clutching with all her meager strength. "Don't leave me. Someone tried to—"

"You're safe now, but you're in no condition to let them in."

She blinked slowly, then jutted her chin toward the door. "Go out there. If we're where I think we are, there are stairs at the far end."

"I'll be right back."

Eyes wild, she hesitantly released me. "Promise?"

"I'm going to do everything I can to make things better for you. I swear." I stood and headed for the door with Reg. With one quick look over my shoulder, I saw her slump forward, holding her head. *Thank you, Fates.*

Once we were outside of the office, Reg took me by the shoulders. He transformed into the hulking skeleton most Reapers knew him as. "Take care of yourself. I'll be back for you in two weeks."

We embraced before he vanished in a puff of black smoke.

None of this was as I'd intended. My plan had been to cross her path a few more times, wave the frozen chess piece off as a trick of the light, and convince her to help me check a few items off my list. I'd help her remember the good things in life, we'd elevate her from damnation, and I could reap her soul as a friend.

And once she was gone, I'd have the first pleasant vacation I'd ever had, content in the knowledge I'd saved her soul.

It was a good plan. It may have been lacking in some implementation details, like how I was going to convince her to help me, but it was still a good plan.

Instead of following it, I'd made another short-sighted decision. She seemed to bring that out in me. I'd broken our cardinal rule and revealed my true nature to a human—all in front of Reg. Although that way, no one could argue when I spent every moment of my vacation with her, so perhaps it was just as well.

With blood from her hair and face smeared all over me, I tore up the stairs to find the police. What was I going to tell them? Why was I there?

I needed a cover story, and fast.

Chapter 9

Danielle

I stretched awake, cracking one eye the tiniest sliver to see the early sun shining through the bay windows by the bed. Best sleep I'd had in years. What day was it? Chess in the park yesterday, so it was Sunday.

Sure enough, John's piano lessons had started downstairs, barely audible over the murmur of the world outside the house: cars, birds, people on the sidewalks. Mom would already be up, cooking breakfast, with Dad stealing bacon as it came off the stove.

Intent on falling back to sleep, I pulled the blankets up to my neck. Maybe I'd pick up where I left off in the dream about the hot trauma surgeon.

I snapped up in bed, reality slamming into me. They died two years ago. I was the only one who lived here. Who the hell was playing the piano downstairs? And where was Byte? He always slept in the room with me.

Call 9-1-1.

My phone. Not on my bedside table, and neither was my smartwatch. Laptop was in the dining room. No way to contact the cops. Shit! But the stairs ended at the front door, so I could bypass whoever was in the parlor if I was quiet enough. Then I'd run over to the Becketts' and call from there.

I tiptoed into the closet and threw on a sweater over my sleep shorts and tank. And a pair of shoes. For good measure, I grabbed a poker from the fireplace in my room. The house was old and had many creaks, but years of sneaking past my parents' room had taught me exactly how to scale the steps.

I inched down the staircase, a baseball bat-like grip on the poker, hooked side down, ready to impale anyone who came at me.

Partway down the stairs, I crouched, peeking between the balusters to the parlor, and saw them. A man with dark hair and a form-fitted navy T-shirt sat on the piano bench with his back to me and... oh god, my little Yorkie next to him, wagging his tail furiously.

The man stopped playing and scratched Byte's head. "Did you like that piece, Max?"

Byte licked the man's hand and gave a high-pitched yip. Byte growled or barked at everyone except my neighbors. What was going on? And what happened to the piano? It hadn't been tuned in years but sounded perfect.

And why did the house smell like a bakery? As if on cue, my stomach rumbled, and I held my breath. Hopefully, he didn't hear that.

"Shh. Danielle's sleeping and we don't want to wake her until she's ready." He returned to the keys. "This one's called 'Clair de Lune.' It means 'Moonlight' in French."

He began, smooth and flowing. His torso swayed gently with the music, fingers flourishing off the keys now and then.

"I met the composer, Claude Debussy, during my last vacation." He looked down at Byte, who put his front paws on the intruder's leg. What the hell? "Fascinating man, although quite ill at the time."

His voice was deep and musical, as elegant as his play. It swirled around in my brain, laughing at my heart for beating so fast. The first time John played "Clair de Lune" for me on that piano, it was the morning of his sixteenth birthday. He made a few mistakes, he said, but I couldn't tell.

The sharp edge of the baluster dug into my forehead, and I straightened. What happened? Was I seriously sitting there listening? I was supposed to be fleeing to the Becketts' next door.

But he had my dog. If I faced off with him, would he hurt Byte? Did he have a gun? If his broad shoulders were any indication, he was strong. Would my fireplace poker intimidate him, or would he laugh it off?

Deep breath in. The only other option was to head back upstairs and hope he left, or at least left Byte alone. But what if he came upstairs to hunt me down?

I crept down the rest of the staircase, winding up near the wide front door, and clenched my weapon tighter. He was still playing, with no reaction to my presence.

"Byte!" I yelled, swinging the inner door open, one foot already through it. We could run out together before the man had time to react.

But the damn dog just tilted his head at me. He was so small, so fragile, he'd be easy to hurt.

The man turned slowly, a broad smile forming as he saw me. Mr. Creepy Hot Trauma Guy from the park yesterday? What was his name again? "The princess has awakened!"

I raised the poker over my shoulder, ready to swing if he closed the twenty-ish foot distance between us. "Byte!"

"Well, that's hardly deserving!" He ruffled the hair on Byte's head, which was welcomed by more tail wagging. "I rush in here to save your life and you command your dog to attack me?"

My stranglehold on the poker loosened while my brain tried to catch up. I was planning to run. Expected surprise or anger or threats. But not— What was he talking about?

"Max and I were spending some quality time—"

"Byte."

He picked the dog up to face him, one hand under his front paws, one supporting his bum. "You won't bite me, will you, Max?"

As if he understood English, Byte licked his face, and the man—Ellis, like the island, why couldn't I remember that?—laughed.

"That's his name." The poker dropped to my shoulder, but I didn't budge.

"You look more like a Max." Ellis tucked Byte against his chest, rubbing his back. He could snap the dog's neck easily. How was I going to rescue him? "Far less aggressive than Bite."

"Byte. With a Y. It's a measure of computer data storage."

"Oh." He finally faced me again, the smile still glowing. "Hungry? I made quite a lot of food. Fair warning, I decimated the kitchen, but your lovely cleaning woman was in and tidied up."

No. She came on Mondays. This was Sunday.

"You had an appalling lack of food in your pantry and refrigerator." He stood, keeping Byte close, a clear message he was in charge. After edging his way out from behind the piano bench, he strolled toward me. "So Abby helped me with some groceries."

Lies! Abby wouldn't have helped a strange man buy me groceries. That was ridiculous. Almost as ridiculous as him buying me groceries.

I pointed the poker at him, trying to look as intimidating as possible with the improvised weapon. And still in my pajamas. "Put my dog down!"

One hand under Byte, he raised his other hand and began counting. "I baked a few loaves of bread, cooked a turkey, made a stew, which I shared with the Becketts—they were quite concerned about you. Oh, and I made an absolutely divine—"

"Who the fuck are you, and why are you in my house?" I brandished the weapon, holding my ground.

Ellis's smile and shoulders fell, head jerking back almost imperceptibly. He placed Byte down, and the dog trotted off to the kitchen. "I also put out food and water for him, which you asked me to do when I told you how long you'd be asleep."

My eyes flicked back and forth from the kitchen to this odd man now standing in my living room, only ten feet away. Talking to me as though we'd known each other for years.

His brows furrowed, dark eyes narrowing to slits. "You don't remember, do you?"

"Remember what?"

His gaze flew heavenward, and the smile returned. He took a few steps toward me, so the poker almost connected with his chest. "The healing. I forgot. Your body spins backward while your brain is still going forward and the signals get crossed."

I lifted the weapon to his face. "Explain."

"TL;DR, you almost died Sunday morning. I healed you, we talked to the police and your neighbors. The medical examiner took the body away—"

"What?" A flash of a memory, of a dream from last night, exploded in my brain. Lying in a pool of blood, fingers and face smashed. I stumbled, colliding with the door behind me, which gave way, swinging open farther, failing to support me. Before I lost my balance and fell, Ellis dodged the poker and caught me.

I shrieked and shoved him away. His hands were as cold as ice. And he smelled remarkably good, like French toast on a Sunday morning, drizzled with maple syrup. Like cinnamon—

Stop letting him distract you!

I took a swipe with the poker, but he easily caught it and wrenched it from my grip. *Oh god.* He was the one who tried to kill me. What would he do to Byte after he—

Wait a minute. "You healed me?"

Men trying to kill you rarely healed you afterward. "Yes, after the other bloke died."

Body. Blood. My knees buckled, and I put a hand on the doorknob to steady myself, black spots clouding my vision.

He reached out as though to help me down, but the closer he got, the colder I became. "I'm not here to hurt you, Danielle. We made a deal Sunday morning."

I waved him off, slumping to the floor, some of the fog clearing. Snippets flashed through my brain: the pain of broken fingers, the scent of sulfur, a giant skeleton—

No. Those were dreams. It didn't happen.

"Dani?"

And this astonishingly attractive guy was not kneeling in front of me with a look of concern. Also a dream.

"Byte!" I hollered, easing to my feet. Nothing. Damn dog. I grabbed his leash from the hook between the inner and outer doors, and he finally came running to me.

"We should talk about this. I have to show you my list."

I clipped Byte's leash to his collar, dealt with the alarm system, and left. Clearly, I'd had too much to drink last night. Maybe I took some sleeping pills and didn't remember. It was all a dream, and I simply hadn't woken up yet. That made the most sense.

Eyes forward, I started down the sidewalk toward the park, still in my ratty gray sleep tank and shorts—thank god I'd grabbed a gray sweatshirt to spice it up. No bodies, no ceiling-height skeletons, no red lights in a secret room in my basement. Byte and I were going to the park like we always did on Sunday mornings.

What time was it? The sun shone from behind the trees, so it was early. Maybe early enough for off-leash hours, and Byte could burn off some energy. That's what we needed.

"Where are we headed?" Ellis walked next to me, a couple of feet between us. The morning was warm, but a cool breeze seemed to follow him.

"I'm going this way." I pointed down the street, then hooked my thumb over my shoulder. "Which means you should go that way."

"The park? Excellent!" He plucked a tennis ball from his backpack. No, my backpack that he was wearing. "I brought this for Byte, hoping we were headed there. I took him the last two days, and he loved chasing it. Oh, and I locked up behind us."

We crossed the street and hung a left, dodging strollers and cyclists. The tags on Byte's collar jangled as his legs moved in double-time to keep up with my stride. The trees were in full leaf, and the constant hum of traffic was familiar, comforting. Not like whatever was going on next to me.

"You and I need to talk about my list and make a plan. We don't have a great deal of time available. You slept longer than I expected."

We turned into the park, through the wide path separating the hubbub of the street from the calm of the green space. Gravel and paved paths zigged and zagged between the lush, mature trees and thick bushes, but I headed straight for Long Meadow.

"So, first—" He lifted a hand and a yellowed piece of blank parchment appeared out of thin air, hovering above his palm. Words began forming in golden script from an unseen pen.

My breath caught, and I snatched the parchment out of the air, swiveling around to find out if anyone else had seen it. Magic didn't exist. It was just another trick, like the cold and the frozen king.

"Wonderful! I'm happy you're embracing your role!"

More memories struck me. Flashlights in the dark, fists to my face, blood in my mouth. I shook my head, trying to clear them as they flooded my brain. Ellis's arms around me. "Who are you?"

"Ellis." A bird chirping in a tree caught his attention, and he inhaled deeply. "This park's a pleasant escape from the city, but truly no comparison to the real thing."

I brandished the paper at him as we left the shade of the trees, the sun lighting up the golden words. A gaggle of runners nearly collided with us on the path, ignoring everything but their own heavy breathing. "What are you? Some con artist? Think you can gaslight me into selling my house? You wouldn't be the first who's tried something dirty like that."

"I assure you, I have no need of your little abode, other than rooming with you for the next two weeks, as you offered Sunday morning. We made a deal, and I expect you to hold up your end of the bargain." He pointed at the sheet, then to a spot on the grass. The open field stretched out in front of us, at least as wide as a baseball field was long, dotted with early-morning patrons. He pulled a blanket out of the backpack and lay it down, far enough away from a mom with a pair of toddlers and another couple to give us privacy.

Balling my fists on my hips, I glowered at him. And at Byte hopping on his lap once he'd sat. "I need answers."

Instead of answering anything, he dug into the backpack and pulled out two travel mugs, a bag of granola, a container of yogurt, some bread, two Danish, cheeses, apples, oranges, and water. "You were asleep for two days; you must be famished! I know I am, and I ate two hours ago!"

He patted the spot next to him, the smile never slipping. He was so freaking pleasant. I had not been asleep for two days. And why did Byte like him so much?

"Excuse me?" I called to the mom with her kids. "What day of the week is it?" I shifted my glare to Ellis, waiting for his easily disproved lie to evaporate.

"Tuesday."

My stomach dropped. Tuesday? I remembered Saturday and bits from that night, but... Tuesday?

She was in on it. He'd picked the spot for us to sit, sure to have his accomplice nearby. Another series of images flashed past me, and my heart took a tremendous leap. The gunshot, the box cutter, and Ellis's hand on mine, him telling me I was safe.

Telling me he was a Grim Reaper.

"Dani, sit. We have a lot to discuss and not much time."

CHAPTER 10

ELLIS

Her face paled, and she sank onto the blanket next to me. Comforting her appeared to be out of the question; she'd swung the fire poker at me when I tried that. With so little time, we needed to focus on my list and her soul, but she was stuck on her mortality or something equally trivial.

She stared blankly at the food I'd brought. In my experience, food made humans happy, so she shouldn't have been so sour. Her dog was better company, despite how poorly she'd named him. This was unfamiliar territory for me, healing a human from near-death and revealing my true nature. Perhaps Reg was right, and this had been a dreadful choice.

I stroked Max's—no, Byte's—back while she continued to stare. How long could this go on? My palms grew damp, and an energy bounced around inside my stomach. What was that emotion? It had been so long, I'd forgotten the symptoms. Not excitement. Nervousness? Why would I be nervous?

Helping with the police, preparing food, speaking with her dog and neighbors, watching over her while she slept—the guilt and sorrow hadn't hit me yet. Those were the ones that brought me to my knees during vacation, and they would weasel their way into my brain soon enough if she and I didn't make some progress.

"So, my list?" I plucked it from her hand, released it, and snapped my hand shut to hide it away.

"You said you were a Grim Reaper." She shuddered and folded her arms. "That's a load of bullshit."

I grabbed the tennis ball and unclipped Byte's collar. An easy lob had him scampering halfway across the green.

Her eyes widened, following the path of the ball. "How did you throw it so far?"

"Open your right palm."

She continued staring after the dog but did as I'd requested.

"What do you see?"

Her jaw flexed several times as her gaze fell to her palm, and the energy in my stomach quickened. "My scar."

"Run your finger over it."

Again, she did as I asked, sending a faint tug through my essence. The hourglass lit up as Reg said it would, and she gasped, transfixed by the golden grains slowly moving from the full top to the near-empty bottom. "What the hell is this?"

"I'm fairly certain you thought I was kidding or not real Sunday morning. And likely still do." The dog returned with the ball and dropped it in front of me. I threw it for him again, and he dashed off. "But the truth is, I'm a Reaper, I saved your life, and you'll die when those grains run out."

She clamped her hand and eyes shut, wavering slightly. Hopefully, more memories were returning. "I was going to die Sunday morning, wasn't I?"

Didn't I already explain that? "Yes, you were."

"Doesn't the Grim Reaper take life?" Her voice shook, but she seemed to be calming.

"I'm not *the* Grim Reaper. There are a great deal of us." I picked up a Danish, with its cherry filling and granulated sugar covering the top. The pastry broke into innumerable buttery thin layers as I bit into it, practically dissolving on my tongue. Food continued improving every century. "We don't kill people; we collect souls and ferry them off to the afterlife. But yes, I have some control of time and can use it to heal a recent wound."

She nodded slowly and looked at me without anger for the first time since swinging the poker at me. "The skeleton?"

"Reg, my mentor and friend." Whom she shouldn't have been capable of seeing. One more mystery to solve. I handed her one of the travel mugs with coffee, another invention which had improved with age. "So, you're remembering things?"

"Yeah. Two more weeks of life, if I help you complete your list."

"Yes! Good!" I slapped my free hand on my knee and retrieved the parchment from my invisible pocket. "Time to get to work!"

She snatched it out of the air. "Okay, let's pretend all this crap is true and you're really a Grim Reaper. And you have some sort of powers. Don't you have rules about not showing them off in public? This paper, throwing the ball so far... Like some Reaper police will come for you or something?"

The tension in my stomach eased, replaced by a lightness in my chest and a laugh. "Reaper police? I'll have to tell the boss that one."

"The boss?"

"Yes, Azrael. But, if we're speaking of those who enforce the rules, that would be the Furies, under Raguel's control." I flicked my gaze across the pale-blue sky, in case naming him would summon him. If I never saw him again, it would be too soon. Why he'd bothered to harass us Saturday was beyond me.

Her brows pinched together. "Furies? Like from Greek mythology?"

"More like from annoying mythology. They're always analyzing things and going on about justice and putting things right. They do a lot of scheming, while we do a lot of working." I took another bite of my Danish, waved it off, and pointed to the first item on the list. "A walk in the park! We're already in a park, and we'll follow the trails after we eat, so..."

A silver line formed through the letters.

She looked from the sheet to me and back again. With a long exhale, she placed it on the ground. "That was easy."

"Indeed!"

She kept her right hand clenched against her chest and dragged her finger down the itemized list. "Two and three, music and laughter. You were playing the piano this morning and laughed about the Reaper police. So you've done those."

I shook my head, accepting the ball Byte dropped for me. He took a moment to growl at a man walking too close to us, but when I cocked my arm back to throw it, he crouched, tail wagging frantically, and was off like a flash when I let it go. "No, they have to be big moments. Special."

"Why?" She maintained a finger on the paper. "And why do you have this list?"

I sighed. We had twelve days to redeem her soul and she was going to consume them by just asking questions. "Every hundred years, each Reaper must endure two weeks in human form."

"I think you mean *is really lucky to spend two weeks.*" She glowered, much like her first reaction to me in Central Park. Somehow, the familiarity felt like progress.

"Our part in the natural order carries significant weight and emotional consequence. If we experienced the horror a soul undergoes when they're cast into the Pit—"

Her eyes widened, possibly recalling the red light and the screams Sunday morning.

"—we'd never be able to do it. Everyone would be sent to paradise. And that's simply not the way of things. Therefore, we exist without feelings for all but two weeks per century."

"What does that have to do with..." She progressed to number four, her brow furrowing. "A birthday party?"

"Imagine every emotion you've experienced for the last decade was held back from you. You felt nothing." I offered her a Danish, but she declined. No coffee, no food. Perhaps her death would be of starvation. "Then they were all deposited in your head at the same moment. All of them. That's what this is like."

"But..." She continued reading. "Delicious meal, dancing, and a sunset?"

"Now imagine the emotions given to you all at once were only the bad ones." I began peeling an orange for her, in case she preferred fruit to sweets.

"Sounds like my life," she muttered, her closed right hand moving, tugging at me, as she rubbed the scar. She did it often, her eyes losing focus when she did. What was going through her head? Sadness? Memories of those she'd lost?

My throat went dry, and I coughed around a bite of the orange I'd unintentionally popped into my mouth. I'd done this to her. Stolen her joy and replaced it with sorrow. The guilt swirled in my chest, crushing my lungs, piercing my heart. I was a horrible, evil creat—

Stop.

I was not about to be swallowed by the depths so early. The sun was shining, the food wonderful, the company distracting. Mostly the dog. I choked out, "Next."

She handed me a bottle of water. "Number eight: Doing a good deed? I still don't understand. What's the point of this?"

"Oh!" I perked up, gesturing at the paper, pushing back the dark clouds before they overcame me. The silver line appeared over number eight. "I healed you! I saved your life! That's definitely a good deed!"

She rolled her eyes. "The point?"

"Ironically, we call this time our *vacation*. We cease work, and instead, we suffer. My goal this century: cram my days with so many good things I don't have time to dwell on the bad." Byte returned, dropping the ball in front of me. "Take Max, for example."

"Byte. It's literally written on his collar tag."

"I know." I gave her a wink. It was met with a quirk of her lip—more progress—which she immediately forced back down. "He helped me muddle through the first couple of days while you were sleeping."

She crawled over to retrieve the ball and threw it for Byte, watching him run. A breeze caught her hair, and she tucked the strands behind her ear as she settled back in her spot. What color was her hair? Caramel? Mahogany? No, chestnut. "You should have picked a better guide."

"Danielle, I feel your pain more keenly than you understand." I put up a hand to stop her before she could protest. Seven hundred years of reaping souls versus two years of missing her family. "I hope experiencing this list with you—if it lightens your burden, even a shred—will make my time all the better."

"You mean you're using me?"

"Yes." And trying to help her, but she was too stuck in her wallowing to see it.

"A good deed is selfless. Healing me doesn't qualify." She tapped the sheet, and the silver line vanished.

My jaw fell open, and I yanked it away from her. "What did you do?"

"What do you mean?"

She'd controlled my parchment. Even Reg couldn't do that. I threw it up in the air, tucked it away in my invisible pocket, and retrieved it again. The paper was in perfect condition, but number eight was still not crossed off. I willed the silver line to appear, but it didn't work.

It hung in the air for less than a second before she had it on the ground in front of her. "Reaper police, remember?"

"Old habits."

How had she done that?

A dirty tennis ball landed in front of me, and Byte climbed into my lap, panting. He'd finished chasing his toy and was ready to be scratched. "It's hard to separate who I am from what I can do. But you're right. We're not supposed to use any powers during our human weeks which might reveal our nature or help us avoid the emotions."

"Makes sense. But doesn't our agreement violate that?"

"Extenuating circumstances." More that I would take whatever punishment the infraction would incur. There were questions I needed answered about her pull on me. Visiting her as a human—and hopefully helping her—was worth the risk.

She hesitated, as though waiting for clarification. When none came, she returned to the last item. She snorted, almost producing a laugh. "Fall in love?"

My stomach constricted like it had when we first sat down, and I closed my fist to make the parchment vanish. Why was this funny? And why did her laugh cause the energy to dance around in my chest? "Yes?"

"You can't fall in love in twelve days!"

"The friend who composed the list assured me I could complete everything in two weeks." I gestured to my chiseled physique and stunning face. "Humans always find me attractive, so surely it'll work."

Her lip curled, a far cry from how she should react to me. "Wow, you're full of yourself."

"No, it's an objective evaluation."

Her scowl deepened. "Right."

I nudged Byte off my lap and stood, turning around slowly, holding my arms out so she could admire my full body. The T-shirt highlighted the muscles I'd chosen, the denim was trendy and cupped my pert rear, and the face and hair caused her pupils to dilate when we met Saturday. "Is there something you'd actually change? Something less than ideal here?"

By the time I was all the way around, she was feeding her dog a treat from the backpack. She hadn't even watched. "You're too perfect."

"There's no such thing. Too perfect is the same thing as perfect." Wasn't that what humans were endlessly pursuing?

"Everyone's got flaws." She ran her gaze over me, head to toe and back again. "You don't have a blemish or a scar anywhere, I'd bet. It's unnerving."

"Really?" I sat, producing the parchment and catching it deftly, so she couldn't complain. My stomach had moved around far too much during this conversation, and it had most certainly dropped at her criticism. "You believe it would interfere with my falling in love?"

"Best I can do is set you up with an app and get you a few dates. Maybe you get lucky and—wait, does that mean actual love or just sex?"

"He said 'falling in love' was the greatest feeling in the world."

"Who's *he*?"

The owner of my second mark. The other human I kept track of and visited, whose contract was guaranteed to come to me. "Perhaps I should change it to sex. That would be simple."

She was right, after all. Sex was easy and familiar. From what little I remembered of love, it required trust and honesty. A belief the other person was good and filled a need in your life.

But why bother? I experienced emotions for two weeks every century, so until I met my Pair, what was the point in going through all that? And even still, the Fates would only tie a

Reaper to another Reaper and didn't provide Azrael with any clue as to who belonged with whom, so it was little more than a crapshoot. If Reg hadn't found his after thousands of lifetimes, what chance did I have? Perhaps the stories about every soul having a Pair were wrong, and Catherine had been right all those centuries ago. I didn't deserve—

Danielle's snapping fingers caught my attention. "Earth to Ellis."

I cocked an eyebrow at her.

"I was saying—" Her cheeks deepened in color, a bright pinkish red. Was she angry? No, anger would usually include narrowed eyes or flared nostrils. She huffed out a deep breath and grabbed the backpack, throwing my culinary offerings into it unceremoniously. "How long do we need to walk for?"

While standing to avoid her wrathful packing, I made the grave error of admiring her figure. Narrow waist, slim hips and chest, medium-length hair falling around her face to her shoulders, and alabaster skin. She was not my usual type, neither voluptuous nor eager, but she was attractive in her way.

It always took time for the emotions to line themselves up on vacation, but lust was a difficult one to avoid for long, even when regarding a woman wearing the clothes she'd slept in. Or perhaps because of? If I swapped the last item on my list, I could simply seduce her to keep myself distracted. Although that also would not redeem her soul.

Either way, he had told me love, so love would remain. She didn't know how to achieve that goal though. Perhaps I could request some advice from her friend Abby, who was in a long-term relationship with someone other than her dog.

Clearly, she understood the emotion better than Danielle, so she would be a far superior guide for number nine.

"I can count on your help?" I picked up the blanket and folded it as she clipped Byte's leash on. "I don't have to reap your soul right here and now?"

She flipped her head up, throwing the hair back from her face, and glared at me. "Whether you're being honest or this is all a demented joke, I can't exactly fault you for anything on your list."

"Except the last one?"

"Yeah. So, sure, whatever." She tossed the backpack at me, doubt still etched all over her face. "But I'll be locking my bedroom door at night."

Perfect. I had help for my list, could steer her toward the light, and she had not changed her mind about my staying with her. "Just so you know, I can literally be anywhere I want, anytime I want. Locks are inconsequential."

"Assuming you are who you say you are." Her face softened to a comfortable granite, and she looked me up and down. "Because if you are, you'll make for one hell of an interesting roommate for two weeks."

I shouldered the backpack, my gaze lingering on her delicate features. Thin lips and wide eyes sparkling in the sun. Until her brow furrowed. Was I staring for an inappropriate amount of time? "How are the memories doing? Are you clear on Sunday morning yet?"

"C'mon, little man." She gave a quick tug to the leash and headed for the paved walkway near us. "Not completely. And I still don't understand most of it."

"But enough that you believe me?" I walked with her, but when I moved closer, she veered away.

She rubbed my mark again, eyes forward. "No, but I can't argue with your paper or the coldness when you're too close."

"Coldness?"

She held up a hand between us, inching toward me. A foot away, she stopped. "Right here. It's like standing in front of an open freezer too long—refreshing for a few seconds, but then you want to slam it shut."

That was new. I'd never had that issue when I was visible, let alone on vacation. The police, Abby, the Becketts, the dog. None of them had reacted like her. "Are you sure? You're the first one to mention it."

"How could anyone not notice it?" She touched my arm with a fingertip—a spark zipped through me, pinging along every inch of my arms and legs, settling unexpectedly in my groin—and she winced before showing me how red it was. "You're freezing."

That touch. It was like the night we met, but infinitely stronger. What was that?

I tore my attention from her, studying the trees we walked underneath, the runners and cyclists speeding past us, the squirrels skittering in the brush. I attempted to focus on the scent of the city, its smog and cloying bodily odors. Its cacophony of cars and voices and machines.

The distraction didn't work. I could still smell Danielle, like coconuts and pears, still hear her soft breath. Bloody Pit, I had questions, and all she was doing was adding more!

And I was already craving another of those touches.

Her head remained down as we continued, paying closer attention to her blue sneakers than the activity around us. "I didn't know that room was down there."

"The room I found you in?"

She nodded, quiet again. "I remember the men asking about a program."

"You told me you didn't know what it was."

"It's still hazy, but I have no idea." She stroked the scar again, and I careened closer to her, the layer of cold causing her to move farther away without looking up.

"Apparently, my father was involved in some things I don't know about. I'll give you fifteen more minutes out here, but I need to get back."

Chapter 11

Danielle

Blood. *Stop thinking about it.* Smooth slice through skin. Knuckles connecting with flesh. So much blood. The box cutter had been sharper than I imagined, the big man's neck surprisingly soft.

Stop. Focus on Ellis.

Ellis strolled next to me, gaze roaming the road, the trees, the houses, as though he'd never seen any of it before.

"So there I was—" He'd talked the whole way, telling stories which could scarcely be true. His arms waved as he described people and places dead for centuries. "—standing in front of the castle church in Wittenberg, and up walks this monk, bold as the day is long, and nails a sheet to the door. I mean, lots of people hung things on that door. It was fairly common, but people started reading it, and I tell you, it caused such a stir. The idea people shouldn't be able to pay to absolve their sins—"

"Wait a minute." I shook my head, which hadn't stopped reeling since I'd met this strange man. "Are you talking about Martin Luther? And the split between—"

"Yes!"

He was, to say the least, a distraction. And given the memories still flooding into my brain about Sunday morning, a welcome one. As long as he wasn't a figment of my imagination, which he could have been.

He continued telling me the story about witnessing the start of the Protestant Reformation. Then it was on to the siege of Caen during the Hundred Years War and something about the Aztecs, but he switched to a language I didn't recognize.

Halfway between the park and the house, Byte lagged behind us, so Ellis scooped him up and carried him under one arm like a football. My dog was going to be spoiled after his visit.

Could it really be true I'd be dead in less than two weeks? "Abby's going to take Byte. It's in my will."

"Smart choice. What about the house? You said people are actively pursuing it?"

"My dad grew up in that house. He'd want it to stay in the family, so I'm leaving it to his brother and sisters." I folded my arms against a wave of cold coming off Ellis, as though his temperature had dropped suddenly. "My aunts live in California, but they can all figure it out."

"Dani!" came a man's voice. "There you are!"

I lifted my gaze from the sidewalk. Dad's younger brother, Mike, was rushing from the landing on the front steps of my house. He ran through the opening in the small wall bordering the sidewalk and threw his arms around me.

Byte growled at him. Thank god. At least one thing was back to normal; my grumpy, jealous dog was still growling at human men.

"You're up and walking!" Uncle Mike pulled back to look me up and down, furrowing his brows, likely at my state of dress. "That's wonderful news!"

He was an inch shy of six feet, with close-cropped light-brown hair, horn-rimmed glasses, and a practiced smile. Despite the warm morning, he was in an impeccably tailored navy suit.

"I'm alright. Just a little tired." And not interested in talking.

"I wanted to check on you before work." Mike released me and took Ellis's free hand to shake, enveloping it with both of his. How did he not react to the cold? "And to thank you again, Ellis. I can't imagine what would have happened to Dani if you hadn't been there."

Well, that confirmed it: the creepy mystery man was real.

Ellis smiled at me and nodded. "I wish she'd woken me up when she went downstairs."

Woken him up?

"That could have been your last glass of water, sweetheart." Ellis tucked Byte against his chest and scratched his head until the growling stopped.

"Dani! You're awake!" Abby dashed out from the garden door of her parents' house. She rented the basement apartment from them and would eventually inherit, like I had, keeping the house in her mother's family. We hugged, then she grabbed Ellis to do the same. "I stopped in yesterday, but you were sleeping. How are you feeling?"

She also didn't react to his temperature.

I took a step closer once she released him, and it was there, just like before. I reached for his arm, growing colder the closer I got, and my fingertips stung when I made contact. He shot me a quizzical look as I pulled my hand away, shaking off the bite of his frost.

And the strange underlying thrill.

"I'm fine." I faked a yawn. "It's been a rough go."

Too much activity. Too many people.

"Do you need anything?" Abby put an arm around my shoulders. "Or does Ellis have everything under control?"

I gave her a tight smile. There were bigger things to worry about than my overall health or groceries, like Grim Reapers being real. And my impending death. And why that room was downstairs.

She leaned in to whisper in my ear, "How long were you planning on keeping this guy a secret?"

"Ellis..." I turned to him, ignoring everyone else. They all seemed to think we were in a relationship, so I'd use it to get out of the conversation. "I want to go inside."

"Need a nap?" he asked.

I nodded, squeezing Abby's arm as I ducked out from under it.

"I'll come in with you." Uncle Mike followed close behind us. "I have an update from the police and want to talk to you about our appointment."

"What appointment?" I opened the door and let the men in, while Abby headed to her place.

Mike shrugged off his jacket and hung it on a hook. "With Neil tomorrow?"

No, I still had three days. It was on Wednes—right. Not only was Ellis *not* a figment of my imagination, but he was right about it being Tuesday. Where was my phone? Or my smart-watch? I wouldn't have lost track of time if I had one of those.

While Mike and I stood near the front door, Ellis let Byte down, undid his leash, and walked into the kitchen with him.

Mike lowered his voice, watching Ellis until he was in the kitchen. "He wouldn't let me see you yesterday. I don't like that, Dani. Tell me about him."

What was there to tell? He was a Grim Reaper, used his magical control of time to heal my fatal gunshot wound, was friends with a giant skeleton, and he produced parchments with golden letters out of thin air.

"That's none of your business."

He huffed and put a hand on his hip. "I need to keep you safe, Dani. Don't you find it strange he didn't hear those guys breaking in? What if he was behind it?"

"Uncle Mike, I didn't hear them, either. They surprised me." I stood by the door and folded my arms, waiting for him to leave. "I don't want to talk about it. I trust Ellis, and I expect you to do the same."

"I know the last two years have been tough—"

"Stop." My jaw clenched as tight as my throat and stomach. John's eyes. The blood. Unable to move.

"But you're not the only one who lost—" He cut off and swallowed hard. "You're not alone."

I closed my right palm, stroking the scar, like I had hundreds of times. Except now, it would glow gold. Little grains running across my palm, counting down to my death.

This was too much.

I wasn't going to die in twelve days.

Grim Reapers weren't real.

Magic wasn't real.

Not real. Not real.

"Dani?" Ellis was next to me, offering me one of the damn Danish he'd brought to the park. "Eat. You need your strength, sweetheart."

I narrowed my eyes at him—*Stop calling me sweetheart*—but accepted it and took a single bite. A fast, angry bite, to make my point. But damn, it was delicious, so I took another.

"I spoke with Detective Riley this morning." Uncle Mike strode into the living room, taking a seat on the couch below the huge mirror, which reflected my haggard state. My hair was a tangled mess, I was paler than usual, and the sweater had a dark smear of something near the neckline.

Had I really gone out in public like that?

His gaze traveled around the house, still the same as my parents left it, with furniture he'd grown up around. He gestured past the parlor to the dining room table. "Why don't you use the office upstairs for your laptop? Working at the dining room table's bad for your back."

Because the office upstairs was Mom's, not mine. As it was, it had taken me a year to move my things into the primary bedroom, and that was only so I'd be closer to the main floor. There was no way I was taking over her office too. "Detective Riley?"

"Right. They identified the man you killed as—"

One step back, and I was against the still-open inner door, clutching the doorknob. Like earlier. More memories, more pain. I sucked in rapid breaths. The blood. I closed my eyes, but the dead man was all I could see. One slice.

You'll die when those grains run out.

"Open your eyes." The air cooled, and Ellis's voice was close, quiet. He took the Danish back before I could drop it. "Focus on this room right now. Focus on my voice."

Blinking my eyes open, I met his gaze. His eyes were my everything, soft and reassuring, like they'd been Sunday morning. A protective blanket wrapped around me, keeping all the dangers of the world at bay. This wasn't the aggressive, arrogant man talking about how easy it would be to find someone to have sex with, or bragging about how perfect he was. This was the man who'd saved me, who'd held me while I was near death and told me I'd be safe.

Uncle Mike walked over to us, stopping next to Ellis. His hand covered his mouth and his shoulders drooped. "I'm sorry, Dani. I wasn't thinking."

He was a numbers man, a banker full of facts and figures, much like my father had been. But my father was the warm one, made of hugs and laughs. Mom once said Uncle Mike spent his life in Dad's shadow and never felt like he measured up.

"I know. It's just been..." I focused on Ellis's eyes, the only thing in the room that comforted me. He smiled, the serenity calming my breaths, slowing my heart. But I kept my hand on the doorknob. Eventually, Mike would take the hint. "It's been a really awful couple of days and I'm tired."

"Alright." Uncle Mike squeezed my arm. "Quick update. He was a low-level thug with a wad of cash on him. They suspect the one who got away paid him to be there. No results from prints or DNA on the other guy, but they're canvassing the neighborhood and will pressure the thug's known associates for information."

Ellis didn't break from our shared gaze. "They believe it was self-defense?"

Uncle Mike nodded. "They found a bullet and casing which matched the gun they found next to him, plus the bruises you'd sustained." He paused, scanning my face. "Although you seem fine now."

"I put ice on it," said Ellis. "She's a tough cookie."

"And they're guessing the intruders snatched Byte and threw him outside. If you insist on living here by yourself,"–he eyed Ellis—"you need a bigger dog."

But I wouldn't be here much longer. It wouldn't matter. "I'll think about it."

"And I want to see the room downstairs. This is the first I've ever heard of it."

His face was tense, brows turned down. I was the one who'd been attacked, but it affected many other people. Uncle Mike, Abby, the Becketts. The looks, the pity on their faces, the worry.

Two years of those looks, and I was sick of it.

They had no idea what actually happened. This dry recall of police information was a far cry from reality. They worried about bruises and break-ins. I was dealing with my impending mortality and the knowledge things existed in this world beyond what I'd ever believed.

My chest and stomach constricted, as if they were being tightened by the giant skeleton. I put my palms to my eyes, trying and failing to shut everything out. To scrub it all from my brain. The screams that came and went with the red light in the basement echoed through my memory, and I switched my hands to cover my ears, to try and drown everything out.

"Mike." Ellis's voice was muffled, but made its way through my failed barrier. "She needs some quiet time. Please come back tomorrow."

"She's my niece! I need to be sure—"

"I know, but she's had a traumatic experience and needs rest. I won't leave her alone, I promise."

"I'll reschedule the appointment with Neil tomorrow." Uncle Mike's arms were around me, and I stepped into the embrace for once. If he had nothing else going for him, other than the lifetime of being there for me, Uncle Mike felt like Dad. Same size and shape, and if I didn't look, I could almost believe it was my father. But he didn't smell right, and his clothes were too expensive. I was going to wrinkle him.

"No, I'll go." I pushed back, taking a deep breath. "What time?"

"Two. I'll pick you up."

My hand flung to the doorknob. "No thanks. I'll take the train."

"*We*, sweetheart." Ellis kept using that word. He was trying to piss me off, wasn't he?

Uncle Mike stepped into the entryway and shrugged his suit jacket on. "Still no cars?"

"Train's faster. I don't understand why you bother." A thousand New Yorkers a year died in car accidents, give or take a couple hundred.

"Your Aunt Kelly said the same thing all the time." He hugged me again before leaving.

I stood at the wrought iron and glass door as he hopped in his car and waved. Once he was safely down the block, I spun on my heel. Ellis was still there with that infuriating smile.

"*Sweetheart?* What the literal fuck was that about?"

He winked and headed toward the back of the house without another word, popping the last of my Danish in his mouth. I followed, unsatisfied with the response.

"You told them we were sleeping together!" I shoved his shoulder from behind, wincing from the cold, but it didn't even cause a stutter in his step. "And why the hell is no one else affected by your cold? And what's with that smile? And your list? And this whole bullshit?"

He slowed, and I sagged against the frame between the dining room and kitchen.

I pressed my palms to my eyes, squeezing my arms against my torso, as if I could stop the tears I knew were on their way. Stop the thickness in my throat. And the shaking which would come next. I'd cried so much since the crash, it had become my default response to everything.

It would have been easier if Ellis had left me on the floor Sunday morning. Then it would be done, and I wouldn't be counting down until it happened all over again. "Why me?"

He gently wrapped his fingers around my wrists, but I jerked away at the burning cold.

"Stop!" I stumbled back into one of the dining chairs. "Don't touch me! Haven't you listened to anything I've said? It hurts! You are so cold, it hurts!"

Ellis stood stationary, so tall and strong I felt insignificant in comparison. He remained far enough away I didn't feel him, his jaw flexing several times, as the tears rolled down my cheeks. For two years, all I wanted in the world was my family back.

Now, I wanted something else. Answers. And he wasn't giving me any.

"You cut our walk short so you could visit the room in the cellar." He turned and headed for the stairs off the kitchen. "Let's go."

CHAPTER 12

DANIELLE

"I told you there were many people who care about you." He was three steps below me, the cold filling the narrow staircase more than his broad shoulders did.

I'd never seen such impeccable posture; the confidence practically wafted off him. A knot formed in my stomach. I wanted to hit him for it. For all of it. For telling people whatever he wanted, treating me like nothing more than a two-week distraction. Like a cheap toy to use and discard without a second thought.

His job held *emotional weight and consequence*, he'd said. As though he actually cared about anything other than getting through his little vacation with laughs, smiles, and sex.

"I can hear your teeth grinding back there." He flicked on a light as he reached the bottom of the steps. The gym lit up, revealing its cushioned floor, treadmill, bike, and weights. Mirrors covered the wall across from us, which reflected his face, just as tight as it was upstairs.

"I'd rather do this alone." I was close with my dad. Hiding things like an entire room in his cellar wasn't like him. Then again, neither was hiding that bank account.

Ellis paused, waiting for me. "You do too much alone."

"How old are you?"

His brow furrowed. "Seven hundred and a few decades."

"So why does this next two weeks matter? You could twiddle your thumbs and barely notice the time go by. Why do you care if I spend it alone or not?"

Before reaching the media area, with its wall screen and six power recliners, Ellis's attention landed on my evidence board. He stopped. "I wanted to ask you about this." He scanned the photos, papers, and notes. "This is unhealthy, you know."

Other than Alex, Uncle Mike was the only one who'd seen it before the paramedics and police Sunday morning. He'd said the same thing everyone else did: 'Dani, this is your grief talking.' It wasn't my goddamn grief. Something happened that night, and it wasn't just an accident.

"Is this what you meant when you told me to give up my hunt?"

"Not specifically." He pursed his lips. "I understand souls, Dani. The anger and obsession inside yours is plain to see."

"I'm not obsessed." Maybe I was, but that was none of his business.

He hummed aloud but didn't look away from the board. "What is all this?"

Not a conversation I wanted to have, but maybe someone who 'understood souls' could help me figure it out.

Just recite the facts, Dani. Facts are easy.

"My family died in a car crash on May twenty-second, two years ago. I got a big payout from the car company because a short in the electrical system triggered the airbags while we were driving." I remembered little beyond that. Highway speed, airbags deployed, swerved into... blank. The police told me we'd hit the median and a few other cars, but that was it. No one else was even seriously injured.

In my dreams, I sat next to my brother as he took his last breaths. Watched the blood trickling from my mother's ear. Saw Dad slumped over the steering wheel. Every. Night.

Deep breath in. Deep breath out.

"That was the crash." I tapped a photo on the left side of the board and continued to the far wall. "Dad was driving, Mom in the passenger seat, and my younger brother, John, next to me in the back. Mom and Dad dead on impact; John—"

My throat clamped shut. *Stop thinking about it. Conversation done.*

I stared at the wall. The door was closed, wherever it was. How did it open? And how had the intruders known about it? Would I find anything inside to answer my questions?

"Going in there is unhealthy as well."

I ran my fingers along the wall, searching for a seam or a button somewhere. "You see the work order in the middle of the board?"

"Mm-hmm?"

"My PI just found it. It's got Dad's name on it, but it's not his signature." There was a black bookcase along the wall, full of programming texts, biographies, and spy thrillers—my father's favorites. It felt off. It was normally centered, but today it was too close to the left wall. Like the entire shelving was out of balance.

"What does that mean?"

"It means I was right all along. It wasn't an accident." I tipped books, moved bookends, ran fingers along the backs of shelves, searching for a trigger. "The door is here somewhere, right? My memories after you healed me are sketchy, and I can't remember."

Healed me. The words came out like they were normal. As if I were talking to a doctor, not some mythical seven-hundred-year-old being. My heart took a brief tumble, rejecting the truth my head was coming to terms with.

"You told the police, correct? What did they do about it?"

"About other things I found, but not that. Not yet. They told me to move on, put it behind me. The PI's digging up more information before we act on that." I kicked the space where the door should be. Next resort, sledgehammer. Did I own a sledgehammer? "There was also some strange bank activity and extra insurance that didn't make sense. I left it for the legal system to handle, figuring justice would be done, but... Six months ago, the car manufacturer case wrapped up and all I got was money. So, I hired some investigators and even got close with a journalist who was sure I was on to something."

"But nothing?"

"Nothing until that work order and those guys who broke in."

"Think of how many more positive things you could have done with that time."

Finding justice for my family *was* positive. "I thought a lot about your warning on Saturday. I even thought about taking the work order straight to the police. But then those guys broke in and—and there's something to all this."

"Something that won't get you to paradise," he muttered.

"How did you know when to show up the other night?" Was it coincidence? Or was he watching me, like some otherworldly stalker?

"Phenomenal cosmic powers." He said no more, just grinned while he studied the notes along the right side of the board. The knot in my stomach switched to a spark. This was going to be a long twelve days.

I shifted my focus back to the wall, throwing a shoulder into it. "A little help over here?"

"I already helped you Sunday morning." He squatted, inspecting the photos along the bottom. "Our remaining time is for *you* to help *me*."

Dismissive asshole. He came barging into my house, sneaking off with my dog, telling me what I should and shouldn't do. Telling my friends and family we were sleeping together. Like he was the only one who mattered.

The spark kindled into a flame.

"You son of a—" I grabbed a paperback, a good five-hundred pager, and threw it at him. The odds of me hitting anything other than furniture were low, but it was satisfying.

It sailed through the air, over the recliners, and stopped. Hung dead in space. I took a step back as the fire grew in my belly. Not using his powers, my ass. How dare he steal this little gratification from me?

I took another book and threw it, then another and another. Each of them stopped midair, and he finally turned, cocking a single perfectly sculpted, infuriating eyebrow.

"Stop being so fucking cryptic!" One more book, aimed straight for his head, but it halted in the air with the others. "And open the goddamn door!"

He stood, brow drawing down and mouth tightening. One hand rose, and he produced a piece of parchment. The golden letters formed one at a time like they had outside, but in a different pattern. He pointed one finger at me, and I froze, mid-reach for another book, held by some Reaper power.

He approached slowly between the books hanging in the air. Bile rose in my throat, the acidic taste mingling with the Danish on the back of my tongue. The starry flecks in his dark eyes flickered and turned to white flame, causing goose bumps to prickle up my arms and legs. The air grew colder the closer he got—far colder than before.

"You ungrateful little child." His growl echoed in the space, despite the acoustic panels and his low volume. "I gave you the greatest gift I could already! A second chance! Despite that, you want more! Exactly like all you tiny humans! Always more!"

"I need to know who killed my family! They need to pay! And not with fucking money!"

"I warned you!" His voice boomed as the parchment floated from his hand, close to my face. His finger dropped, freeing my body, and I slumped to the ground, unable to rip my eyes from the sheet in front of me. "Behold your fate!"

The words danced on the page in a flowery script, making it hard to read. But the letters at the top were clear: *Danielle Cristina Edmonds.*

As was the word at the bottom: *Damned.*

With shaking hands, I covered my mouth. Damned? How? Why? I wasn't a bad person.

This wasn't real. None of it was real. I clamped my eyes shut and repeated the mantra over and over.

Not real. Not real. Not real.

But when I looked again, everything was still there. The parchment, the books in the air, the flames in his eyes.

My vision blurred as tears collected against my lower lids. Again! Goddamnit, he was making me cry again! "I don't deserve that."

"Then prove it, Danielle." He snapped his hand shut, and the parchment vanished, his face softening, fire extinguishing. He knelt in front of me, a foot away, dropping his voice to a whisper. "I've given you a chance. Take it."

"Can I change that in twelve days?" I swallowed hard as the tears fell. How could any of this be true?

"Anything's possible in twelve days." He gave a weak laugh. "Except love, right?"

I leaned my head into my hands. "What did I do?"

His voice remained soft, soothing my nerves. "The gates to paradise and damnation are inside you. You simply must choose the path for yourself."

"I choose paradise."

"Do you deserve it?"

I clenched my jaw and took several deep breaths. "Yes?"

"Humans, Dani..."

The air next to my head cooled, and I looked up. He'd reached for me but was withdrawing.

"Humans are weighed down by guilt and shame. The most deserving person might say they deserve damnation for fear of sounding boastful. While the most evil will claim they deserve paradise, because they feel the afterlife owes them everything, just as the mortal world did."

I brushed the tears from my cheeks but couldn't control the shivering. "I don't understand."

"There's a difference between what you say and what your soul believes. My primary job is collecting those whose fate is undetermined upon their demise." His shoulders eased down. "Those souls are committed to neither damnation nor paradise, and I remind them of why they deserve the latter."

He opened his hand, and his list appeared, showing the first item crossed off. "You accused me of using you, and that's true. But I'm hoping this will remind your soul of what it truly deserves as well."

"But why am I damned? What did I do?"

"I'm still trying to figure that out." He closed his hand and the list vanished. "The nearest I can figure is wrath. You said it yourself: You want the people who killed your family to suffer. You say you want justice or the truth, but what you really want is vengeance. That belongs in the hands of the divine, of those who create and weigh these contracts. Not you. Any other belief is nothing but pride, which is your second great sin."

"But I haven't hurt anyone." Other than my friends, by shutting them out. "Don't actions speak louder than words?"

"Intentions speak loudest of all."

I rubbed my thumb across the scar on my palm and the hourglass lit up. Ellis drifted toward me, the temperature dropping as he did.

"Danielle, the black cloud surrounding you has darkened your horizon, leaving you surrounded by a stormy and unpromising sky." He clenched a fist and held it to his mouth. "Let me bring your soul into the sunshine. Don't squander this gift."

What did all this mean? Was I just another job? If any other person—actual human person—looked at me the way he did, I'd think there was something else behind it. The way he leaned forward, the intensity in his gaze, his tight shoulders—I could almost believe he cared.

But he was a Grim Reaper. His job was to collect souls, not save them. Unless their fate was undetermined, which mine wasn't.

"I still want answers, Ellis. I need to know."

His head dropped as he exhaled sharply and stood. The books all released from his control at once, continuing their flight and slamming into the wall together. With one hand and no effort, he moved the bookcase along the wall by a foot. It *had* been off-center. And how did he move it so easily? There were easily four hundred books on the shelves.

"You're really strong."

"Yes." He pulled three books from the shelf to show me a button. When he pressed it, the door popped out slightly, the seam behind where the bookcase had been.

I leaped for it and swung it open. Time for answers. "Thank—"

Blood. Smooth slice through skin. *Stop, Dani.* Knuckles connecting with flesh. So much blood.

My heart hammered in my ears, fingers prickling. Why was there still so much blood on the floor? The man. That was his.

I took a step back.

Two steps.

Three.

My breaths grew ragged, and the spots drifted through my vision again. Again! This was a terrible idea. Why did I think I could come down here?

There it was. The floor where I'd almost bled out. Where Ellis had appeared. Blood splatter covered the walls, but where I'd lain was clean.

Why was it clean?

Fourth step back, bumping into a recliner.

He'd healed me. Held my hand. "Why weren't you cold Sunday morning, Ellis?"

"You can do this tomorrow."

"No. Now." I took a few deep breaths and held the last one, moving through the doorway, finding a light switch, and avoiding the sticky pool. It spread out like an inkblot, tendrils creeping in at least a dozen directions, a torso-sized smudge where the body had been. Where the giant skeleton had stood. The red light and the screams. And the smell like rotten eggs and decay. I'd caused that. I'd taken a life. "Add murder to my list of sins."

Ellis appeared ahead of me, and I startled. "Focus on me."

"Where's my blood?" I clenched my hands together at my chest. The smooth skin of the scar. *Breathe.* Everything dies. *Breathe.*

"Look at me."

My eyes snapped up to meet his.

His arms were outstretched, halfway to an invitation, and I wanted to collapse into them. He was so broad, he'd envelop me, and I'd be safe there. No matter how scary he and his powers were, how they shattered everything I believed about life and death... He could be flippant, rude, and dismissive, but when I needed him, he was there.

After one night and one day, I knew, deep in my soul, to the bottoms of my feet, that Ellis would protect me.

The room became fuzzy, and bile creeped up my throat. "I'm going to pass out. Or vomit."

The corner of his mouth quirked up, the sparkle returning to his eyes. "You haven't eaten in days. How about we start with the broth I made from the turkey, then we'll come back down here? Resume with the list tomorrow?"

I nodded and kept my gaze as far from the blood on my way out as possible. "I just need to go into the city tomorrow—"

"We, remember? Your uncle will expect both of us." Ellis walked behind me this time, likely to herd me forward. "What's the appointment for?"

"Neil's our family lawyer. Uncle Mike suggested creating a scholarship in their memory with some of the payout. We're finalizing the paperwork."

"Splendid!" Ellis clapped suddenly, his mood shifting so quickly it would have made me dizzy if I weren't so nauseous already. "That's a fantastic deed! I'll come with you, and we can cross that off my list!"

I paused at the bottom of the stairs, glancing over my shoulder. "It has to be *your* good deed, not mine. That doesn't count, either."

CHAPTER 13

ELLIS

"Ellis? You still here?" Danielle's voice was distant.

"I'm in the creepy secret room in the cellar!" The door was open a crack. If I'd had it my way, I would have sealed it shut for eternity, but that was hardly my choice.

After she'd eaten yesterday, we'd pulled a few drawers out of the office and inspected some papers, but her emotions were brittle. She'd grown tired quickly and slept the afternoon and night away. Just as well. The less she discovered about her family's death, the better for her. Any shred of fresh evidence would only ignite her need to follow a dark path.

I'd promised her one day to indulge her curiosity. She had very little time yesterday, so today was the day. The odds of experiencing a good laugh with her were slim. I was too cold for her to touch, so there'd be no dancing. Powers that be, the odds of her helping with anything on the list weren't looking good.

Unless I added *Have books thrown at head* to the list. Or *Get yelled at*.

I breathed slowly, deliberately, easing the rapid beat of my heart. I'd deserved it all. Empathy was a skill, not an emotion, and I'd honed mine razor-sharp for dealing with souls, not for humans.

The jangle of Byte's collar grew louder, and he squeezed through the space to settle in my lap. Without a thought, I leaned toward the door. She was stroking her scar, tugging me toward her.

It was humiliating she had that control over me.

"Come inside, Dani. You'll be fine."

She creaked the hidden entrance open, breathing like a rhinoceros. I looked up at her from my cross-legged position on the floor, waiting to gauge her reaction. Prepared to catch any books she might bring with her.

She made it no farther than the blood stain.

Rather, where the blood had been the day before.

"What the...?" She surveyed the rest of the room, taking a hesitant step inside.

I'd rotated the furniture one wall counterclockwise, so the filing cabinet covered the space where I'd found her, and the desk was no longer next to the door. And I'd removed the blood. The room was spotless, other than the six piles of paper surrounding me on the floor.

"When did you do this?" She was a far sight better than yesterday. Showered and dressed in something more appropriate than pajamas. Slim jeans and a fitted blue V-neck shirt, her mid-length chestnut hair pulled into a ponytail. She seemed rested. The dark circles under her eyes had almost vanished. Thank the powers that be.

"I don't sleep."

"Oh." She didn't budge, just hovered in the doorway, staring at the floor. "How...?"

More questions? She was always asking questions.

"A few years ago, I reaped the soul of a crime scene cleaner. Lovely woman, despite her ghastly job. She had a great deal to get off her chest about things she'd done, and I learned a lot from her. You'd be amazed at what a little baking soda and vin—"

She took an unsteady step backward, careening into the doorframe. Danielle was clearly not as interested in the intricacies of cleaning the floor as I was. "I want to apologize for yesterday. It was, um... it's a lot to process."

"I could have been more considerate." I stood, cradling Byte in my arms. "My emotions are unstable for the first few days. It's just as well you slept through most of it."

She waved a finger around the room. "You did all this?"

I pointed to the desk, not prepared to address the look in her eyes. The shame mingled with gratitude spilling out of them. "And there's your phone and watch. I found them tucked in a chair in front of your board."

Danielle took a step in, and I took one back to match. "I don't remember going to bed last night. Did something happen that's going to embarrass me in an hour or two?"

"You were exhausted and fell asleep in one of the big chairs. I assumed you'd be more comfortable in your bed, so I carried you to your room." And checked in on her several times to ensure she slept peacefully. Twice, she'd begun writhing from a nightmare, but a few soft words put an end to that.

Such fragile, easily disturbed creatures.

She chuckled and strapped on her watch. "Surprised I'm not a popsicle."

Jokes were a positive step.

"I wrapped you up in a few blankets before I picked you up." To me, she didn't feel any different than the others, like her uncle and friends. Or even Byte. But none of them flinched like she did. "Which reminds me: I told them we were sleeping together because the police needed a reason I was here before they were. It was the first thing that came to mind."

Her gaze crawled up from my feet, up my khaki shorts, past the dog, my white polo, and finally settled on my face. Why so slow? She tilted her head, crinkling her brow. "You have a scar."

Warmth climbed from my chest to my cheeks, clearly from holding the dog against me. I touched the small mark by the corner of my right eye and shrugged. "Not too perfect now, am I?"

A jumble of energy crashed around in my stomach as she smiled. I could pause her right there and maintain that smile all day. Over the last two years, I'd sought her out multiple times for the peace her presence instilled in me. I never knew how it happened, nor why it weakened each time I saw her.

But this feeling inside me was different. Very distinctly not peaceful. It was similar to the jolts I'd felt when she touched me yesterday. What was that?

And why were we just standing there in silence? I hadn't accidentally stopped time, had I?

Byte licked my chin from his spot on my chest, and Danielle and I laughed.

"I started sorting things—"

"It wasn't there yesterday. I'm sure of it." She reached toward my face, pulling back when she got too close. "Did you hurt yourself and heal? Or can you control your appearance?"

"The latter."

Her body bounced ever so slightly, and she clutched her hands in front of herself. "Okay, that's kinda cool. Can you show me?"

"With pleasure." I handed Byte to her, ignoring how she winced as our fingers touched during the hand-off, and grinned. "He may not handle this well, so hold on."

First, I bronzed my skin, lengthened my muscles, and increased my height. My nose became broader, hair buzzed short and white.

Danielle's eyes went wide, and her mouth gaped. "Wow!"

I'd found her happiness, so switched to another. Short, narrow waist, paling my skin and adding a pink undertone, widening the space between my brown eyes. Taller again, olive undertone with blue eyes. Added weight, porcelain. Hazel eyes, glasses, robe, beard, bald, straight teeth, crooked teeth.

She gasped with each transition, eyes shooting open wider and wider, magnifying the energy inside me.

Finally, searching for a laugh, I turned my skin a brilliant shade of blue, releasing a tail and pointed ears. Byte barked and squirmed, snapping in my direction, so I quickly reverted to my regular form. He whimpered and continued struggling until Danielle let him go, and he tore out of the room.

But not her. Things were different between us today.

"I recognized the second last one."

She'd caught me.

I wasn't prepared for this conversation. "I think we should start with this pile. It has—"

"We've met before, haven't we? Before Saturday?" The lightness in her eyes dimmed.

"—the most recent paperwork, from the six months—"

She took a step toward me, so she was at the edge of the layer of cold around me. Only a foot away, so close I could smell her minty breath. "I'll be dead in eleven days. What does another mystery of the universe matter?"

"—before the accident."

"The hospital. After the crash?" She gazed at the ceiling, eyes flicking back and forth. "Was it a... nurse? In the trauma un—" Her mouth fell open, hands raising to cover it. Not from excitement and joy this time, but apparent shock.

Maybe this was the right point to freeze time. Or keep talking to distract her. "There's a gun in the bottom right drawer of the desk."

Her gaze traveled to the desk for a half-second, then was back to me. So much for that tactic. "When you said you worked in the trauma unit... You meant you *work* at the trauma unit."

"It can be a busy assignment for a Reaper."

She didn't budge, didn't lower her hands. But more importantly, she didn't step away from me. Our reality was sinking in, and she wasn't panicking. "Why did I see you there?"

"Because I let you." A lie. To this day, I had no idea why she'd been able to see me. "Like Saturday, I can take human form temporarily to interact with mortals."

"And why are you using this form instead of that one?" She gestured up and down, her hand coming closer than before. "I might not have freaked out so much with a familiar face."

"It's my default—the closest I can remember to how I looked before." With a few tweaks she seemed to like. I pointed to the stack of papers at the end. "Now, as I said, we should start here."

"Before? Were you human? Or are Reapers just spawned?"

"Both, actually." More secrets of the universe. Distractions, all the same. "Reapers are born with what we call Grace—akin to a genetic mutation triggered by the soul entering the body—and we live human lives with no knowledge of what we are. Upon death, if we've lived a good life, we're offered a position and are taught how to manifest our powers. It's the same for all immortals. Balance for the Furies, Oracle for the Fates..."

She was still so close, the energy began zipping through my insides again.

"How did you die?"

I had to step away. Look away. This was getting too close to a story I didn't want to share. "Protecting a cow."

"A cow?"

"It was during what became known as the Great Famine. Food was scarce, but we scraped by, in part because we owned a few cows and just enough grain to keep them healthy. I lived with my sister and her husband until one of our neighbors ran out of food. He thought his only option was to take one of our cows for his own family."

"He killed you for it?"

I shook my head. The memory remained so distant, and yet so clear. Edward, named after our king, lying dead in the field. "I was a strong young man, and he was starving. But he landed a lucky blow and sliced my leg open. It became infected, and that was it." My sister and brother-in-law tried their best, but there was nothing they could do.

"And you became a Reaper after that?"

"Somewhat. Another Reaper arrived, offered me the choice to join them or pass into the afterlife."

"You chose this?"

"I did. It's a tremendous honor." For all the guilt I held and how difficult our vacations were, I was lucky to have received this blessing. "And I was fortunate enough to have Reg assigned as my mentor."

"The giant skeleton?"

I leaned on the surface of the desk, crossing my ankles and folding my arms, creating a barrier between us. This was a more comfortable conversation than the direction we'd been headed earlier. "He was one of the first of our kind, initiated when the human population grew too large for Azrael to manage everything on her own. He's a kind being and wonderful friend, but he's perfected his horrifying performance. I've never heard a soul scream as loudly for anyone else."

She crossed to the desk and sat on it, two feet away from me. "Well, he scared the shit out of me Saturday."

Other than my first few reapings, I couldn't remember him ever calling the Stairs or mentoring anyone else. "When I met him, he appeared to me as a stout blond man with blue eyes, who baked the best bread I'd ever eaten."

Her head fell back with a loud laugh. "Bread? The skeleton?"

"Have you tasted any of the loaves I baked yet? They're up-stairs, and he taught me everything I know."

"This is ridiculous. I cannot believe I am standing here, talking to a Grim Reaper about a giant skeleton who bakes bread."

"And yet here we are." I shrugged. "And I have six piles of papers for us to go through before we leave."

She stared at the piles, biting her bottom lip. Not pouncing on them. If I could stoke that shred of hesitation, we'd be that much closer to my end goals.

"Or we could go into the city early, and you could show me around?" Crossing fingers was a silly human superstition, yet I found myself doing it anyway.

Kneeling next to the six-month pile, she shuffled some papers from the short stack, not truly looking at anything. One-hundred-thirty-six sheets of paper. The more absent her flipping became, the louder my heart beat. She was almost there. Almost making the right choice.

"Knock off the delicious meal for lunch?"

She pushed papers aside, toppling the pile, fanning it out. "What do you consider delicious?"

"Anything I don't cook."

With a chuckle, she gathered the sheets together and tapped the bottom edge against the floor to re-form the perfect stack, nodding. "That's because you haven't eaten anything I've made."

"Perfect." I walked to the door, giving her plenty of space to stand with the pages.

As she placed them on the desk, one slip fell out. She leaned down to pick it up and froze. "Oh my god."

No.

"The money!" She snatched it. "The hundred and fifty thousand."

"What?"

"It's a carbon copy from a check. From my father. For the hundred and fifty thousand dollars." She flew out of the office, while I nearly had to slow time to get out of her way.

She'd found something important, throwing my hopes of a delicious meal out the window. Why hadn't I noticed what it was and destroyed it?

At her evidence board, she jabbed a finger at a piece of paper near the center. "My father had this private bank account, despite swearing he shared all of his money with Mom. There was a deposit of four hundred thousand into it before his death, then this came out of it. I never knew who received it. Until now!"

I didn't want to know. But I promised her a day for the secret room, and I wouldn't break my promise. "What does it say?"

"It's written out to my godfather, Chris Beckett. For a river scene painting by Henry Moret."

"So, the money isn't a clue after all? This proves it's a legitimate expense?"

She turned to me slowly, mouth gaping. "My parents didn't collect art!"

Chapter 14

Danielle

"You gave us a real scare, Dani." Wanda rounded the kitchen island with cups of coffee for Ellis and me, setting them down on the dining room table. She and Abby were the spitting image of each other—petite and blond, with perpetual smiles. Wanda's hair was fair enough the gray was hard to see unless you were close, and she always kept her glasses on top of her head.

The Becketts' house was almost identical to mine on the outside, but the interior couldn't have been more different. My country-rustic kitchen and formal dining room were inspired by the original house design. Wanda and Chris had made dramatic renovations, converting the interior to open space with modern touches like gray counters, stainless everything, and sleek white chairs.

"Thanks, Wanda." I clasped my hands around the mug. This house had been the site of countless sleepovers, birthday parties, and play dates. Living next door to your best friend and godparents had benefits.

"You have a beautiful home, Mrs. Beckett." Ellis took a sip of his coffee, staring at me over his mug, eyebrow cocking. "And a lovely art collection."

He didn't want to be there. He'd told me three times in the one minute it took us to walk over from my cellar. I had a twinge of guilt over changing my mind about lunch, but we could grab food in the city after the meeting with Neil. This conversation was more important.

"I can't believe what happened. Attacked in your own home?" She shuddered before she sat. "The gunshot woke me. Thank heavens he missed you."

In my brain, I was barely a day past the incident. For everyone else, it'd been three.

Smooth slice through skin.

My heart quickened, and I held the mug tighter, breathing through it.

"Dani." Ellis's voice was quiet, but it held weight for me. He smiled, a movement I echoed, calming. If only I'd met him under different circumstances. Like having more than eleven days left to live and him not being Death itself.

Wanda leaned her folded arms on the table. "So, how long have you two known each other?"

"A couple years." I stuck with the ridiculous cover story. "We met in the hospital. He works in the trauma unit."

Wanda placed a hand on my wrist, her lips tight. She and my father had grown up together, next-door neighbors and close friends, like Abby and me. She married Chris a year after my parents married, and they'd been the center of their social circle. Then Abby and I were born a couple of months apart, and we were inseparable. The Becketts were there for me after that day, as much as Uncle Mike.

But I wasn't there for memories. "I don't know if you heard, but Sunday morning, we discovered there was a secret room in the cellar."

"Secret room?" She jerked her hand away and covered her mouth. "What does that mean?"

"It means my parents hid some things from me."

"And from me." There was a tremble in her hand, which fell to the table. "Why would they do that?"

I pulled the carbon copy from my rear pocket, folded perfectly in quarters. "Did my parents buy a lot of art from you?"

Wanda chuckled, looking from me to Ellis and back again, as though waiting for the punchline. "Good heavens, no!"

Ellis's smile dimmed. "Maybe they went through your husband?"

She shook her head at him, turning a smirk on me. "Your mother once bought a piece while we were out shopping. I can't remember how much it was exactly, but less than a thousand." She laughed, a wistful look on her face. "When she brought it home, we could hear your father from here!"

I turned the paper over in my hands, chuckling. "I remember that. Mom said it was my graduation gift, but Dad made her return it. A new laptop was far more necessary for a comp sci grad, and he'd picked out a powerhouse for me."

"Wild and crazy guy." Ellis grinned before taking another sip.

"Do you remember buying a river painting by Henry Moret, by any chance?"

Wanda's laughter faded. "Yes, we have one downstairs in Abby's—soon-to-be Abby and Grayson's—apartment."

"He's moving in?" What kind of best friend was I when I didn't even know that? They'd been dating for over a year, so I should have seen it coming, but... but what? I'd avoided her and all my other friends too much.

"Yes, they're moving his stuff in at the end of next week."

I unfolded the check copy and stared at it for a moment. Bad friend, bad goddaughter. What was I going to find out from this? Was this part of the evidence like I'd thought, or a misunderstanding? I slid it over to her. "I found this in that room in the cellar."

Wanda pulled her glasses from the top of her head and inspected the copy. She frowned, flipped it over, and handed it back to me. "I'm not sure what this is. I only remember the one Moret river scene, and I don't recall Luke ever paying us that much money for anything."

"Do you think Chris might know more?"

She pushed her glasses back up. "He might, but he's at work for the morning. Why don't you come by later?"

Ellis was on his feet before she finished talking. "Perfect. Let's go into the city and find something to eat."

"When do you expect him home?"

She collected the mugs—mine still full—and took them to the sink. "An hour or so. He's working from home this afternoon."

I mouthed to Ellis, *We're waiting*.

His shoulders dropped. "Or I can make us lunch?"

"A man who cooks!" Wanda turned to face us, fluttering her eyelashes. "He's a keeper."

"I always play for keeps." He winked at her. Did he have any idea how creepy he sounded?

Wanda walked us toward the door. "Good. Our Dani could use a little of that."

I rolled my eyes. Apparently, he wasn't creepy to her. "Don't encourage him."

Before we arrived at the front door, a painting over the sleek fireplace in the living room grabbed Ellis's attention. He detoured into the room, past the two wing chairs which sat opposite a sofa, all upholstered in green. Two dark-wood curio cabinets sat on either side of the fireplace with its white marble mantel. The painting was large, different shades of blue fading into white, all in a jumble.

"This is lovely," he said. "The thin gold frame accents the colors perfectly. Not too heavy or ornate, which would be too much in a grand room like this, but just enough to enhance it."

"Are you a collector?" Wanda stood next to him, close enough I would have been shivering, but she didn't react to his temperature either. I was the only one, wasn't I?

"A connoisseur only."

Having inherited Dad's lack of appreciation for fine art, I lingered behind them, leaning on the back of one of the wing chairs.

"We picked it up at a local gallery—"

They continued talking about artists, techniques, and museums. He knew a surprising amount about art. Did Grim Reapers have hobbies? Things they did when they weren't collecting souls? And did that mean when I'd attended museums in the past, there would have been invisible beings standing with me, admiring the same displays?

Art, baking, and piano. When did he have time to master those things? And where did he practice?

A small, dark-wood table sat between the two chairs. It held a reading lamp, a crystal bowl with individually wrapped candies, and a black Moleskin notebook. A prickle ran up my spine as I stared at the notebook. Surely, it wasn't—

"Did you really?" Wanda gasped, laying a hand on Ellis's arm. She left it there, not cringing, and looking at him in a way she really shouldn't have been. "Chris and I missed that exhibit."

Heat flushed through my cheeks. She was flirting with him. Were Chris and Wanda having marital problems? Or was this a Reaper-magnetism thing? Must be. It explained why so many people had been craning their necks to check him out at the park.

I shifted back to the notebook. Much of Sunday morning was still a haze, but the surviving intruder took a laptop and a notebook. Dad used Moleskin exclusively for programming notes and forced the obsession onto me when he began teaching me coding as a kid.

Chris and Dad had worked together at a software company until five years ago, when Dad retired to focus on private consulting and teaching at Columbia. It wouldn't be odd if Chris used the same notebooks.

I grabbed a candy and slipped the elastic from the cover, careful not to make any noise. The *In case of loss* information on the inside cover wasn't filled out, but I flipped to the bookmarked page. It was covered in pseudo-code, with a single data flow diagram and notations.

Ellis and Wanda made their way to one of the curio cabinets, as she explained where they'd purchased a few small sculptures. Was he intentionally distracting her? Or was this what interested him?

I turned a few pages, finding more of the same. With each page I skimmed, the faster my heart beat, and the surer I became. Unless Chris and Dad had the same handwriting, this was my father's notebook.

Why was it here? Surely, Chris wasn't involved with what happened?

I took slow, measured breaths, trying to calm myself.

No. There was no way.

None.

Just breathe.

This was an older notebook of Dad's. They'd worked together, so there would be a good reason for Chris to have it.

The front doorknob turned, as did Wanda and Ellis. I flipped the notebook shut and reached for another candy. Hopefully, no one would notice I'd moved the book and hadn't done up the elastic.

Chris opened the door and froze halfway through. His eyes met mine, then quickly flashed to my hand with the candy, then down to the table. There was no way he was the one in the cellar. He hadn't taken the book, told that man to make sure I didn't talk, then brought it here to read.

No. Way.

But the glazed-over deer-in-the-headlights look in his eyes screamed guilt. So did the weak feeling in my knees.

"What are you doing, honey?" Wanda crossed the living room to Chris, who came out of his stupor and snapped his attention to her when she kissed his cheek. She closed the door behind him and ushered Ellis over. "Have you met Dani's boyfriend, Ellis?"

Ellis followed and held out a hand without correcting her. We'd apparently moved up from *sweetheart* to full-on *boyfriend* without discussion. "Good to meet you, sir. Wanda was showing me some of your art collection, and I must say, you have wonderful taste."

"Uh, thank you." Chris shook hands, even though his narrowed eyes stayed on me. "You look good, Dani. Healthy. From what Michael told us about the other night, I—"

"Ellis works at the hospital." Wanda took Chris's messenger bag and hung it up. "He's been taking wonderful care of her."

Chris hurried from the entryway to the living room, stopping next to me. His face tightened for an instant before he threw his arms around me. He was thin and didn't have the same protective feel Uncle Mike had. "I was so worried about you."

As he held me, his familiar musky cologne washed over me, and a lifetime of memories flooded back. Fourth of July picnics, Christmases together, barbecues in our backyards. He couldn't have been involved, but the acidic taste of bile flowed up my throat.

I backed out of the hug and took the check copy from my pocket, handing it to him. My stomach twisted at the thought of what the notebook and money meant. That there was a possibility one of my father's best friends—my godfather—was involved in the break-in Sunday morning and my family's murder. Surely, he'd have a good explanation. "I found this in some of my father's things. Do you know anything about it?"

Chris unfolded the paper, eyes widening as he read it. "Did Wanda offer you anything to drink?"

"She did." I tapped the sheet. One hundred and fifty thousand dollars wasn't something you just forgot about. "Wanda didn't recognize this."

"It's nothing." He took a deep breath and folded it. "We were drunk and got to talking about surprising your mom with it. She always wanted to start a collection, and he was going to do it as an anniversary gift."

"But the painting's still downstairs?" said Wanda.

Chris handed the copy to me and spoke to her. "Luke sobered up and decided he didn't want to buy it after all. It was too much money, so I tore up the check."

That didn't make sense. The money had come out of the account. Unless there was another carbon copy somewhere that would point to another expenditure in the same amount. On the same day.

But then there was the notebook. Was it my father's? Say something about it or not? I reached for the notebook, but before my hand landed on it, Chris hooked his arm around mine and led me toward the door. My brain spun. He was steering me away from the book. I was sure of it.

Chris gave a weak smile. "Sorry, you two, but I came home from work early because I'm not feeling well and would like to go for a nap."

Ellis offered his hand, causing Chris to release me. "Our apologies for the intrusion."

My heart raced. It had to be my father's notebook, which meant Chris had either been in the room Sunday morning or knew who had. And he was almost surely lying about the money.

Chris was behind the break-in. My father's best friend. My godfather.

But why?

CHAPTER 15

ELLIS

"Think about it, Ellis!" Danielle had been on edge since we left the Becketts' house, unable to settle on a single emotion, whether rage, sorrow, or confusion. She'd charged down to the office in the cellar, tearing the place apart for evidence. She was hurt, certain Chris had her father's notebook and had lied about the money. She needed more proof, but we found nothing.

With one tiny slip of paper—the check copy—my hopes of touring The Big Apple of the twenty-first century with Danielle had vanished. At least for the morning. Perhaps the meeting with her uncle and the lawyer would refocus her on my needs and on resolving the situation with her soul's damnation.

Or perhaps all I'd see of the city was this dull elevator.

"Of course! That's why Byte didn't wake me up! Chris and Wanda take care of him all the time, so he's practically the only man on the planet Byte doesn't bark at. Chris could have easily thrown him outside so there'd be no noise." She strode out of the elevator, through the landing with its gray marble walls, and into the pale-blue hallway. It was lavish, decorated with plants, artwork, and soft lighting. "And why they didn't trigger my alarm. Chris has my codes!"

"That makes sen—"

"Shit!" She halted so suddenly, I nearly ran into her. "I need to change my alarm code."

"Deal with that later."

She spun to me, eyes wide. "What if he's in the house right now? What if he saw us leave and—"

"Calm down." This, I could fix. I inclined my head toward the men's washroom down the hall. "I just need a moment. Old code, new code, and instructions on how to change it."

The vibration in her stopped, and some of the stress released. "What do you mean?"

"I'll do it, but I need the information. I'll duck in there to ensure no one sees me, travel to your place, and change the codes." And maybe I could find her smile again after that.

"You can—" She lowered her voice, scanning the empty hall-way, as though some invisible person would overhear her. "Just go there?"

"I told you yesterday morning, I can be literally anywhere I want."

Suspicion crept across her face as she narrowed her eyes. "And my locked bedroom door?"

"I'll ignore whatever locks I need to, to keep you safe." Whether that was safe from intruders or nightmares, I'd do what she needed.

Her shoulders loosened, face relaxed, and she blinked several times. She stood there, doing nothing of any use, other than staring at me.

"Do you want me to change the codes or not?" Hopefully, an infraction like this wouldn't result in disciplinary action. Since it would ensure no one else snuck into her house and potentially discovered who I was, I had a solid defense.

"Uh, yeah." She jostled her head and pulled her phone out of her bag, tapped the screen several times, and handed it to me. "What about the Reaper police?"

I chuckled. "As long as I'm not seen and I'm not avoiding emotions, this should be akin to jaywalking." Granted, knowing Raguel, he would be the one to punish a jaywalker to the fullest extent of his powers.

Danielle explained how her phone worked, leaving it on a screen with instructions, and I ducked into the washroom. It was vacant and devoid of security cameras, so I entered a stall, locked the door, and moved to her house. A cursory check of each floor told me no one had been there.

She wasn't wrong to be paranoid, but I'd be with her every moment until her death, and I'd protect her if someone else broke in. Unless I was destined to fail and another would take her soul.

Was this all one grand lesson from Azrael? Punishment for delaying my vacation so long?

No.

Azrael would have encouraged me to complete my two weeks before Danielle's contract came due as a kindness. Reaping her soul while even a hint of emotion churned inside me would be near-impossible. This way, all the guilt and sorrow would be safely tucked away in time to escort her to the afterlife.

And to imagine, after that, she'd be gone. No more visiting her, watching over her. No more peace from the strange woman who could see me when no other human could. Who made me *feel* when I shouldn't have.

A knot formed in my stomach, accompanied by a most irritating stinging behind my eyes.

Gone.

My throat tightened, making it difficult to swallow.

In eleven days, I wouldn't even be capable of caring anymore. She'd be damned, and it wouldn't matter to me. My memories of her would be nothing more than photographs in my brain until a hundred more years passed, and I'd finally mourn losing her.

Between discovering the money and the notebook, she was worse off than yesterday. Her rage was peaking, not diminishing, and I was no closer to my goal of saving her.

The first tear rolled down my cheek.

The worst thing was, the longer I was human, the farther I'd fall into anger on her behalf. I'd forget my list and drag her down instead of lifting her up. That was how my vacations always wound up.

How much time did I have until I descended into my own rage and despair?

I wiped the ridiculous tears from my cheeks and re-programmed her alarm system. Undeath was easier, shuttering away feelings far more efficient. No standing around and debating how you felt, wondering how someone else might react to the things you did. These emotions were infuriating.

Her uncle Michael had sent her a get-well bouquet, which sat on the table in the middle of the living room. An explosion of colors, it stood in stark contrast to the white furniture and walls.

White and yellow roses, pink lilies, with smaller blue and purple flowers, all surrounded by green foliage. Once she'd calmed enough yesterday to notice it, it had cheered her up.

Plucking one white rose, I twirled the stem between my fingers. Maybe it would have the same effect today.

I moved to the washroom near the lawyer's office, into the stall I'd left from. Only a few minutes had passed, and the room was still empty.

When I exited, she was leaning against the wall, arms tight against her chest. The anger wafted from her, filling the hallway.

"What's that?" She pushed off the wall, pointing at the flower.

I handed her the phone, careful not to brush her fingers, and bowed with a flourish. "I thought this might brighten your dour mood."

She took the offered rose, barely glancing at it. Her eyes pinched and shoulders eased until she eventually smiled. It was slight, but it was there, and as it formed, the tightness in my chest released.

"You know, Ellis, you can be charming when you're not being an ass." She suppressed a larger smile, which caused a different tightness to form in my chest.

"Why, Danielle Edmonds, are you flirting with me?"

With a huff and a roll of her eyes, she started down the hall without me.

"Should I go back for a few more of those flowers? I rather enjoy flirtatious Danielle." I chuckled, but from the way she increased her speed without looking back at me, the wisest course of action was merely to follow her.

The double glass doors at the end of the hall bore simple black letters: *McEwan and Associates*. To the right, a large dark-wood reception desk with a serious young woman in a pale-pink hijab and well-kohled eyes. To the left, beige leather chairs and a couch, sleek and refined, with long paintings of the New York City skyline above them. A conference room stood opposite the doors, while a hallway ran off behind the reception desk.

Music filtered into the room from speakers in the ceiling—violins and a solitary piano. Another thing which had improved over the centuries: the ability to retrieve any music you wanted in an instant.

Dani marched straight up to the desk. "Danielle Edmonds for Neil McEwan."

The woman stood and motioned for us to follow. "Can I get you anything to drink? Coffee, tea, water?"

"No, thanks." She forced a smile, flirtatious Danielle transitioning back to irritated Danielle. "We won't be long."

With a nod, the woman led us down the hall, her wide-legged black pants and long jacket swaying as she walked. Closed doors to our right, glass walls and doors to our left, allowing a view of the tall buildings across the street. These structures made them feel so powerful, yet it reduced them to little more than ants in a colony. Moving their pieces of sand about, following the scent of the worker ahead of them.

We were shown to a large office at the end of the hall, with windows along two walls. On the far side of the room, a desk with computer monitors; closer to us, a seating area with three black leather couches around a short table. A few art pieces decorated the walls, but awards and other documents proclaiming

Neil's prowess as a lawyer outnumbered them. At the center of the room, two men—Danielle's uncle Michael and the one who must have been Neil—sat together at a round mahogany table, with two empty chairs. They stood as we entered.

"Dani!" The unfamiliar man hugged her. Three-piece navy pinstripe suit, sleek graying dark hair, tall and slender. He reeked of lawyer and was a perfect complement to Michael; the only difference between their outfits was Michael's lack of pinstripes. "Mike gave me an update on what happened on the weekend. I'm astonished you made it today!"

"Thanks, Neil. I hope it's okay, but I brought my..." She separated from him, gesturing to me and clenching her jaw. "My boyfriend, Ellis."

Neil offered a hand. "Ellis...?"

"Grimm." I shook, but he squeezed, as though attempting to exert dominance over me. I could have shattered every bone in his hand with little more than a thought. Neil was on my bad side from the beginning. "Like the fairy tales."

"And you're here because...?" He didn't let go of my hand, but cocked an eyebrow and leaned his head back to glower down his nose at me.

How many tricks did I have to reduce him to a quivering pile of jelly? The cloak and scythe to start with. The flaming eyes, red lights, skeletal face. The aura of fear I could project through the room. Perhaps the cold I could freeze him with?

I squeezed a tad tighter until he winced and pulled away. Generous creature that I was, I allowed it. Perhaps that was my good deed? "I'm here because someone tried to kill Danielle, and I don't intend to let her out of my sight."

Neil put the hand into his pocket and nodded, stepping away from me to sit. "A bodyguard?"

"He's whatever I need." Dani flicked a brief look at me, and I couldn't help but smile. That almost sounded like she enjoyed my company.

She and Neil sat, while Michael and I shared a far more hospitable greeting before he joined them. His eyes narrowed briefly as well. He didn't trust me, had told Danielle to be wary of me, and I appreciated that. At least someone watched out for her.

Neil distributed stacks of paper to Dani and Michael. "We've already worked out all the details, and nothing's changed since our last meeting. You can read the paperwork, but essentially, it explains—"

I walked to the windows while they spoke, looking down on the scurrying little ants twenty-five stories below me. For blocks, up and down the street, not a Reaper in sight. There were likely many at work inside the buildings. Perhaps even Jessica alongside whomsoever took over her training after my abrupt departure. A person died every nine minutes in this city, but the death wave was muted during vacation, so I wouldn't feel the passing of a life unless it was close.

Over the last hundred years, metropolitan centers like this had inspired Azrael to zone our work, so I'd rarely seen the outside of New York City in sixty years. Perhaps after this vacation, I'd ask for a transfer out of the city which would remind me of Danielle. Anywhere but London, which would remind me of Catherine.

In the window, I watched Danielle's reflection. She remained agitated, fiddling with the rose every now and again, looking up at me when she did. Our gaze didn't meet, so she may have thought she was stealing glances. The flower had been a wise tactic; she didn't rub her scar once during the meeting. I had to get her mind off Chris, for both our sakes. How hard should that be when her death was approaching?

I let out a slow breath. She was a stubborn one.

"Sign here," said Neil.

I turned to watch the three of them flip through pages, adding signatures next to little flags. First to Dani, then Michael, then Neil.

Neil collected the papers and slipped them into manila envelopes, pushing copies toward Dani and Michael. "I'm glad you're doing this. Your parents would be proud."

"If only it could bring them back." She pushed away from the table and held the rose under her nose, inhaling gently. For a moment, she smiled at me. The world, its weight, its horror—and its too short future—all faded away. It was her and me and the calm.

What caused it? How did she do it?

But almost as soon as it began, the cloud came over her again, and the peace faded. "Lunch?"

"About time!" I nodded curtly to the men, scooped up Dani's copy of the paperwork, and held the door while she said her farewells.

In the waiting area, a slight man in a black suit sat on the couch with a well-coiffed and adorned female companion. His jaw was set like granite, and he glared as we walked past him. I moved closer to Danielle in response, only half a foot separating us, and she didn't deviate from her path. This should have been too close for her comfort.

The woman behind the reception desk jumped up. "Mr. and Mrs. Fitch, I can take you back now."

Mr. Fitch kissed his wife on the cheek. "Wait here, darling. I won't be long."

I held the glass door open for Dani, evaluating the man in the reflection. He was bad news, but I couldn't quite read the headline.

"Thanks. Not sure how good company I'll be for lunch, and it's pretty late. We should just head home." She tapped the petals of the rose against her lips. "Order delivery or something."

"How boring!"

She jabbed at the elevator button. "Ellis, maybe you missed this, but we discovered this morning my *godfather* broke into my house and told someone to kill me!"

"Let the police worry about that. You need to focus on me."

The doors opened, while her face tightened, and she waved the rose in my direction. "Why? Because you're more important than I am?"

I ushered her into the elevator, which was thankfully empty. Once the doors closed, I pulled the papers out of the envelope. "No, because of this. This is who you are. A kind, giving woman who sees the good in people. Sees their promise."

"People are shit." She snatched the contract, staring at the front page.

"The woman who did this wouldn't subject me to miserable delivery food when we can find something fresh, local, or unique. I don't care what, just an experience."

"Michael strong-armed me into this." She dropped her arm, the papers smacking against her thigh.

"You didn't want to do it?"

"No." She sighed and gave a tremendous heave of her shoulders. "When we started the process a year ago, I didn't even want to leave the house."

My own shoulders fell, chest constricting. I stepped closer to her, raising a hand toward her back. I wanted to wrap her in empathy but stopped. Touching her would bring nothing but pain, and I'd already hurt her so badly. How could I make this up to her? "I'm sorry, Dani. I didn't realize—"

"Do you think I'm wrong about Chris?"

The elevator stopped at the eleventh floor, and the doors opened to welcome more passengers. Five of them. It was so tempting to freeze their time and continue with her alone, but I behaved myself. A well-dressed group, they spoke and laughed, discussing the meeting they'd come from.

At the back of the elevator, I maintained enough distance to keep Danielle at ease, but leaned closer with a brief whisper. "I think you're wrong about this entire approach."

Instead of responding, she bent her head, focusing on the contract and tuning me out. A few more stops on the way down had the elevator packed by the time we continued from the fifth floor. Almost everyone stared at their phones, rather than participating in life. This was something which *hadn't* changed for the better.

One of the crowd, a curvaceous woman with dark hair and bronzed skin, lowered her phone to give me a blatant once-over and a wink. "You heading out for lunch?"

"That's up to my girlfriend." I gestured to Danielle, and the woman frowned.

"Too bad."

Danielle made no reaction. So much for the flirting earlier.

The elevator doors opened on the main floor, and everyone filed out, except for Dani, still staring at the contract. She was on the last page, the stem of the rose strangled in her left hand.

I placed a hand behind her, cooling her enough to attract her attention. "We have to exit the car. There are others waiting."

She moved away from my hand, as expected, holding the pages in front of her as we dodged our way between those in the lobby.

We were soon outside on Madison Avenue, the buzz of the city energizing me. People of every shape and size filed past us; cars, vans, and cabs inched their way along the road; and shops littered the street-fronts of the buildings. A myriad of scents fought for attention—the roasted nuts from the cart nearby, the flowery perfume on a woman passing us, the Mexican restaurant next door.

Large urns overflowing with greenery dotted the edge of the wide sidewalk, separating us from the vehicles. Dani flagged against one of the planters, her face growing pale. She dropped my rose, looking as though she were about to pass out. "This just got a whole lot worse, Ellis."

I stepped close enough to catch her if she collapsed. "What did?"

"Neil McEwan was one of Dad's friends. He's also friends with Chris." She braced a hand on the urn, her breath picking up.

"Dani? Look at me. Talk to me."

"You remember I said Dad's signature was wrong on the receipt? The E was wrong." She held the last page of the contract up to me, stabbing a finger at the signature. "Neil McEwan. Same E."

CHAPTER 16

DANIELLE

I cradled the phone against my shoulder as I tore the signature page off the scholarship contract and added it to the evidence board.

Alex answered after a single ring. "Danielle! I was just thinking about heading over to see you."

"Did you have something on the mechanic?"

"Not yet. Neil told me your house was broken into?"

An icy breeze blew past me as Ellis paced. He'd brought up lunch at least a dozen times on our way back, focusing more on his stomach than on me. He could skip eating until his little mortal holiday finished and barely suffer. But his damn list was all he talked about. "Call the police, Danielle, not a PI."

"Are you safe?" asked Alex. "I can come over and—"

"Don't worry, I'm good." I stalked toward the secret office, my steps slowing as if I were wading through tar, coming almost to a stop. I shot a glare over my shoulder at Ellis, whose expression mirrored his temperature.

With a huff, Ellis released whatever time freeze he was exerting, and my pace resumed.

"It sounded serious."

"Alex, I need you for two more jobs."

"Neil said they stole items from your office." He was barely listening to me. One more man who thought his needs were more important than mine.

"I don't want to talk about that right now."

"Dani." Alex's voice was sharp. "What did they get away with? Did the police find anything?"

Why did he care so much? Why were he and Neil talking about me in the first place? If Neil was behind part of this, could Alex be in on it? They'd known each other long enough. What was Alex's background? I'd hired him blindly at Neil's recommendation. What if he was holding back information from me?

"How close are you and Neil?" *Great question, Dani. Way to smoke out the lies.*

"He's a client. And the only job I've done for him in the last six months is for your scholarship."

At Dad's desk, I pulled open the top right drawer. Pencils, ruler, erasers, stapler. Not what I wanted. "If I wanted you to investigate him, would you?"

"You *are* talking about Neil McEwan, right? Your lawyer?"

I slid open the bottom right drawer an inch, and it stopped, stuck. "I'll pay you double your fee."

Alex was silent. Was that a good sign or a bad one? If he took the job, maybe it was good. If he rejected it, I could call it a loyalty test or something. With how few days I had left, I didn't have time to find another PI, so he was what I had.

"I'll triple it. You swore you'd help me balance the scales."

"Those were the magic words."

Magic words? Which part? Tripling his fee, bringing up his promise, or the balance?

A pen clicked on Alex's end. "What do you need?"

"Dirt. Anything you can find. I think he's the one who signed the mechanic's work order." I pulled the drawer again. It didn't budge. I called over my shoulder to Ellis, "I need help opening this drawer!"

"Alright, that gives me something to work with," said Alex. "What's job number two?"

I chewed on my bottom lip. Was I really doing this? Was I siccing a PI on two of Dad's best friends? Could they really have been behind this? Or was Ellis right, and I was overreacting?

"Danielle? Number two?"

Ellis made little noise as he stepped into the room, coming no farther than the doorway. I pointed at the drawer, but he folded his arms and shook his head.

"Chris Beckett. He's a software architect with..." With the same company Dad used to work for. Where I'd worked until I couldn't face everyone anymore. "With Hargrave Security Systems."

"Got it. What are you looking for?"

"Same." I gestured to the stuck drawer, mouthing, *Please?*

"Okay, I'll see what I can find. Maybe I can tie Neil in with the mechanic." He jumped on this too easily after working for Neil for years. Why weren't they working together anymore? "Did you get into their computer system like we talked about?"

"No." I'd been too busy being nearly killed.

"Too bad." Alex let out a long breath. "And a word of warning: I've had my eye on a few of Neil's clients for some time now.

Powerful people you don't want to get on the wrong side of. You watch your back."

My back? Apparently, I should have been watching for them to come straight at me. "Thanks, Alex. I will."

As soon as I hung up, Ellis started. "You have more details now. Talk to the police. Surely, they can match the DNA they found here with Chris."

I tossed my phone onto the desk. "You don't think that occurred to me? He's here all the time! I'd be stunned if his DNA *wasn't* all over this house!"

"Fine, then Neil. Have him questioned about the car. Why did he take it in for maintenance and use your father's signature?"

"Who'd believe me? All I've got is a suspicious E in the signature." I heaved on the drawer, and it suddenly released, sending me sprawling on the floor. Pain ricocheted from my hip and tailbone up through my spine. "You fucking asshole! You froze it shut, didn't you?"

If I had books within reach, I would have thrown every damn one of them at him.

His jaw flexed, arms tightening in front of him. "You take that gun out, and we're done! I refuse to help you anymore."

"You don't understand!" I struggled to my feet, rubbing my sore side.

The tears threatened behind my eyes, but I wasn't about to cry in front of him again. Hit him, though; that was what I wanted. Punch him in that broad, muscular chest, which I knew could take the beating. Over and over and over until all the rage flew out of me, pummeling the truth of my life into him. "I dream about them every night! When I wake up, it's like I lost them yesterday! You feel a little sad for two weeks out of every fifty-two hundred. Two fucking weeks, Ellis! I've dealt with this for two years!"

His fists clenched and nostrils flared. "Bloody Pit, Danielle! You have eleven days left to secure a ticket out of damnation! Don't throw it away!"

I turned to the desk, placing my hand on the cool surface of the gun. It was so small but held all the weight of the world within it.

"Danielle, I'm tempted to freeze you, but I won't. You remember what I said about intentions?"

I'd never fired a gun before. It looked simple in the movies. There'd be YouTube videos to help me figure it out. Put in the bullets, point, and shoot. Done. Take everything away from Chris and Neil.

Avenge my family.

And if I got caught, who'd care? Everyone I loved was already gone, and I would be, too, in a week and a half. Besides, I was already going to Hell anyway.

"Dammit!" He came close enough I was in his circle of cold. "I'm here for you! Get that through your thick skull!"

"For me?" I spun to face him, body trembling as fire coursed through my veins. "Why do you care? You said it yourself the day we met in Central Park: Hundreds of people that week alone. I'm nothing but your next job!"

He closed in on me, causing goose bumps to crawl up my arms.

I smashed a hand against his chest, hurting myself more than him. "You're here for yourself, you selfish asshole!"

"Selfish asshole?" He bared his teeth, and the specks of stars in his eyes swirled, faster and faster, until they became white flames. "Your insignificant brain can't comprehend the weights and measures of what I am. You are so constrained by this flesh sack you inhabit for less than a century, you think you know better than me. I've walked this world for seven hundred years, witnessing the extent of human brutality, all in the name of want. 'I want more! I want what he has!' Progressing no farther than Cain and Abel. It's no wonder you're damned!"

"Big words from the tough guy with the powers. How unfortunate you have to stoop to my level for a whole two weeks and spend time with a pathetic little creature like me!" I hit him again as I backed into the desk, my hand stinging from the contact.

"We had a deal!" He planted one hand on the desk, the temperature dropping as his decibels climbed. "You agreed to help with my list! It's supposed to be the greatest things in life, but all I'm getting is the same torment I suffer every time! If I wanted to spend my vacation in misery, I wouldn't have bothered healing you!"

"Then maybe you should leave me the fuck alone!" The temperature had dropped so much, my breath came out in a silvery burst and frost crept up the wall. I trembled and my teeth clattered, the wind circling, lifting my hair around my face.

"Why do you humans do this? Why, Dani? Explain this to me!" His leg came in contact with mine, so cold it burned. "True justice is beyond you and your trivial existence!"

Catherine knelt on the ground, not ten feet from me, covering her eyes as she wept over William's body. A pale-yellow linen cote pooled around her kneeling form, there in the middle of the paddock, in the worked-up dirt.

I shook my head to clear the image of—who?

Catherine?

What just happened?

Ellis's body followed mine as I leaned back to put whatever distance between us I could.

"You're too close, Ellis."

The room darkened, an inky cloud spiraling around his feet, climbing up our bodies. His eyes transformed, the white fires becoming golden. "You are a drop of water in the ocean compared to me!"

I knelt next to her. "He's in Heaven now, Catherine, I promise. I took him there myself."

Every breath I took seared my lungs, and my vision swam with the woman in the yellow dress.

But the cold overwhelmed me, bringing my focus to him. He'd sworn to take care of me, protect me, but every fiber of my body screamed. "Ellis, stop!"

"I could take your soul—" His face neared mine, everything vanishing but the flames in his eyes and the agony spreading through my body.

"Ellis, stop!" I shoved him with all my might, doing nothing more than moving his shirt.

"—with less effort than you'd use to swat a fly."

He'd warned me his emotions would be volatile. How could I snap him out of it? He needed a shock.

She fell back at the sight of me, arms and legs flailing to escape.
She ripped the paternoster from her belt, beads scattering across
the ground, clutching the cross at its end, screaming, "You're dead!
You're dead! Monster! Demon! Begone! Go back to Hell!"

Blinking away the vision, trying to find control in the moment, I took a deep breath, like someone about to walk across a bed of coals. I clamped both hands on the sides of his too-close face and planted a kiss on his lips. My eyes remained open, watching his surprise, the flames vanishing and frost receding.

A jolt of electricity jumped between us, and something deep inside me sighed, *It's him.*

He pulled away and took several steps back, while I sucked in warm air to replace the stabbing pain in my chest.

Eyes wide, he gasped, "What was that?"

God help me, I was still shivering, but I needed to kiss him again. Hear that sigh inside. It was like an unseen hand pushed me toward him that I couldn't—didn't want to—fight. I closed the distance, the cold penetrating my light summer clothes, bracing for another. It was like wrapping myself around a snowman in the dead of winter, but my soul craved another touch.

I grabbed the back of his neck and kissed him, my mouth urging his to open. For a heartbeat, he softened, and I let out a hungry moan. As I inhaled, the piercing cold came with the breath, but so did an all-encompassing joy that flowed through my being, from our joined mouths to my stinging fingers, all the way to my toes.

The sigh came again. *It's him.*

He grew rigid and separated from me. "Don't do that; you said it hurts."

"I don't care." I would take hypothermia over never kissing him again. It was exhilarating, the most wonderful thing I'd ever felt. Energy zipped around inside me, and every cell in my body urged me forward.

"But I do!" He stumbled back, running into the door. "I—what was I—"

With a hand over his face, he vanished in a puff of black smoke, leaving nothing but the scent of cinnamon on the air.

Come back, Ellis. Please come back. Don't leave me. "No using powers to avoid emotions. Isn't that your cardinal rule?"

The room remained silent, other than the background buzz of the electrical and the hush of the air conditioner. Was he still there and invisible? Had he gone upstairs? Halfway across the globe?

As intense as the argument had been, I was unbalanced without him. My skin prickled at the cosmic unevenness of his sudden absence. We had to make up, apologize or something. Anything. I needed him back. "I don't want to be done with you, Ellis."

He coalesced slowly from nothing—from a vague outline to transparent, gradually becoming whole—holding a white rose. "I'm sorry."

The pain and anger I'd felt when we originally came downstairs had melted. The burning desire slowed. What did that leave me with? Confusion. The one emotion I'd felt more than any other since I met Ellis in Central Park. The emotion which only grew the longer I knew him. "I don't understand why all of this is so important to you."

"If Chris and Neil make their penance, they can find their way to paradise. If they don't, they'll suffer the Pit. But if they don't deserve the opportunity, how can you? Everyone must be worthy of a second chance." He held the flower out to me. "I have to believe that."

"You have to? You mean you don't?" How was I supposed to put faith in everything he was saying if he—the one who lived it—didn't have faith?

"I take people from their loved ones for a living." His face and hand fell. "Danielle, I'm going to be perfectly frank. I need help with my vacation. The negative emotions are taking over, and I don't know how much longer I can push them aside without you."

"I can't let them get away with what they've done."

"But you can, you see. That's the whole point. Intentions first, then actions, and finally words. Let the divine powers decide what happens to them, and by doing so, save your own soul." He raised his empty hand, and my contract appeared above it. The letters at the bottom were still the same: *Damned*. "You deserve more than this, but it's not my choice. I'm merely the delivery man."

I swiped the parchment in his hand aside and it vanished. He was offering me a chance, a lifeline, but it'd been so long since I'd thought about anything other than who did this to my family. It was all I had left, and giving it up was like heading out to sea and losing sight of land. I'd be adrift in unfamiliar waters.

But somehow, in some strange twist of the universe, I now had *him* until the day I died. Eleven days. Revenge, justice, and damnation. Or a shot at paradise and Mr. Hot Grim Reaper Trauma Guy.

I sagged onto the desk, head falling into my hands. Did I believe what he was telling me? How could I not? I'd seen him do things that were either true, or I was losing my grip on sanity. If it was the latter, then everything else—the intruders Sunday morning, the notebook, the signature—was up for question, too.

But if it was all true, I had to believe in second chances. I didn't want Chris and Neil to have theirs, but if they didn't, how could I? If I killed them, how was I any better than them?

I rubbed my hands up and down my face. Inhale, hold, and exhale. *Don't cry. Just don't cry again.*

My voice quavered. "It's not fair, Ellis."

"I know it's a cliché, but life isn't fair, Danielle." The air cooled around the side of my head, and I opened my eyes. His fingers lingered near my cheek, eyes soft and full of hope. "But I guarantee the afterlife is."

"Including mine?"

He fingered the hair at my neck, touching me, and yet not. "Except yours. But I swear, I'll do everything in my power to fix that."

"Why?" I shivered from the prolonged nearness, and he backed away.

"Because I'm a sucker for a pretty face?"

I paused, staring at him, which he met with a wink. When he smirked and tilted his head in that way Byte did, I spluttered a laugh. Charming and handsome, so full of himself, and yet he was there for me. On an eternal-soul level, he was there.

"Okay." I nodded slowly, the words sitting heavy on my heart. "I'll give Alex the week, then add anything he finds to what I have already. And turn it over to the police."

Ellis threw his hands in the air and looked heavenward with a laugh. "Thank you, Dani. Those are the sweetest words I've ever heard."

"You need to get out more."

"I do." He tapped me on the nose with the flower and smiled, soothing the ache inside my stomach, releasing the tightness in my chest. That was the best power he had: the peace he instilled in me.

We stayed like that for too long, until his gaze fell to my mouth and he moistened his lips. The desire to kiss him surged.

That was the cue to leave, so I stood, and he stepped back. "Let's go grab some food. There's a ton of restaurants within a short walk."

"How much did it hurt?"

He should have chosen a less appealing physical form—one I didn't want to climb on top of. The more we talked about it, the harder my willpower would have to work. "Sushi, maybe?"

He came closer, my body reacting to every twitch of his impressive muscles, the emotional roller coaster climbing, preparing for another descent. His fingers brushed my cheek, so frigid, but it was feather-soft and didn't last long enough to hurt. "My touch makes you shiver?"

"Yes." Heat spread out from my core, almost strong enough to compensate for his cold. "For more reasons than one." Temperature, lust, desire, fear.

He took another step, leaving us half a foot apart, and the mercury dropped. I looked up at him, his spectacular dark eyes narrowing as he cupped the back of my neck.

I gasped and spun away from him, scrunching my neck into my shoulders to clear the sensation that someone had dumped a handful of snow down my jacket.

He came close to me again and stood there, his breathing as deep as my own.

"You realize this is half the distance it was yesterday?" The corner of his perfect, bowed lips quirked up. "You're warming up to me."

"You have that the other way around." Heat flushed through my cheeks, betraying me.

"I know I said it already, but—" His mouth hardened, along with the rest of his face. "I'm sorry for my outburst earlier. I was hoping you wouldn't see that side of me."

I shrugged, the room still spinning from everything I'd seen, the kiss, how much more I wanted, and my choice to let my revenge go for a week. And Catherine? Who was she? A ghost? A memory? "You're not a monster, Ellis."

"I—" He flexed his jaw and blinked slowly, dropping his gaze. There was the bottom of the coaster. "Thank you."

He held the rose delicately between his fingers—the gift I'd rejected. There was such pain inside him, and instead of helping him fix it or avoid it, I was compounding it. But didn't I deserve a little selfishness in my last weeks?

And yet I was overcome with sympathy. For the Grim Reaper! The creature who stole people from their families. Plucked children and loved ones away from— No. That was how stories and myths portrayed him, without ever knowing who he truly was. He was the delivery guy, carrying out contracts someone else wrote up, and it weighed on him.

He hurt. So deeply.

We had too much in common. Most significantly, an emptiness we needed to fill with joy, but neither of us could find it on our own. I wanted to hug him, let him know everything would be alright. But I'd be lying. Maybe if I could keep him smiling, things would be better for both of us. Maybe we could find joy together.

"Let's not do this again." I plucked the rose from his grasp, tapping him on the nose so he looked up at me.

His smile was tight, not offering my soul the comfort a genuine smile did. He'd saved my life, and now he was asking for my help. A Grim Reaper was asking for *my* help. I had to give it to him.

"Let's order food. I'll hit the sack early, then we'll go out tomorrow." I headed for the door, not giving him time to argue. "It'll be fun. I promise."

CHAPTER 17

DANIELLE

"We're going to hit!" Ellis yelled, as our caged-in Ferris wheel car rolled forward, careening toward the stationary one ahead of us. It took a sudden swing upward at the end, and he whooped. Screams, laughter, the whir of the coasters, and loud music filled the air. I'd chosen one of the swinging cars on the Wonder Wheel in Luna Park for maximum Reaper thrill.

He had the front bench, and I took the rear, allowing us our own space and temperature. He'd squealed the first time our car hurtled forward as the staff filled up the other cars, looked back at me with a smile, and my heart was glad. Seven hundred years old, but it reminded me of the first time I'd brought Johnnie with me.

"We didn't hit last time. Why would you think we'd hit this time?"

"I don't know!" He looked out the left side, to the boardwalk and the beach. "The sensation in my stomach, combined with this strange tightness in my chest—"

"Fear?"

He spun in his seat to mock-frown at me. "Fear? Reapers don't experience fear!"

"Maybe not when you're immortal and stuff."

Swiveling to the front, he pointed to the Sling Shot, hurtling people into the sky. "Can we do that one next?"

My stomach lurched as the wheel brought us closer to the ground, making the gradual descent. "This wheel was built more than a century ago. You didn't do stuff like this the last time you were human?"

"My last vacation was during World War One." His shoulders sagged, and the joy melted out of the car like an Italian ice sitting in the sun, leaving nothing but a hot, sticky mess. "That was my worst one yet. I spent most of my time at field hospitals and evacuation stations near the front lines, comforting the dying."

What could I say to that? *Yeah, war sucks.* How enlightened. Or better yet: *You must have needed a break after collecting so many souls.* No, there wasn't anything I could say.

I touched his shoulder, a shiver running up my arm, and his hand lifted, as though to grab mine.

"Don't." He shifted away, voice sharp. "I don't need your pity."

Darkness had descended upon Ellis, in the center of an amusement park, full of laughing children. I'd promised him a better day and no more arguments like yesterday. Then I landed us smack dab in the middle of his sorrow.

I slid to the edge of my bench and gripped the back of his. "You know, I really suck at emotional shit."

"Me, too."

"I'm more of a bottle it up and push everyone away kinda gal. Pretend everything's okay, while more and more of the people I thought I could count on deserted me."

He turned in his seat, causing the car to sway.

"Not that I can blame them." I clenched the wooden slat at the top, digging my thumbs into the gap between it and the one below. Its bright-blue color matched the cage walls, the paint thick as if they'd added an inch over the years. It was lumpier than it should have been, and I picked at a glob with a fingernail. "How many times can someone hear 'I'm not ready to be around anyone' before they stop asking?"

He propped an elbow on the back of his bench, leaning his head onto his hand. "Tell me about yourself before the accident."

Before? I dragged my right palm across the slat, trying not to close the hand to stroke it. It was a bad habit, but it was my anchor, the physical remnant of my last day with them. Before was a place for fairy tales and dreams. Real life was after.

I rubbed the scar—now covered with his golden hourglass tattoo—across my forearm. No, not enough. Balling my hand, I ran my fingers over the smooth skin and exhaled. Could other people see the grains falling or was that just me?

The Ferris wheel came to a stop and the cage doors slid open. The girl working the wheel—who couldn't have been more than twenty—gave Ellis a blatant once-over as he climbed out. I'd noticed it happen at least a dozen times since we arrived at Coney Island. He was hot, no denying, but there was something else at play, as though supernatural pheromones wafted off him, attracting everything in a ten-foot radius.

"You were saying, sweetheart?" He grinned, shoving his hands into the back pockets of his faded jeans, accentuating his broad chest and narrow waist. He did that on purpose. Probably attempting to pull her attention to his firm ass. Never mind the way the heather-gray T-shirt revealed the outline of his pecs.

I pointed to the Nathan's hotdog cart nearby, and we made our way, keeping our distance from each other. "What's with that?"

His gaze lingered on the Spook-A-Rama, with its cheesy skeleton decorations. From the flexed jaw and loss of focus, he seemed bothered by it. "With what? Me wanting to know about what you were like before?"

"No. With that girl working the ride." I tugged his sleeve, stretched tight across his bicep, bringing his attention back to me. "She looked like she wanted to go for a ride, if you know what I mean. That happens a lot."

He glanced over his shoulder, in her direction, and she was still eyeing him. She needed to get back to her job. Or maybe one of the cars should hit her as it came around.

"I don't know what causes it. Power, inevitability, darkness." A smile tugged at his lips as we got into line. "And I'm kind of cute, aren't I?"

Yes. I pointed at the menu on the cart. "What do you want?"

"For you to answer the question I asked all the way back before that woman recognized my obvious qualities."

It was a lifetime ago. I was a different person. Maybe if I was going to live more than ten days, I could have gotten back there somehow.

The guy in front of us was short, with dark, greasy hair and a white T-shirt which should have been in the laundry. Cargo shorts and sandals with black socks, one pulled up to his shin, one slouching to his ankle. He needed to fix that sock.

Ellis waved a hand in front of my face. "Which one of us is distracted now?"

"I worked a lot, played video games, D&D with my friends, movies. I enjoyed touring museums alone, though, losing myself in another world. And chess, of course, every Saturday." I stepped to the front to order. He didn't tell me what he wanted, so he was getting my standard. "Two chili cheese dogs and two lemonades."

"Are there any movies you want to see?" He paid the man at the counter. "We could go tonight."

"I'm not really up for it. All this activity..." I waved my hand around at the rides, the flashing lights, the people, the music. "It's exhausting."

He tipped his forehead down and frowned at me, deeply enough the scar by his right eye puckered. The look—a combination of irritation, disappointment, and somehow amusement—tore straight through me, lodging itself in the pit of my stomach so firmly I took a step back.

"You really know how to make me uncomfortable, Ellis."

He leaned closer, keeping his voice down. "In my estimation, the only place you're comfortable is in your grief."

"That's not true." I was plenty comfortable doing all sorts of things. By myself.

"It is." He accepted the chili dogs from the man working the cart. "Perhaps a little discomfort will help get you out of your rut. Friendly discomfort."

A little? He was way more than a little discomfort.

I took the lemonades, and we sat at the only free table next to the bumper cars. Arguing wouldn't get me anywhere, so movies it would be. "I'm assuming tear-jerkers are out?"

"Definitely out." He took a giant bite of his dog, the chili falling onto the table, and his eyes went wide. "This is delicious!"

"Crossing-off-a-list-item kind of delicious?"

He shook his head and took another bite. One more, and he finished in hotdog-eating-contest speed. "Starving man who's been denied food for too long kind of delicious."

With a laugh, I pulled out my phone to check movie times as he cleaned his mess. He was over-dramatic, but the enthusiasm coming off him was refreshing.

Ellis shot up out of his seat. "I'm going to buy another one of those chili— Hold on."

"Hold on what?" I looked up to see him staring at a carnival game nearby, where people used water guns to make frogs race. "Don't even bother. Those things are rigged."

"You doubt my skill?" With a mischievous look in his eye, he bounded off for the game. I watched him for a moment as he stood behind the current players. It *was* like bringing Johnnie here when he was little. The excitement, the attention bouncing all over the place, wanting all the food and eyeing up the impossible prizes.

This was a good day. A better day than I'd had in a long—

Stop.

I took a bite of my chili dog—definitely crossing-off-a-list-item good—and returned to finding a movie. Nothing serious or sad. Action movies were probably out because they'd include death. Comedies? Maybe a romcom? Would he like that? Would it be awkward to watch with him?

I laughed around my straw as I took a sip of the lemonade, tart and super-sweet. No, he'd probably make inappropriate jokes through the whole movie. Not that it would be a bad thing. It was entertaining and a little flattering. Well, a lot flattering when he aimed them at me. *Just forget about all the other women drooling over him everywhere we go.*

A pulse ran between my legs, and I adjusted in my seat. The kiss yesterday. I blew out a long breath and closed my eyes. As kisses went, it was awful. Too cold, he was too rigid, and he barely participated. But the thrill of contact with him, of my lips against his. The spark was stronger than anything I'd ever—

"Victory!"

I startled, nearly spilling my lemonade all over my phone.

There stood Ellis, both hands behind his back, an infectious, beaming smile on his handsome face. Everything was the same as the day we'd met in Central Park, from the artful mess of his hair to the full stubble. Other than the little scar he'd added. "Left or right?"

"Right."

"Sorry, no, you meant to pick left first." He whipped his left hand around and produced a large stuffed animal. A gray-and-white dog, two feet high.

"You won?"

"Of course!" He held it out for me, and I put it on the table.

"So, right hand?"

He slid onto his bench, hand still behind his back. "Did you pick a movie?"

"Yes." I flashed my phone screen at him, showing the movie poster. A woman between two men, and a ghost in forties-style clothes. "It's a romcom about a woman who moves to the Jersey Shore to look after her family's house. Then her grandmother's ghost interferes in her love life."

"Sounds perfect." He stared at me, the triumphant grin fading to a more serious one. "Close your eyes."

I leaned away slightly. What did he have behind his back? Was this going to be a cream pie in the face moment? Or would he try to feed me something gross? "Why?"

He cocked an eyebrow. "Do you trust me?"

"Not really." A complete lie, but it felt like the right answer.

His head fell as he laughed. Once he'd regained his self-control, he smiled, and I couldn't help but mirror it. "Yes, you do. Now close your eyes."

I moistened my lips, which had gone strangely dry, and did as he said. It was intimate, between the music, bells, and squeals all around us; the smell of my chili dog mixed with the faint scent of propane and the nearby garbage bin. There I sat, eyes closed, trusting nothing bad was about to happen. With a complete stranger. Who was also a Grim Reaper.

My reality had reached a whole new level of weird.

"I won't touch," he whispered. "I promise. But keep them closed."

Something soft brushed my cheek. *Open your eyes, Dani.* A nervous laugh escaped, and I clamped a hand over my eyes to fend off the temptation. I trusted him. For some reason, I actually did. "What is that?"

"Shh."

It moved down my cheek to my jaw, skimming across my skin. Electricity and heat followed it, my nerve endings on high alert, causing me to bite down on my lip. What was he doing? And could the increasing tightness between my thighs calm down already? "Can I open them now?"

"No." His voice was quiet, but it filled my ears over the noises all around us. His fingers would be tender like this, like the way they danced across the keys on the piano or how he held his chess pieces.

As it approached my mouth, I caught a whiff of vanilla and caramelized sugar. Cotton candy. I spluttered a laugh and pulled away, releasing the hand from my eyes.

"Open your mouth." He winked at me, causing the stubborn throbbing in my core to escalate.

"You're getting creepier every day." I leaned forward and took a bite of the airy pink confection, letting it melt on my tongue, the sugar coating my taste buds as it disintegrated. "Which is really saying something, considering some of the days we've spent together so far."

"Creepy?" He took his own bite and licked his lips clean. "I thought I was charming?"

"You're a handy distraction, I'll give you that." And ridiculously charming, yes.

He switched onto my bench, straddling it, his knee approaching and passing the cold barrier. When I flinched, he inched back and lifted the cotton candy for me to take another bite, while he did the same. The warmth inside me spread, his danger and mystery as powerful an aphrodisiac as his handsome face, firm body, and elegant fingers. What those fingers could do if they weren't so cold. And those lips—

"Only a distraction?" He moved the whipped sugar from between us, playing at a pout. "You're hurting my feelings, sweetheart."

I leaned closer, to the point I cooled, and narrowed my eyes. Holding my smirk down was harder than I'd expected. "I sincerely doubt that."

He laughed and launched off the bench, tucking the stuffed toy under his arm. "Fine! Grab your chili dog. We need to hit the roller coasters before we head to the movie."

CHAPTER 18

ELLIS

"Happy birthday toooo you!" Danielle flourished her arms as she dragged out the last notes of the ridiculous song.

It was Friday morning, and we sat on a red picnic blanket at Brooklyn Bridge Park. The rhythmic buzz of traffic on the bridge and dozens of conversations around us provided a special kind of privacy this city excelled at. I stretched out on my side along the blanket, propping my head up with an arm, while she sat on one hip, legs curled beside her. It was another warm and sunny summer day, and she wore blue Capri pants with a white V-neck shirt which highlighted her collarbones.

She dropped her head, laughing at herself, her chestnut hair covering her face. "I can't believe I just did that."

"A deal's a deal!"

We'd avoided the cellar since Wednesday's episode. She didn't mention the evidence, Chris, or Neil; and I didn't mention her contract. Regrettably, the kiss was also off our discussion list, but it wasn't far from my mind.

The first one had been a surprise, nearly bowling me over with the strength of a dozen simultaneous death waves. Lust was a difficult emotion to avoid, but there'd been something else behind it, as though an unseen hand had pushed me toward her during the second kiss. An almost imperceptible whisper telling me not to stop.

Until the guilt settled in, and I realized how much the contact hurt her. Memories had flooded over me from her family's car accident, bringing with it the terror she'd felt that night.

I'd never experienced anything like it. The incredible high followed by the incredible low.

Yesterday's trip to Coney Island and the movies, however, had been a tremendous success. Not only were the distractions working, but the more time I spent with her, the more distracting she became. The cotton candy had begun as a joke. I'd planned to tap her nose and be done with it, like she did to me with the rose on Wednesday.

But watching her in that moment, I'd felt a great desire to touch her. The wisp of sugar had been a stand-in for my fingers, which longed to caress her cheek. Sampling its sweet flavor at the same time she had sent the blood rushing to my core. If I didn't warm up around her fast, I might have to resort to—what was there even to resort to?

My birthday cupcake sat in her hands, its small candle flickering in the light breeze. She held it in front of me, with its swirl of pink and blue frosting and tiny silver beads. "Now make a wish—keep it secret—and blow out the candle."

"Hmm." I considered the candle and the woman holding the cupcake. The birthday party was far smaller than I'd expected, but it had everything I needed to cross off the fourth item on my list. I was at peace, and she was smiling. "Careful you don't drop that thing, or the blanket will go up in flames like in the movie yesterday."

She grinned. "I'm glad you enjoyed it."

"I haven't laughed that much in years!"

"But..." She lowered the cupcake. "I'm assuming without emotions prior to Sunday morning, you wouldn't have laughed at anything anyway, so that's not saying much."

I tossed my head back with a laugh, my belly full of delicious energy. "You're too smart for me, Danielle Edmonds!"

"Of course, I am." She smirked and shot me a wink. Ooh, she was becoming playful. This would be fun. "Now hurry up and make your wish, slowpoke."

"Let me think." There'd been no yelling, tears, or frustration in almost forty-eight hours. I'd stood guard while she slept and kept her safe. We'd enjoyed each other's company, watched movies, played several card games I'd never heard of, and gone for walks in the park with Byte. What else was there?

Another kiss would be nice.

Pulling her soul up from the depths would be better.

I blew out the candle, and a pair of children sitting on the grass near us clapped. Looking at their mother, I held out my cupcake, but she shook her head.

"Don't accept food from a stranger." Danielle withdrew the candle, sucked the frosting off the end, and handed the cupcake to me. "Don't you know anything?"

I grinned at her and accepted my treat. "Haven't we already established I know more than you think I do?"

She feigned a glower and peeled the wrapper off her own cupcake before taking a bite. A big, unladylike, loves-her-food bite. As she chewed, she closed her eyes and moaned deep in her chest, a noise echoing the one she made the second time she'd kissed me. My manhood stirred at the sound and the memory, and I admired her while she lost herself in the moment. Her uneven face, awkward sitting position, and long legs. And the hair which never stopped moving.

What else might cause that noise to erupt from her?

After a swallow and another moan, she opened her eyes, immediately wiping the corners of her mouth. "What? Do I have icing on my face?"

I'd been staring. "Can I change my wish?"

"No!" She frowned. "Birthday rules 101: You get one wish, and you have to make it before you blow out the candle."

"I want to hear you make that noise again." I tilted my head and touched my tongue to the frosting, twirling the cupcake to take a layer of the decorations off it.

Her face contorted. "For one, I'm not making that noise again. And for two, that's how you eat an ice cream cone, not a cupcake."

I held mine out to her. "Maybe you can show me the proper way?"

She rolled her eyes and took another bite of hers—a very intentionally silent bite.

"What if I put it on my list?" I put the cupcake down and raised my hand to retrieve my list, which I snatched from the air immediately.

Her eyes widened as the golden letters flashed in the sunshine: *10. Hear Danielle make that noise.*

"I already made it." She cocked an eyebrow, and a silver line appeared through the entry.

"Oh, no you don't." I lifted onto my hands and knees, crawled closer to her, then knelt. My eyes remained fixed on her. If she manipulated my list again, I'd catch how she did it. Holding the paper up between us, I smirked. The word *again* appeared at the end of the entry and the silver line vanished. "What are you going to do now? You're contractually obligated—"

"To help you with the original list." She leaned forward, narrowing her eyes. "As it existed when we entered our agreement. Modifications must be agreed to by both parties."

We sat two feet apart. Practically together, but an ocean separating us. She held up her cupcake and took another huge, exaggerated bite, keeping her mischievous eyes on mine, completely silent.

"Alright." I flicked the page for effect. "I hereby accept your amendment to the list, as proposed on Tuesday morning. Number nine shall be changed from *Fall in love* to *Have sex*."

She spluttered, covering her mouth as she coughed on the food she'd foolishly attempted to devour in a single bite.

"Are you alright?" I inched closer, closing my hand to hide away the list, without actually changing number nine. This woman was my priority; she certainly wouldn't die on me again.

She nodded, putting me off with a hand. Fighting to keep the food down, she chewed and swallowed deeply, patting her chest. "Are all Reapers as forward as you?"

"Oh, *sweetheart...*" I drew the word out, causing her mouth to tighten. She despised that word, but I adored her reaction to it. I moved closer, our faces a foot apart. "If I recall, you're the one who kissed me."

"You have a point there." She licked some frosting from the corner of her lips, which wasn't actually there. Her eyes fell to my mouth. Was she toying with me? "And you definitely weren't kissing back."

"I might if you try again."

She moistened her lips and leaned in, causing my heart to leap.

My eyes closed and lips drifted open as she neared me.

Her warm breath brushed my mouth, then my cheek, finally my ear. "Sorry, Ellis, but that's not happening again."

I cracked one eye open and pivoted my head to look at her, so close she was blurry, but her grin was evident. "You're declining my invitation?"

"You told me no kissing if you were too cold." She pulled back far enough I could see her clearly, and she shrugged. "And you still are."

"Not one of the smarter things I've ever said." I ran my fingers through the ends of her hair that fell loose by her neck, not touching her fair flesh.

"It was pretty smart." Her gaze flicked to my lips and back to my eyes, brows drawing together. "You're sure this has never happened to you before?"

"Never as a human."

"Kiss him already!" shouted a woman nearby. We turned as one to see an attractive young redhead thirty feet away, with a few friends, all staring at us. "Or I will!"

Danielle gestured to the woman, her voice dropping. "Your Arctic layer probably wouldn't affect her."

"True. That does seem limited to you." I separated from her, resuming my casual position at the edge of our blanket. Picking up my cupcake, I held it toward her. "Don't suppose we could try that noise again?"

"He's all yours, if you want him." Danielle smiled at the redhead and popped the last of her cupcake into her mouth. She dug into the backpack next to her and withdrew a wooden tube.

I grinned at her and helped take the soft leather from the tube. "You're no fun at all."

She unrolled the board, its alternating squares of dark and light dyed into the leather. "Sorry, I'm going to be too busy kicking your ass to make any noises other than cheers of victory."

We took our pieces from their bags, and I turned them over in my hands. The workmanship was impressive, the knight's mane carved with such talent, it appeared to be blowing in the wind. "This is gorgeous."

"Birdseye maple and African ebony. My father had it custom-made by a friend and we used it for the first time the weekend before—" She drew her right hand into a ball and stroked the scar once, unintentionally tugging at me.

I glanced at her, then resumed placing my pieces. "You don't have to talk about it if you don't want to."

She carried so much sadness inside of her, and there was barely an hour that went by that something didn't trigger it. I understood all too well; my vacations were typically the same.

Sorrow at every corner, loneliness, a turn of phrase pulling me back to a moment shared with people who were long dead.

And all I wanted was to wrap my arms around Danielle and tell her it would be alright. But if I did that, she would freeze, and it most distinctly wouldn't be alright. Once she died, I'd be able to hold her soul and confess how much I'd wanted to do that in life. Confide all the lovely things her father said about her, describe how peacefully her mother and brother met with the Grim Pair, Anya and Katrina, before ascending the Stairs.

She picked up my king and pointed it at me. "No destroying this set."

"How about a wager?" I held my hand out, and she dropped the king into it.

With a grin, she straightened all her pieces and moved her pawn to e4. "What did you have in mind?"

"So many ideas…" I countered with a low-commitment e5 and resumed eating my cupcake.

"Alright." Her knight to f3. "If I win—"

"You get to kiss me." I winked at her, and she rolled her eyes. "That's not how this works."

My knight to c6. "But it could be."

"I was thinking more like…" She fluttered her fingers over her bishop.

"Are we doing this again?"

"The Evans Gambit?" She leaned over the board to whisper, as she moved her bishop to c4. "Isn't the Grim Reaper supposed to be a chess expert? Or are you afraid of a little competition?"

"Never taunt a Reaper, Dani." I picked up my bishop, considering it and how far I could push my luck. "If I win, we go out for our delicious meal tonight."

"Try again. That's tomorrow night." She pointed at c5, where my bishop belonged. "Abby texted me this morning. She snagged a reservation at Di Sano's and has two seats for us. It's one of the best Italian restaurants in the city, and their waitlist is usually months long."

"You didn't tell me."

She shrugged, tapping the leather board. "It was going to be a surprise."

"In that case..." I placed the bishop down but kept my fingers on top, signaling I wasn't finished yet. "If I win, I choose what you wear."

She narrowed her eyes, pursing her lips. She was thinking, but it felt like a delectable invitation. "Alright. I'll take that bet, as long as I get a veto if you pick something inappropriate."

I laughed and released my piece. "Fair. And if you win? Even though you don't have to answer, since you don't stand a chance."

Danielle leaned onto an arm, stretching out a leg, brain churning.

"I could suggest a few—"

She held up a hand, shaking her head. "If I win, you have to play our second game—which will not have any wagers associated with it—without that shirt on."

"Pfft, that's hardly a bet." I teased with the hem of my polo shirt at my hip, sliding it up to reveal a strip of skin above my waistband. When she didn't react other than a twitch of her lip, I sat up. I took hold of the back neckline and inched it up, watching her eyes widen as it revealed my waist, navel, then abdominal muscles.

When the shirt covered my face, she whispered under her breath, "Holy shit."

That was more like it.

I let it fall next to me once I was done. "All you had to do was ask."

Her gaze was busy trailing down my chest and along my stomach. Her breaths paused. A wolf whistle came from the direction of the redhead and her friends.

I snapped my fingers near my face, and her eyes launched up to meet mine. "My face is up here, sweetheart."

She laughed, crossing her legs in front of herself, and leaned forward on her elbows. "That's going to make it difficult to concentrate."

"I can take the shorts off, too, if it would guarantee my win?" I sprawled out along the blanket, propping up my head.

"If you get us kicked out of the park, I win." She picked up her pawn sitting at b2 and curled her fingers around it.

"The goal of chess, my dear, is to remain comfortable in your own game while making your opponent uncomfortable." I rubbed a hand across my abdomen, leading her gaze with it. A fantasy flitted through my brain about it being her hand moving against my skin. Or maybe her mouth. "How are you feeling right now?"

She bit her lower lip and returned her focus to the board, her cheeks reddening. "Like you're cheating?"

"I'm merely using the resources at my disposal." I leaned forward and lowered my voice. "For the record, I have a wealth of remarkable assets you're welcome to sample. Say the word, and I'll happily oblige."

A wicked smile spread across her face, and her eyes lit up. She placed her pawn on b4, maintaining contact while establishing the rules. "If I win, you have to stop flirting for twenty-four hours."

"No." I waved the option off and resumed my original position. "I would combust."

She cocked an eyebrow, not letting go of her pawn, fluttering her long eyelashes. "What happened to Mr. Danielle-doesn't-stand-a-chance?"

"Ooh, I like this side of you." I waggled my eyebrows. "You're on!"

"Excellent!" She released her pawn, but as I reached to make my next move, she rotated my c6 knight ninety degrees counterclockwise.

I pulled my hand back. That was the same odd setup as Saturday in Central Park. The one I'd tried to correct, but she'd thrown her book to the ground in an effort to stop me. "Why do you do that?"

Her right hand clamped shut, fingers moving across her scar. This had to do with her father and her family's death. Was it related to the story she'd started telling me when she unrolled the leather board?

"Dani, do you trust me?"

Her emotions constantly bubbled at the surface, but she tucked any thought of discussing them deep inside. She chuckled, opening her palm and swiping across the mark. It lit up, the golden hourglass with the shimmering grains falling through it. "I haven't had any nightmares since Sunday morning."

"You have them a lot?"

"Every night." The mark faded, and she swiped it again. "I tried psychiatrists, medications, alcohol, sleeping pills strong enough to put an elephant down..."

I did this to her. The shirtless flirtation was childish; I should put my clothes back on. She was hurting, and I was making jokes.

"I don't know if it was the near-death experience, the realization there's more to this world than I thought, or just having you here, but..." She took a few breaths, continuing to stroke the mark, watching the grains fall. It was roughly one-third done. "We were out of town for the weekend, the four of us. Dad and I normally played on Saturdays at the Chess House with the set I had last Saturday."

"I am sorry about that." I hadn't expected the king to shatter, only for it to be cold. It was supposed to snap her into paying attention to my warning. I'd failed her so significantly, and that just added to the tally.

"You really freaked me out that day." She chuckled quietly. "Although that was nothing compared to what happened that night."

"I was trying to warn you."

She looked up at me for a second with a rueful smile. "You knew I was going to die soon?"

How much to tell her? I had to balance enough truth to satisfy her without damning myself at the same time. "The Fates

draw up contracts fifteen days in advance, and angels dissemi-
nate them to all required parties."

"Must be some big-time logistics going on there."

"Angels are masters of multi-tasking."

She laughed and leaned forward to smack my shoulder,
pulling back when she was a couple of inches away. "So, angels
are real?"

I nodded. "There are many of them. You remember I mentioned my boss is Azrael? She's the Archangel of Death."

Her laughter faded away, a somber tone taking its place. "Do
humans become angels when they die?"

"That's an odd question."

"I have this weird memory that…" Her gaze fell away, returning to the mother with her small children. "That an angel kept
me company until the ambulance arrived."

My breath hitched. Powers that be, she remembered me. She
just didn't realize it was *me* she remembered.

"Maybe it's just a dream I've had so many times it feels real or
some figment to deal with what happened. He looked exactly
like my brother, and I always thought he was watching over me
that night."

"Dani." The pain in her voice ate away at me. Should I tell
her the truth? Would it set me free, bring us closer? Or would it
destroy whatever comfort the memory gave her?

She took a deep breath and shook the moment away. "So,
anyway, Dad and I sat down to play a game with the new set.
We got this far, he was fiddling with the knight, then he said
something about how chess notation would be an excellent
password."

"Odd."

"Not really. He was a systems security expert and he trained me, so we talked about stuff like that all the time. The odd part was that he ran off to find my mother right after. He left the knight twisted like that."

"Did he come back to finish the game?"

"No. Something inside me feels like he's here if it's pointing the way he left it."

"Was he given to erratic behavior like that?"

"Sometimes, but he always explained it. He was—"

She blinked, a long, slow movement, which crawled to a stop. The children nearby paused in their running about, the buzz of the cars went silent, and the giggling redhead with her friends halted.

The air and positivity and fun all rushed out of me.

A flash of white and gold caught my eye.

Great. Just what I needed.

CHAPTER 19

ELLIS

I craned my neck toward the top of the blanket.

Raguel straightened from his landing, golden wings unfurled. Ready to attack, as always. His voice was immense, like a human's boom, but an angel's whisper. "Golden boy! How has your vacation been going?"

"As well as can be expected." The last couple of days had been far better than I was expecting, given the first few. I was hardly going to give him any reason to ruin it.

"Fascinating outfit you're wearing."

I was not putting my shirt back on for him. For Danielle, I would have, but not for this celestial pain in the ass.

"Didn't I warn you about playing with this human?" He strode around the blanket, crouching next to Danielle.

"What else am I supposed to do?"

"What you normally do. Cry, mourn, weep for all the pain you've avoided for a century?" His wings remained out, hovering just above the ground, as though he were too good for Earth. "This one's different from the companions you usually choose."

I shrugged noncommittally. No need to bring more attention to her. "She'll suffice."

"More than suffice, I think." He leaned closer to her, his face nearing her cheek. "There's something special about her to garner your interest?"

My breathing deepened, and I used every trick I'd learned on my vacations to control the rage. *Breathe through it. Ignore his words. This moment is temporary. It's all a test.*

She was not mine, and he wasn't just an angel, but an archangel.

"She deserves more than you." He faced her, but his gaze drifted to me, loathing pouring off him. "Perhaps I'll have a go with her."

Fire burst through my veins, and I shot to my feet. "Don't you—"

One of his wings met my throat, and he turned to face me. All angels possessed voices like music, but his was like a contra-bassoon. Deep, rumbling, incapable of holding a steady note. "Don't what, little collector?"

Every molecule in my body wanted to tear him to pieces, throw him into the Pit, and watch as he turned to ash. But it was a fight I'd lose. Even if he showed mercy and didn't anni-hilate me, Azrael would never abide one of hers challenging an archangel. So, I did what I could. I remained still and breathed, with his bloody golden wing on me again.

"That's what I thought." Raguel narrowed his eyes and shoved me. Far. As I sailed through the air, he returned his focus to Danielle, whispering something in her ear. In a flash, he stood, and with one tremendous flap of his wings, ascended as a blur.

I moved back to the blanket, into the casual position I'd been in when Raguel arrived, prepared for Danielle to finish her sentence. What were we talking about?

Right. Her father and the chess set.

"—a big spy novel and movie fan, which I think inspired his career choice."

Why had Raguel come? He'd whispered something to her. What influence was he attempting to exert? And why did he care if I took an interest in *this* human?

"Although now that I'm thinking about..." She picked up the c6 knight, turning it over in her grasp.

Damn. He was the Archangel of Justice. And vengeance. He must have told her something about the piece, so it had to be a clue. But Raguel had the Furies to do this type of work, just as Azrael had the Reapers for hers. Why would he come all this way? Why did it matter to him? Was he simply manipulating her to make me suffer more?

That must have been it. Her continued want for vengeance and her damnation were part of *my* punishment.

"I followed him when he ran off..." She tilted her head and closed her eyes, scrunching her face up in thought. "I missed most of the conversation, but he told Mom..."

Double damn. If Raguel had reminded her of a lost memory which contained a clue, what then? Would our temporary reprieve be over? Would the fun and flirtation end?

Her eyes flashed open. "He said if anything happened to him, he'd hidden something in the knight." She gripped the bottom and held tight to the top, attempting to twist it, pull it, snap it in half. It didn't budge.

"I believe it's my turn?" I accepted her gambit and took her b4 pawn with my bishop, attempting the distraction.

Move on, Danielle. Stay with me.

Ignoring me, she grabbed my other knight and did the same thing, but the top and bottom separated. She gasped, dumping out a small square of black plastic which had been concealed inside.

I reached for it, every intention to freeze it into oblivion, but she withdrew her hand. If I stopped time, I could take it from her and no one would be the wiser. But everyone had phones with cameras and any number of people might catch something. Plus, she'd be furious. "Dani, please don't."

Don't leave me for this. Don't let Raguel win.

"It's a memory card. It holds data. It's a—" Her face and eyes wide, she clamped her fist around it and shot up from the blanket. "It's a clue or a message! It's got to be!"

My heart sat firmly in my throat. What could I say that I hadn't already? What other obstacles had he planted in her brain that I'd have to surmount?

"He *knew* something was going to happen! That explains the life insurance policy." She waved her free hand as if it would release the frantic energy bouncing around her. "We have to get home! I can read it on my lap—"

"Dani?"

She crouched down on her side of the board, eyes wild. "Let's go!"

"Is this the point at which I kiss you to snap you out of your downward spiral?"

Falling onto her knees, she screwed up her face. "Huh?"

"That's what you did for me Wednesday. You reminded me I was going down the wrong path, so at the risk of sounding like a broken record... Dani, leave it be. You promised to wait for the investigator before you did anything else."

"But"—she held up the little square—"this could be the key to the whole thing!"

"Is it the key to this?" I produced her contract, pulling it from the air and pointing to the word at the bottom.

Her shoulders sagged as she stared at me. "That's not fair."

"You're right, but life's no more fair today than it was on Wednesday." Not fair for humans, nor for Reapers, apparently.

"What's so wrong about wanting justice?" She took the sheet, clenching it in her free hand, so it creased and wrinkled. More ideas from Raguel.

"I don't write the contracts—"

"I know, I know." She handed it back to me, swiping at it so it vanished. *She* made it vanish. "Just the delivery guy."

We sat in silence. She stared at the chessboard while I stared at her. It'd been going so well. But one visit from *him* and everything was ruined.

Not ruined. She wasn't throwing things into her bag, which meant I had a chance. How to snap her out of this? Wait or push her? Say something or let her work through it on her own?

"Hi." A voice interrupted us. I sat up out of my lounging position to see the redhead standing next to me. She'd added a shimmering lip gloss since she'd originally caught our attention. "My friends and I have been trying to figure out if you two were together or not. On the off chance you're not..." She held out a slip of paper with a wink and a bite of her lip. "Here's my number."

Dani huffed out a quick breath and turned her head away from the charming young woman.

I held up a hand to decline the paper. "Thank you, but no. I am most definitely spoken for."

The woman shrugged, placed the paper in my hand, and curled my fingers around it. "If anything changes, call me." She sauntered off and gave me a wave as she joined her friends leaving the park.

Danielle's words came out sharp. "Could have taken care of number nine, I expect."

I ripped the paper and tucked it into the empty cupcake container, which I'd throw out. Then I held my hand out, palm up. "Give it to me."

"What?" She kept her gaze out at the water, at the slow movement of a long, glassed tour boat motoring along the East River.

"The black square."

She frowned. "What are you going to do? Freeze it so I can't ever find out what's on it?"

"No. I'm going to put it back inside that knight." It was a risk, but one I'd take. What other option did I have?

She turned to face me slowly. Maybe I still had her. She'd calmed from her earlier excitement and hadn't packed anything yet. But I'd have to tread carefully.

"It will still be there later." I flashed my most debonair smile, hoping for a laugh. "But I'm also going to do my best to distract you."

She didn't laugh, but the frown loosened a little. "How do you intend to do that?"

"By beating you at chess." I threw my wadded-up shirt at her, hitting her square in the face.

When she threw it back, she was working hard on suppressing her smile.

"And by continuing to flirt with you. Because there's no way you're going to win this little bet." I couldn't touch her, but I could wait. The temperature problem was resolving slowly, but still, it was actually resolving. There were plenty of days left to win her over, or at least to have fun and laugh and not focus on the bad things.

I winked at her, which was met by a tolerant smile. Perhaps she felt the same about her final days.

And thank all the powers that be, she relinquished the memory card. Against my better instincts, I returned it to its hiding spot in the knight, rather than sending it to join my paperwork and scythe.

We were back to where we'd been on Wednesday. The dark cloud hung over her, but I had more tricks up my sleeve.

Including choosing a beautiful dress for her for Saturday night.

Because I was not about to lose this game of chess.

CHAPTER 20

DANIELLE

"Don't hate me, but I'm officially leaving Grayson for Ellis." Abby wrapped her arm through mine as we left the restroom together. "I can't believe you've known him for two years and never mentioned him!"

We dodged tables in the dimly lit dining room, zigzagging our way to the back where the men sat. Red and gold pendant lights on long chains descended above each table, illuminating them like private islands. Along the walls, art spotlights shone down on murals in deep hues, with women frolicking in forests. Ellis said they were impressionist styles and mentioned a few artists they reminded him of. He hadn't said as much, but I had the distinct impression he'd met some of the people he'd named off.

Soft voices and quiet classical music melded in the background, and the scents of garlic, bread, and sizzling meats wafted by. After years of closeting myself away in the house, it had taken my impending death to remember what life was really about.

"And his eyes!" Abby slapped a hand against her chest.

"They're weird, aren't they?"

"I mean, they're so blue! Like sapphires or aquamarines or something! I can't stop staring at them!"

His eyes weren't even close to blue. They were like coal or onyx, with white specks. "Blue?"

"They're blue, right? Or are they gray? Whatever they are, they're gorgeous!" She squeezed my arm tighter as we neared our table. "And speaking of gorgeous! Your dress!"

I ran my hand along my free side, delighting in the way the silk jersey caressed my skin. The dress was a brilliant amethyst color, with a neckline too deep, and a sway to the skirt which made me want to spin endlessly. "I bought it yesterday, specifically for tonight."

She swatted at my arm. "You did not!"

"Ellis and I had a bet over chess." I cleared my throat when he looked up at me and smiled, the little scar by his right eye deepening as he did. *Had* he added that for me? He and Grayson had been having a good laugh over something. "The bastard wiped the board with me, so he got to pick what I wore tonight. Said I didn't own anything nice enough and we went shopping."

"Love him even more." As we reached the table, she threw her arms around me—she'd had too much wine. "I've missed you so much."

Ellis stood to pull out my chair, and my heart skipped. He was spectacularly handsome in his black suit, which he'd paired with a gray dress shirt and striped pocket square. He'd originally gone with a matching tie, but when I told him it was dressier than need be, he removed the tie and left the top couple of buttons undone. I was happy he had.

It was too easy for him to find the right outfit. I showed him some photos of men at an upscale restaurant, and he pulled clothes from wherever he stored his sheets of paper. He could have simply changed how people perceived him, like he'd shown me that day in the secret office, but he said this dinner was special, so he chose to wear actual clothes. I was pretty sure that meant he was normally naked, but he refused to answer my questions on the matter.

He pushed the seat in as I sat, and I waved him close to whisper in his ear. The layer of cold between us had been steadily shrinking, and, a week after meeting him, it was only a couple of inches. He was close enough I got a heady whiff of the scent of cinnamon which lingered around him.

"Abby says your eyes are blue."

He nodded. "Mm-hmm?"

"They're not, though."

His head jerked back slightly, and I could see him clearly. The restaurant lighting was dim, but they were definitely black with flecks of white.

"Here we go!" Grayson clapped his hands together, startling me. He reminded me of Ellis in many ways, both of them tall and broad, with ready smiles, loud laughs, and infectious charisma. They even shared the close-cropped facial hair. But Grayson's bald fade and waves hairstyle was far less chaotic than Ellis's artful mess, and his skin was a rich, deep brown, compared to Ellis's golden beige.

I turned as a server in an all-black uniform unfolded a standing support, setting his large tray on top. He placed desserts in front of Abby and me—dark chocolate mousse with light-brown drizzle for her and a tiramisu with vanilla drizzle and sliced strawberries for me. "I didn't order—"

"We did." Grayson took Abby's hand and squeezed it, while the server placed red and purple gelato at Ellis's setting and a small chocolate cake at Grayson's. "Happy anniversary, Abigail."

Her shoulders softened, and she let out a sigh. "Thank you."

They leaned into each other and kissed, her hand brushing his cheek, his caressing her arm. They'd met a couple of weeks before my accident, which meant I hadn't gotten to know him as well as I should have. She was in love. They were happy, moving in together, and all was right in their world.

Maybe they'd get married or have kids, be a couple forever. Maybe they'd split up in a year's time. No matter what, I'd miss it all.

I reached for Ellis's hand, slipping my fingers into his palm. A jolt of energy coursed through me, hitting my toes, careening all the way back to my fingers. Sadly, within a few seconds, the cold began burning, and I had to pull away.

Dragging my eyes away from Abby's joy, I focused on my plate, trying to steady my breath and slow my heart. Did he feel it when we touched, too? Or was it another one of those Reaper things, him exerting some strange power over a human?

Ellis leaned toward me, keeping his voice low. "Be happy for them."

"I am."

"Good." He gestured toward my tiramisu. "Because there's a surprise in your dessert and you'll only find it if you're in a good mood."

"Even creepier today," I whispered back, which was met with a wink. I picked up a spoonful of my dessert and placed it in my mouth, closing my eyes to savor the first bite. The custard was soft on my tongue, the espresso and cocoa exploding across my tastebuds. The spongy ladyfingers at the center practically melted. He'd chosen well; it was divine.

The cold approached my ear and his scent combined with the flavors in my mouth to overpower my senses. A shiver ran the length of me as Ellis's deep voice reverberated in my chest, "Number ten, check."

My eyes snapped open, and I swallowed hard. "Did I just...?"

"You made that noise again." He nudged my chair and laughed, biting into his gelato.

"That was the surprise?"

Ellis grinned mischievously. Having soundly beaten me at chess, not only did he *not* have to abstain from flirting for twenty-four hours, but he cranked it up several notches out of spite. "You're getting to know me too well."

The men continued telling each other ridiculous stories and laughing, while we all polished off our meals and the remaining wine. I was pleasantly giddy by the time we finished. Abby fluttered her lashes at Grayson—clearly wanting to get him into bed—so I signaled for the bill, which Ellis paid in cash, despite polite protests from everyone at the table.

As we stood, Ellis brushed the small of my back. "I'll grab your jacket from the coat check. Meet you at the door."

There was cold when we touched, but another jolt, a thrill, coursed through me, lingering for a moment after he left us. Four glasses of wine may have been too much.

"You brought a jacket?" asked Abby.

I shrugged and took her arm in mine, like we'd done earlier, Grayson walking ahead of us. "We're going to stay in the city a bit longer. Go for a walk, take in some sights. Might walk across the bridge or something."

She pulled my arm tight. "How romantic!"

Romantic? Yeah, right. "Thanks for inviting us, Abby. This was the perfect dinner."

"Don't thank me, thank my dad! It was his reservation!"

I stiffened. Chris's reservation?

"He'd planned to bring some client here or something but had to reschedule unexpectedly. He insisted I take you and Ellis."

"Insisted?"

"Oh, right! He told me to tell you he's sorry about what a tough time you've been going through lately."

This dinner was supposed to be an apology. How could he think there was any way to apologize for what he'd done? Or maybe he didn't realize I knew—

A woman in a yellow dress walked past us, and the vision from the secret office washed over me like a wave. My breath caught, the memory trying to suffocate me. Catherine, in the paddock, crying over a body. Her screams of 'Monster!' echoed in my head.

I'd left her there, without any comfort, alone in the world. How could I have done that to her?

What kind of monster was I?

My shoe landed funny, the heel went out from under me, and Abby caught me before I tumbled to the floor.

"You're cut off, girl!"

I gripped her arm as though my life depended on it and blinked until I saw her clearly. It was the most vivid daydream I'd ever had. Even today, it left me short of breath, with my heart pounding. I couldn't shake the image of her, like a character out of a medieval drama, in her long yellow dress, carrying a cross at her waist. "I'm fine. Just a little distracted."

Where was Ellis? I scanned the restaurant. I needed him. Coat check? Faces, so many faces, until—

He stood at the door with my jacket over his arm, that smile on his gorgeous face. The smile that brought me calm and serenity. That told me things were going to be alright, despite how dire they were. My heartbeat slowed, and a sigh escaped my lips.

"Wow." Abby nudged me. "I was starting to think I'd never see that look on your face."

My eyes stayed on his, and I echoed his smile. "What look?"

"You know exactly what I mean."

I did, but she was wrong. Couldn't have been more wrong. I mean, he was a Grim Reaper. And I was going to die in a week. No future there, despite the warmth spreading through my body as we approached him. Or the way my knees were still a little wobbly.

Grayson and Ellis held the double-doors open, and we stepped out, the scents of the restaurant giving way to the homey smells of exhaust. Diners sat at small white tables nestled along the front of the building and along the street, where cars would have normally parked. A half-wall of planters and greenery separated them from the slow-moving traffic beyond, while small lights wound up the tall trees growing from the sidewalk.

"Thanks for dinner, Ellis." Grayson shook my and Ellis's hands, while Abby shared hugs with each of us, and we parted ways. They headed to the train, while Ellis and I made our way the half-block to Central Park.

It was one of the longest days of the year, and the sun had set while we were eating. The city that never sleeps could be gorgeous at night.

"I like them," he said.

"You and Grayson really hit it off, and Abby's totally in love with you."

"Of course, she is! What's not to like?"

I rolled my eyes dramatically, settling on him with a raised eyebrow.

"I've met many people in my time but haven't made friends since I became a Reaper. This is..." He chuckled, smiling as he looked up at the buildings, to where hidden stars were twinkling high above us. "It's different."

We walked side-by-side, arms swaying, almost touching, but having to stay apart. My shoulder felt it most keenly, since the cold emanated off every inch of him, my hand only cooling when it swung by his.

"Can I have the jacket?"

We stopped, and he held it as I shrugged it on.

"Chris asked Abby to take us out tonight." My stomach tightened. I'd agreed to stop pursuing the crash, wait for Alex's results, but how could I get away from it? For two years, my entire life was about finding out what happened, and the clues were right there. The check copy, the notebook, Neil's signature on the scholarship paperwork, and whatever was on the drive inside the knight.

Ellis came around to face me, his soft smile taking the edge off my nerves. He reached around me to pull my hair out from the neck of the jacket. "Don't let him ruin the evening."

I closed my eyes as his arms withdrew, some aroma sitting underneath the cinnamon, like vanilla or lavender. "It's not him, it's the whole thing, the—"

"Stop." He leaned down to look me square in the eyes. Gray specks, floating in inky darkness. Bowed lips, still curved up slightly. "Do you prefer what you're feeling right now, or what you felt in the restaurant?"

This wasn't about feelings. It was about Chris. And my family. But still... "The restaurant."

"Excellent!" His smile broadened and my remaining doubts vanished.

Maybe it was mind control, the way he soothed me with that smile, but I'd take it.

"Although, I must say..." He stood back to look me up and down, slow and deliberate, lingering at my ankles, the hem, and neckline. "The jacket does nothing for the drape of your skirt."

I chuckled at the silly remark, pulling on the gloves from the pockets. "You've seen a lot in your lifetime. Lifetime? Is that the right word?"

"Works for me." He shrugged, and we resumed our pace down the sidewalk, dodging people coming in the opposite direction. "When I was human, the hemline of that dress would have had you burned at the stake."

"Seriously?"

"Perhaps not that severe, but you would have gotten into a lot of trouble showing so much skin." He looked over at my legs. "There are many things which have improved over the centuries, and hemlines would be at the top of my list."

He was incorrigible.

"I swear, I am never losing another game of chess to you. How long do I have to put up with this?"

He put a hand to his heart in mock offense. "I thought I was doing a rather good job of controlling myself."

"The subtle art of distracting yourself?"

"And you, my dear." He leaned close enough the temperature dropped. "How's it working?"

Very well, Ellis. Too well. Especially after the wine. "It was a good evening."

"Good? It was a far sight better than good!" He threw up a hand in that way that he did to produce a sheet of parchment, this time the one with his list on it. It vanished again before I caught more than a glimpse. "Not only did we check off number ten, but also a delicious meal. At this rate, I won't need you much longer!"

My mood deflated again at those words. I was feeling better than I had in years and wanted him to continue needing me. I enjoyed spending time with him.

He nudged me, the cold buffered by the jacket. "I suppose I'll just have to suffer your company because I enjoy it."

CHAPTER 21

ELLIS

"And finally, Times Square!" Danielle spread her arms wide to showcase the mass of bodies, dazzling lights, and vehicles. Nearly midnight and the crush of people on the sidewalks remained—tourists milling about, taking photos, locals with their heads down, flashing lights on the billboards, rickshaws moving faster than the cars.

The constant buzz of voices, vehicles, and late-night hawkers filled my ears. "I've spent more time in this city than any other. But seeing it with the emotions, taking the time to appreciate its eccentricities, is an extraordinary experience."

"I probably shouldn't be giving you the first-timer tour?" She'd walked me around some well-lit paths in Central Park, bought honey-roasted nuts from a street vendor, and watched late-night buskers. "Empire State Building's definitely off the list now!"

"I shall follow wherever you lead." I remained a couple of inches away from her while she kept the jacket and gloves on. Three times during our two hours, I offered her my elbow, but she declined each time. Was it only the cold? Surely, it wasn't disinterest?

"We're stopping for a bit." She headed for the Red Steps at the north end of the square, taking a seat halfway up. She slid off her shoes and rubbed her feet.

"Tired?"

She gestured to the flashing billboards all around us. "There's an art show that starts a few minutes before midnight. I thought you'd enjoy it."

My heart skipped a few beats at her thoughtfulness. This was the first time I'd chosen a constant companion through a vacation, and certainly the first time I'd ever revealed myself to one. It allowed for a rapport to form between us I hadn't experienced since I'd been human. It was both exhilarating and somewhat terrifying.

Not that Reapers ever felt fear, of course.

"Brace yourself." I sat on the step below her and took one of her feet in my hands. I clasped around the narrow arch, enveloping the delicate foot, sighing deep inside at the contact with her bare skin.

She sucked in a quick breath through gritted teeth. Time slowed for her aching foot. A faint glow shimmered underneath my hand, but between how minor the healing was and the flashing lights around us, it didn't seem to catch anyone's attention. I released my grip once time had ticked backward to the point at which we'd left the restaurant.

Her shoulders fell, and after circling the ankle a few times, she held the other one out to me. "This won't make me forget tonight, will it?"

I took the offered foot, keeping the smile at her invitation at bay. "This healing's small enough you may miss a minute or two, but no more."

"Good." She held tight to the step until I let go. "Perfect timing! It's starting!"

I took a seat next to her as dozens of advertising screens gave way to a synchronized art exhibit. Polka dots in vivid shades flashed across the screens, on their own, in waves, within other forms, zooming in and out. I whispered the artist's name, "Yayoi Kusama."

Some of the activity in the square slowed as people paused to watch the artwork, and several sitting near us oohed and ahhed, pointing in every direction.

Danielle's gloved hand slipped into mine, like it had at the restaurant. As breathtaking as the display all around us was, my eyes found hers and held there, heart beating an unsteady rhythm. She smiled, the flashing lights reflecting off her face, illuminating her with dozens of colors.

Energy jostled around in my chest, traveled into my stomach and through my extremities. This need to be with her in all ways was new and strange. Lust. I'd felt it every time I was human, and I indulged it at a whim. But as much as I felt that when I looked at her, as much as I wanted to indulge, I couldn't. There was the cold, but then there was a desire to encourage our connection to blossom more first.

Or should I revel in lust and allow the blossoming to come later? *Perhaps I should get her opinion on the matter.* "In case I haven't been clear enough, Danielle, I am profoundly attracted to you."

"Really? I hadn't noticed." A grin spread across her face.

I moved closer, and she moistened her lips, leaning in to meet me. My mouth brushed hers gently, and I ran my fingers through the loose hair at her neck. Her free hand grazed my cheek, but she pulled back, sucking her lips into her mouth.

"So close," she whispered, her deep breaths answering my earlier question. It was certainly not disinterest. "But still so cold."

I squeezed her hand that was still in mine. "But the jacket and gloves seem to work."

The art display ended at midnight, the giant screens returning to their advertisements. The synchronicity vanished, plunging the evening into chaos and overwhelm.

"If the Empire State Building's out, that was the last thing I had planned." She rose, still holding my hand. "So, our options are to take the train straight home so I can get some sleep or take a slight detour to walk across the Brooklyn Bridge, then head home?"

I stood, admiring her beauty, wanting little in the world other than to kiss her again and hold her body next to mine. To feel the electric charge that jumped from her skin to mine when we touched.

But she deserved more than that. More than a single week with a man she barely knew, who was simply there to collect her soul. Deserved more than mere lust. I ran my fingers through her hair again, trying my best not to touch her for too long.

"I have a better idea." Releasing her hand, I descended a few steps to a young man sitting near the bottom, a violin case at his feet. "Excuse me, but is that yours?"

He barely looked up from his phone. "Yeah."

"Are you any good? Would you play for my girlfriend and me?"

"Sorry, man. I'm not a busker."

I pulled out my wallet and withdrew a hundred-dollar bill, inserting it between his eyes and whatever was so important on his phone. "Do you know any classical waltzes? Strauss, perhaps?"

He snatched the bill from my hand, tucking the money in his pocket. "Damn straight. 'Blue Danube' or something less common?"

"Whatever you've got." I held out my hand for Danielle, who was coming down the steps.

Her thick black coat was out of place in the warm evening, with so many people in shorts and T-shirts. The amethyst skirt bounced as she walked, taking each step carefully in her high heels.

"What's going on?" She eyed the young man with the violin.

"Two and six."

She paused before taking my hand, tilting her head. "Music and dancing?"

I nodded.

"Here?" She looked around at the other people, the incredulity practically dripping off her. "Wouldn't a club be better?"

"Carpe diem, my dear." I reached out and took her gloved hand, encouraging her to the sidewalk and around the ominous statue of a rather dour man.

She put her hands on my shoulders, remaining a foot away. "The only dance I know is the slow back-and-forth sway."

The musician had his violin out, playing long, slow notes as he tuned it. He took a few steps and hopped up onto the low barrier off to the side of the stairs. He may not have been a street performer, but he was clearly comfortable in the role.

"We will most certainly not sway. I've been dancing the waltz for two hundred years. It's as natural as walking."

She laughed, as she often did when I spoke of my past, as though I were inventing each story.

"In fact, two vacations ago, I attended a splendid party in Brighton, in honor of a visiting Grand Duke of Russia."

I grasped her right hand, taking it from my shoulder, and slid mine to her shoulder blade.

"I don't know how to do this."

"Just follow my lead. You step back, bring your feet together—" I went slowly as the violinist began.

"Tell me more about the party."

"—to the side, together. Forward and repeat."

She kept her eyes on her feet, stumbling more than once, as we practiced the steps.

"I spied a charming young thing with her miserable husband, who was at least ten years her senior, if not twenty. As the Grand Duke began the dance, the husband excused himself, so I snuck in, taking on his form. It only took one dance before she pulled me off the floor, into a private corner."

Danielle's face shot up, eyes wide, but she stumbled again and laughed. "Sorry, I'm having a tough time paying attention to both my feet and your words."

I pulled her closer, my hand traveling down the curve of her spine to the small of her back, our bodies not quite touching. "Are we alright here? The closer we are, the more I can support you."

"We can discuss how far apart we need to be after we get through one dance without me breaking an ankle." She closed the distance, her thick coat pressed against my suit jacket. "Unless I develop hypothermia."

I inhaled deeply, taking in her jasmine perfume, which was the faintest hint stronger than her coconut shampoo. "She'd figured me out, you see!"

Danielle cocked her head, her feet finding the rhythm when she couldn't see them anymore.

"I took one glance at her bosom, and she knew I was an imposter! Apparently, her husband was more interested in one of his grooms than in her!"

She laughed, a rich and hearty sound. "That's ridiculous."

"You likely would have said the same about dancing in Times Square a couple of weeks ago."

"You have a good point there."

Other couples danced around us, and some phone camera flashes went off. I stepped out of our starting box, rotating the dance slightly, and she held on. "You're a wonderful tour guide, Danielle."

She smiled, laughing as she stumbled when I tried to spin us too quickly, and held tight. "The jacket was a smart idea."

"I have a confession." The song ended, but the violinist continued seamlessly into another piece I didn't recognize. I stepped away from Danielle for a moment, encouraging her to spin slowly, and pulled her against me. "Too cold yet?"

"That wasn't a confession."

"Nor was that an answer." I swept her to the side, forward, side, and back, her cheeks flushing.

"To be honest, I'm a little warm. If I'd known we'd be dancing, I would have brought something lighter." She halted and undid the jacket to tie it around her waist. "Let's try this."

I put a hand to my heart, taking in the way the dress followed her curves, the tie at her waist accentuating her slimness, the deep-cut neckline highlighting her gentle cleavage. "My confession: She was nowhere near as stunning as you."

"Stunning?" She looked down, then returned her gaze to meet mine, her face squirreling up. "Is this another crack about my hemline? Or number nine on your list?"

"You should learn how to accept a compliment when it's freely given."

Her mouth opened and closed, as though about to say something, but no words came. Instead, she took in a deep breath and her chest swelled, igniting a flame inside me. With the gloves still on, she took my hand and slid her grip to the back of my neck, moving her body closer to mine. The movement was tentative, stopping at each interval we'd suffered the past week. One foot, six inches, four, slowly, and gradually, together.

She blinked slowly at me. "You're cool, not cold."

We moved to the music, her body against mine the most glorious feeling I'd experienced this century. Her breasts against my chest, my hand spanning her waist, the staccato of her warm heart. Her groin close enough that mine reacted, and I reveled in the pleasure for a moment before calming it.

I trailed my fingers along her forearm to test flesh-on-flesh. Her eyes fluttered closed, but she shook her head, and I returned my hand to her glove.

In the span of six days, we'd gone from a foot of separation to a layer of fabric between us. What would tomorrow bring? Perhaps I'd be able to touch her, hold her, comfort her like I'd wanted to all along. Was it inevitable, or was our growing friendship allowing the closeness?

The third song ended, and I spun her slowly, her balance significantly improved. Her body returned to mine, and I kissed her forehead.

She sighed, placing her head against my shoulder. "One more week."

I stiffened, holding her tighter. "Don't think about it."

"How can I not?"

"We still have a great deal of living left to do this week."

"I wish you were warmer." She tilted her head to look at me, squeezing my hand as we continued to sway gently.

My heart beat faster, in concert with hers, and I leaned close, our breath intermingling. I paused, waiting for her to pull back if it was too cold, if it hurt. A whisper echoed inside my essence, urging me to press on, to feel her surrender in my arms.

But it could hurt her, and I didn't want that.

She touched her lips to mine, sending a wave of pleasure through me, which battled with the despair of how few days we had left together. Each time she touched me, I felt a rush of delight, which was only magnified by the hesitant kiss. Not simple lust, but something deeper, as if our souls recognized each other.

My tongue reached out, prompting her mouth to open, and it met hers. Soft, warm, strong, and with the faintest taste of the candied treat we'd shared earlier. Her tongue slid against mine, a ripple on the bank, portending the coming tidal wave. I could have drowned inside her kiss. It was so perfect, so tender.

The whisper reverberated deep inside me.

It's her, the whisper said.

"Sorry, man, but I gotta go." The violinist was next to us, apparently no longer playing. Danielle and I separated with a start, the moment ending as quickly as it had begun. All the other couples had already drifted away.

"Thank you." I dug into my wallet and tipped him another hundred.

Once he was gone and we were as alone as one could be in Times Square, even after midnight, she whispered, "Where do you get your money?"

I laughed at the question, strangely logical after our romantic moment. "Reaper bank."

She furrowed her brow.

"One of the first stops on any vacation is the bank, to obtain appropriate currency for wherever we'll be spending our time." When she didn't unfurrow her brow, I added, "It's currently in Switzerland."

"Of course, it is." Danielle took my hand, her jacket remaining around her waist. "On to more normal discussion points, straight home or bridge walk?"

"Is either one of those a pickup line?"

"Ellis!" She nudged me with her hip, rolling her eyes.

I gave a wink, which didn't earn any conciliation from her. "I choose bridge walk; more time together before you go to sleep."

"Good choice. We can take the—" She cut off abruptly. As her eyes had finished rolling, they'd apparently found something. She squinted at a restaurant across the street and took a half-step toward it. "What's he doing here?"

CHAPTER 22

ELLIS

"He who?" I was losing her to another mystery already. "Are you alright?"

Her gaze snapped from the crowd across the street and back to mine, as if my words had brought her out of a trance. "I... um, I thought I saw someone."

"There are many someones here." I squeezed her hand, unprepared to let her escape from our moment together. "We were heading to one of the bridges? Shall we take the train? Or are your shoes up for the trek?"

She glanced across the street again. "I could have sworn I saw—"

"And I need Mr. Fancy!" A loud, shirtless man in long shorts threaded his arm through mine. A rather athletic-looking fellow, he sported dark locs held back with a red bandanna. "Let's get a round of applause for all of our wonderful volunteers!"

A nearby semi-circle of people clapped. Wonderful. Another busker.

Danielle let go of my hand, and he pulled me by the arm toward the center of his performance, where five other people stood together. She clapped with the crowd and waved for me to take part, her focus split between me and whoever she might have seen.

I joined the rest of the people in the lineup, eying Danielle to ensure she didn't run off across the street.

She gave her head a shake and smiled at me, hopefully flinging the other person out of her mind. So long as it wasn't an ex, Neil, or Chris, she should be able to ignore them.

"Everyone put your arms out in front of you, then lean over and touch your toes!" The busker demonstrated for us, corrected a couple who weren't leaning down properly, playing to his meal tickets the entire time. "No matter what happens, don't stand up!"

I was at the end of the line, and a young girl with curls stood beside me. "Whatever are we doing?"

"He's going to jump over us!" She clenched tight, bouncing when she said it, her hair following her frantic movement.

"My name is Joe, and I want everyone to clap for me! Let me hear you! Let's go, Joe!" He forced an opening in the ring of spectators, clapping over his head. The crowd joined him in unison, as did the girl next to me. I craned my head up to find Danielle, but she was hidden amongst the onlookers. *At least, she'd better be with them.*

"Let's go, Joe! Let's go, Joe!" shouted the crowd over and over, and the man began running at us. He took a tremendous leap and soared over me. The spectators yelled their appreciation and—

And the shock wave hit me.

Not the one signaling death, but the warning wave that told me one of my marked souls was staring into the abyss.

Danielle.

I stumbled forward and shot up as the first scream sounded. I scanned the throng frantically for her, ice splintering in my veins. Where was she? I couldn't find her.

No, no, no, no!

More screams, and the crowd scattered, people running every which way to escape the unseen danger. The wave finally collapsed, pulling me toward Danielle.

"Call 9-1-1!" came one voice, as I burst through the remaining people who hadn't fled.

"Did anyone see what happened?" came another.

I pushed them aside until I found her, lying on the dull-gray paving blocks, clutching at a wound in her side. Blood stained the sidewalk a deep crimson. She stared up at the sky, tears streaming down her face, silently mouthing something.

Ellis. Ellis. Ellis. She was trying to call for me, so desperate I almost heard it inside my head.

"Dani!" I fell to the ground next to her and pulled her head onto my lap.

"Funny meeting you here." She grimaced, whimpering, gloved fingers stretching out, as though searching for my hand. "Guess we don't have that week left, do we?"

"Quiet. I'm not done trying to seduce you yet." I sniffled, and she almost smiled at the lame joke. Leaning over her, I cradled her like I had a week ago in her cellar, gripping her hand.

"Let me use that jacket to slow the bleeding." The busker knelt beside us, gently pulling the jacket from Dani's waist.

What could I do? If I healed her, everyone would see the light, and I'd reveal myself. Sick gawkers would be recording this, so if I did anything, it would be all over the media.

"Reg!" I yelled, my voice strangled. It was an outside chance, but he might hear me. He'd come when I needed him to take over Jessica's training, so maybe it would work again.

"Take off my glove," whispered Danielle.

"Hold on. I need to check your injury." I slid my hand underneath the jacket the busker was pressing against her side. The blood soaked her dress, a warm, slick layer covering her side. The cut was narrow, an inch wide, likely from a knife. Her jacket hid the dim light as I slowed the progression of her wound. Any more and the blood would vanish from the sidewalk, the light so radiant it would stream through the crowd. People would know.

"Reg, please!" I pulled her glove off and swiped at her palm, finding that the grains were still counting down. She was already cool to the touch, but she had time left.

"You're not cold, Ellis."

I wrapped my bloody fingers around hers and leaned close. Blocking her face from the crowd, I kissed her gently. "No, you're just approaching my temperature."

Her face contorted, and she writhed slightly, a fresh panic appearing on her face. "You can't reap me as a human, can you?"

"There's a way out of this. I just have to figure it out." I couldn't let her go alone, couldn't let her go at all. We needed another kiss, another dance. We had to walk across the bridge.

Reg, please!

"Bloody Pit, Ellis!" Reg coalesced next to us as a towering skeletal figure, billowing cloak and scythe at the ready.

I let out a sigh of relief.

No one in the crowd could see him, so I continued whispering into Dani's ear. He'd hear that. "Reg, I need help. I can't heal her here."

"Let her die. It's her time." He transformed into the blond man with the blue eyes, my old mentor, but his voice remained gruff. "I'll take her."

She sucked in air and groaned, leaning into the wound. It wasn't getting worse, but a lot of damage could have been done. "It's alright, Ellis, let me go. Thank you for giving me such a wonderful final night."

I pulled back to look at her. Her face was far paler than usual.

"Where's the ambulance?" the busker yelled to the crowd.

"Any chance a dying woman could get a last kiss?" Danielle smiled weakly. "And pretend it means something special?"

"What is she talking about?" growled Reg.

"Dammit, Reg!" I flicked my eyes up to him with a glare, the people standing near him backing away from his cold. "Do something."

Reg vanished.

Danielle chuckled and winced. "He's pissed at you, isn't he?"

The busker craned his neck to check behind himself, to where Reg had stood, then back to me. "The ambulance will be here soon, man. She'll be fine."

I touched my lips to hers, then to her forehead. *Please, Reg, please.*

Her eyes fluttered closed. "You can do better than that, Ellis."

"The grains are still falling, Dani. I'm not done with you yet."

"Alright, back up, back up, people." A blond, blue-eyed paramedic barged through the small crowd. Thank the powers that be—it was Reg. "Make some space here."

The busker moved away when the paramedic took hold of the jacket.

"You're kind of cute for a skeleton," Dani whispered.

Reg glared at me but said nothing. The way she continued bleeding, something vital must have been pierced. But he was here, he'd fix this.

"I just got off duty. Didn't come in an ambulance." Reg spoke loud enough everyone nearby could hear and slipped a hand under the jacket. A faint light appeared from where he touched her, winking out almost immediately. "But I think the wound is stable enough for us to get her into a taxi."

"No!" Her eyes shot open, locking with mine. "No cars!"

I kissed her forehead again. "We have to get you somewhere to heal."

"Can you carry her?" Reg asked me.

I nodded to him, then to the busker in thanks, and put my arms under her, trying not to jostle her body any more than necessary. Her head fell against me, the same way it had when we were dancing. "I've got you, sweetheart."

Reg charged ahead of us, stepping right in the way of oncoming traffic, shoving a hand onto the hood of a cab.

The tires squealed before the driver hit the brakes, and he hollered out his window. "Get outta my way, asshole!"

"My confession?" She yawned, pressing a hand against my chest, over my heart. "I know you say it to piss me off, but I kinda like it. No one's ever called me that."

"Then you just need to hold on a bit longer, sweetheart. Once we're in the taxi—"

"Please, no cars. I can't lose you, too."

"I promise we'll be safe. Trust me?"

"I do." Her voice trailed off as her eyes closed. "Completely."

Reg opened the rear door for us to get in. He crawled in behind me and slammed the door shut, ducking down before making himself invisible to human eyes.

"Park Slope," I said, and the driver was off, miraculously oblivious to what was going on in the back seat. Eyes narrowed and lips tight. He and Reg must have had words I'd missed.

Reg put his hands on Dani and threw a dark shadow over the back seat, concealing everything that happened. He held her side, slowing and reversing time for her body, soaking up the blood, healing the wounds, and delivering her into a deep sleep. When it was done, he let the shadow evaporate. "I'm reporting this to Azrael."

"Figures." I held her next to me, heart and lungs still racing. I would take whatever punishment she handed out. It didn't matter anymore. The dance, the kiss, the horror when I felt the wave. I couldn't lose her already. "I just need seven more days, Reg."

"What's that?" asked the driver.

"Nothing!" I raised a shoulder to wipe away my tears. "Muttering to myself."

He waved and nodded, continuing on our way.

"You owe me big, Ellis." Reg converted from paramedic to skeleton, making his features impossible to read. And he vanished.

CHAPTER 23

ELLIS

Danielle's breathing was soft and rhythmic as she slept, curled up on her side, tiny under the piles of blankets on her four-poster bed. I'd pulled the oversized wing chair from the window to her bedside, so I was close enough to touch her, while Byte watched from his guard position on a pillow.

Reg saved her. She'd be alright. But if last weekend was any indication, she'd be asleep for two days.

How was I going to get through those two days without her? The gnawing feeling in the pit of my stomach grew with every second. I'd left her side for no more than ten minutes, and I almost lost her again. Twice now, since the day in Central Park, someone had tried to kill her.

Who had she seen? And dammit all, why hadn't I gone to check? This was my fault. I'd been too distracted by the physical sensations we'd shared and didn't pay enough attention to the risks around her.

Darkness swirled at the foot of her bed, and Byte shot up off the pillow, yapping. The cloak formed first.

"Byte, calm down." I tucked my hand under her blankets and wrapped my fingers around hers. "Cut the theatrics, Reg. She's asleep."

Byte scurried to the end of the bed, growling quietly as Reg appeared in full reaping attire, scythe and all.

"I spoke with Azrael," he rasped from deep inside his hood.

I brushed Danielle's hair back from her face, tucking it behind her ear, maintaining my focus on her. "And?"

"She's figuring out your punishment." He put a hand on his hip, the movement inspiring Byte to move closer and growl louder. "Which will come after you've finished your vacation. Why you get the reprieve, I can hardly fathom."

"Fine." I bowed my head, exhaling slowly. She wasn't forbidding me from seeing Danielle for the rest of my time here. That was a blessing. "I assume you still don't approve."

"Dammit, Ellis!" He slammed the butt of his scythe on the hardwood floor, a booming noise which echoed through the room. It vanished, and he tore back his hood to reveal a gleaming white skull with red flames for eyes. "What are you doing with her? She's a human!"

"She's special, Reg." I squeezed her hand under the blankets.

"I warned you!" He strode forward, his feet clacking on the floor. "You've been avoiding this vacation because you *think* you felt something before it was time."

"You're not listening to me!" I launched out of the chair. Byte began yapping, but a glare sent him cowering, tucking his tail between his legs. Poor thing only wanted to protect Danielle. With a sigh, I picked him up and held him against my chest.

"Something happened the night I met her. This vacation, my emotions, everything... I feel different with her."

"She's little more than that thing." Reg pointed at the dog. "A tool to facilitate your emotional experience."

I ran my fingers along Byte's spine, calming him. "She's so much more. She sees me when I'm hidden, sees my true eyes, controls my list. She even saw you!" I looked at him, everything suddenly falling into place as I said it out loud. "Of course! She's a Reaper! Her contract would say that if she wasn't damned. Maybe she's my—"

"She's not a Reaper, Ellis. So she's not your Pair, if that's what you were going to say." He placed a bony hand on my shoulder when I opened my mouth to protest, his voice softening. "I asked Azrael point-blank."

"Then why—"

"She's more sensitive to our kind, that's all."

"That's all?" I dropped into the chair, staring at her peaceful face. "But that night in the car? The way I feel with her? Like I want to spend all my time with her, protect her, make her smile?"

"Nothing more than guilt." He knelt next to me, bones clattering from the move. "Ever since her accident, you've been fixated on her. That's about you and Catherine, not you and this one. It'll all go back to normal once you finish your two weeks."

What if I didn't want it to go back to normal? What if sitting on the Red Steps and dancing was the normal I wanted? I shut my eyes, focusing on the way she'd looked at me after our dance. But that wasn't an option for me. I'd be back at work in a week, and this version of Danielle would be gone forever. Her soul would do its time in the afterlife, then it would find a new body and be different. Not her.

I took in a stuttering breath, my throat thick. "How am I going to take her soul, Reg?"

"With the same care you always do." He ruffled the hair between Byte's ears, the dog tilting his head to snap at Reg's bony hand. "This isn't why I'm here, anyway. I have someone for you to meet."

I placed Byte on the bed, and he returned to his sentry post. "I'm not leaving her."

Reg lifted a hand, a parchment appearing above it. "I think you will for this."

The contract bore the name Hayden Joseph Younge, a name I didn't recognize.

He heaved his shoulders as though taking a deep breath. "Raguel came to visit me after that little stunt you pulled in Times Square."

That was not a good sign. I sat back in the chair, trying to disappear inside of it. "Sorry."

"He told me the man's contract was coming due, and I had to mark him so it would come to me." He paused. With Reg, that was often for dramatic effect, but this almost felt like regret. "Because he wanted you to see it, Ellis."

An even worse sign. "What?"

He tilted his skull heavenward, shaking it slightly.

I sat forward in the chair. "Reg, tell me."

"This"—he held the parchment forward—"is the man who stabbed her."

Heat built inside my stomach, and I lunged for the contract. Images of the Pit flashed in my imagination, throwing him into it, condemning him to the horror he tried sending Danielle to. I growled, "Give it to me."

"You can't reap right now." He snapped his fingers shut, and the parchment vanished. "But he's bleeding out from the same knife he used on her, and I can give you a minute to talk to him."

My cloak unfurled, black and tattered like Reg's. I buried my face deep inside the hood, flared the red flame in my eyes, and reached into the ether for my scythe. "I'm right behind you."

We moved as one, to an unlit path in the heart of Central Park, to a trail people shouldn't take at night. A man in a dark shirt and pants lay in the bushes, propped up against a tree, bleeding from a wound in his side. How ironic.

"Hayden Younge." I spoke slowly, deepening my voice so it would lodge in his stomach.

He mewled, looking around for the source of the noise. I raised a hand, bringing forth my golden hourglass, glittering grains of sand falling from top to bottom. It illuminated the space amongst the trees and brush, light pouring from each speck inside. The top was almost empty.

"Who—who are you?" He cringed, lifting a bloodied arm to block out my light.

"I am eternity. I am penance and absolution."

His shoulders relaxed slightly.

"But I am also vengeance and wrath. And a higher power has found you guilty of crimes deserving of damnation." I moved closer, keeping my face in the shadows of my hood, allowing him to see only the fire in my eyes. I lowered my voice to a whisper. "But more personally, I am the one whose girlfriend you tried to kill in Times Square two hours ago."

He attempted to inch away from me, flailing the blood-soaked hand between us. "I'm sorry! I didn't know!"

I checked the narrow hole in his side, just as I'd done with Danielle's injury. Someone had sliced the outer layer of his earthly shell cleanly, and his life was slipping away. Rage washed over me. This was why we had to control our emotions when we reaped. I could have healed him over and over, just enough to maintain his agony for days.

"Ellis!" Reg smacked my leg with the shaft of his scythe. "I said you could talk to him. So, talk."

I growled a response, emphasizing each word for Mr. Younge. "I am a Reaper, you pathetic little worm. And when you try to hurt the things that matter to a Reaper, you must pay."

Every soul was pure, but this one had been tainted by his choices in life. He had to be cleansed.

"It wasn't my idea." My victim sobbed, as though begging could save him. How strong had he thought himself as he slid the knife into Danielle? And how weak was he now? "It was a job."

A job?

I tossed aside the Reaper pretense. The cloak and scythe, shadows, and flames vanished, while the hourglass hovered next to me, providing light. "Who?"

His eyes widened. "You!"

"Who paid you?"

He reached a shaky hand into his pocket and handed me a photograph: Dani and I leaving her house. "He told me she'd be at Di Sano's tonight. Follow her. Do it when her boyfriend wasn't around."

I'd only left her for the busker. I wanted to make her smile, and it almost cost her life. My stomach churned, and I knelt next to him, bile coating my throat. I raised a hand, producing a parchment with the sketch of a man's face in golden ink, and shone the hourglass on it. *Let me be wrong.* "Is this the man who paid you?"

He nodded slowly, gasping for breath, slower and slower, until finally his eyes glazed over and he stopped.

I stood, balanced against a tree, emptiness swallowing me. "He's all yours, Reg."

"I am here to—" he intoned behind me, but I walked a few steps down the path to a bench and slumped down.

Once more, it was all my fault. I'd told her to give up her hunt, promised to protect her, distracted her with my pathetic little list. Good things in life? After seven hundred years, I should have known better. Humans were creatures of want, and never an appreciation for what they had.

The red light lit up the path, Hayden Younge begged for mercy, and then he was gone. The scent of sulfur lingered in the air, as did the echoes of his voice and visions of his nodding head.

"I taught you well." Reg spoke lightly and joined me on the bench. It creaked under his enormous weight. "You certainly terrified him in record time."

"I need to get back before he comes after her again."

"He?" Reg gestured a skeletal hand to where the Pit had been.

"The man who paid him was behind the break-in last weekend. She wanted to go after him, and I talked her out of it." I leaped across the path, swung my arm, scythe coalescing in my grasp, and swept it through the trees in front of me. The cut was so clean and sharp, so fast, they remained in place. Taunting me. Reminding me I was a failure at everything, even this.

I yelled, an extreme pitch inaudible to humans, the vibration knocking the trees and bushes over.

"Ellis, calm down." He was a man again, turning me to him. "Leave her. Give me her contract and go somewhere far from here for the next week."

"No!" The flash of red in my eyes reflected off his face. "I swore to her, the night I cast her father into the Pit..."

There it was. Out in the open, the words hanging in the air, my throat too tight for more. Saying it out loud, after all I'd been through with her the last week, watching her sorrow and calming her rage... saying it out loud was like a shard of ice splintering in my heart. It physically hurt, from chest to stomach, all the way to my toes.

I took her family away from her. *I* ruined her life. If I'd healed one of them the way I'd healed her, she wouldn't have gone down this path alone. Or if I'd let her die the way she was supposed to, she'd be in Heaven, preparing for another life on Earth—another chance to find her Pair, like she deserved. Instead, all I gave her was suffering.

I swallowed the lump and cleared my throat. "I promised her that night I'd be the one who took her. If I can do nothing else for her, I swear I'll do that."

"Ellis." He placed a hand on my shoulder. "Think carefully about this."

"I have." Donning my cloak once more, I set my jaw and my infernal intentions. This *was* my fault. She'd seen him in the crowd. But I ignored it. "And right now, Chris Beckett has to pay for hiring that man to hurt her."

Chapter 24

Ellis

Danielle and Byte were tranquil when I returned. She would sleep two more days. While Chris Beckett would wake in his bed in the morning, warm and comfortable. He'd broken into her house, brought a killer with him, left her for dead. Then paid another man to kill her a week later.

Her godfather. Paid a man. To kill her.

I stood next to the bed, watching her as I breathed. Always breathing. This infuriating heart hammering inside my chest. Lungs burning. Fists clenching. Teeth grinding.

And the bloody inconvenient emotions. Fear. Guilt. Disgust. Sorrow.

Absolute, all-consuming rage.

The scythe remained in my hand, cloak moving about me in the frigid wind that followed my Reaper form. I could go next door and scare him. Take him. Heart attack. Hypothermia. Push him out of his window. How many weapons were in the house? Bash his head in with the laptop he stole from Danielle.

But... I raised my free hand and searched for his contract. If he was going to die anytime in the next fifteen days, it would be there, somewhere. Unless he was marked and someone else had it.

If I went next door, and it wasn't his time, something would save him. If it was his time, I could avenge her.

I sank to the edge of the bed, and she rolled toward me, hand landing on my leg. Just like last weekend, when I'd saved her, and she'd put her head on my lap while she slept. She was close enough to death, my temperature was no match for hers.

Her hair fell in front of her eyes, and I pushed it back to watch her. A smile crept across her face, and some of the rage clouding my brain faded. What was she dreaming about? Was I in there? It certainly wasn't the nightmares she used to have. I'd seen her at the start of those, her face contorted in panic.

Panic that Chris Beckett was at the center of. I could reach into his chest and wrap my fingers around his heart to stop it. Make sure he saw me do it. Inspire all the terror Reg taught me to inflict on souls, but on a living human. How long could he survive that?

I rose from the bed.

Longer than Dani would have survived the stab wound. Or the gunshot.

I moved.

The Beckett's house had the same floor plan as Danielle's. Their primary bedroom sat in the same place as hers, making it easy to find. But Chris wasn't there. Wanda slept soundly in the large bed, the other side undisturbed.

Was he awake in another room? Or did they not share a bed?

Remaining invisible to humans, I moved again. Living room, kitchen, basement, office, and two bedrooms, until I found him. Asleep in another room, a floor away from his wife.

Good thing. I wouldn't have to navigate Wanda. She didn't deserve a fraction of what he did. Unless she was in on it as well. Time would tell that tale, but I was short on patience.

Humans were so frail, he would be easy to take.

Then Danielle would be safe again.

Cold radiated off me, and I crystallized all hints of moisture, the air itself sparkling. Frost spread across the floorboards from my feet, creeping up the bedposts. I could slay him without lifting a finger, but I wanted to see the look in his eyes when he realized what I was.

I was power.

I was vengeance.

I was a monster.

Chris's breath slowed so easily.

Before the ice reached his blankets, his breathing stopped altogether.

Bloody fucking Pit!

I drove the cold harder but hadn't reacted fast enough.

The white and gold streak came as no surprise, and it fueled the inferno blazing inside me. He should keep his angelic little ass in the heavens and leave me to my work.

Raguel slammed into the small space between me and Chris's bed. As he straightened from his landing, his lip curled. The glint in his eyes told me he was already enjoying this. "I warned you about playing with humans, little collector. Twice, if I recall."

I pulsed the cold, but with time frozen, it didn't budge. The archangel who should have been rejoicing in my vengeance was saving this pathetic little ant. "What kind of angel of justice are you, if you'd stop me here?"

He tucked his wings toward his sides, ready for a fight. "*Arch*angel, you mean."

"He paid someone to kill—" I lowered my scythe to point at Chris, and Raguel snatched it with a wing, forcing it into the ether. *My* scythe!

"Your pet human?"

I took a step toward him—the last thing a Reaper should ever do with an archangel—and the curl in his lip lifted. He would not speak of her like that. I bared my teeth, unable to control my contempt for him. "Return my scythe."

"You can ask Azrael to fetch it for you." He tilted his head as he stepped closer to me, wingtips pulling up toward my chest. "If you still exist by the time we're done here."

I took a tremendous breath—nostrils clogged with cloyingly sweet angelic scent—and I didn't hit him. At least, didn't bother trying to hit him. For all my strength and speed, he was stronger and faster. My powers were nothing compared to his, but maybe he'd be so stunned I'd dare attack that I could land one punch before he obliterated me.

Then where would that leave Danielle? Alone in the world again. Unprotected. And without me to collect her soul when she died.

Raguel stood eye-to-eye with me, a hair taller for good measure, full of exasperating superiority. He governed justice, vengeance, redemption, and harmony. He sometimes worked with Azrael to weigh the death contracts, but also had his own team to mete out divine justice on Earth, cleansing souls to prepare them for paradise.

Again, why was he doing this instead of sending one of his Furies? A Fury I could have argued with, fought, defeated, and then exacted my revenge. If I'd been lucky, it would have been one who truly believed in balancing mortal scales, and they would have helped.

"He deserves justice—" I stepped back and gritted my teeth. Conciliation was difficult while the troublesome human emotions swirled inside me. "Archangel."

"And he'll have it. But when has that *ever* been your decision?"

"Why did you force the killer's contract on Reg?"

"Because Reg was what he earned. And the truth needed to come out." Those were the first words he'd spoken plainly, without malice. But what did it mean? I knew the truth: Chris was behind it all. So why was Raguel stopping me from taking the life?

"Is Chris Beckett's contract ready?" If it were, even if I weren't the one to take him, that would give me some solace.

"That is none of your business, unless it comes to you when he's done." His wings stayed up, following me as I took another step back. His nostrils flared. "Golden boy."

He wanted me to know about Chris but not do anything about it?

Raguel and his Furies often harassed us Reapers, but this level of venom was new. Had something changed? Or was it always this bad, and I only noticed it because of my vacation? My delay and the strange emotions I was feeling? Had I just never realized how angry he was all the time and how he loathed me?

"What's your problem, archangel?"

"You are!" His wings ruffled, as though a shiver ran through them. "You are out of order! You are not the way of things!"

Reapers sometimes killed on vacation. Less and less as the rule of law became stronger and we didn't have to protect ourselves, but it happened. I'd never heard of him going after one of us for it.

"You are a collector of souls! Decisions are not yours to make!" He flexed his wings, balling his fists. Had he been a Reaper, I expect his eyes would have flared to red flame. "Just because Azrael treats you like you're more important than every angel in the heavens doesn't mean you actually are!"

Me? What?

"Plush assignment. Letting you interfere with that human. Not punishing you for avoiding your vacation for two years. Two years!"

"I don't think—"

"Shut your mouth!" His voice rose to deafening volume, vibrating through my body. He was as unseen and unheard to humans as I was now, able to pass through anything substantial, but the furniture still shook at the sound. "There will be order! You take your vacation when it's your time. You collect souls when it's theirs. When the Fates decide! Not when *you* decide!"

I stepped away, heart lurching back to life. An archangel's ire was bad, but his rage was not a thing to trifle with.

"You are not his judge! I am!" His face flushed red, and his wings smashed together in front of me, the buffeted wind pushing me another step away. "Now get out!"

His wing curled, and my scythe appeared. I snatched it and moved as quickly as I could.

Back to Danielle's room.

To her resting body.

"I'm sorry, Dani." I collapsed next to the bed, releasing my cloak and scythe into the ether. My first tears fell before my knees hit the floor. I brushed the hair back from her face, reaching under the covers to grip her hands. "I couldn't do it. It's not—"

The words caught in my throat, and I pulled my hand from her. I didn't deserve her warmth. I'd failed her again. Again! Over and over, I continued failing her.

All of this had been a terrible idea. From the moment I'd sat in the car with her, my existence had been a string of horrid choices. I swallowed the thick saliva down my scratchy throat before it choked me.

My head rolled forward onto the edge of her bed, and I breathed in the fresh linen scent of her sheets. Was there any point in trying to stem the flow of tears? Didn't I deserve that sorrow? Just let it all out until she woke up?

Five million souls taken away from their families, and the one that changed my existence had been Luke Edmonds. He'd been a good man at his core, but with troubles which earned him the Gray Hallway. He could have waited. He could have chosen paradise, if it were in him. But for all my time speaking with him about the good things in his life and his past, something weighed on him he wouldn't speak of, and he chose the Pit. A fifty-year cycle until he could return and search for his Pair again.

And once he was gone, something pushed me to heal his daughter.

Raguel was right—as much as I hated to admit it. No matter how many times Reg told me I'd made a mistake that night, it hadn't been Danielle's time. If it had been, I wouldn't have been able to save her.

Just as much as I wouldn't be able to take Chris unless it was his.

"Ellis." Danielle's voice was quiet, no more than a breath.

My head snapped up, but her eyes were still closed. "Yes?"

She mumbled something, which she did often in her sleep. They were merely sounds strung together, but my long-dead heart told me she was trying to comfort me. True or not, I had to hold on to that, if I was going to make it through the next two days.

Her hand pushed out from under the blankets, limp. Definitely asleep. But I'd take what I could. I pulled the chair closer and sat, slipping my hand into hers. She smiled, breath deep and rhythmic, and I tried to match her speed. It calmed me, like her smile always did, the feeling of her skin against mine giving me strength.

How did she do that?

Reg said she was more sensitive to our kind. But what did that mean?

If she wasn't a Reaper, then what was she?

CHAPTER 25

ELLIS

"Good morning, Danielle." I kept my voice soft as she stirred, not wanting to wake her before she was ready, but unwilling to lose another moment with her. A myriad of smells blanketed the room from the two breakfast trays I'd brought up. Coffee and chai, bacon and fresh bread, pancakes, jams, whipped cream, and four types of fruit. "Based on last weekend, I thought you'd be up soon, so I made a little of everything. It may be too much, even for me."

She'd tucked the duvet under her chin, so all I could see was her peaceful face and a vague shape under the blankets. With a small sigh, she cracked one eye open, moving no more than that.

I leaned forward in the chair—still next to her bed—putting on my best smile. Considering the circumstances, it wasn't a very good one.

"Do Grim Reapers normally get dark circles under their eyes?" She yawned and stretched her arms out.

I forced a chuckle at her lame attempt at a joke. There would only be circles there if I put them there. "I thought my being slightly less than perfect might make you feel better when you see what a state you're in."

"Gee, thanks." She laughed, sitting up and pulling her knees to her chest, snuggled underneath her blanket. She looked around the room, paused on the crackling fire and breakfast trays on the bed. I'd had to shove Byte out before he consumed the whole thing. "How long was I out?"

I shifted from the chair to the spot where her feet had been, rubbing along the sides of her legs through the blanket. She'd slept for fifty-four hours again; two days full of rage and sorrow, like every other vacation. It would have been easier had I not spent any time with her. Never realized how she filled the hollowness inside me, nor how great that void was without her.

"It's Tuesday morning."

Her eyes widened, and she sucked in a deep breath. "Five days left?"

The sands in the hourglass were gaining speed, and we were running out of time together. And again, it was Chris's fault. He'd stolen four days from us. She didn't need to know that though. We had to focus on the good. "Plenty of time. Five nights to find the perfect sunset and one good deed to wrap up my list."

She tried to smile, but the corners of her lips fell. "Just leaving number nine."

"That was a terrible choice." But was love so bad? I kissed her knee through the blanket. "I never should have added that."

"Exactly. Although you just had two days on your own to take care of it." She laughed, but it was awkward. I shouldn't have shown her my list. Shouldn't have made those comments about humans finding me attractive. I should have stuck with the original eight items and not added number nine.

Who was I fooling? Falling in love? Me? Even less likely, someone returning my love? The stories were wrong. Not every soul would find their Pair. My destiny was a solitary one, and I had to accept that. It would be me and Reg alone until the end of time.

I looked away from her weak smile, pulling a mug from one of the trays. "I made coffee but thought chai would be easier to digest?"

She reached for it but snapped her hand away before she touched it.

The air rushed out of me all at once, and my heart froze. "No. It's back?"

Danielle fell on her pillows and stared at the ceiling, rubbing at her cheeks. We'd been so close Saturday night. Only a layer of fabric between us. I'd held her in my arms as we danced, she'd tucked her head against my shoulder, and we'd kissed. Those memories helped me through her slumber, along with the promise of what else we might do when she woke. But now? Our chance was gone?

She tented her hands over her mouth and squeezed her eyes shut. "Are you doing this on purpose?"

I dropped the mug on the tray, spilling it, and launched off the bed, pacing across the room. She had the audacity to ask that? "What a ridiculous question."

"Then come back and try it again." She sat up, hugging the blankets. "Maybe it's because I'm just waking up."

Returning to the chair, I put my hand out, and she did the same, inching toward me. Sure enough, she had to stop, unable to come closer than a foot. I strode back to the fireplace, stoking the logs, throwing a fresh one on. "Eat something, Dani. You need your strength."

She patted the bed next to her. "Come sit with me. Let's pretend it's another picnic."

I should have taken her far away instead of staying in New York. Somewhere no one would be after her, and she'd have no triggers reminding her of her family. Before joining her, I opened the door, and Byte came scampering in. He bolted up the steps at the side of the bed and leaped onto her.

She squealed and laughed as he licked her face. Their joyful reunion should have been ours. We should have been able to pick up where we left off.

"He barely left your side since you came to bed."

She giggled, trying in vain to control him, her laughter quelling some of the fire inside me. Perhaps we could put the attack behind us and move back to happiness. He twisted in her grasp and bolted for the bacon.

"This is not for you, Byte." I crawled up on the end of the bed to grab him and sat with my legs crossed. He settled in my lap when I began scratching his head.

Danielle plucked a piece of bread from a tray and cocked an eyebrow at me. "So, I noticed I'm not in the same outfit as I was Saturday night...?"

Had I needed to, I would have helped, but she'd woken up just enough to change before she climbed into bed. "I wish."

She extended a leg under the blankets to nudge me. "Right. Any exciting memories tucked inside my brain this time?"

"Not as much as last weekend." I rubbed along her leg, wishing for more contact, to feel the spark travel through me again as it did when I touched her skin. "It was just the three of us."

"And..." She took a sip of the tea and another bite of bread. "Reg healed me, not you?"

I nodded, continuing to scratch Byte, to fend off his jealousy at the attention I gave her.

"What did you do while I was sleeping?"

I slathered some strawberry jam on a piece of the bread and left it on her plate. "Try this. It's homemade."

"Did you stay here, or did you go traveling?" She swapped pieces of bread and took a bite, savoring it, making that low rumble she did when she ate something she adored. At least she liked my jam. "Maybe pay a visit to that redhead from Friday's birthday picnic?"

Her lips tightened, and she glanced away.

Jealousy? Seriously?

Were it not for the accursed cold, I would have stripped off the blankets and taken her in my arms that very moment, ran my fingers through her hair, and kissed her deeply. Shown her how preposterous her question was. But I couldn't, because it would hurt her. That left me on the outside of the blanket while she nestled underneath, and our only shared contact was with her damn dog.

"That's ludicrous." I swung my legs off the bed, releasing Byte to the floor. The fireplace needed tending. The floor needed to be paced.

"You did, didn't you?" Her voice was quiet, accusatory. Shocked, even. "Was it the redhead? Or the dark-haired one from the elevator? Oh, no, wait. The one from the Wonder Wheel? I mean, there've been so many, how can you even keep track?"

The words stung. She thought I'd discard her so easily? I'd sworn to protect her, to watch over her. I wouldn't leave her side for something as insignificant as lust. Some petty human need I hadn't felt a single time while she slept.

I spun to face her, waving the question off. Nothing could be right, as long as we stayed in New York. "Let's go somewhere. How about Rome? I love that city."

"That wasn't an answer."

Voice light, playful, I attempted to veer her away from the discussion. Surely, something would catch her interest. "Or Paris?"

"It was two days. I suppose you had time for more than just one."

My shoulders sagged, dreams of taking her far away fading. So stubborn. She wasn't about to let this go, was she?

"I was there." I pointed to the chair. "Or downstairs or taking Byte out. But mainly right there."

She curled her legs underneath herself, kneeling. "Why?"

"I had to keep you safe." I returned to the bed, crawling on top of it, so my face was just outside the barrier of cold. "Since we met at the Chess House, I've only left you alone twice, and you nearly died both times."

Her mouth slowly eased open, the realization awakening the fire which had lived inside me since I'd met Hayden Younge. "You don't think this one was random, do you?"

I was a Grim Reaper. I collected souls and did not mete out my own justice. But I battled with myself every moment she lay sleeping. Stay with her or go after Chris, to the Pit with what Raguel said. I could have struck fast, before he could catch me, and dealt with the consequences. "The man who stabbed you is dead."

"Did you—"

"No. Someone else did. I didn't care to find out who. But Reg received his contract and brought me to him."

"Who was it?"

I resumed pacing. If I told her this, it would change things for her. Chris would no longer be a simple suspect in the break-in. To her, her godfather would, without question, be the man who paid to have her killed.

He tried to take her away from me before her time. Twice.

My plan had been to hide it from her. Keep her on the path toward redemption. We were making progress toward paradise.

But the adrenaline pumped through my veins, and my heart raced. My lungs demanded extra air to fuel the knot squeezing my stomach tight. I wanted him to pay.

"Ellis?"

I turned to her, unable to filter out the memory of her lying on the ground, blood all around her, asking me for a last kiss.

"Your eyes..." Instead of backing away, she crawled out from under the blanket, coming to the end of the bed. "They're burning."

With a deep breath, I extinguished the flames and reverted my eyes to blue, even though she saw through that. Her head on my shoulder, hand on my chest, carrying her to the taxi so Reg could heal her away from prying eyes. I should have protected her. We should have spent the two weeks in our own little paradise. Whatever it had taken, whatever I had to say to get her to go with me, that's what I should have done.

A piece of toast covered in jam hit me square in the chest. "Talk to me, dammit!"

"Chris paid him."

She deflated and turned as pale as each time I'd held her near death. Eyes glistening with tears, a shudder wracked her body. "Are you sure?"

I rushed to the foot of the bed, kneeling in front of her, wanting nothing more than to hold her. I dug my hands under the blanket and grabbed her hands, maintaining the layer between us. "His name was Hayden Younge, and he had a photo of the two of us with instructions to follow us from Di Sano's until we separated."

"The reservation." A tear fell down her cheek. "It was Chris's. Abby said he insisted she take us."

"I showed Mr. Younge a picture of Chris, and he said that's who paid him."

She trembled, maybe from the cold seeping through the blankets, maybe from the revelation. Releasing my hands, she pulled the blanket up over her lap. "He's like a second father to me. My godfather. It really was him last weekend, wasn't it?"

I pushed farther under the blanket, spreading my arms around her legs, around her waist, laying my head on the covers atop her lap.

She brushed her fingers across the side of my head, briefly, before she had to withdraw. "This is the point where you're supposed to tell me to take my information to the police."

"I know." I looked up at her, her face hardening behind the tears. "I have no evidence of his link to your attacker, other than a dead man's word."

"And all I've got is a notebook he could claim was his. Or say Dad gave it to him. And maybe Dad's laptop somewhere in their house, with the same excuse." She wrapped the edges of the blanket around my back and held me. "The police wouldn't do anything with that."

Damn him to the Pit. "And the bastard was there watching."

"He was what?"

"You saw him before the busker grabbed me." I'd convinced myself of that two days ago, but from the blank look on her face, either she didn't remember, or I was wrong. "He *was* the one you saw, right?"

"No." She trembled in my arms, hopefully not from the cold. "It was Alex. My PI."

"Are you sure?"

"I'm not sure of anything right now."

Neither was I. Had telling her the truth been the right choice?

"What do we do now, Ellis?"

"I have a really terrible idea, and I can't believe I'm saying this, but..." I'd gone back and forth a thousand times while she'd slept, debating whether or not to bring it up. I still wasn't sure if it was the right choice. But I leaned back and dug a hand in my pocket, producing the ebony knight. "It's time to find out what this is."

CHAPTER 26

DANIELLE

"I'd say it's all Greek to me, but I speak Greek, and I don't understand this." Ellis sat in the chair next to me, leaning closer than the temperature barrier, staring at the flashing cursor in the *Enter your password* box. My laptop sat on the dining room table, as usual, and he'd brought the breakfast trays.

"If you're going to sit that close, can you go grab my Columbia sweatshirt?"

He finished his sip of coffee, nodded, and vanished.

Had I really seen Alex at Times Square Saturday night? Was he part of all this? He knew Neil, but did he know Chris? Or had I just seen someone else who looked like him? In a city with this many people, doppelgangers were common enough. Something told me I could trust him; almost as deep in my soul as I knew I could trust my guardian Reaper.

Ellis reappeared with the sweater, and I accepted it, but just sat there, staring at him.

A week and a half ago, I believed I'd live another fifty years, at least. Wasn't sure I wanted to but knew I would. I believed in humans and dogs and all the things I could see with my eyes.

Creatures of myth and legend didn't exist. No Grim Reapers, angels, or pits to damnation. No contracts for souls.

Now what? A shudder ran through me, and goose bumps prickled my legs. What did I even have left other than lies and betrayal?

I had Ellis. Two days ago, he was warm enough I could have fallen into his arms, he would have wrapped them around me, and I could have believed—for just a second—that everything would be alright. He was so thoughtful. Healing my sore feet, paying that guy to play for us, always looking out for me. Why couldn't I have met him under different circumstances?

Dammit, why couldn't he have been human?

Leaning an elbow on the table, I dropped my head into my hand. "You can't turn time all the way back to last Saturday, can you? Let me make different decisions? Not be here during the break-in?"

"I can't sugarcoat this, Danielle." He placed a hand on the table, and I reached for it but could hardly bear to be within six inches of him. "When your contract's up, it's up. There's nothing I can do to change that. There are so many things I should have done differently, but I just can't."

I gritted my teeth and pushed past the freezing barrier, relishing in the thrill of contact for a second before retreating. "Am I going to regret looking at the information on this drive?"

He clenched his fist and pulled away so I couldn't touch him again. "Put your sweater on."

Right. He was close, and I was cold. How could one man turn my insides to liquid fire and my outside to frost at the same time? "In case I didn't tell you before I was in the near-death stupor on Sunday morning, I had a really great time."

His jaw flexed, as did his other hand. "Me, too."

I'd expected to come home after that evening and... and what? If he weren't so cold, I would have told him to change number nine to sex and taken care of it with pleasure. A man who could be any size and shape he wanted to would probably be the best lay of my life. His lips were soft, his body strong, hands delicate. He was gentle and caring, not to mention confident.

No, not confident. Ellis was cocky.

And then there was the thrill that came from touching his skin. The electric charge that spun through every cell in my body.

A Danish appeared in front of my face. "You're staring."

"I need caffeine, not carbs." I'd already polished off my first coffee, plus the tea.

"Your wish is my command." He stood and bowed, calling over his shoulder as he stepped into the kitchen, "*Sweetheart.*"

"I didn't mean that!" My memories were hazy from Sunday morning, but I certainly remembered telling him I liked it. Not one of the smarter things I'd said. It was true, but he'd use it against me.

"Yes, you did!"

I stared at the window on the screen, which demanded a password for the drive. That was as far as I'd gone.

"Maybe there's a clue inside one of the other pieces or on the board itself?" Ellis brought me a steaming hot mug and the aroma of rich, dark beans surrounded me. "One Caffè Americano."

"Just what I needed." I took a sip of the coffee. The faint roasted caramel flavor mixing with the slight bitterness was a surprise. "I didn't notice with the first, but you bought new beans, didn't you?"

"Focus."

"I'm pretty sure I already know what it is." Another sip, while I continued the war raging inside my head. Look or don't look? "Considering my dad told me chess notation would make a great password before he ran off and told my mom about the drive being hidden in the knight, that's got to be it. It's easy to reproduce if you know the game or the opening it's for."

"But you aren't sure which opening he would have used?"

"We'd played that game up to the end of Evans Gambit, so maybe that. But he was fiddling with the knight, which was only on the second turn, so that's another option."

"And if you guess wrong?"

"If he went to all this effort to hide the drive, odds are good too many incorrect answers will cause the program to wipe the entire thing. Three tries on the low end, ten on the high."

"I may not be as qualified as you are in this respect, but by my count, you have two guesses, which keeps you under your limit of three."

Good point.

"Alright. Here goes nothing." I typed in the shorter notation and received an error. My stomach clenched. What if my theory was all wrong? What if I ruined the drive and all this was for nothing? What if I got in and the whole thing was empty? Next, I tried the full Evans Gambit notation and the drive unlocked. "Got it."

"That was easy."

"That was only step one." The drive displayed a directory. There were several files on it: a compiled software program, source code, technical documentation, and a data dictionary.

"What is it?"

"Not sure yet." I launched the compiled program, which prompted me for a first and last name, with no hint as to its purpose. But whose name? Dad's? Mine? Someone else's? "I should check out some other files first."

"I mean, I know what a password is, but I only understand computers as a concept." He gestured vaguely at the laptop. "You obviously know far more than I do."

"It's what I did for a living. Software programmer for a security company." I turned the machine to show him the code for the main executable. "To put it in the simplest terms, there's a lot of information tucked away inside this laptop. I have a password to unlock it and gain access to that data. When I'm connected to the Internet, someone else—who knows what they're doing—can also gain access to this laptop and the data on it."

"That doesn't sound particularly safe."

"There's extra security, like a firewall, encrypted partition, multi—" I stopped. I was lecturing. "Suffice to say there are a ton of ways I can protect it. But there are people out there who spend their whole lives trying to figure out how to get around all the security measures. That's something my father was amazing at, and he trained me how to do it, too. We spent a lot of hours bonding over ethical computer hacking."

"Computer hacking? You mean you and your father broke into people's laptops together?"

I raised a finger, ready to correct him, explain about caches, packets, and the cloud, but what did the details matter? They didn't. "Yeah. The company we worked for developed advanced security systems to keep those people out. His specialty was finding loopholes and gaps in security. By finding all the flaws and closing the doors, they wrote programs in high demand."

"And that's what this is? A way into something?" He leaned closer, scanning my screen.

If only the filenames gave me any hints. I pointed to the last two comments at the top of the code. "CB: Version 9.5 – Final. LE: Version 10.0 – bug fixes. Final-final."

"What's that?"

"Programmers annotate their code, and this part's a revision log. CB for Chris Beckett, I'm guessing. LE for Luke Edmonds. Chris and Dad developed this together."

"If Chris helped him create it, why break in here to find it?"

"Chris's last comment says it's the final version, then Dad's says he fixed some bugs—problems—with it. I'm betting Chris never saw the final version, and whatever he's got doesn't work." And he broke in, looking for the working version. "This must be the program the thug was demanding."

"What would it do if it worked?"

"No idea. But if Dad went to all this trouble to hide it—if my family died for this—I need to figure it out."

CHAPTER 27

DANIELLE

After a couple of hours, another coffee, a Danish, four slices of bacon, and a croissant covered in jam, I pushed my chair out from the table. Pain stabbed through my left shoulder. I stretched out my neck and back, digging my fingers into the knot. "It's a software program designed to bypass the security at Empire First Bank."

Ellis stopped playing the piano and headed through the dining room to the kitchen.

I let out a long sigh as he did something with the microwave. "The account my dad—" I made air quotes. "—paid Chris for the artwork from?"

"Empire First?"

"Yeah. All our accounts are with them because Uncle Mike works there." Was Dad working on a proposal for them? Show how vulnerable they were in order to secure a contract?

Ellis returned with a heated beanbag, pinching the corner between his thumb and forefinger, and placed it around my neck. "What does that mean?"

The heat eased my sore muscles, and I closed my eyes to relax. I'd hunched over the laptop for too long, so engrossed I'd forgotten to move. "Nothing, if they've updated their security since then."

"Only one way to find out." He slid his icy fingers under the bag, onto my warm skin, and the knots slowly came undone as he did his magic. His hand lingered after the healing was complete, energy zipping around inside me, pinging off every nerve ending. I edged away when the cold overpowered the heated bag, and he withdrew, leaving me warmer but empty.

"Thank you." I pulled the seat back in and launched the program. When the name prompt came up, I entered my own. It churned for a moment and produced a list with three Danielle Edmonds, only one with my address. A tremor ran through my hand as it hovered over my keyboard. The results from a name search meant the program hit the bank's client list, at a minimum. Unless it was a central repository from elsewhere, which would route me to the bank systems.

How illegal was this? Did it count if I was only looking at my own information? Of course, it counted. I was hacking into a bank. I'd done it before as part of my job, but that was always with the company's consent because I was helping them by finding holes. Then again, I was dead in five days anyway, so what did it matter?

If Chris didn't make it happen sooner.

I hit the key to continue, and a list of my bank accounts appeared. I gasped, tapping another key to drill into the first account, and it presented us with all my recent transactions.

Ellis leaned in to look at the screen. "It works."

Oh, god. "It does."

Byte shot up suddenly from his pillow in the parlor and bounded into the room, dropping a ball at Ellis's feet.

"I'm of no use here. I'll take him out back." He picked up my little Yorkie and started with the baby talk. "And wet him stwetch his wittle wegs."

Damn, that was cute.

He left with Byte, out the back door from the kitchen, while I explored the program's interface. A button labeled *Transfer* caught my attention. Clicking it produced a dialog asking for an account number. I returned to my account list and jotted down my savings account number, entered my checking, and executed a transfer between the two. A quick cross-reference with Empire First's online banking showed that, sure enough, the money had switched accounts.

So many questions, so little time. But the first one: Did Chris have an account there? And if he did, the second: Was there a deposit for one hundred and fifty thousand dollars to match up with my father's check? The one Chris said he'd torn up.

Through the glass door at the back of the house, I glimpsed Ellis. The backyard garden was half a story below, but he was tall enough I could see him bobbing and weaving around the small space, playing with Byte. Coral honeysuckle wove through the trellis behind him, and no doubt there would be an irritated butterfly or two trying to avoid them. Trying to avoid the Grim Reaper, jumping around like a fool with my dog.

I shook my head, unable to keep the smile down, until I turned back to the hacking program.

And Chris.

But first, I disconnected from my router and signed onto the Becketts'. If something went wrong, at least any investigation would point them toward Chris's IP address, not mine.

With very little effort and only ten minutes, I had the answers to my first two questions: Yes, he had an account, and yes, he'd deposited the check from my father. There was even a digitized copy, so there was no debate. I dug deeper and deeper, the rabbit hole taking me places I wouldn't have believed two weeks ago.

The back door opened, closed, and locked. Ellis smiled when our eyes met, the genuine smile that made my insides melt and almost convinced me to close my laptop. Byte scampered to where I kept his treat container. Ellis spoiled my dog rotten.

"Find anything?" His cheeks were flushed and there was a flower petal stuck in his perfectly messed hair. It wasn't fair he was so gorgeous. How was I supposed to resist that perfect face with the tiny imperfection he'd added?

"I thought you never got tired?" I pointed at him, while Byte trotted to his pillow with a rawhide bone the size of his little body. "Your cheeks are red."

"Trust me, I don't." He waggled his eyebrows and grinned, hopefully not noticing the way my breath caught. He returned to the dining room, grabbed a slice of watermelon, and sat next to me. It was very ripe, so when he sank his teeth into it, the juice dribbled down his chin. He wiped at it with the back of his hand, sucking the juice off his fingers. "See anything interesting?"

"That wasn't subtle." I plucked the petal out of his hair, cold though it was.

He pointed at the laptop. "Clearly, I meant on there."

"Clearly." I stared at him an instant longer as he took another bite. He ate a ton. "Do you eat when you're off vacation?"

"Sadly, no. While at the same time, thankfully no. We have little spare time for food, sleep, or other things which preoccupy humans." He took another bite, winking at me. "So, did you learn anything?"

"A lot. The information is all transparent. Account numbers, names, transfer histories. It's amazing!" I'd known my father was good at his job, but I didn't realize how good. And how poor Empire First's security was. "Chris and Neil also have accounts with the bank. Neil's the one who transferred the four hundred thousand to my dad, the same day he transferred a hundred thousand to Chris, and two hundred and fifty thousand to someone else who no longer has an account with the bank, so I can't get their details."

Ellis dropped the watermelon and his pretense. "Neil doled out all that money on one day?"

"Yeah, right after he received a deposit of one million from someone named Isaiah Fitch."

"Fitch? Do you suppose that's the same Mr. Fitch from Neil's office last week?"

"Who?"

"He had an appointment with Neil after we did."

None of that rang a bell for me. "No idea, but if it is, that tells us they know each other."

"I doubt it would be a coincidence."

"Me, too. So, once my dad transferred the money to Chris, that makes four equal shares of two hundred and fifty thousand."

"Equal shares for what?"

"No idea." I flipped the view to show him Neil's account. "But Neil has a long-running history of receiving large amounts of money and immediately dispersing it. All the other ones came out of his account via check or cash withdrawals, except this one instance."

"Something to do with his law practice?"

"This is a personal account, not corporate or a trust or anything." I rubbed my forehead, as though it could clear away everything I'd just learned and return me to a normal world. But I had all the proof in front of me. "Maybe I've read too many of those thrillers my dad loved, but I'd bet Neil's laundering money. Plus, given Chris and that thug were looking for a program and willing to kill me to keep it secret, this seals the deal. This is the program they were looking for. It's why my family's dead."

Ellis exhaled sharply and shook his head. "So, this is enough to take to the police? Send Chris to jail before he can come after you again?"

That thought had already crossed my mind while he was outside, and I'd discounted it. "No, because it's still all conjecture. Coincidences and guesses. The CB comments could be just about anyone. Plus, this is all obtained illegally. There *might* be a way to get the police investigating Neil, which *might* eventually pick up some proof about Chris, but it's doubtful."

Ellis stood and rounded the table to the fireplace on the opposite side of the room. "Chris, Neil, and your dad were involved with Isaiah and someone else." He ran his long fingers along the mantel, looking up at the family portrait hanging above it. "But you can't prove anything."

"No, I can't. But..." I'd had an idea, but it would definitely send me hurtling further away from Heaven. Before I'd met Ellis and heard his revelations, I would have done it.

Maybe?

He took a seat opposite me at the table, leaning forward. "But what?"

"If I transfer money from Neil and Mr. Fitch's accounts to Chris's, I can report it to the bank. They'll investigate, check with Neil and Fitch, and unless they protect Chris—"

"They'll think Chris stole the money, and he goes to jail?"

I nodded. "Even if they search his house, they'll find Dad's laptop and notebook, with evidence of this program. And maybe something linking him to the break-in last weekend. Divine justice."

Ellis swept a hand across the table, absently clearing away crumbs which weren't there. "Far from divine, Dani. That's a Fury's job, not yours."

"That's why I'm hesitating." My heart thundered. This was the wrong side of the law and ethics, and definitely not the right thing to do. But it was all I had left. If Ellis gave me even a hint of approval—if he thought it wouldn't guarantee my damnation—I'd do it.

"He's tried to kill you twice over this." He clenched his fists and waved me out of the seat. His mouth clamped shut, and his eyes hardened, as though they were about to switch to flame again. "Show me how to do it. It's as much my intentions as yours now. But it will only be my actions."

CHAPTER 28

ELLIS

"I don't feel comfortable being out here." Danielle's eyes darted over every surface, to every shadow. "I've only got four days left, and no one's come for Chris yet. If something happens to me…"

Then I'd save her, she'd fall into another slumber and wake on Saturday. Giving us that day and night, plus perhaps a morning together. The layer of cold between us was decreasing faster than last week, but I wasn't about to hit that reset button again. Today, we were only two inches apart, just as we'd been when we walked out of the restaurant Saturday night. Close enough I could feel her heat before she had to back away.

"Do you want to go home?"

"No. Alex doesn't trust sending information via email, so if he really found something about Neil, an in-person meeting is the only option."

"Why a cemetery?" We waited for him at the northern end of Green-Wood Cemetery, atop Battle Hill. Next to us, the nine-foot-tall statue of Minerva—Roman goddess of wisdom and strategic warfare—stood on her grand platform.

I touched Minerva's bronze arm, darkened to near black from the century she'd stood there, her hand raised in salute to the

Statue of Liberty three miles away. Draped in classical Greek dress and scaled armor, she held a laurel wreath in her lowered hand. Her helmet was decorated with braids, creatures, and a tremendous double-plume.

She looked quite a bit like several angels I knew.

"The view's changed so much." I let out a sigh. To all but the west, the city was virtually hidden. Trees buffered the buzz of traffic, but the nearby condos and apartments in their uninspired beigeness blocked out most of the bay. From our perch atop the hill, all we could see over them was the jungle of New Jersey across the water. "I can't even see my island anymore."

"Ellis Island?" The wind caught her hair, sending it dancing about her face. She tucked it behind her ears, but it quickly escaped.

The ground was thick with monuments, dotted with smaller gravestones, and graced by grand mausoleums. Now and then, we'd passed a grave marker without a name, their letters and memories erased by time. The cemetery was a large, remarkable park with manicured lawns and lush trees. Behind us, the crypt of the man who'd erected the statue loomed.

"I remember being here for the Battle of Long Island in 1776. Three hundred and sixty-four dead. There were a lot fewer of my kind back then, and of yours, as well. Less than a billion humans, and now there's almost eight."

Eight billion creatures full of want, with no regard for the others around them.

"Bloody Pit, when I was born, there were only three hundred fifty million. You spread across the planet like a pestilence, infecting every inch you find. And what's the result?" I faced the break in the trees, sweeping my hand across the bay. "A world made of concrete, metal, and plastic, where people kill each other over little letters on a computer screen."

"Grief and revenge haven't changed since you were a human, Ellis." She stared off toward the statue in the distance, holding her hair still, jaw clenching. "Just the way they're delivered."

With a wave of my hand, her hair froze, the strands suspended in midair like the writhing snakes on Minerva's armor. I calmed each one, flattening or tucking them behind her ear, while her coconut scent wafted over me. "Neither have hope nor love, Danielle."

Her gaze drifted to my face. It was a gentle moment made all the more intimate for the death surrounding us. Until she shivered slightly and stepped away, her face hardening. "Well, I *hope* what Alex has is good enough that the people responsible for my *loved ones'* deaths will pay for what they did."

I'd worked so hard my first week with her, pulling her away from her thoughts of vengeance, hauling her soul away from damnation. And for what? A second attempt on her life, and both of us plunged into anger and despair. "And you're certain you can trust him?"

Danielle's assailant had clearly pointed to Chris being behind the attack in Times Square. She'd grown gradually less sure this PI of hers had been the one she'd spotted nearby that night, but what if he was part of it? "Not sure, but I think so."

She'd also thought she could trust her godfather.

"Doesn't he work for Neil?"

"Not really. He's worked contracts for him, but he's not an employee." Her eyes flicked back and forth, from me to the shadows and to me again. "Alex was the first one who saw my evidence board and didn't judge me for it."

"How many people have seen it?"

She shrugged. "Some police officers, my Uncle Mike, Alex, and the three PIs I hired before him."

And me. I'd told her to give up her hunt, but it kept coming after her anyway.

"He's the only investigator who found anything valuable." She ran her fingers through her hair, releasing the time freeze, sending strands every which way. "If he wasn't on my side—if he was involved with Chris—why bring me the mechanic's slip?"

"As a distraction? Perhaps it leads nowhere and he's trying to get your hopes up before smashing them—"

"Dani!" An attractive man her age strolled across the grass from the direction of the Higgins mausoleum. A couple of inches shorter than me, he wore jeans and a black polo shirt, with close-cropped strawberry-blond hair. He smiled, his perfect teeth lighting up blue eyes and his smooth-shaven jaw. Save for the outfit, lack of wings, and my not wanting to smash his face in, he bore an uncanny resemblance to Raguel.

This was her private investigator? I'd imagined someone far older, given his mistrust of technology. Someone significantly less handsome and who didn't look like he spent quite so much time at the gym.

Unfortunately, it was unlikely anyone else would approach her with familiarity and a manila envelope in a graveyard.

"Hi, Alex!" She headed in his direction, a broader smile on her face than I was used to.

"How are you doing?" He placed a hand on her arm, stroking it with his thumb.

Hands off.

"Excuse me." I approached them, sporting the most brilliant smile I could manage while he was manhandling her. "Where are your manners, Dani? Weren't you going to introduce me to your friend?"

"You can call me Alex." He scanned me from head to toe, producing a smile which didn't reach his eyes. "I'm her private investigator."

"What do you have for me?" Danielle asked, before I could introduce myself.

"Any news from the police?" Alex maintained focus on me. "On your break-in, that is?"

"Nothing yet." I extended my hand to shake, which he accepted and squeezed. Bad choice. I squeezed back, but the insolent human didn't flinch. "But she's fine."

Danielle smacked my chest, and I let go before I broke any bones. "*She* is anxious to find out what Alex brought her. And *you* are going to be nice in the meantime, Ellis."

Alex turned to her. "Your guard dog seems a little grim, doesn't he?"

Apparently, attire and wings were the *only* differences between him and Raguel.

She held out her hand, palm up.

"Can't say I blame you for hiring protection."

"I'm not—" I clamped my lips shut at her glower.

The corner of Alex's irritating mouth quirked up, highlighting the dimple in his chin. A chin dimple! Who has a chin dimple? Mr. Perfect handed her the envelope. "You're dealing with some dangerous people."

Did he have evidence of Chris's attempts on her life? I leaned closer to her as she slipped a series of photos out of the envelope. Four large photographs of Neil McEwan and a woman; exiting a car together, embracing, and walking into a house.

"I recognize him, but who's she?" Danielle flipped through the photos, inspecting each.

Alex stepped beside her and pointed at the woman in the image. "That would be Natalie Fitch. Wife of none other than Isaiah Fitch."

Danielle and I looked at each other, the words unspoken. The million-dollar man from the bank accounts.

"So..." I began, but Dani widened her eyes at me, the message clear: *Be quiet.*

"Who's he?" She blinked rapidly at him and tucked her hair behind her ear, despite the wind having died down. No, wait. That was eyelash fluttering! What was she doing?

"On the surface, a successful business owner who attends a lot of political fundraisers." Alex lowered his voice, cocking an eyebrow at me. "He also coordinates all sorts of goods—if you know what I mean—moving through the ports in Jersey."

She pursed her lips, nodding slowly. "And you're sure this is his wife?"

He eliminated what little distance there was between them, standing closer than I could without causing her to edge away. I should have frozen his hand while I was busy not crushing it.

"I got an excellent shot here." He pulled out his phone, fiddled with it for a moment, and showed her. "And here they are at a fundraiser in May. It's definitely her."

Danielle smiled at him again. "You have digital copies for me?"

"As much as I hate it, yes." He lifted his phone toward her. "Turn on yours so I can airdrop them."

"And what about Chris Beckett?" she asked as she pulled out her phone, as requested.

"He's been out of town since Sunday. I tracked him down to a resort in Grand Cayman."

She glanced at me. "What's he doing there?"

"He went alone and is scheduled to return tonight." Alex shrugged. "Lot of dirty money still goes through the Caymans, but that's all I have. Didn't think you'd pay for me to travel to the Caribbean. Do you want me to tail him when he gets back, even if it's after your deadline?"

"No, I think we're good." She pulled an envelope from her small crossbody bag and handed it to him. "I threw in a little extra for speed and discretion."

Alex peered at me and leaned toward Danielle's ear. "Have you vetted your bodyguard?"

"She has." My words must have come out sharper than expected, as they both frowned at me. "And what about you? Have you been vetted? She saw you in Times Square just before the attack, you know."

His head jerked back, and his brow furrowed. "Attack? What attack?"

I had centuries' worth of experience gaging human reactions. This one seemed genuine, as much as I didn't want it to be.

Dani's frown deepened. "I said I wasn't sure if it was him or not."

"But you're alright?" Alex sidestepped so he faced Dani, gaze roaming over her. "That's why he's with you?"

"I'm with her because I'm her boyfriend, not her body-guard."

He gave me a tight smile. "She needs a balance of both, I suspect."

"Thanks for the concern and the photographs, Alex." Danielle separated from him and returned to my side, reducing a tad of my desire to freeze the pretty boy. "I have some follow-up to do on this."

"What's your plan?" He gestured to the envelope as she slid the photos inside. "If her husband finds out, things won't go well for anyone involved."

Dani nodded, the breeze catching her hair again. "I have to think it over."

"This is a dangerous game. Call me if you want to discuss anything or have any concerns. I have experience dealing with his type." Alex gripped her upper arm again and she smiled, but he looked directly at me. "And watch your back."

That sounded like a threat.

I did my best not to narrow my eyes or send the cold creeping across the ground toward him. "I would, but I'm busy watching hers."

"Try doing both." He gave me a curt nod and sauntered off.

"I don't like him." My lip curled, and the words came out as a snarl. Completely unintentional.

"He's harmless." She ushered me along the path toward the exit. As we walked, she kept her eyes on her phone. "But I know someone who'll want to see these photos. Neil's well-respected as an up-and-up lawyer, so I bet it'll tank his reputation if he's in bed with some underworld guy's wife."

"Not to mention she's the wife of one of his clients."

She paused typing on her phone and grabbed my arm. "This is going to be good!" She let go quickly, clenching the hand and shaking it. Too cold.

Not like that tosser Alex. He wasn't too cold.

"You're getting too much enjoyment out of this, Dani."

"I've been looking for the truth for two years, Ellis. They're going to get what they deserve." She chuckled, deep and throaty, but the twinkle was missing from her eyes. It wasn't a cheerful laugh. It wasn't the laugh that would get her out of damnation. I shouldn't have told her about Chris or encouraged her to open the knight. Why didn't I take her far away?

"Hey, Morgan!" She had her phone at her ear as she strode down the path, weaving between monuments and gravestones. "I just sent you an email with some photos—" She paused, nodding, watching the ground ahead of her. "No link back to me?"

We approached the grand gate at 25th Street, and she finally hung up.

"Morgan has a contact at a website where they do scandal pieces. He said they'd pay well for the photos I sent him."

"That easily?"

"Yeah, apparently, Fitch is a big deal." She stopped to watch a group of lime-green Monk Parrots returning to their roosts in the center spire of the Gothic Revival gate. "They'll have them up tomorrow."

I'd admired the gate many times, how it reached toward the heavens, but all I wanted to admire was her neck. Long, elegant, stretched the way it was, so she could watch the birds. I could reach out and touch it, run my lips against it. If I were Alex's temperature.

"If Alex gave you digital copies you could send to anyone you want, why did we have to meet him in person?"

She cracked a smile, shielding her eyes from the sun. "I told you—he doesn't trust technology. Figures the airdrop is safer, since it's a direct phone-to-phone transfer."

"And you were..." I clenched my jaw, chest tightening. This wasn't my business, was it? "You were flirting with him."

"Flirting? I was being polite. He's a nice guy who gave me the information I need."

I shoved my hands into my shorts pockets, not interested in pointing at her or shaking a finger like some controlling boyfriend. "A little too polite, if you ask me."

She didn't turn away from the parrots or the architecture, but she didn't seem to be looking at them anymore, either. "What are you? Jealous?"

I scoffed. "Reapers don't get jealous. I get emotional. Angry, sad, happy, disgusted—"

"Jealousy's an emotion." She lowered her gaze to me, continuing to shade her eyes so I couldn't see them.

But I caught the sharpness in her voice.

"You would have let him believe I was no more than your bodyguard." I most certainly was not jealous.

She resumed her walk under the giant archway, avoiding the slow-moving traffic. "I thought about telling him you were my 'soulguard' but figured it would require too much explanation."

Another joke. Was that all I was to her? The creature who followed her around until she was dead, nagging her into behaving herself?

"Danielle, if I weren't..." My longing to be close to her, to touch her, was overwhelming. Surely, I wasn't the only one. I mean, her dying wish in Times Square was a last kiss from me, wasn't it? But this Alex fellow comes along and—Wait. *Was* I jealous? "What's going on here?"

She hooked her thumbs around the strap of her bag. "That depends on what you mean."

I stopped, and after a few steps, she did the same, turning to look at me. She knew bloody well what I meant. She just wanted me to say it.

"To be clear, I didn't take care of number nine while you were asleep."

Redness spread across her cheeks. "Did you consider it, at least?"

"I considered doing to Chris Beckett what he tried to do to you."

"Why didn't you?"

Raguel hadn't left any room for debate. For all my powers, my immortality, my role in the natural order, I was nothing.

Replaceable. A delivery guy. I didn't make decisions; I merely followed orders.

Bah! To the Pit with his rules.

"I was warned that if I hurt him, the price would be never seeing you again." I walked toward her, stopping far enough away I didn't freeze her, but close enough she had to tilt her head up to keep eye contact with me. "And I'm not willing to pay that price."

She sucked in a quick breath and touched my chest for too brief an instant, sending a flutter through my heart. Those were the right words, yet so wrong.

Because in four days, I'd escort her to damnation.

And lose her for all eternity.

CHAPTER 29

DANIELLE

"The colored pebbles in the path were supposed to depict the emperor." Ellis placed his tiles on the board, an O and an R off my F on the top row. "But I thought I'd have a little fun."

"Why do I suspect your idea of fun didn't mesh with everyone else's?"

"Because you're perceptive." He placed a B.

The wink he gave me lodged in my windpipe and caused heat to flush through me. It was Thursday lunchtime, two-and-a-half days since I'd woken from the evening in Times Square. One of the greatest and yet worst nights of my life.

Our kiss at the end of the dance had been like a dream. Soft, hesitant, caring. Holding more desire in it than any kiss I'd had my entire life. Maybe that's what kissing a Grim Reaper was always like?

Or maybe there was something different between us.

Then the stabbing, me sleeping for two days, and the revelation about Chris. And finally setting an actual plan in motion like I'd wanted for too long.

All of it paled compared to that kiss.

But since then, nothing. Lots of flirting, banter, and innuendo, but he hadn't touched my cheek or my hair once—let alone tried to kiss me.

He placed an I with a wicked smirk. "I created images of women punishing their husbands for their various misdeeds."

"Of course, you did." I laughed. "So where was this?"

I hadn't powered up my laptop since we returned from the meeting with Alex. It remained on the sideboard behind me, while we played Scrabble at the dining room table. Of all the games we'd played together over the last week and a half, this was one of my favorites. Watching him move his tiles around in the holder and place them on the board was strangely erotic. His fingers were one of the first things I'd noticed about him in Central Park, how long and elegant they were.

And he never left his tiles crooked. Every time I played with anyone else, I'd have to straighten things constantly. But Ellis? He was my perfect Scrabble opponent.

"You have to guess." He held up four tiles, hiding their faces from me.

The word was obviously FORBIDDEN, and he was referring to the Forbidden City in Beijing. But maybe I could wrangle something out of this. Folding my arms and settling my elbows in front of me, I narrowed my eyes at him. "What do I get if I guess?"

The way his smirk deepened from wicked to devilish triggered another wave of heat inside me. Before we'd started the game, he'd placed his hand on the table, and I'd brought mine down to less than an inch away from his, until the cold crept up to meet me. As he'd withdrawn the hand, he raised a single finger to trace the length of my palm, the contact sending shivers and sparks through me. Shivers and sparks which had continued pinging around my core the entire game.

"I was thinking, Danielle, that we should—"

A car door slammed shut outside, ripping my attention away from him. A fist pounded on a door close by—one of the neighbor's doors—and a man yelled, "You fucking son of a bitch! What have you done?"

I scrambled from the dining room to the front bay window. Byte's head shot up from his pillow in the parlor as I passed him, and he bolted after me, like it was playtime. The window provided a perfect view of Neil McEwan, in a charcoal suit and white dress shirt, continuing to pound on the Becketts' door.

He'd tucked the nose of his car into the spot in front of my house, running over the orange traffic cones Abby had put down for the impending arrival of Grayson's moving truck.

"Open your fucking door, Chris! I know you're in there!" Neil tried turning the doorknob, to no avail. He peered into the bay window of their living room and rapped on it.

The door whipped open, and Chris appeared, looking around frantically. Ellis's arm wrapped around my waist, and he hauled me back from the window faster than I could react. I collided with his chest, sucking in air from the surprise as much as the cold.

"Sorry." His word was quick, quiet, and he immediately separated from me. When Byte barked, wagging his tail, Ellis snatched him up to calm him.

We plastered ourselves against the wall, my heart beating in overtime. The shirred window coverings allowed us to see out, and with the sun shining outside, our lurking wouldn't be obvious unless they looked right at us. But after two attempts on my life, we couldn't be too sure or too safe.

Chris had arrived home late last night, and the knowledge he was so close, right on the other side of a two-foot-thick party wall, had me on edge. Ellis had made me chamomile tea, drawn me a hot bath, and sat in the chair by the bed until I slept. He'd promised again to watch over me and protect me for the night.

I should have been the one to tell Alex that Ellis was my boyfriend. He was the closest thing I'd had in a long time, and he seemed upset by me not acknowledging him. Like he was believing our little ruse. Or maybe it was turning into more than a ruse. Now he stood next to me, a thin layer of cold between us, as though we'd known each other for years.

"Keep your voice down," snapped Chris. "Get inside."

"You figured it out!" Neil's voice grew louder, and Byte yapped at the noise.

Ellis vanished, a door closed upstairs, and he returned. "He's locked in your bedroom for now."

He could move from place to place—Magically? Supernaturally?—with things, but this was the first time he'd done it with a living creature. Now was not the time to ask about that.

Indistinct mumbling came from next door, so I peeked through the window again. They were agitated, and Chris grabbed Neil's arm as Wanda joined them.

"For the last time, I'm not coming in!" Neil wrenched his arm from Chris, red-faced, but speaking more quietly. "I went to pay for brunch with a client and my fucking credit cards were declined. I know you did this! You figured it out and thought you'd screw me right back, didn't you?"

"Neil." Wanda came out to stand next to him. "You're upset. Why don't you come inside, have coffee, and we'll sort it all out?"

"All my Empire First accounts are empty and the cards are maxed! You took it all, I know it!" Neil narrowed his eyes at Chris, pointing a threatening finger. "And if you think that's going to save you from Fitch, you've got another thing coming."

Save him from Fitch? Was there something else going on? Something predating me screwing with their accounts?

Wanda pulled her phone from her pocket, while Chris professed his innocence and tried to get Neil into the house again.

She shook her head. "Neil, there's nothing out of the ordinary in our bank accounts. Chris hasn't taken anything from you."

Chris gestured through the front door. "Exactly! Now come inside and stop making a scene."

"Fuck you, Chris." Neil turned to Wanda. "Did you check your Empire First accounts?"

"No, we closed those after Luke and Vicky—"

"You mean Chris told you he closed them?"

Wanda looked back and forth between the two men and returned focus to her phone. My father wasn't the only one who kept secret bank accounts?

"Honey?" Wanda's hand clapped over her mouth. "You said we closed this account but—but we have over a million dollars in it. Transferred—oh my god—transferred Tuesday? You didn't tell me anything about this. What's going on?"

Chris gaped at Wanda. "We what?"

"Don't you play innocent with me!" Neil poked Chris in the chest. "You've got twenty-four hours to put it back before I go to the cops!"

"You can't go to the police," hissed Chris.

"Watch me!" Neil spun on his heel and marched back to his car.

"Mom? Dad?" Abby's head popped over the other side of their steps as she arrived in their tiny front yard from her apartment downstairs, Grayson at her side. They looked at Neil's car as he sped off and back to her parents. "Is everything alright? We heard banging and yelling."

"Come on." I plucked at Ellis's sleeve and headed for the door, a different type of energy bouncing around inside me. If the commotion brought Abby outside, I could certainly leave the house and appreciate my handiwork. This was going to be good.

"Everything's alright." Chris held out his hands when he saw Ellis and me. He repeated it to people on the street, to other neighbors who'd come out to see what the fuss was about.

"Explain this!" Wanda shoved her phone in Chris's face. She seemed confused, upset, frantic even. "Where did this money come from, and what was Neil talking about?"

The peal of sirens caught everyone's attention, and we all turned to look down the street where an NYPD squad car and two large black SUVs were approaching. I spun back around to see Chris's face grow pale.

"Everything alright, Chris?" I shivered as goose bumps prickled my arms, and I walked down to the landing on my front steps.

Abby climbed up to her parents, while Grayson focused on the sirens. "Dad?"

"Explain this!" shouted Wanda, tears in her eyes.

The squad car and SUVs stopped in front of the Becketts' house, one after the other. Two officers, three men in dark suits and a woman with them.

"It's happening," I whispered to Ellis, the energy growing so intense I practically bounced.

The six descended on the man who tried to have me killed. Twice. The suits revealed badges, the front one speaking. "Chris Beckett?"

He nodded, leaning against the carved pillar at the side of his door.

"Special Agent McDonald with the FBI. We have some questions for you." He looked at Wanda, while one of the police officers placed Chris in cuffs. "Are you a resident here?"

She waved her hands as she took in shaky breaths, and Abby rushed to her side. Visions of Wanda reading us stories during sleepovers, braiding my hair, and taking Abby and me to the park as little girls flooded my memory.

Abby spoke up. "I'm his daughter. This is my mother. Yes, she's a resident here, as am I."

Curtains opened all around us as people spied out their windows. We lived in a safe neighborhood where things like this didn't happen. The FBI agent held out a piece of paper. "We have a warrant to search the premises and take into custody any and all computers, tablets, and phones."

Ellis grabbed and squeezed my hand so quickly I would have questioned if it really happened had I never seen how fast he could move. "Chris, I have an excellent lawyer I can call. Name's Hayden Younge."

Chris's gaze flew to Ellis, then to me, the name of my would-be murderer as clear a declaration as we needed. *You found it!* he mouthed, as the officer read him his Miranda rights before leading him to the squad car.

"It's okay, Mom. Everything's going to be alright." Abby helped Wanda slide down onto the wide limestone railing next to the door, leaning her against the house. "Dani, can you come sit with her while Grayson and I go in with the officers?"

No, no, no.

Chris sat in the back of the police car, head down. I was right about him. He had something to do with my family's death. He broke into my house and told someone to make sure I *didn't talk*, then he paid someone else to kill me a week later. After two long years, Chris Beckett was finally staring down at the consequences of his actions.

But Wanda... what had I done to her?

"Help me, Ellis?" I whispered as I nodded to Abby. Slowly, I climbed down my stairs—my muscles protesting the entire time—then up hers, taking her in my arms when I got there. *I'm sorry you have to go through this, but your father's a horrible man.* "We'll wait here for you."

Abby, Grayson, and the FBI agents went into the house, and I sank down next to Wanda. She took my hand, tears streaking her face.

Ellis knelt in front of her, resting his hand on her knee. How could he offer that kindness to everyone but me? "I'm sure they'll sort this out quickly."

Wanda blinked rapidly, nodding. "How much of Neil's accusations did you hear?"

I put an arm around her shoulders, while Ellis maintained the conversation.

"Most of it. Something about Chris stealing his money?"

"What could that mean?" She stared at the police car. If I'd thought for even a second she'd been in on it, this would have sealed the deal for me. Wanda had been betrayed by Chris just like I had.

"I don't know. Do you want to try figuring it out or tell me about something else?"

Four quarter-million-dollar payouts. Dad was dead. Chris was in custody. And Neil's punishment would come soon. Who was the fourth? The two men who'd attempted to kill me were strangers. Had one of them been in on the original crime? Maybe someone Dad and Chris had worked with?

Not Fitch, if Neil said Chris needed saving from him.

Maybe the mechanic? No, the mechanic came into play after they stole the money.

Wanda patted Ellis's hand and smiled weakly. "You're a good man, Ellis. I'm glad Dani met you."

"So am I." He smiled at her, then turned the handsome face to me.

My nerves relaxed as I lost myself in those strange, dark eyes. I wanted to take his hand from Wanda's knee and hold it, thank him for being my strength the last week, just like he was doing for her. What a cruel irony. I was going to Hell right after the universe dropped the most perfect man in my lap.

"Now—" Ellis squeezed Wanda's hand. "Shall we talk about what's going on, or shall I distract you?"

"For right now, I think a distraction's what I need."

"Perfect. Why don't I tell you about the last time I was at the Louvre, three years ago?" He was calm, speaking quietly and slowly, and she clung to his every word like a life preserver. Another police car arrived at the end of our one-way street and blocked off the traffic. The roadway became still, and the gawkers eventually stopped once the police had taken Chris away.

Then, it was just the three of us sitting on the stoop, chatting like old friends. Me, the wife of the man who killed my family and nearly me, plus a Grim Reaper. Just an average Thursday morning.

CHAPTER 30

DANIELLE

"Ellis, I—" My knees gave out as soon as I reached my living room. I slumped into the chair closest to the door, tears finally spilling free. "What have I done?"

We'd spent an hour with Wanda, sobbing, worrying, fidgeting with the twenty separate tissues she'd used for her eyes and nose. The FBI agents left with three laptops, two tablets, three phones, and a box full of notebooks. From Neil's accusations, it sounded like Chris had been trying to finish the program but hadn't been able to. That meant one of his laptops would have at least enough on it to tell the authorities he was guilty, even if they didn't find Dad's.

The only track I'd had to cover was the IP address. It was too easy.

I had my revenge.

But Wanda's face. And Abby's.

The perpetual hole in my stomach widened, and I dropped my head into my hands, trying to stem the tears. This would destroy the two women who'd stood by me through everything.

I did deserve Hell.

"Chris will go to prison. Maybe once he's fingerprinted, they'll even find a link between him and the break-in." Ellis knelt next to the chair, placing his hand close to my arm, fingers flexing as though to reach for me. "Isn't that what you wanted?"

"I did. I mean, I do." What I wanted was to have his arms around me again, so I could cry on his shoulder. To have him warm and comforting, like he was with Wanda. Not cold. Not the fucking cold. "I just—I wasn't thinking about Abby and Wanda."

He vanished and returned, placing Byte in my arms, who wagged his tail and licked my face, forcing my head up. Ellis smiled, but it was rueful, not transferring the peace it usually did.

I focused on him, on his peculiar dark eyes, his handsome face, while I scratched Byte's back. I had three days left with Ellis. Would my soul remember him after I died? Would I miss him? "What's Hell like?"

His gaze fell. "I don't know."

"But you've taken people there?"

"We throw them in the Pit." He shook his bowed head. "Other than that, all I know is that they spend fifty years there before they take on a new body. I don't know what it's like or what happens during that time."

I put Byte on the ground, and he stared at me, tilting his head. He placed a paw on my foot until I waved him toward the parlor, and he scampered to his pillow next to the piano. "I'm still damned, though, right?"

"I don't want to look."

That meant yes. "Fifty years isn't so bad, is it?"

He swallowed hard, then launched to his feet. "I'm hungry. You hungry?"

"Not really." I wanted to keep crying, like I deserved.

He held his hand out to me, sporting the fake smile, the cocky one, or maybe the one that was hiding his genuine emotions. Either way, it was the one that didn't reach his eyes. "I want a sandwich. Come help."

"The subtle art of distraction?" I stood, wiping tears away instead of taking the offered hand.

He covered his heart, feigning offence. "I don't know about you, but I'm certainly not going to spend the next three days moping."

"Moping?" I chuckled and sniffled, nudging his shoulder with mine as we made our way to the back of the house. "What's the alternative?"

"Celebrating."

I cleared the last tears from my cheeks. If I'd had him in my life two years ago, even just for a couple of weeks, would things have turned out differently? Would he have held my hand through all of it, not letting me push him away, like I pushed everyone else away?

"Celebrating what?"

He selected a tomato from a basket on the counter, a cutting board and knife, and placed them on the butcher's block island. "Whatever we want. And for right now, that's my sandwich."

"It's remarkable." I rinsed the tomato and returned to the island to cut slices, while he retrieved more ingredients.

"Yes, I rather think I am." He winked over his shoulder and smiled. And there it was—the peace, the calm. The way he helped me let go of my regret for just a moment. My life defi-nitely would have turned out differently if he'd been part of it.

"You're seven hundred years old. You've seen all the wonders of the world, hidden treasures, met the most fascinating people, yet the smallest things still make you happy. I'm barely thirty and can't find happiness in anything."

He placed bread, lettuce, and a package of cooked bacon on the counter. "It's all perspective, Danielle."

"After the car accident..." I stopped, one tomato slice cut, and opened my right palm. I'd stared at my scar, massaged it, stroked it hundreds of times as a reminder of my family. If I did that now, it would light up with the hourglass, a reminder of my deal with Ellis instead. "I can't tell you how often I heard that time would heal the wound, but it never did."

"Because you wouldn't let it." He tore off enough lettuce for the sandwich and took it to the sink. On his way past me, he leaned close, coolness brushing my ear. "Try now. What have you got to lose?"

He settled at the sink behind me and turned on the water. What *did* I have to lose? Three days left, and I was going to Hell. Not like things could get any worse.

I cut another slice.

But it couldn't get any better, either. Of all the things I thought I wanted in the world, my time with Ellis showed me that the thing I was missing was connection. But I couldn't connect with him, could I? Not the way I wanted to. Not with his soft breath on my cheek and his body next to mine, wrapped up by those strong arms against his broad chest.

Going out for dinner and walking around the city with him Saturday night was like a different time. A different me. An old me I missed. I'd been alone for two years, and having him here made me feel... what? Like I was part of something? Like I wasn't just the girl everyone felt sorry for?

What I was going to lose was him.

I shut my eyes and—

"Ow! Shit!" I dropped the knife and clutched my thumb, drops of blood falling on the counter. I spun from the cutting board, shouldered Ellis aside, and shoved my hand under the tap. He'd abandoned the lettuce to the bottom of the sink, and I covered it in blood, diluted by the still-running water.

He flipped the tap to hot and grabbed my hand before I could tell him to stop. His eyes closed, and a white light spread out from between our hands, bright enough I had to look away. The tingling I'd felt in my feet Saturday night crept through my hand, up my arm, as he turned back time to heal the wound.

A wave of joy radiated through me. Every molecule in my body moved a little faster, my breaths bringing more oxygen than I needed.

His touch, under the scorching water to stem the freezing cold, was magnificent, filling me with an awareness of everything around us. Dust motes hanging in the air. Byte's soft snores two rooms away. Ellis's rapid pulse thrumming next to me.

Too soon, the light dimmed, and he opened his eyes, brows drawn down. "Are you alright?"

"Yes." My voice trembled, something deep inside screaming at me to hold on to him and never let go. "Did you feel that?"

"What?" He began to retreat, but I caught his hand and held it under the water. It was smooth, despite being so strong, so ancient. And it was the first time his skin had touched mine without pain, cold, or death. "Don't, Dani. I don't want to hurt you."

I interlaced my fingers with his, heart thundering in my chest. What did I have to lose? "Letting go would hurt more."

He hesitated, scanning my face, flexing his grip in mine. The emotions whirring through him were so clear—like I was feeling them myself—from the initial concern, to hope, to confusion. "Are you sure?"

"I haven't been sure of much the last couple of weeks, Ellis." I took a stuttering breath, unwilling to tear myself away from him. "But I want whatever part of you I can have, even if it's only this."

"Danielle." His voice rumbled deep in his throat as he broke our grip to run two fingers across my palm. Across his mark. His lips parted slightly, eyes falling to my mouth, and he settled on a single emotion: desire. He stepped closer, the cold coming with him, and I wrapped my fingers around his. He stroked my palm, in and out of my loose grip, our hands speaking need and consent. "I've wanted all of you since we met."

"There's still time to change number nine." My lungs heaved, another vision of his body next to mine flashing through my brain. But this time, the vision included less clothing.

A lot less.

His T-shirt pulled across his chest as always, and I lifted a tentative hand to touch him, like part of me had wanted since the day in Central Park. Ten seconds, and I had to pull it away.

But the one under the hot, running water continued. He caressed that hand, his grip shifting to explore the length of each of my fingers, sparks lighting up my entire body from the small contact.

"Is that what you want?" His eyes narrowed, and he closed the distance between us, launching goose bumps up my free arm. He leaned in and touched his lips to mine. When his tongue slid out to open my mouth, I shuddered. But my tongue greeted his, desperate, like he was the very air I breathed.

Arctic air. I stepped back with a shiver, wanting more, but unable to continue. My wet fingers slipped between his, and I gripped tight. "Oh my god, Ellis. So much."

Breaking contact from the water and his hand, I cupped his cheek, running my thumb across the short facial hair, and urged him forward.

His wet hand grazed my throat, circling to the back of my neck. Droplets rolled down my chest, falling between my breasts. My skin begged for more, for his hungry mouth, his soft fingers, his scratchy stubble. With the residual heat from the water against his cheek and my neck, the kiss lingered. His teeth brushed my lips, tongue sweeping across mine. He tasted like vanilla cupcakes, complemented perfectly by his cinnamon scent.

As one, we stepped together, bodies coming flush for the first time since he'd healed me in Times Square. But my warm hands were no match for his frigid body, and I separated from him, his lips sucking on mine as we broke apart.

"I'm too cold, Dani."

"This is wrong." Cosmically wrong. I intertwined my fingers with his, which were ice again. But when we placed them under the running water, the stab of pain eased, and my lids fluttered closed. "I want to feel you."

The growing bulge in his shorts told me he wanted what I did, that the need pulsing through my veins was in his as well. I constricted my throbbing inner muscles, urging them to stop reacting, yet pleading for the possibility to find release with him.

"Lust..." His lips hovered near mine, not touching unless the warmth was nearby, the hunger in his eyes palpable. "It's a powerful emotion."

Was this lust? Or was it more? He was so tender, the word didn't seem to fit. If that was all it was, he wouldn't have returned his fingers to the water. He would have taken what he wanted and laid waste to me, while I screamed for more.

But no. We had a connection, a caring, something special which sparked from the day we'd met in Central Park.

He withdrew his hand from the water and pushed it under my shirt. His splayed fingers spanned my back, and I was suddenly, unavoidably aware of his height, his breath, his all-encompassing physical presence.

It wasn't new, but in that moment, my fragility compared to his strength, his immortality and power... he could consume me in one breath. And yet, together we were something greater. Grander. Stronger.

I sucked in his air, craving his scent and his taste, and our mouths met again, far too briefly. My wet hand landed on his waistband, aching to undo the button. Such a bad idea. If he lost any clothing, it would be near-impossible to deny what we both wanted. "Do you use protection?"

His hand left my back at the first goose bump, and he warmed it under the water.

"I do whatever my partner wants." He laid his warm hand against the side of my head, ghosting his tongue along my upper lip.

I stepped forward, dipping my fingertips below his waistband, running my knuckles across the trace of hair on his abdomen. Any lower, and the button wouldn't matter. But I had to put my hand back under the water; we were so far into this peculiar dance it barely phased me. "Including tasting like cupcakes?"

The corner of his mouth quirked up. "You like that?"

"I do."

Our first kiss, I'd winced through the pain of holding his face. Maybe I could do it today without hurting. I put my second hand under the tap.

And it struck me.

The single greatest idea of my life.

I turned off the water and tugged on his T-shirt. "Follow me."

We made our way to the front of the house, to the staircase. Savoring the moment and doing my best not to run, I ran my hands down my sides, all the way to the hem of my shorts. How would his fingers feel on the tender skin at the back of my thigh? Or inching up my ribcage to my breast?

"Where are we going?" He brushed a frigid hand along my rear, eliciting a gasp and a sigh from me. Yeah, lust—or whatever this was—was a pretty strong one.

A jingle and claws on hardwood brought my attention to Byte following us. Ellis's fingers grazed mine, my back, my legs, as we went up the stairs. He stayed far enough away and touched me only briefly, each contact compounding pleasure with the last.

Flames licked through my veins, and my body, my very essence, screamed for surrender. If it weren't for his icy touch, I would have pulled him down on the stairs and given myself over right there. Screw the discomfort. I needed him, and fast.

We arrived on the second floor and made our way to my bedroom, nudging Byte out as I closed the door. He barked incessantly, but for once, I didn't care.

"This won't work, Dani."

"We have options. We can pleasure ourselves together, try toys to keep us at a safe distance, or..." I turned to face him and bit my lip. We could do this. "Or we can take a chance on something else."

He snatched the hem of my shirt and balled a fist in it. A low noise, a rumbling, sounded in his chest. "From the look in your eyes, I think I choose number three."

I held up a finger, and he let go of my shirt, so I could grab a couple of condoms from my bedside table. This had to work. I returned to him, walking backward, towing him behind me by his shirt. We stepped through the door to the ensuite, and I tossed the condoms on the counter.

The room was bright, white marble sinks with a large mirror, patterned tile floor, and an immense shower enclosure with pale-gray tiles to the ceiling. Two showerheads, one on each wall. My parents had installed it—

Stop. Not the time for memories. This was the chance of a lifetime, and I wasn't about to let it slip through my fingers. Especially considering my life would end in a few—

Stop. Focus.

I swung the shower door open and turned on the water—all the hot water from both showerheads—and ushered him in. He obeyed, stepping under the cascade, leaning his head back so streams poured through his hair, over his face, soaking his clothes. His shirt clung to every ripple of muscle on his torso and shoulders, a wisp of steam circling around him. I'd never been as jealous of water as I was at that moment.

"Smart woman." His mouth opened, tongue rubbing along his upper teeth, like it was waiting for mine. He held out a hand.

Was it enough?

I slid my fingers into his palm, as warm as it had been under the tap in the kitchen. As I stepped into the shower, I inhaled the steam, the lingering scent of coconut shampoo and soap, plus the vanilla cupcakes.

Tentatively, I reached for his chest. *Let it be enough.*

"Is that alright?" His fingers interlaced with mine, free hand paused just shy of my face.

I closed the shower door behind me, smiling up at him. Before I could nod, we crashed into each other under the onslaught of heat, mouths frantic for each other. His tongue was cool but refreshing and delicious under the scorching water.

His hands drove into my hair, mine around his upper back, as our chests crushed against each other. He ground his hips against me, side to side, his hardness becoming more pronounced with each swipe. "Still okay?"

"More than okay." The cold was still there, if I held too long in one spot, but never so much I feared going numb. My soul rejoiced. This was going to work. "Take off your shirt."

He stepped away, and the spray blasted his neck, sending a fine mist into the air, which mingled with the steam. It was slow, how he peeled the wet shirt from his body, revealing inch by glorious inch of his flesh. He let it fall to the tiled floor with a splat, splashing our ankles. The way it had clung to him revealed so much of his form, he'd been practically shirtless with it on. But the perfect skin underneath sent another round of energy pinging through me, rattling around in my core.

Seeing him remove it at the park last week been thrilling, but this held a different promise. This man, this creature, wasn't teasing today. He would be inside me, satisfying my compulsion to be closer to him.

The layer of frost we'd suffered for almost two weeks un-balanced my world. Being separated from him felt off. Wrong. Like the way a crooked picture on the wall made my skin crawl. But finally, we'd be together, and we'd revel in the release and completion we ached for.

When I moved toward him, my hand slid down the muscles of his abdomen, over his button, to his shorts. He groaned low in his throat as I stroked his length through the fabric. It grew under my touch, the thick shaft becoming more prominent, his want propelling my own.

He undid the button and zipper of his shorts, letting them fall open, revealing a black D&G waistband. "Do you want me to take these off?"

"No." At least, not yet.

He arched an eyebrow, teasing at the elastic with his thumbs. "You sure? Because I really want to."

I licked my lips, stepping back to tilt my head to my showerhead, smoothing my hair under the water. Heating my body under the blistering spray, my skin reddened to a point I couldn't take it anymore. I returned to him, my hands covering his. "Let me."

As I dug my fingers under his clothes, he captured my mouth with his. Easing the shorts and underwear along his backside would have been easier dry, and I giggled in the kiss when they clung to the curve of his tight ass. He laughed with me, our mouths locked, and he took over, leaving me to savor the lift of his perfect rear.

"Your turn," he whispered, lips remaining on mine, his fingers popping the button on my shorts. "If you're still warm enough?"

"I am." I separated from him, only enough to scan the length of his naked body. From the faint hair across his chest to the defined muscles, and the happy trail leading to thick hair around his full and ready cock. His kindness, the way he kept me laughing. How much he enjoyed every board game, card game, and video game we played. His amazing body. I couldn't have designed someone more perfect for me.

Except the cold and the death.

I stripped off my shirt and bra without pretense. My body was about to explode.

He came back at me, pulling my shorts and underwear down. He got them as far as my thighs and stopped to take one nipple in his mouth. Sucking on it, caressing it with his tongue, sending a groan echoing through me. An excruciating moment later, he continued pulling down my bottoms and freed my feet one at a time.

He stayed kneeling and kissed my ankle, my shin, skimming along the inside of my knee. I balanced my arm against the wall while he inched his way up my body. The need intensified with every touch, throwing me closer and closer to climax before he'd even reached my sex.

His hands on my hips, he nudged me to the wall and draped my leg over his shoulder. Hesitantly, he ran his mouth along the soft skin of my inner thigh, his short facial hair tickling, magnifying the fever his lips were creating. Every inch, he looked up at me. "Is this alright?"

And every inch, I echoed, "Don't stop."

He continued exploring until he reached the top of the thigh, tilted his head, and I edged my hips forward, inviting him. His tongue danced across to my clit.

I squealed—like a fucking glacier between my legs—and grabbed his hair to yank his head back.

"Too much?"

"Shit, yes." I stomped my foot back on the ground, sending a spray of water around the shower, squeezing my thighs and inner muscles together as hard as I could. So close, but still not enough. Unfair. So fucking unfair. This wouldn't work after all.

He stood, reorienting one showerhead to beat against us at the wall, and gathered me in his arms. It was a hug, an embrace, an all-encompassing security blanket. I was safe. Secure. Like I hadn't been in two years.

Not because I was dying, but because he cared.

This wasn't just lust. It was tenderness. I wanted *Ellis*, not just anyone. And he'd had so many opportunities, but he chose me. There was more between us.

"You said there are other options, Dani?"

I didn't want other options. I wanted him, and I wanted him for more than a few more days. His powerful body enveloped mine, and I held on tight, breathing him in. The hunger pulsing through me relaxed as we remained still. Together. My head fell against his shoulder like it had when we danced, and he stroked the length of my hair as I nestled in closer.

What I wanted most was just beyond my grasp. The story of my goddamn life.

CHAPTER 31

ELLIS

"Shh, Dani." Her breath hitched, and I held her tighter. Lust and passion had given way to something I hadn't felt before. A need to protect her—not just her body, but her heart. I wanted to rescue her from the pain each time it overcame her. To simply be *with* her in any capacity, stronger even than in Times Square. "I only want to see you smile again."

Without unwrapping her arms, she tilted her head so I could see her clearly. And she was smiling, the glitter back in her eyes, like every time she laughed. I bent to meet her lips, soft and inviting. Her tongue slid against mine, and my erection throbbed, begging to be inside her.

The thrill which accompanied human mating was spectacular. It had overcome me in the kitchen, more quickly than Saturday night while we danced. But now what? My tongue on her hidden sex was too cold, yet she clung to me, so the shower was fulfilling some small part of the role she'd hoped for.

She touched my cock, closing her hand around it, as she'd done with my fingers downstairs. But this time, she stroked, and I moaned into her mouth, not daring to break contact with her. Her other hand grasped the base of my shaft, squeezing a tight ring and cupping my balls as she encouraged my arousal. The confidence and reciprocated need spurred me on, magnifying my desire for her.

I broke from our kiss, my thoughts becoming fuzzy and singular. "Do you want to try?"

With a tentative nod, she escaped the shower stall and retrieved one of the silver packets she'd brought from her room. I wasn't about to argue how it wasn't necessary, even if she was going to live beyond Sunday morning. This was what she needed, so it was what I would do for her. Perhaps the layer of the condom would even act as a buffer to the cold.

She tore it open and beckoned me to the door, rolling it along my length. "We don't actually need this, do we?"

"Whatever makes you comfortable." I grinned, holding it with one hand, stroking myself with the other, while she re-entered the shower and resumed her position against the wall. "Is it warm enough?"

She bit her lower lip and nodded. I slipped my hands to the backs of her thighs and lifted her, skimming her back along the wall. As she wrapped her legs around my hips, I pushed against her gently. She kept her eyes fixed on mine, my concern reflected on her face. But once I entered her—eased in as her tight walls stretched around me—she relaxed, and a broad smile took residence.

This moment, this perfection, this radiance, would be what I remembered of my twenty-first century vacation. Seeing the smile on Danielle's face. How it lit her up and stirred my ancient heart.

I buried myself deeply, crushing my hips against hers, until she gasped, and my stomach lurched. "Are you alright?"

"Yes," she breathed. "That was a good noise."

My gaze locked on her as I pulled back slowly, watching for any hint of the cold or pain. But I was met with her rapture. Her delight. This was the Danielle I'd longed for. Joyous Danielle. We'd brought her back from the edge together.

Together.

We moved as one. The spark that surged through me every time my skin touched hers was nothing compared to this. Being inside her felt like home, like the place I'd missed for centuries. Somewhere I belonged, where I was welcome and wanted. With a woman who didn't see me as a monster, but as someone to be vulnerable with. Someone to trust. Not a one-night stand nor an unknown man who would vanish in the morning, but a lover. Someone who cared. Someone who might be in lov—

Mom's head twisted awkwardly, streams of blood running down the side of her face. From her ear. The airbags had gone off too early.

What? The echo of a reaping? Now?

"Don't stop." Danielle groaned, bringing me back to the moment. She rolled her hips in my grasp and captured my mouth with hers as I sank into her warmth. It was slow and intense, and I was aware of every inch as I slid in and out, over and over. The pressure built swiftly, and she encouraged me to speed up, countering my desire to freeze time when I plunged fully inside her.

I quickened the pace, the ecstasy growing, consuming us both. Her gasps and moans fanned the flames of my need, bringing me closer and closer, as we cried out for each other.

"Oh yes, Danielle!" Her name was a prayer on my lips, purity and bliss and wonder. If this lasted until her final morning, it would be too little. How would I get enough of this woman? How could fate have thrown us together, only to rip us apart again?

John blinked slowly, and I reached for his hand, but my body rejected the command. I couldn't even move a finger.

I lost my rhythm, but she picked it up, dragging her nails across my back and through my hair.

What was going on? The aftermath of her car accident had flashed through my brain. Like the first time we'd kissed, it was as though she were in my head. But she wasn't a Reaper, so she wasn't my Pair, and we weren't Bonding. It was my imagination. My guilt.

"I'm almost there." Her fiery breath on my ear propelled me back into the moment. My need and want rekindled, I leaned into her, growing more fervent by the second. I twisted my form, thrusting against her most sensitive spot in a way no human could, ensuring she reached her peak first.

Her eyes shot open. "Ellis! Oh, my god!" Her inner muscles clamped, pulsing in rapid succession. She bit down on my shoulder, suppressing a scream, while I exploded inside her, pumping the empty seed out of me, clutching her tender body against mine.

Continuing to move until we were both done, the bliss coursed through my veins, relaxing every ounce of tension. Her legs loosened as our breaths eased, but I kept rolling against her, unready and unwilling to be singular again.

He laid a hand on my chest, a small light emanating from the touch. Stars swirled in his eyes until I could feel my fingers again.

"Is it too cold?" I leaned against her on the wall, and she shook her head. I clung to the euphoria, pushing aside the guilt and memories. That night after her accident, I'd taken her father. I'd saved her when it wasn't my decision. Not a day had gone by that I didn't think about her. I didn't deserve her. Didn't deserve anyone.

Focus on her, Ellis. Not on all of that.

She was so soft, and all I wanted was to hold her next to me for eternity. She'd found her vengeance. It was behind us, and we could concentrate on *us* for the time we had left.

"That was amazing." Danielle's words were so quiet, I almost missed them over the continued pummeling of the dual showerheads. No wonder she spent so long in here every morning. "Not to inflate your ego, which is already immense, but that was easily the best orgasm I've ever had."

"Thank you." I pulled out, placing her back on her feet, and kissed her temple. The serene look on her face and subtle laugh caused something to skip inside me. As though my chest had expanded and found a fertile space for my heart to regrow. "I can do it again, if you'd like?"

"I'll turn into a prune." She grinned, removed the condom from me, and left the shower to dispose of it. "But so worth it."

I braced my arms against the glass at the door, kissing her deeply when she was close enough. She pulled back with a start, brows drawn.

"What's wrong?"

"Oh my god, you're—" She yanked me out of the shower, a puddle forming on the tiled floor underneath us. She prodded my chest, twisted me around, ran her hands over my back, through my hair. A brilliant smile creased her face, which lightened my entire being. "You're warm!"

"I'm what?"

"It's not just the water. Was it the sex? Did that do it?"

"I don't know." Her happiness washed over me and the swelling in my chest grew. *Was* it the sex? Or the connection between us? And did it even matter? "Whatever it was, I think we should continue in your bed."

CHAPTER 32

ELLIS

I lay under the covers next to her, my arm wrapped around her waist. Naked—gloriously naked—and fitting together as if the universe had designed us for each other. We'd had sex, eaten delivered food at the dining room table in scant clothing, and gone back to the bedroom for more. I'd tasted every inch of her delicious body, and I was sated.

Until she woke up, at least.

For the first time in seven hundred years, I longed for sleep. A way to pass the hours until she wakened and I could bury myself inside her, caress her breasts, suckle the soft flesh of her neck. And her mouth. On mine, wrapped around my length, bearing down on my shoulder while she climaxed.

My cock stirred at the thought of my body entwined with hers. She moved in her sleep, nestling closer to me. I could scarcely wait for morning, when the exploration would continue. Two full days wouldn't be enough, but I would settle with what I could have before I lost her.

Two days. That was all we had.

Then I'd be alone again.

Forever.

One hundred years before I could mourn her properly. One bloody century before I could even care that I was alone and she was gone.

She moved once more, faster this time, but brief. This wasn't turning over or switching the position of her legs, which she'd done eight times thus far.

There it is again.

Was it a dream? A nightmare? She hadn't moved like this any of the nights I guarded her sleeping body.

And again. A shudder wracked her. A seizure? It continued, rocking the bed, her breath coming as quickly as her movements.

I moved out of the bed, forming in front of her to see her face. Her lips were pale, and the shaking didn't stop.

No, no, no! My stomach sank.

My cold was back.

No! We'd been fine since the shower. Not a single problem!

She halted, and a white puff hung in the air when she exhaled. Not shivering anymore was worse than shivering. I slowed her—all of her—giving me a chance to act. To the kitchen, microwave a beanbag. To the other bedrooms, retrieve blankets and add them to her bed. Grab Byte and throw him under the covers. Light a fire in her fireplace. Toss the beanbag under the blankets.

And wait.

Put on pajama pants.

Wait more.

She began shivering slowly—a good sign—so I released the slowed effect on her and sat still. Hoping.

I'm sorry. I'm so sorry. This is my fault.

Her exhales grew clear, and her lips returned to pink.

I should have known better. Vacation wasn't a time for joy; it was for suffering. To remember everything I did every day, the souls I committed to the Pit, the families I broke apart, the sorrow I caused. It was to remind me I was a monster, undeserving of the happiness I could have had in life.

And Danielle suffered for it. She'd spent two years in agony because of me, and my being here was nothing more than salt in her wounds.

Why did I do this? Why did I think it could be different this time?

Nothing more than ego.

I pulled the wing chair to her bedside and sank into it, my head falling to my hands. "I'm sorry, Danielle."

Byte wriggled out from under the pile of five blankets on top of her and whimpered at me. I picked him up and snuggled him against my shoulder, appreciating the warmth I could share with him that I couldn't share with her.

"I'm sorry, boy," I whispered, not wanting to wake her. "I'm going to have to take Dan—"

My throat closed over, and a shiver ran along my spine. A shiver? When had that ever happened? Byte fought against my grasp, so I let him into my lap, where he curled up, watching Danielle with me.

The pit in my stomach widened as I continued stroking Byte's back. His head eventually drooped against my leg.

With my free hand, I produced her contract. The letters flared as they appeared, dancing with their elegant script. It was Friday morning, and the collection date was Sunday. And the letters were all the same.

Damned.

I'd reaped over five million souls over my centuries. I knew the hallmarks, what it took to earn the Pit, the Hallway, or the Stairs. Her sins weren't so awful she deserved this, but it wasn't my choice to make. The Fates wrote the contracts, while Azrael weighed the souls—sometimes with Raguel's input. She didn't make mistakes, so maybe it was his influence. Either way, this was wrong. So wrong.

My vision blurred as tears collected against my lids, and Byte raised his head to look at me. I rubbed his back and vanished the parchment as the tears fell. "Abby will spoil you, I promise. We'll write her a note to be sure she knows which treats are your favorite."

He dropped his head to my lap, letting out another whimper.

"I'm going to miss you, too, Max."

Danielle's breathing regulated, and her face grew rosy. She was probably overheating now. Humans were such fragile things; it was easy to forget.

I let out a long sigh. That's why Reapers had to do this, wasn't it? To remember what we once were, so we'd hold *them* in the esteem they deserved.

Reg was wrong. This human was different. She wasn't simply a tool to help me experience my emotions. She was special, and all I wanted in the world was to hold her and change her contract. But how?

I pulled a few blankets off her, doing my best not to disturb Byte, who'd drifted off. She rolled over, facing away from me, so all I could see was her wavy mass of hair. Picking Byte up, I rounded the bed and climbed onto the other side. It dipped as I moved, but she didn't stir. The bed was large enough I could lay three feet apart from her, far enough she wouldn't feel my cold.

Byte snuggled against my chest and dozed off quickly.

What was the key? Why was I warm to her all afternoon and evening? What magical thing happened at three in the morning that caused this?

Was it nothing more than a celestial joke, all the angels and Reapers laughing at my misery? Additional penance for delaying my vacation so long?

I reached over to brush the hair from her face.

Or was it penance for falling for a human?

CHAPTER 33

DANIELLE

"Good morning, handsome." I padded into the kitchen where Ellis was making breakfast. The scent of banana bread in the oven and frying bacon competed with the aroma of fresh-brewed coffee. But the real feast was him.

He wore blue lounge pants, no more, doing the impossible: cooking bacon while shirtless. The pants slung low on his hips had my body firing on all cylinders.

"I expected you'd still be upstairs when I woke up. Get bored waiting for me?" Arms out, I approached him. I'd rushed through my morning routine, freshening up enough to race down and find him. Excited to feel his skin against mine, I'd only thrown on little shorts and a tank top to maximize surface area.

Yesterday had been mind-blowing, and he'd promised me another day of it.

But he backed away with a grimace before I could touch him. He put out a hand, keeping me at a distance. "Sorry, Dani."

"Sorry what?" The bacon spit, searing my forearm, and I jumped away from the stove. "Ow!"

My heart sank as I took in his defensive posture. And how he inched away. Oh, god. It *was* just lust for him. He'd used me to satisfy an emotion. He'd changed number nine on his list to *Have sex*, we'd crossed it off, and he was done with me. Everything I'd felt, the joy, pleasure, adoration, excitement...

Something on my face must have betrayed me, because his eyes flew open, and he closed the distance quickly. The layer of cold hit me before his body did.

"No." My shoulders fell as his fingers twined in my hair. "That's why the fireplace was coals this morning?"

He gestured to the pan on the stove. "I need to get this before it burns."

"Yeah. Right." I backed away and leaned against the black countertop, watching him work. Watching his narrow waist, thick biceps, corded forearms. Those arms should have been around me at that moment. He moved the bacon from the pan to a plate next to the stove and shut the flame off.

His mouth was tight. "Three in the morning."

"What?"

"That's when it happened." He rested his palms on the counter on either side of the stove, tilting his head to look at me. "You were curled up against me and began to shiver, then shake, and your lips turned blue."

I wanted to lash out at him, hit him, throw something at him, accuse him of doing it intentionally. But it was all over his face—it hurt him as much as it hurt me. "So, yesterday was a onetime deal?"

The doorbell rang, and someone pounded on the door furiously. At the same time, a notification buzzed on my watch.

Ellis pushed off the counter and was past me in a flash. "I've got it."

The message was from Alex: *We need to talk*

I hit a quick-response as I followed Ellis: *What?*

The inner and outer door opened by the time I'd reached the parlor.

"Where's Dani?" It was Alex's voice. Why text me when he was outside?

I hit the main hallway in time to see him dodge past Ellis. "Who did you send those photos to?"

"What?"

He thrust his phone in my direction, playing a live news feed. The headline scrolled across it: 'Prominent New York lawyer dead.'

I gasped and nearly dropped his phone. The highlight reel looped through professional shots of Neil from his law office's website, the photos Alex had given me, photos of Isaiah and Natalie Fitch at a fundraiser. All followed by late-night video of police working a scene, two sheets covering bodies, evidence flags, and lengths of yellow police tape.

Ellis came closer—so close the temperature dropped, but I couldn't move.

A woman's voice played over the video. "Details are still coming in, but the NYPD has confirmed they've taken a man into custody in connection with the murders. An anonymous source has reported that Natalie Fitch's husband, Isaiah Fitch, has been identified as a person of interest in the case. We're not yet sure if he's the one in custody at this point. We've contacted his office, but they declined comment—"

Oh god.

Bile burned up my throat, and I dropped the phone into Ellis's hands before tearing out of the living room. I sprinted to the bathroom, fell to my hands and knees in front of the toilet, and threw up everything in my stomach. Neil was supposed to be discredited and embarrassed—maybe disbarred for being involved with a client if I was lucky—but not dead. And not Natalie Fitch with him.

Two people's lives gone, and it was all my fault.

Ellis and Alex continued talking in the foyer, but I couldn't make any of it out over my heaving and shuddering breaths.

Abby's father arrested. Wanda's life ruined. Now Neil. I flushed the toilet and leaned against the cool wall, but no tears came. They should, shouldn't they? Tears of regret, of guilt, of relief? Of something? Anything?

I *did* belong in Hell.

CHAPTER 34

ELLIS

"Who did she send them to?" Alex swiped his phone from me and tucked it into a pocket. "I need to know."

"You should leave." I was in a foul enough mood after Dani's late-night freezing that I was liable to do something I shouldn't. From down the hallway, I could hear her retching into the toilet.

"Neil wasn't supposed to die," he hissed.

"A lot of things shouldn't have happened." I took a step toward him. Toward his cocky, handsome face and his ridiculous statement. Neil's and Natalie's times had come and gone, but that was determined by the Fates. Not by any of us. "She feels awful enough every single day, but you had to put those photographs in her hands, so now she'll blame herself for what happened."

"I didn't see that ripple, Ellis."

I froze, straightening. Ripple? The Furies didn't implement punishments and rewards for souls one at a time. They plotted one action, which ricocheted through countless people, sometimes spreading through entire communities. They called them ripples. "You what?"

"She was supposed to send them to a gossip site—"

"She did."

"Natalie and Isaiah were supposed to fight, and she was supposed to be hurt. Neil would find her in the hospital and..." He dragged his hands through his hair.

The toilet flushed, and I took another step toward him. "What do you mean by supposed to?"

He gripped the back of his neck with both hands. "Are you really this blind when you're on vacation, Ellis?"

I leaned closer, keeping my voice down so Danielle couldn't hear us. "You're a Fury?"

His eyes rolled heavenward. "Didn't I give you enough hints on Wednesday?"

Hints? Of course. Balance, protection, warnings about watching our backs. And that explained why he hadn't flinched when I squeezed his hand. "You *were* involved in the attack on her at Times Square, weren't you?"

The water began running in the bathroom, and both Alex and I looked down the hall. Almost as soon as it started, Dani shut it off to vomit again.

"I didn't even know about it until you brought it up." He folded his arms across his stupid chest. "I've been trying to help her balance the scales for months."

"Balance the scales?" This was the moment I should have hit him. Instead, I lifted my hand to pluck her contract out of the ether. "Is *this* how you balance scales?"

Alex sucked in a breath and grabbed for the parchment, but his hand passed through it. "That's not right."

"Not right? You've been stoking her obsession. All you've done is condemn her soul to the Pit!" I snapped my hand shut, hiding the contract. Rage coursed through me as strong as the night I'd gone after Chris, but still I whispered, "Now leave her alone."

"That's not right." His gaze fell to the door next to us.

"I'm trying to raise her soul up, but you're making that near-impossible."

He nodded slowly, then looked directly at me. "Your best bet is to take her out of town. The ripples are too unpredictable around here right now."

"What does that mean?"

"Neil and Natalie weren't supposed to die." His jaw tightened. "And she's not supposed to wind up in the Pit."

Furies didn't have the power of foresight like Fates did, but from what I knew, their awareness of consequences was near perfect. Perhaps those were just stories, like the ones that said every soul had a Pair, whether they were still mortal or not.

"Sounds like your powers aren't working so well these days, Alex."

His lips tightened, a venomous light flaring in his eyes. "Powers that be, you Reapers are jerks when you're on vacation."

The toilet flushed and the water ran again.

"Feel better, Dani!" he hollered in her general direction. He headed for the door, but while he was halfway out, he said over his shoulder, "Heed my warning. Take her out of town."

I helped the door shut behind him, more forcefully than needed. Bloody Fury! He shook his head as he made his way down the steps, probably at me. *I* was the jerk? I wasn't the one who was manipulating the world around Danielle, so she was damned to the Pit. My every effort had gone into saving her soul. But him? He'd made everything worse.

The water in the bathroom stopped, and I took a long, slow breath to center myself. She needed my support, not my rage or even my irritation. *Focus on Danielle. On her soul.*

I moved down the hallway, appearing outside the open bathroom door.

She rested her hands on the sink counter, staring at her pale face. Red-rimmed eyes met mine, and I could almost hear the thought in her head, *Things just keep getting worse.*

Without thinking, I reached for her, but the subtle movement away from my hand reminded me of the awful situation we were in. Twelve hours ago, I could have wrapped my arms around her and comforted her. Now, all I had were words. "Are you alright, sweetheart?"

CHAPTER 35

DANIELLE

I looked at him in the mirror, standing in the doorframe behind me. The softness in his eyes, the way he reached for me but pulled his hand back... I had revenge against two of the three who were behind it all. But now what? I felt even worse than before, my stomach rolling, heart aching, and I just wanted to crawl into a little hole and pretend it was all a dream.

I stared at the sink in front of me. "You should have let me die."

"Don't say that." He stepped into the room, placing his fingers on the small of my back, the cold easing some of the nausea. "Did you hear what Alex said after you left?"

"I couldn't hear anything."

"Neil made his choices. From everything we've learned, he's made a lot of bad ones. You added one extra thing to that pile, but the foundation was of his making."

"But the woman he was with? Natalie Fitch?" I looked up at his reflection. "She had no part in all this."

He brushed the hair away from my face, keeping his fingers off me. "That's the limitation of human justice, Dani. You can't isolate it to a single person."

He was right. Of course, he was right.

I'd thrown a stone into the pond and expected no ripples. But they were all around me, waiting for me to drown. "And we still don't know who the other quarter million was, Ellis."

"Does it really matter anymore?"

Good question. Maybe leaving it in the hands of the divine was the right choice after all.

"Where did Neil go? Heaven or Hell?"

"I don't know." He gestured toward the door. "But I do know I'm hungry."

I nodded, following him to the kitchen. "Do you know who... collected him?"

"There are hundreds of us assigned to New York City. I choose to believe it was Reg. He takes the worst of the worst."

The scents in the room were distinctly less appealing than when I'd first walked in. I'd expected to wrap myself up in Ellis's arms, kiss him, eat the food he'd prepared, and make love. That's where we should have been at this moment—naked, lost in each other. Instead, Ellis was too cold to touch, I had vomit-breath, and Neil and his mistress were dead.

Ellis put a couple pieces of bread down to toast. "If he and Natalie were in love, maybe Anya and Katrina took them, to remind them of what they could have had."

"Anya and Katrina?"

"They're the only Pair allocated to the city."

"Pair?"

"The strongest of my kind. Bonded pairs of Reapers, never one without the other." He took the toast and spread a thin layer of butter, pushing it in my direction. He stared at it while

I sat on a stool at the island and took a tentative bite. "They sometimes collect couples who die together to help the souls see the difference between their human belief in love compared to the union of true souls."

The thick, chewy bread, with all the little grains and seeds in it, was exactly what my stomach needed. He really did make amazing bread. "I'm not following."

"As a Reaper, I only know the stories passed on from Fates and angels. But as it's told, souls wink into existence in pairs, tied together by a golden thread. When they enter their first body, the tie is severed, and they spend every life searching for their other half again."

"Every life? You said Hell is a fifty-year punishment? Are souls reincarnated after that?" At least I hadn't sent Neil there for eternity. That settled my stomach a little.

"Fifty years for Hell, one for Heaven. Just enough for the soul to separate from its human identity and prepare for a new life."

"And when they find their Pair?"

"When the circumstances are perfect, a Fate will tie their threads back together, and they can reform their Bond in a moment of intense emotion." He crossed to the counter where the coffee had brewed before I came downstairs. "Mortal Pairs go to Heaven and never leave again. Immortal Pairs are given the option to continue working. Few of them do, but Anya and Katrina did."

"That's beautiful." I took another bite of the toast.

"It's complicated. Too complicated. There are far too many rules around it. The Fates only tie souls who've earned the White Stairs, only two mortals at a time, or if they're immortals, they have to be the same type. And for a Reaper?" He dumped two mugs of coffee into the sink and returned to the coffeemaker by the stove. "That moment of intense emotion can only spark two weeks out of every century. Try lining up two Reapers at the right time! Powers that be, Reg hasn't found his after more than a hundred thousand years."

The topic bothered him. Had he lost someone? Had he been Bonded before he died? How did that work?

"Did you lose your soulmate?"

"I've never Bonded." He waved a dismissive hand. "Can you imagine? Never being alone? What a bother!" The weak laugh and slumped shoulders that followed betrayed his truth. He was lonely. My Grim Reaper was sad and lonely and trying to brush it off.

Never alone.

Before I met Ellis, that would have sounded awful, but now? After this time with him, I could almost imagine always having someone there by my side. My parents did it for thirty-five years, and before the crash, I dreamed of having the same thing.

If he ever did Bond, that Reaper would be a lucky one.

Why couldn't he have been human?

I rounded the island to stand next to him and took an oven mitt from a drawer by the stove. Slipping it on, I put the hand on his shoulder and turned him to me. "You're not alone now."

"Neither are you." His voice dropped as he took the hand from his shoulder and squeezed it. "Never say that again—that you wish I'd left you in the cellar to die."

As one, we stepped closer, to the edge of the cold, and he held my mitted hand.

"I'm really going to die in two days, aren't I?"

He kissed my temple, lingering long enough it stung. "Yes."

"It's funny. After the crash—" A lump lodged in my throat, and I swallowed hard, gripping his hand like the lifeline it was. "I didn't want to go on."

There'd been so many options. The pills, a rope, a knife, the train. It would have been so easy, and the pain would have stopped. No more watching Johnnie's last breaths in my sleep, seeing the pity in people's eyes, walking through the quiet house. No more crying in the shower. No more staring at the ceiling for hours. No more sleeping for days.

Just no more.

My head fell, almost resting against his shoulder before I had to straighten. I wanted to tuck my face against his neck and live inside his embrace until it was over. Why did he have to be so damn cold again? Last night, we'd shared space, breath, joy. Our skin and arms and mouths had found each other finally, and all I wanted was one more warm hug.

"Neil pushed me through the first year and a half, going after maximum payouts from the insurance company and the car manufacturer." The irony. He killed my father for money and swore he was working for me pro bono because he was so upset over it.

"But it was only money?"

"Yeah. No real justice. I was sitting on my bed, every leftover bottle that every doctor had given me spread out in front of me." A strangled sob burst from my chest. I would not cry over this. Not again. "I don't know how long I sat there, staring at them."

Ellis pressed my hand against his heart. Its rhythm was rapid but steady, and I stood still, feeling it beat through the thick fabric of the oven mitt. I hadn't even said this to any of the doctors. They all asked, assumed, but I told them what *I* wanted them to hear, not the truth.

Give me the drugs, spare me the lecture.

"I remember opening one bottle and counting the pills I had left. I don't even know which one it was, or if it would have been enough. But I remember there were twenty-four of them. I scooped them up—" My shoulders shook, but I held the tears back, instead pressing my lips to his hand and taking a deep breath. These words had never come out, but I needed to tell him. He thought he was alone, just like I'd thought I was. "I didn't have anything to wash them down with, so put them back in the bottle and came downstairs for some vodka."

As if on cue, the sound of claws on hardwood and the jangling collar announced Byte's arrival. We watched him approach, a tennis ball half the size of his head gripped in his mouth, which he dropped at our feet. He put a paw on my foot, and Ellis scooped him up. Once he straightened, I placed my protected hand against his chest and the other on my dog.

"And this little shithead..." I leaned close enough to Byte that he licked my nose, pulling a quiet laugh out of me. "He'd gotten into the bag with his treats, and the place was a mess."

Mess was an understatement. Half-eaten food scattered across the floor, shreds of the bag they'd been in, doggie vomit, and he'd used the bathroom in the corner.

"I lost it on him. His tail tucked between his legs, and he whimpered and cried." I scratched Byte's chin, his head tilting, the way it always did when I was upset. He was the best little pup I'd ever had. "My exact words—I'll never forget them—'I can't leave you alone for one second, can I?'"

I touched my nose to Byte's, and he rolled his head to lick me again. His little tan face and black ears, tiny wet nose, and dark eyes. So like Ellis's eyes. Byte was my sunshine.

Shaking my head, I let out a long, uneven breath, and all the stress that came with it. "And that was it. That was when it hit me. I'd been planning on leaving him forever, and I just couldn't."

"What did you do then?" Ellis's voice was deep and soft, not a hint of judgment or disapproval, but caring. His gentle gaze hadn't left me the whole time.

I cleared my throat, forcing the thickness from it. "Cleaned the fucking kitchen and called the first PI."

"And you never thought about it again?"

"I thought about it a lot, but that was the only time I got close to acting on it. I focused on my hunt." I screwed up my face, trying to lighten the mood, trying to pull us out of the emotional hole we'd fallen into. "Ellis, I've been living in the past for two years, only looking to the future as the place where I'd find revenge. I thought it would make me happy, but now that I have it, I'm even more miserable."

He leaned down so our foreheads almost touched. "Humans have so many blessings, so many things to be grateful for. But instead of living in a moment and appreciating the bliss which surrounds you, you're scheming for tomorrow, looking for the thing that can make you happier. When in reality, happiness only exists in the now."

"Are you happy? In the now?"

"Dani…" His face pinched. "I'm with you. Of course, I am."

My heart tumbled, and I took a half-step back. "With me? But I'm the least happy person I know."

"Thus proving my point. Air in your lungs, roof over your head, and plenty of food to eat. Powers that be, you have people who love you, an adorable dog—" He jostled Byte, who craned around to lick Ellis's chin. "And most of all, a charming yet delusional man who calls himself your boyfriend, and who had you panting and moaning for several hours yesterday."

I stifled a laugh, visions of our time together flashing through my brain, echoing through my body, and landing squarely between my thighs. He was right, but baring my soul made me want him even more than I had yesterday. "But today—"

He tapped a finger on my lips. "But today, there's still the shower."

"Maybe I should eat something first."

"Yes, you'll need your strength." He winked and put Byte down, returning to his gigantic plate of food. "And I have a surprise for dinner. We're going to meet someone very special to me."

CHAPTER 36

ELLIS

"Ellis Grimm! Where have you been, young man?" The stout woman in blue scrubs ahead of us folded her arms. Nurse Chase guarded the hospice wing at St. Christopher's with cool precision and could have thrown us both out on our tails if she wanted to.

"I know, I know!" I raised my hands in surrender. "But I only missed one Friday."

She glared over the thick-framed glasses sitting low on her nose. "Some people around here don't know if they'll have another Friday."

Danielle wore black Capri pants with a white T-shirt and carried an insulated bag with food and drink in it, while I held a half-dozen helium balloons with Happy Birthday written on them. As we'd made our way in, I greeted several people who knew me, and Danielle became more suspicious by the minute.

"Well, I know I didn't miss Glenn." As my other marked human, a copy of his contract would have been sent to me the moment it was drawn up. And since I'd not yet received it, he had at least fifteen days left. I pointed to Dani's bag. "We come bearing gifts."

Nurse Chase—who I was certain was born without a first name—frowned deeply, looking Danielle up and down. "Who is we? You know I can't let just anyone in here."

"Nurse Chase, I'd like you to meet Danielle. My helper for the—"

"Don't toy with me, Ellis. Tell me this is your girlfriend!" Her frown cracked, and she spread her arms wide, grabbing Dani.

"I think I'm supposed to say yes to that." Dani stiffened and patted her gently on the back, unable to do anything else in the woman's vice-like grip.

"Hearts must be breaking all over the world!" The nurse released her and stood back with hands on her hips. "I tell you, this man comes here every Friday like clockwork. When he misses a week, I worry."

I withdrew a white pastry box from Dani's bag, full of decorated cookies. "This is for you, my dear."

"Charmer." She winked at me and gestured to Glenn's door. "Go on in."

"You come here every Friday?" Danielle leaned close as we headed down the hall, and I caught the scent of her hair, reminding me of our time in the shower that afternoon. We'd satisfied our physical desires, I'd washed her hair, and we'd held each other. We hadn't been as lucky as the day before, but the intense thrill of being in contact with her for that hour had left a near-complete peace deep inside me.

"Like when I visited you in Central Park, I can make myself visible to humans at any time." I touched the small of her back briefly, like an instinct, but she edged away from it. "Normally, the cold vanishes when I'm visible."

"What I'd give for normal." She frowned but shook it off. "But why come here?"

It was the type of training I'd chosen centuries ago. I regularly visited the dying when most others wouldn't. The Black Death, lepers, yellow fever, Ebola, AIDS, all the worst humankind had endured since I'd become a Reaper. A kind face made so much difference to those accustomed to being treated like something to be feared. "Mercy? Kindness? Empathy?"

I knocked—three taps, a pause, then another two—and opened the door. The pale-orange walls of the hallway gave way to a cheery yellow inside. Two light-blue patterned chairs sat below the picture window at the far end, next to a hospital bed and its accompanying wheeled table with water and a book. Covered by a thick navy flannel blanket lay a tiny wisp of a man with glasses and tubes in his nose.

As we neared him, Glenn turned his head with a frown. "You're late!"

I held my smile at bay and snapped back. "I was busy, old man!"

He laughed, which changed rapidly into a cough and a wheeze. When it passed, he looked at Dani, his teasing eyes softening, and he settled a papery-thin hand on his chest. "And who is this beauty?"

"I'm Danielle," she said, smiling. "I'm apparently here for a birthday party?"

"You know, young lady..." He reached for Dani's hand, and she acquiesced. "All the nurses insisted this strapping young lad had to have a woman in his life. He swore to me in confidence he didn't. Don't break my heart and tell me he lied."

"That's enough flirting, Glenn. We have a lot to do tonight." I took the bag from Dani and put out the boxes of food, while she got out a small speaker and put on some light jazz—his favorite. "Now, I made all the food, so no complaining about it."

Dani placed disposable plates and cutlery on the low table by the chairs.

"You know I can barely eat anything, Ellis."

I stopped what I was doing and put my hands on my hips. "Who do you think I am, you old goat?"

He wheezed again. I'd started visiting Glenn three years ago, before meeting Danielle. I'd been one of the Reapers collecting at the car accident which took his wife, daughter, and two others. He was in the midst of chemotherapy at the time, but he kept on fighting, searching for the beauty in every day. Sadly, it wasn't a battle he was going to win, but he was a light in the darkness. He'd easily earned the White Stairs and would return stronger a year after that.

"Should have had the pretty one cook," he grumbled.

Dani's shoulders shook as she laughed quietly, carrying a small container and spoon to Glenn's table.

"She was busy in the brains line when they were handing out the cooking skills." I opened my small container with pale-green soup in it, steam curling off the top. I inhaled deeply, the seared onions and pepper striking first, followed by the hint of lemon and broth. "Leek and asparagus soup to start?"

Glenn's eyes lit up, and he pressed the button to lift the head of his bed. "Roll that table over here, please."

She opened his container and pivoted the table for him. "How do you two know each other?"

I looked out the window as Glenn took his first few spoon-fuls; the sky was growing dim, but sunset wouldn't be for an-other hour. On the other side of the building. Dani settled into the chair next to me and opened her own soup.

"He's a busy volunteer. Used to help with my groceries while I was still at home, and when I moved in here, he was playing piano out in the common room."

"And he told me I was the worst piano player he'd ever heard."

Dani laughed, almost losing some of her soup. "He's fantas-tic!"

I nudged the bed with my foot. "Glenn's an old grump. It's how he shows his appreciation."

He wheezed again and took a couple more mouthfuls. "This is delicious, Ellis."

"After this, I have lemon garlic pasta with scallops—had them brought in special from Digby, Nova Scotia—and chocolate brownie cupcakes with peanut butter frosting."

"You make the cupcakes with those damn avocados again?" He put his spoon down in his cup, already finished.

"I did, because you love that recipe."

Dani closed her container. She hadn't finished, but we'd keep to Glenn's pace. "I tested one. They're amazing."

"You mean you tested two?" I winked at her and stood while she portioned out a bit of pasta for him. I switched his cup for the plate.

Glenn inhaled deeply and coughed a couple times as Dani and I got out our own. "How do you expect to kiss her if your breath reeks of garlic?"

"Because mine will reek of the same thing." She looked at me from the corner of her eyes, pretending to be coy. "Plus, he'll taste more like chocolate and peanut butter by then."

He choked out a few more laughs before indulging in his food. We made our way through the meal, eating slowly and laughing, concluding with a round of the "Happy Birthday" song before enjoying the cupcakes. Once we finished, I brought around the wheelchair.

Glenn waved it off. "I don't have your energy, Ellis. It's time to call it a night. You two go make the best of it."

Danielle cleaned up the food, packing everything away.

"Lazy old man." I parked the chair next to the bed with a grin and pulled down the railing. "The sun's going down."

"Sunset?" Dani tilted her head. We hadn't crossed that one off my list yet, but tonight was Glenn's night, not ours.

I nodded. "There's a reflection garden on the west side of the building, and I expect the sun going down beyond the fountain will be breathtaking."

Dani remained paused in packing. "We're hitting an awful lot of—"

Pressing a finger to my mouth, I nodded to her, but continued harassing Glenn. "What do you think, old man? Indulge a couple of young lovers who want to experience what you said were the best things in life?"

He harrumphed and shook his head. "That's extortion."

I laughed, pulling back his blanket and tucking my hands under him. "Bribery is probably the correct term."

He settled in the wheelchair with the blanket wrapped around him, and I set up his portable oxygen tank. As we left through the west entrance, he breathed in deeply, a rattle sounding in his lungs. Danielle walked next to him, and he held her hand the whole way. We toured along the path, between flower beds, under trees, ending at the fountain.

Brickwork surrounded the round pool, and two small sprays threw water into the air on either side of a cherub at the center. I parked the wheelchair next to a bench where Dani and I sat.

"I know it's not a park, Glenn—"

"Ellis..." He reached for my hand, and I took it. His damp eyes were off to the west, to where the sun was going down. "Where's my dance?"

"Fortunately, I taught Danielle the waltz last weekend." I looked over at her, her eyes wide. I stood and took the back of the wheelchair, inclining my head to her. "Shall we?"

She stood hesitantly, started some music on her phone, and came to the front of Glenn's chair. I flicked my eyes down to his hands, and she took them, keeping them on the armrests. I wheeled him forward, and she stepped back, twisted his chair to the right, pulled him back, and twisted again.

He wheezed, she laughed, and we fumbled our way through the awkward steps.

"Danielle, my darling..." He lifted his arm, unable to raise it above his chest, so I reached under and helped. Together, we elevated Danielle's hand high enough she ducked under it to spin slowly. "This is the best dance I've had in years."

She smiled as we let his hand back down, and she held them on his armrests, stooping slightly to remain close to him. "Me, too."

"Now tell me you'll leave this horrible avocado lover and run away with me."

She laughed when I moved the chair again, taking a misstep and colliding her knee with the side.

"I don't know." Her eyes rose to mine, catching the setting sun in their reflection, and she smiled. The smile that warmed my heart and made me want to remain human forever. "I'm kind of fond of him."

Perhaps suffering the emotions of a full lifetime wouldn't be so bad. There'd be valleys, but the mountains could be so high. Suppressing everything protected me from sorrow, but I missed the joy, the passion, and love.

Number nine.

Have sex would never make up for sacrificing the ability to *Fall in love*.

Glenn coughed a few times, and we paused in the dance, but he waved his fingers, encouraging me to continue. "What if I confess my undying love for you? Would you run away with me then?"

The song ended, and Danielle curtseyed before him, likely signaling her shins and knees were finished. "You're the one who wrote Ellis's list of the best things in life?"

"That I am!" Post-dance, his face was peaceful, contented. "I've lived a decent life. Faced some rough times, but you have to focus on the good. I had fifty-three wonderful years with my wife, forty-eight with my daughter, and my son and grandkids still come to visit me. Life is a blessing, but dear Ellis seems to struggle with that."

I nudged his chair. "I do not."

"You see," he continued, ignoring me, "he works too hard. I gave him that list to remind him to stop and smell the roses." He winked at her. "Or the coconut-scented shampoo. Looks like it worked."

He shivered and coughed again, gasping to catch his breath.

"We should get you back inside." I stood to maneuver the wheelchair, and Dani resumed her position next to him, hand-in-hand.

CHAPTER 37

DANIELLE

"That was…" I paused, looking all around us—at the street-lights, the people on the sidewalk, the cars, up to the stars in the sky. "The only word I can come up with is humbling."

"An appropriate word." Ellis stuffed his hands into his pock-ets and smiled up at the heavens. *Do a good deed* must have been crossed off his list, if nothing else.

For almost two weeks, we'd been trying to get through life's best things together, but it had been difficult with me bringing the mood down. But with Glenn? One evening saw every single item crossed off.

"I wish I could have been more like that. You know, at peace with the universe despite everything?"

"It took him time." Ellis nodded, a far-away look settling over him. "But he learned joy and misery are nothing more than comparisons to each other. Once he came to terms with his grief, he gradually found comfort in the small things he hadn't appreciated before. He told me that when he had everything his heart desired, he forgot to watch the sunsets for the miracle they are."

"Thus, the list." My gaze fell to the sidewalk in front of us. How many doctors, friends, and family had told me essentially the same thing? If only I'd listened.

"Danielle, you lost a great deal, but not everything. You haven't run out of time to choose happiness until you've drawn your last breath."

Was it really that simple when I was heading to Hell? "I don't know about all that, but I do know one thing."

"What's that?"

"I'm so happy I got to spend the last two weeks with you." I raised my head to look at him and take in that gorgeous face. I touched his arm—not cold—then slowly threaded mine around his. Still not cold!

He jerked away, but I held tight, and we stopped. A couple nearly collided with us, but they moved out of the way in time.

"It's not cold." I placed my other hand on his chest.

He sucked in a sharp breath, the corners of his mouth begging to lift. "Not at all?"

I shook my head and slid my hand up his right cheek, the electricity sparking when my skin touched his, and stopped at the scar he'd placed by his eye. "I love this scar."

His breath deepened. "I added it for you, you know."

"I suspected." I stroked it with my thumb, thinking back to our first day in Prospect Park when he proclaimed how perfect he was. "We've come a long way in a short amount of time."

He canted his head to place a kiss on the side of my hand. "We have."

From three in the morning, when he had to separate from me, to this. Could we have another night like the one before?

My fingers combed through the hair on the side of his head, settling at the nape of his neck. "This isn't what your vacations are normally like?"

He tucked my hair behind my ear, moving closer. It was tentative, like every time he was checking for the barrier of cold. "If they were, I would have asked to retire a long time ago."

"What does *retire* mean to a Reaper?"

His big hand circled my waist. "Hang up the scythe, go through the white door, and come back in a year."

"Not as a Reaper, though?"

"No." He pulled me tighter against him. "In a fresh body, ready for the roller coaster of the human experience."

With no guarantees whether that experience would be happy or sad? "Maybe you'd have an easier shot at finding your Pair that way?"

"I couldn't care less about that right now."

Me, either. I pulled his face to mine, and our lips parted when our mouths met. Not a single degree of temperature drop. One of us deepened the kiss, maybe both of us, and the overwhelming sense of serenity and rightness flowed over me. My hand explored his hair while his ran just under the hem of my shirt.

My world was at peace, and the whisper came on the wind again, *It's him.*

"Get a fucking room." Some jerk passed us, staring at his phone.

We broke from the kiss and laughed quietly, and he dropped his forehead to rest against mine. This was new and wonderful; we hadn't even needed the shower this time. It was Friday night.

We had until Sunday morning. If the cold could stay at bay that long, I would finish my days and his vacation in a state of bliss.

"We need to get home." He caressed my cheek and sucked on my bottom lip.

"Glenn was right." I grinned and interlaced my fingers with his, tugging him along the sidewalk. "That garlic's pretty strong."

Chapter 38

Ellis

"I thought you didn't sleep?"

I opened my eyes at her words and smiled. "Just passing time."

We nestled under the covers of her bed, three feet apart, separated by the ever-present Byte. After nearly freezing her to death last night, we'd taken precautions. I extended my hand toward her, and she reached out to me, our fingers intertwining without hesitation.

She yawned and stretched her body. "Not cold."

I lifted the blankets and slid across the distance to her, as her arms and legs wrapped around me. Byte hopped over me, yapping his disapproval at being awakened.

"Last day." She sighed, nestling her face against my chest. "I keep hoping I'll wake up and find this has all been a wild dream. That you're just a normal guy who was hitting on me in the park."

"It would have taken more than a normal guy to cut through the attitude you were slinging."

She chuckled, holding tighter. "That no one had died, no one was in jail, and you were just the one who saved me from myself.

That you were actually my boyfriend and not just playing with your pet human."

I jerked back, seeking her face for some indication of whether she was being honest or making an absurd joke. "We've spent nearly every minute together for the last thirteen days, made love multiple times, enjoyed each other's company, and both your dog and your best friend adore me. If that doesn't make me boyfriend material, I don't know what does."

Her face tightened. "You're going to kill me tomorrow."

I shot up to sitting. The words were a stake through my heart, a slap across the face, a punch to the gut. How could she say that? "I'm going to help your soul transition to the afterlife!"

She rolled up onto her knees, the veil of sleep fully pushed aside. "And feel nothing when you do! Isn't that right? I become another random soul in your list of—how many?"

"Dani—" I put a hand to her cheek, but she swatted it away.

"Cold again." She turned from me and left the bed with a huff.

Powers that be! Again? Why couldn't I stay warm long enough to spend one full day with her?

She crossed to one of the windows, staring down to the street, dressed in her pale-pink tank top and shorts. "So there you have it. You've finished your little list, so feel free to go find someone else to nag for the rest of the day. Ooh, or maybe go sample someone else's *assets*. Sex is easy, right? Isn't that what you said?"

Surely, she didn't mean all this. This was inevitability talking, her future coming to a premature end. It was anger that I'd be involved. She had to understand.

I picked up the thick blanket and followed her to the window, wrapping it around her, holding her with the layer of insulation between us. "My list isn't finished yet, and I need your help."

She folded her arms around mine, breath shuddering. "What's left?"

"I need a sunset. A special one."

"We did that last night." She sniffled, wiping her cheek with the blanket.

Oh, my heart. "No, that was Glenn's sunset, not ours."

Her body relaxed, and she pressed her cheek against the blanket piled up between our faces. "Ours?"

"Dani, I don't want to spend time with anyone else, and I don't want to cross off my last item unless you're there with me."

She turned to face me, still bundled up to keep warm. "And I don't want to spend my last day without you." One of her hands wriggled out of her cocoon and her short nails brushed across the stubble at my jaw, then her fingertips, finally her palm. "And it's gone again."

I let go of her so the blanket fell and wrapped her in my arms, her head falling against my shoulder. We had less than twenty-four hours left together, and I wasn't about to risk losing a moment of that to any other attempts on her life or reminders of the horrible things she'd been through.

It was time I took Alex's words seriously.

We were leaving.

"If you could go anywhere in the world right now, where would it be?"

"Quite the change of topic." She chuckled. "By physical travel or magically, like the way you move?"

"My way."

"Tough choice. There's so many." She lifted on her tiptoes and kissed my cheek. "I need to clean up, then we can talk about it over breakfast?"

"No breakfast." I released her, taking a hand to usher her to the bathroom. "Cleanup, then travel. I have an idea. We're going to visit a lot of places, eat a lot of food, and enjoy a lot of sunsets. Wear a bathing suit under your clothes."

"What about the Reaper police?"

Raguel hadn't descended from his holier-than-thou perch since I invaded Chris's house. If he showed up today, he could bloody well fly into the Pit.

"They'll have to catch me first."

CHAPTER 39

ELLIS

"This is the best sunset of the day." Danielle sat next to me on her beach towel, head on my shoulder.

I draped my arm around her, committing the moment to memory. Her fresh scent, soft skin, the freckle on the back of her hand running absently up and down my thigh. The heavens blazed with reds and oranges, reflected across an endless sea, the darkening sky full of unseen stars high above. Gentle waves lapped on the white sand of our private beach, inspiring a calm which almost rivaled Danielle's smile.

"We still have Las Vegas, if we hurry." I kissed her temple, brushing my lips across her silky hair.

"No, this is where I want the day to end. Paradise on Earth." She let out a long breath. Neither of us said it, but we were undoubtedly thinking the same thing: This was the closest she'd get to paradise this time around. "If all the other sunsets didn't finish your list, this one has to."

"It does." My entire list was complete, but I refused to show her, or she'd know about number nine. Let her believe what she wanted, that I'd changed it to *Have sex*. I'd come close to telling her so many times today, but that would make things

THE REAPER'S GAMBIT 337

more difficult for her. I didn't want to give her one more thing to lose, so I kept it to myself.

The voice in the back of my head wanted to confront the truth, that I was afraid of what she'd say. Reapers didn't know fear. We were confident, powerful, eternal. And we certainly didn't fear rejection from mortals.

No, I was protecting her, not myself.

"Tell me..." She interlaced her fingers with those on my arm around her shoulders. "Which sunset was your favorite?"

We'd made sixteen stops, from Lhasa to the tiny, deserted atoll in French Polynesia where we currently sat. It was little more than a crescent-shaped strip of sand dotted with palms and brush, the brilliant-blue water in the lagoon our own private pool. This was the only stop where we'd been entirely alone. No voices, no lights, no hum of electricity. Just me, Danielle, the crackle of our small fire, and the setting sun over the ocean.

My power to move from one place to another wasn't designed for humans, but it worked. And she squealed each time with greater excitement than she'd expressed on the roller coasters. The sun set early here in summer, and it was nearing eleven at night in New York. One hour left of her last full day.

"Honestly, we missed the one I wanted to take you to the most. If it were August, I would have taken you to Sendai, Japan, for the Tanabata Festival. We would have written our wishes on slips of paper and tied them to the bamboo."

She kept her eyes on the horizon as the sun sank. "What's that?"

"The Star Festival." I leaned my head against hers. "Orihime, the daughter of the Sky King, wove beautiful cloth out of the heavenly river—the Milky Way. But she was sad. She worked so hard, she never had a chance to meet someone, so her father introduced her to the heavenly shepherd Hikoboshi, who lived on the other side of the river. They immediately fell in love and married. Her father grew angry because Orihime stopped creating her weavings, and Hikoboshi let his cattle roam across the heavens. So, he separated them by the river and forbade them from meeting again."

She heaved a deep sigh. "Literally star-crossed lovers."

"Very true. But Orihime missed her husband desperately and begged her father to reunite them. His daughter's tears moved him, and he promised they could meet on the seventh day of the seventh lunar month—as long as she finished her work."

Danielle laughed. "Sounds like a bit of a tyrant."

"Sky Kings usually are in the stories." The sun sank rapidly, darkness creeping all around us, fended off by our little camp-fire. "The first year they were to meet, they found they couldn't cross the river. She cried so much a flock of magpies came and created a bridge over the river for them. And the magpies return every year to reunite the lovers."

"I don't suppose magpies can create a bridge out of Hell?"

I kept my eyes forward on the sun as the horizon swallowed it, transforming into a line of red and orange. The intense blue above was almost as breathtaking as the woman next to me. I would miss her like the weaver missed the shepherd. But not for another hundred years. A prickling began behind my eyes, but I blinked it away. Even my grief over losing her would vanish when my vacation ended.

"Part of my job is to visit undecided souls and transfer them to paradise once they're ready. Maybe I can plead your case and get you in there."

Her gaze fell away from the sunset, to our joined hands. "Like conjugal visits in prison?"

"I wish I could give you more, Danielle. I'd give you all the stars in the heavens, if they were mine to give." My blinking wasn't enough, and a stray tear made its way down my cheek. I leaned back on the towel, easing her with me to look up at the sky.

"That's what your eyes look like." She raised an arm, sweeping it across the darkness above us. "Like eternity."

"Yours look like topaz."

She nestled her head into the dip at my shoulder. "I had a boyfriend once who referred to them as shit-brown."

"He wasn't a very good boyfriend."

"No, he—" Her hand zipped to the left. "Did you see that? Shooting star!"

I rolled over and clamped a hand across her eyes. "Make a wish."

She grasped at my hand, startled, but laughing. I made my wish the second I spotted it: that when I reaped her soul, I wouldn't have to call the Pit. That was all I wished for since I received her contract, and I'd continue wishing until the moment I was doing it.

Maybe I should also wish to maintain my feelings for her until she was gone, so she wouldn't feel so alone when I escorted her.

"Okay, okay, wish made." She tugged on my hand, and I released it, hovering over her. The firelight danced across her face, her soft smile, her bikini-clad body.

"Is this like birthday wishes that have to stay secret?"

The laughter faded, and her features darkened. "Does the reaping part hurt?"

I brushed my fingers through her hair, trailing my gaze over every feature, tucking this moment away so I'd always have it. Her squared jaw, uneven smile, the way her left eye was a little lower than her right, and her sharply angled eyebrows. Death was inevitable and so unwelcome. "You're beautiful, Danielle."

She blinked slowly. "That doesn't answer my question."

Of course, it didn't. She wanted to speak of the end, and I was still thinking about beginnings. There had to be something I could offer Azrael to either extend her life or get her out of damnation.

"Ellis, please?" Her chin quivered and eyes tightened. "The distraction's nice and all, but I'm scared."

My chest ached. How could we be so close to the end already? "No one's ever told me it did. I've only had a few people resist letting go, so maybe it did for them, if I had to force them."

She nodded. "Step one, don't resist."

"And I'll be there." My voice cracked as I pulled her up to sitting, facing me. I swiped across her right palm and the hourglass lit up, the top almost empty. "This mark is my promise. No other Reaper can take you unless I allow it."

The promise was actually the mark underneath, the one I'd given her two years ago. The one she didn't need to know about.

"So, you could just refuse to end your vacation, and I could go on living?"

I lifted her hand to my lips and kissed the scar, shaking my head. "If only it were that simple."

"Why me, Ellis?"

"Why you what?"

"Of all the contracts you take on, why did you show up and warn me? Why have you spent all this time trying to fix things?"

"I didn't think you'd been judged fairly." And I was sorry for what I'd done. I ruined her life and needed forgiveness, but I didn't deserve it. My eyes slid closed as I nestled my cheek against her hand. I didn't deserve the look in her eyes, the feel of her heart beating against mine, or the—

"Whatever you're doing, stop it."

I straightened, the crackling fire the only light left for her, but I still saw her so clearly.

"Because I can literally feel your temperature dropping, and I can't face the end of my life without touching you."

Clutching her hand, I relaxed. That was it. A physical manifestation of my doubts and guilt. My words created my reality—so long as I didn't believe I deserved her, I couldn't get close to her. I *had* been doing it the whole time. "Tell me I deserve you."

"Of course, you deserve me." She placed the hand on my chest and eased me back onto the towel, crawling up over my body, straddling my hips. "You gave me a taste of paradise."

"But I can't give it to you in the afterlife."

"Remember, Ellis, intentions speak loudest of all. You wanted to, and you tried." Tugging at the ties at her neck and back, she removed her bathing suit top, revealing her exquisite breasts, the nipples dark and tempting in the twilight. Next came the ties on her bottoms, and she slipped them off. "You deserve me, and I deserve you, even if it's just for a little longer."

CHAPTER 40

DANIELLE

I inched his bathing suit down, traveling along his body, revealing the dark hair and his swollen cock. His toned muscles twitched as I moved, and I bit my lip, aching to connect one last time. On my return up his body, I took his tip into my mouth, swirled my tongue around it, and let it drop to his groin.

He groaned, lifting his hips for more. "Did you pack the condoms?"

"I'm going to die tomorrow, Ellis." Goose bumps prickled up my arms as a cool wind blew off the water. Or possibly off him again. "Protection's a bit pointless."

He extended his hands and slipped his fingers through mine as I straddled him. "No more talk of the end."

I rubbed my sex along his, encouraging him to grow. "Today was the best day of my life."

He sat up, wrapping one muscular arm around me, tilting his face. "Mine, too."

The towel under me dug into the sand as I moved my hips back and forth, stroking him. "There is no way this little day was the best in seven hundred years."

"True." The corner of his mouth quirked up. "We're closing in on midnight and I haven't been inside you yet today. Maybe if we did that, then it would be the best?"

I leaned in to kiss him, the warm breeze and his hand caressing my back, the fire crackling, and the rush of waves lapping on the shore. He was eternity, and I was a second, a grain of sand. But for this fleeting moment, being together was all that mattered.

Our mouths joined, his tasting like the coconut he'd ripped open for us. He separated and lay back at my urging, while I lifted onto my knees to tip his cock up. As I lowered onto him slowly, he ran his palms up my thighs. My walls stretched around his thickness, sending a flood of heat through my being.

"Yes," he moaned. "That's what was missing."

As expected, Ellis had turned out to be the best lover I'd ever had. Thoughtful, enthusiastic, and eager to please, with a hint of magic no human could match.

I rolled my hips, grinding my clit against him, teasing my fingers along his abdomen. How long did we have left? Would it be two weeks to the minute of when he healed me the first time? What time was that?

His palms eased up to my waist, lifting me so I rode him, swelling when I landed and lengthening as I reached the top. Once we hit our rhythm, I planted my hands on his stomach, closed my eyes, and let him guide me into oblivion.

I was the waves crashing on the beach; the stars shimmering overhead. I was the leaves rustling in the breeze; the scent of salt and smoke in the air. I was his, and he was mine.

Bright lights flashed behind my eyelids as we gained speed, and I indulged a glance at him. By the dim fire's light, I could just make out the stars dancing in his inky irises. He smiled, a smile that took my breath away. In it was all the peace of the universe, the smile of the man I lov—

Catherine knelt on the ground, not ten feet from me, covering her eyes as she wept over William's body. A pale-yellow linen cote pooled around her kneeling form, there in the middle of the paddock, in the worked-up dirt. The charger that'd thrown him stood at the fence, stomping a hoof to express displeasure with its former rider, oblivious to the damage he'd wrought.

William was gone, through the white door and up the Stairs, but Catherine collapsed on him, wailing, "Get up, William! Get up!"

Everything was as I remembered. The stone house, the little garden, the pigs at the trough. Her long, plaited hair. Only a year gone by since my death, but she looked at least five years older.

"Danielle!"

Catherine was alone; William was beyond her grasp now. I'd seen to that. Helped lift him up to paradise. But her grief... her tears... how could I let her go on like that?

"Dani! Come back!"

I had to help her. Reg pulled at my scythe. It was time to go. But he'd taught me how to will myself visible to humans, so I did, and I knelt next to her. "He's in Heaven now, Catherine, I promise. I took him there myself."

She fell back at the sight of me, arms and legs flailing to escape. She ripped the paternoster from her belt, beads scattering across the ground, clutching the cross at its end, screaming, "You're dead! You're dead! Monster! Demon! Go back to Hell! Begone!"

I could comfort her, help her through this, even just an embrace. "Catherine—"

"Monster!" She stumbled to her feet and ran, leaving William in the dirt.

"Danielle! Stay with me!" Ellis pushed up from his position on the towel. His eyes were golden flames, like they'd been that day in the secret office. The first time I'd seen *her*, whoever she was. And again, our first time in the shower.

"Ellis? What's—" I was still moving on top of him, more out of instinct than anything else.

"Stay with me." He grasped me, spinning our bodies so he was on top, between my legs, still thrusting, driving me toward climax. "Just focus on us."

I clutched his back, and he lowered to his elbows, continuing to move inside me. Molten heat flowed through my veins, his body burning with fever. "Something's happening!"

"I know." He threw himself into me, over and over. "It's glorious!"

"Don't be afraid. I won't hurt you." I appeared in front of her, keeping my voice quiet—

"Danielle!" His tongue plunged into my mouth, snapping me back to the island.

I returned the kiss, searing hot like my blood. Like him. And I broke away. "You're burning up!"

"Ellis, leave her alone." Reg coalesced next to me, invisible to her. "She can't fathom what you are now."

"But she's my sister. How can she say—" My voice caught, and he—

"It's us." The whisper was in my ear. I was whispering.

"Yes!" I screamed. "Yes! Oh god, Ellis, yes!"

I was inside Ellis. Inside myself. The orgasm came, and I let myself go inside her. Inside me. Pouring all of who I'd ever been, ever would be into her, while my muscles spasmed around him. We continued moving, slowing, existing as one.

One being without a start or an end.

We were perception.

We were finally whole again.

My body was numb. Exhausted. His legs—no, my legs—collapsed against the towel, the sound of the waves and the fire coming back to me. Another streak of light across the heavens, dust and debris falling to Earth.

He pushed up on his elbows, the flames in his eyes flickering and waning until nothing but the dancing stars remained. "Are you alright?"

I sucked in a breath, fingers digging into his arms, spots crowding my vision. Lips tingling. "What—what happened? I saw a woman. I've seen her before."

He ran a hand over my cheek. "Catherine?"

Of course, he knew her. He was in the dream.

No. He wasn't just in it; it was his dream. Or his memory?

I gasped and tried to roll out of his grip, but he held me steady. The house was such an old style, like out of a medieval village.

Oh, god. A medieval village.

Seven hundred years ago.

"I just saw..."

"My sister." He nodded slowly, tears welling in his eyes. "And I saw your family at the crash."

"You saw what?" The island spun around me, and I clamped my eyes shut.

"I don't know how to prepare you for this..." He ran a finger over one of my brows, and I looked up at him. "But that was only the first step. I expect there's going to be a lot more memories coming."

A shiver ran through me, rapidly progressing to a full-body shudder I couldn't stop. Faces began flooding my brain. Men, women, young, old, happy, sad, all colors and races. Ellis moved fast, sitting me up, moving me next to the fire. One towel was under me, the other covering me.

"Stop." I pressed my palms to my eyes, but they came faster and faster. Faces, then bodies, then places. Voices. Pits and Stairs and a Gray Hallway. I was cold, so cold, but not from him for once. "Stop! Ellis, make it stop!"

He rubbed up and down my arms. "Am I still warm?"

I nodded frantically and reached out for him. He took me on his lap and held tight, rocking me while I whimpered. A weight settled on my heart, and my head swam, breath coming in ragged spurts. "What's happening?"

"I'm sorry, Dani. I had no idea." He held my head against his chest. "I never imagined this would happen."

Hairstyles and clothing styles changed, clean people, dirty people, burned, stabbed, dismembered. Every one of them, I held up my hand, read from a parchment, and escorted them to their portal. Blood pumped through my veins with increasing speed, hammering in my eardrums. "I can't do this, Ellis. Make it stop!"

"Look at me." His voice was quiet, and it shook as much as mine.

I pulled back, peering into his dark, tear-filled eyes, the faces continuing to suffocate me. Hanged, diseased, quiet in a bed. "Is this because we didn't use a condom?"

"No." He sniffled, blinking rapidly, the smile forming. "Danielle, it's a miracle. We Bonded."

I shook my head. On horseback, at sea, falling from a cliff. "We've been bonding for two weeks."

"That's not what I mean." He wiped the tears from my cheeks and from his. "I mean, you're my soulmate. The one I was created with. We're a Pair."

"No. You said—" Short hair, long hair, no hair. The Pit, the Hallway, the Stairs. I sagged, dropping my head, but he lifted it back up, returning my focus to him. The faces became more familiar, styles I recognized from the last century. *Please let it be over soon.* "You said that happens between mortals or the same types of immortals. I'd have to be Reaper to be your Pair."

"I know." He touched his lips to my cheek. "And Azrael says you aren't one. But the memory exchange is something that happens when... it's only supposed to happen to souls once they're finished with their human bodies."

"When I saw her before—the visions were incomplete."

"The Bond must have been trying to cement itself all along." He kissed my temple. "It explains why seeing you always calmed me."

"And the feeling of your skin." Flapper dresses, ballgowns, and war. So many from war. The faces slowed, each one clearer. "Oh god, there's so many faces."

"Seven hundred years of memories. Eighteen from a human and the rest from a Reaper." He ran a hand across my cheek. "Humans aren't designed to hold all that sorrow."

"And guilt." I clasped his hand, grip tightening as the agony spiked through me. Operating rooms, airplanes, and overdoses. "How do you handle it?"

"That's why we have to suppress our emotions." His brows tightened. "Are you there yet?"

"Where?"

He squeezed my hand, the smile faltering. "You'll know it when you see it."

Happy Land fire, September eleventh, Hurricane Sandy, and a car accident. My heart skipped and the air rushed out of my lungs. A sedan.

Sitting with the soul of a middle-aged man of undetermined placement, talking about his life, and what he wished he'd done differently. About his children, his wife, and his regrets. Escorting him to the Pit, to cleanse his soul. Moving into the car to sit between his children, next to his daughter in her yellow sweater.

Yellow had been Catherine's favorite color.

Time slowed as I took her hand, and a spark traveled up my arm. Something drew me toward her, as if her face were tattooed on my unbeating heart. Warmth flowed through her into me, and I felt... felt? Peace.

I shouldn't care, but I did. It was too early. My vacation wasn't due to start yet. But I had to comfort her, help her through this. I shifted my form so I resembled her brother. That would help her.

"I don't think we're okay, Johnnie," she whispered.

"We're not, Dani." I brushed her hair back from her face, blood trickling over her eyes. I placed a hand to her chest and turned back time for her body. It was against so many rules, but it was as though a tiny voice urged me forward. It told me I had to save her—and if it were truly her time, the Fates would take her anyway. Light filled the vehicle as I shifted time, healing the break in her spine, healing the internal damage, healing all but the minor cuts and bruises marring her body. "But you'll be alright."

Once she was healed, she shook and gripped my hand. "Don't leave me. Please."

I shot to my feet, clutching the towel around me, stumbling back as the faces continued, overlaying with the visions of Dad. And me. The faces, the horror, the sorrow. "You!"

A pit opened in my stomach, wrenching and twisting at the thought of leaving her. I couldn't abandon her. Not her, not now, not when she needed me. "I'll wait until the ambulance is here. But then I have to go, sweetheart."

She nodded, her tears mingling with the blood, no doubt clearing her vision somewhat. "You're not John, are you?"

I shook my head and smiled gently. "John's in Heaven, I promise. I watched him go there myself."

Her trembling stopped, and she let out a long sigh as she closed her eyes. "You're my guardian angel?"

No, I was the one who took her family from her. No different than with Catherine. I was leaving Danielle alone in the world.

My sister was right all along.

I was a monster.

Still, I lifted her palm to my lips and kissed it, searing my mark into her skin. "It's not your time yet, Dani. When it is, I promise I'll be the one to come for you."

"You? You took them?" I floundered around in the sand, searching for my discarded clothing. "You sent my father to Hell, but you healed me?"

Ellis stood, bathing suit already back on, holding his hands between us. "Dani, you know I didn't make the choice—he did. I'm just the—"

"Yeah, the delivery guy, you've said that!" I found my shirt and hauled it on, trying not to let the towel fall. I was naked enough as it was. "But you could have sent him with Mom. You could have convinced him! Changed his mind! You son of—"

I collapsed to the ground, landing on my shorts. My memories of the crash had always been hazy, but now I saw all of them again, clear as day. And my father—cast into Hell. It was a million times worse than every time I saw it in my nightmares. It ripped my heart out, leaving a gaping hole inside me. The wound was raw all over again.

The wound. The scar. I held my right palm up to him. "You put this here, didn't you? You branded me like cattle?"

"It's not like that." He took a half-step toward me. "It was my promise. That mark told me where you were and whether you were alright."

"I haven't been alright since the crash, Ellis!" I threw a handful of sand and shells in his direction, missing completely.

"When you touch it—"

I clamped the hand, stroking the scar like I had thousands of times since the crash. His feet remained steady, but he leaned in my direction.

"Your soul calls to mine, Danielle."

"The soul remembers," I breathed. The line from *The Count of Monte Cristo* he'd read to me in Central Park. Ellis was the one in the car. The angel I thought was my brother. I hadn't dreamed it. "You knew all along?"

He laid his hands over his heart. "I only knew there was something that drew me toward you, but not why."

Everything suddenly made sense, yet absolutely nothing did. The crushing weight sitting on my chest. The faces, the guilt, and the memory of the accident.

Soulmates.

That's why his smile calmed me, why I felt drawn to his voice. My soul knew him, even if my body didn't.

But how could he be my soulmate and have done that to me? Taken my family away and forced me to live through the grief every day for two years? Every sleepless night, every tear, every wish for it to be over. It was all his fault.

And what did it matter? It was after midnight at home, my last day. And the one man I thought I could count on had betrayed me before we'd even met.

I hauled my shorts on, still holding the towel in front of me. "I want to go home."

"Dani." He knelt next to me and took my hand. We had to be in contact to travel, but it made my skin crawl. His face, his sad little face which needed to be punched. Or avoided. Or something. "I didn't know this would happen."

"I don't care!" Faces continued clicking forward in my brain, so vivid, but unable to replace my memory of Dad and the Pit. "Take me home. Then leave me alone."

We moved together, arriving in my bedroom. He began to wrap his arms around me, but I pushed away and headed for the door.

"I can't, Ellis. I'm done."

"Danielle!" He appeared in front of me and smacked a clenched fist against his thigh. "You can't run away from this! The Bond is eternal!"

"No!" I held up a finger, jabbing it into his chest. "Did you forget? My forever ends today! And you'll throw me in the Pit along with my father, and I'll just be another memory you can pass on to the next little human you fuck!"

His shoulders and face fell. "That's not what happened!"

"Enough! I'm going downstairs to die in peace!" I shoved past him, tears clouding my vision. It had all been so perfect. The day of sunsets, making love on the beach. I could have died happier than I'd thought possible. But no, he was a traitor, a liar, and he'd damned my father. "Leave me the fuck alone!"

I hit the top of the stairs, groping for the smooth, wide railing.

"Go ahead. Blame me, just like everyone else does! Sacred and holy! I don't know why—" Ellis's voice faded into mutters behind me.

Three steps from the bottom, my legs grew weak, and I sagged, gripping the balusters as I eased down to sitting. This had been coming for two weeks. I should have been ready for it.

But Ellis had changed everything. Given me hope and a chance to be happy for the blink of an eye. And now it was gone.

John, Mom, Dad. Gone. And a memory as fresh as the day it happened. Fresher even, without the haze of human memory. I should have died that day with the rest of them. But here I was, about to die anyway.

I was a monster, just like Catherine said.

No. I wiped the back of my hand across my face to clear the damn tears. That was his memory, not mine.

More faces, more John, but interspersed, memories of me. Selling me a coffee. Helping me reach a book from a top shelf in the library. Holding a door open for me. Across a crowded street.

Oh, god, he really had been checking in on me for the last two years.

I bit back a sob, so he wouldn't hear. Every time he'd seen me, I'd smiled, and he felt the same peace I did. But he didn't know why. He never knew why.

Fucking soulmates.

Why? Why did this have to happen now, right at the end?

Byte's collar jangled as he stretched and climbed off his pillow in the parlor. When he reached the living room, he stopped, growling.

"What's wrong, boy?"

The outer door creaked open. Was this how it would end? Another intruder in my house? My mouth opened to call for Ellis, but my time was up, so why bother? Maybe I should make him watch me die, and he'd understand a fraction of the hell my life had been.

Before the sound erupted from my throat, I recognized the figure.

Uncle Mike flipped on a light and punched in his security code. He smiled through the glass of the inner door. "Didn't expect you'd be up, Dani."

I sniffled as he walked through the inner door. "This isn't a good time, Uncle Mike."

Of course, it wasn't a good time. It was one in the morning. And he'd just come in with his own key. Why wouldn't he call before coming over?

Or wait until morning?

Wait. Why the hell was he walking into my house at one in the morning?

His gaze rose to the top of the stairs. "Ellis, so glad you could join us."

"Michael." Ellis's voice behind me was loud, commanding. He came down the stairs, some of them creaking under his footsteps. "It's late. You shouldn't be here."

"Funny, I was thinking the same thing about you. I come in here, see my niece sobbing on the stairs, and then I see her angry boyfriend coming after her." Mike's lip curled and nostrils flared as he stepped aside to show Ellis the door. "I had a feeling you couldn't be trusted."

Ellis stopped on the step behind me. Byte continued to growl, like he always did when any man other than Chris came in.

I swiveled to look up at Ellis, so tall and strong from my spot on the steps. "It's nothing. We were just having a—" 'Existential crisis' would need too much explanation but was accurate. "A fight."

"No." Ellis's word carried, a trick of sound that took up more space than any one person's voice should. "I'm not leaving her."

"Fine. Have it your way." Uncle Mike sighed and swung the door shut. He reached behind his back and drew a gun from his waistband.

And pointed it at Ellis.

Chapter 41

Ellis

"Dining room." Michael gestured with the gun, then pointed it at Danielle. "I'm assuming your laptop is there, like usual?"

"Well, would you look at that?" I opened my hand, searching through all upcoming contracts nearby but couldn't find his. Either someone else already had it, or the Fates had missed the fact that I was about to obliterate this insolent pissant. She was my soulmate, and he would not take her before her time. "And you were trying to tell her *I* was the bad guy?"

My heart rate accelerated, and I fought to control my breaths, which became so thick his stale scent invaded my nostrils. She still had another hour until the two-week anniversary of our deal. Then, and only then, she'd fade into my arms, Reg would end my vacation, and I'd escort her to her final destination.

Before she stood, I was between her and her uncle. I could protect her from his puny metal toy. "And if you harm her, I'll shove that gun so far up your ass, you'll be coughing up bullets."

More than once, I reminded her there were people who loved her. How foolish had I been? I should have known better. These petty humans and their exasperating squabbles. Their need to feel more powerful than others.

"Brave boyfriend." Michael smirked at me. "Not too smart, though."

"Smarter than you may think." I raised my hands. Before she left, he would confess everything. "Let's go, Dani."

"What the hell are you doing, Ellis?" she hissed from behind me. "Just take the gun from him."

"Do you trust me, sweetheart?"

"No." Her voice was petulant, no doubt still reeling from what she'd discovered after the Bonding.

I had one hour to secure her forgiveness. In the seven hundred years since my death, one hour had never seemed like more than the blink of an eye. But tonight, I wanted that blink to last forever—once we were done with Michael, and she knew the truth.

Heaving my shoulders, I blew out a long breath, attempting not to break my teeth from clenching so hard. "Yes, you do. I want you to head to the dining room."

"Fine," she grumbled as she shouldered past me on the bottom step.

I walked backward, not taking my eyes off Michael. She picked up Byte on the way, and from her grunts and his growls, he was resisting. Smart little animal.

"Neil told me you found the program, Dani."

"No, Michael." I smiled, taunting him, ensuring his focus and the gun remained on me, the immortal. "I believe you mean Chris found it?"

"Right. Neil told me Chris figured it out and stole all his money." He snorted. "Chris was never smart enough for that. Luke was the brains all along. You wouldn't believe the shit he did in that little office. There's a reason he didn't tell her about it."

"What? What did he do?" Desperation tinged Dani's voice. She wanted to know what happened so dearly.

"Ethical hacking, my ass. You know, I never did figure out where he stashed his money."

We stopped in the dining room, at the far end of the table. She'd told me about the money she'd inherited and received as payouts, but this sounded like something more.

One subject at a time though. "Let's go back to what Luke did in that room for a moment."

"And then Chris got stupid." Michael shook his head back and forth as he talked, gaze wandering. "Neil introduced him to Fitch last year. One bad choice after another, until Chris promised him a foolproof way to hack anyone's bank account. He's been trying to complete the damn thing for the last six months and got the bright idea to break in here. Like Luke would have just left it lying around?"

He was lost in his own world. The odds of Danielle learning the complete truth vanished faster than Michael's grip on reality.

"But you found it, didn't you, Dani? So, I guess Chris was right all along."

I glowered at him. "What did Luke do in that room? Danielle deserves the truth, doesn't she?"

He smiled—a lopsided, tolerant smile—attempting to telegraph that he was the clever one. Instead of answering my question, he inclined his head toward her laptop on the table. "Just give me the program."

"Uncle Mike, please." Danielle tried to step around me, but I caught her in my periphery and shifted in front of her. "Tell me?"

I had a plan. Couldn't she hear it in my voice? "Dani, stay behind me."

"Fuck, Ellis, I'm going to die, anyway. What does it even matter?"

My hands still up, I suppressed a growl. "It matters to me, dammit!"

"Shut up!" Michael's hand shook, his face reddening. "It's obvious you figured out what happened to your dad. You took out Chris and sicced Fitch on Neil, which leaves me!"

Danielle sucked in a shaky breath, and I sensed the distance between us increase. Up to that moment, it had been hearsay and conjecture. Now, there was an admission of guilt and confirmation Michael was the final quarter million.

"And I won't be next!" Michael's smile gave way to a wild look in his eyes as he took a step to the side, aiming the gun at Dani. "So, give me the program or start it on your laptop or whatever you do, and no one gets hurt!"

"No one gets hurt? Like Mom, Dad, and John?" She burst out from behind me, and Byte sailed to the floor, yapping incessantly. She raised her fists like she was going to attack. "My family died because of that thing! I'll never give it to you!"

"Dani, stop!" I spun to grab her by the forearms, and she struggled against me, her miniscule strength no match for mine, but I was as gentle as possible. "You have the truth now. Just give it to him so he leaves!"

"No!" Her eyes were wide, teeth bared. "You need to stop him!"

"I can't! You know that!" I leaned in, forcing her to look me in the eye. "I can't reveal myself."

She wrenched her arms free and shoved me with all her human might, not moving me an inch. "What's the worst they can do to you?"

I put my hands up again, partially to calm her, partially to satisfy Michael behind me. "Sweetheart, they could extend my vacation so I can't collect your—"

A deafening crack sounded, and licks of flame pierced my back. Dani gulped in a deep breath as her hands flew to her mouth, and I crashed to my knees.

"Get the program. If you're fast enough, you'll have enough time to call 9-1-1 for him after I leave."

What was happening?

I was immortal. I was perception.

But I hurt. Infinite. Pain.

And blood?

"Ellis!" She let out a strangled wail, shuddering as she fell to the floor next to me. "No! Ellis! Get up!"

So much blood. How strange. I couldn't stop it. Couldn't transform to heal the wound.

Byte whimpered somewhere nearby. He was alright, wasn't he?

Michael's voice behind me was cold. "Now, Dani."

I balanced on my knees, staring at Danielle. "What do I do now?"

She eased me down to the floor, hand resting on my cheek as her tears fell. "Call Reg. Like at Times Square."

"Vacation's almost over." That must have been it. Or perhaps Bonding with a human took some shred of my power? "I suppose I should have revealed myself after all."

Byte resumed barking, and Michael aimed at him.

"I'll get it, Uncle Mike. Just let me—" She edged away from me, latching onto Byte's collar and scurrying through the kitchen with him.

"You run and your boyfriend's dead!"

"I know!" The back door opened and slammed shut—the yapping continued, but muffled—then a drawer, and she returned with several cloths, which she wedged under my shirt, against my back.

"Clock's ticking, Dani," said Michael.

"Don't die on me." She kissed my forehead and launched up to the table, waking her laptop and glaring at her uncle. "The police will already be on their way after that gunshot."

And the barking dog in the middle of the night. Smart woman.

He trained the gun on her while she worked. "Possible, but even if they are, it'll take time to figure out which house the shot came from. And I'll be gone by then."

Her fingers flew across the keyboard, casting glances at me every few seconds. "What do you want me to do?"

Michael dug into his pocket and withdrew a slip of paper, dropping it close enough she grabbed it. "Move all the money from Chris's account into that one."

"You won't get away with this."

"Of course, I will. The bank didn't notice it when your dad did it, and they only caught Chris because there was an anonymous tip. I wonder who called that in? I warned my manager three years ago the security wasn't tight enough, and he didn't listen. Serves them right getting hacked like that."

"Fitch never figured it out?"

His lips tightened for the faintest moment. What was that look? Regret? "Neil put him on a false trail two years ago, and Fitch thought he took out the guy behind it. Until Chris opened his big mouth and told Fitch he could hack into the bank."

"What about Aunt Kelly and Ollie? Do they know about this?"

"She hasn't let me see him in—" He cut off and extended the gun toward her, his voice strained. "Stop talking."

Dani shoved the chair away from the table so hard it banged into the sideboard behind her. "I'm into the program. Do the rest yourself. I won't have any part in this."

Without another glance at her uncle, she came to me, sinking to the floor.

"Ellis," she whispered, adjusting the cloths on my back. "You'll be alright."

"I'm not so sure of that." I was supposed to be her protector. She wasn't supposed to be kneeling next to me while I bled out. And the pain. I'd forgotten how awful a sensation it was. She wrapped her hand around mine, and our eyes met. Peace. I blinked slowly, the world returning to focus, the pain ebbing.

"But just in case our schedules don't sync up properly in the next life, I want you to know what you did for me. I'd lost track of who I was and pushed away everything I had left. But with you..." She laid on the floor next to me, like when we'd woken up, side by side. "With you, I remembered what it was to be part of the world. How to choose happiness, even for a little while. Thank you so much."

"Thank you for letting me, sweetheart."

"And more importantly, I forgive you."

"Forgive me?"

"For Dad." She caressed my cheek, sending a jolt of energy through me. From the held hand to the contact on my face, we were a continuous loop, power flowing between us, returning some semblance of my strength. "I know it's your job and it was his choice."

"It really is that simple!" Michael tapped a key on the laptop.

"I was angry and freaked out about everything."

"Sorry, Dani." There was remorse in his voice, but not enough to stop him.

It all happened in a blur. The click of the hammer. The tiny explosion in the barrel. The rapidly expanding gasses from the end of the gun creating the loud crack. The hiss of the bullet in the air.

My eyes on the bullet.

It stopped.

She'd given me enough strength and power I could still protect her.

I let go of her hand and pushed myself up to sitting. A pain so great I wanted to vomit ripped through my back and chest, but I pushed past it. She was not his to take.

"Ellis?" Her voice trembled.

As I fought my way to my feet, my cloak unfurled, and I transformed my eyes to white flame. I held out a hand and pulled my scythe from the darkness which swirled around me, leaning on it for support.

Michael's eyes bulged, and he slammed the laptop shut, throwing it under his arm. He grabbed the gun and stumbled back, knocking one chair over, pulling the next in front of himself, as though it could stop me.

Searing pain coursed from my back, through my veins, but it was no match for the rage bubbling like magma from my heart. He'd tried to take her! His own flesh and blood. And for once, I was there to prevent it.

I pointed at Michael, ricocheting the sound off every surface. "You are neither judge nor jury nor executioner! You do not decide her time!"

"What—what are you?" Every inch of Michael shook, and he dropped the gun.

"I would have let you go without punishment, if you'd let her be." I increased my height to tower over him like Reg did and flipped the table, throwing it across the room to shatter against the fireplace. The flames in my eyes reflected deep crimson off the walls, like the blood which had flowed out of me. "As you'd promised to do!"

"Chris—Chris said she was shot and stabbed. I thought he was crazy! But she's—You're why she survived?" He tripped on the rug in the parlor and fell back, gripping the laptop tight to his chest, unable or unwilling to look away from me. "Please! Please don't—"

"You fucking asshole!" Danielle was beside me, extending the gun toward Michael. "You killed them! All of them!"

"It wasn't me!" Michael flung his hands out in front of us, letting the laptop clatter to the ground. "Your dad was going to talk to the FBI. I was going to wipe all our data from the bank's computer systems to get rid of the proof, but Chris swore it wouldn't work. So he and Neil did something to his— You never took that car as a family. Never!"

Her shaking voice dropped to a whisper, full of anguish. "But you knew?"

"I didn't want anyone hurt, but— Luke was the only one who was supposed to die!" He edged onto his knees, eyes glistening, hands folding together in prayer. "I've been trying to make it up to you ever since."

"You fucking liar! You just tried to kill us!" Her voice raised, and she took a half-step forward, finger flexing on the trigger.

"Don't damn yourself now, Dani." I moved in front of her, blocking the gun, and hid my Reaper attire. As I returned to my normal height, the bullet dislodged, shifting inside me. A stabbing pain tore through my chest, and I grunted but fought it as much as I could. For her.

"Listen to him," whimpered Michael.

"He knew what was going to happen, Ellis! He could have stopped them!" Tears streaked her face. She sidestepped me and pointed the gun in his direction. "He took everything from me!"

I grimaced and let out the quietest groan I could. "Not every-thing, sweetheart. There's still hope."

"Hope?" She spluttered a laugh. "I'm already dead."

"'Until the day when God will deign to reveal the future to man, all human wisdom is contained in these two words—'"

She squeezed her eyes shut and shook her head, completing the passage. "'Wait and hope.' *The Count of Monte Cristo* is a crock of shit. Where did waiting or hoping ever get me?"

I lifted my hand, and her contract appeared with the change I'd discovered after she left me upstairs. I pointed to the bottom where the word was now: *Undetermined*. "Dani, we can work with that."

She lowered the gun, reaching for the parchment, but not touching it. "I don't understand. How?"

Fabric rustled behind me. Michael was trying to sneak away. Let him. Her final minutes would be about us, not him.

"You thought you wanted vengeance, but when you had it, there was no joy, only regret. You're a good person who's been through a nightmare, without justice for the crimes you suffered. Your heart..." I placed a hand on her chest, the action causing the pain to streak through me again, and I wavered, leaning some of my weight on her. "It deserves paradise, but your sorrow has dragged you down."

"I didn't think it was possible."

"Anything"—I closed my hand to hide away her contract and pulled another document from the ether: my list, fully crossed off—"is possible."

She blinked rapidly and tore the parchment away from me. Her brow flexed, as though trying to change it, like she'd done before.

"The list doesn't lie, Danielle." Number nine, still at its original *Fall in love,* was crossed out. "I know you could never feel the same way about a creature like me, but—but I love you, Danielle. And if I can't have you beyond today, all I need for eternity is to know you've gone to a good place."

"You're not a monster," she whispered. "Catherine didn't understand. You're compassionate, kind, and thoughtful. Ellis, you're the most wonderful man I've ever met." She closed her hand, and the list vanished. Of course. My Pair could control my list. "I love you, too. So much."

"Thank the powers that be." I reached for her, to hold her, and a wave of pain, stronger than anything I'd ever felt, washed over me. I sucked in an excruciating breath, like breathing underwater, no air reaching my lungs. There was a dull thunk on the far dining room wall as the bullet I'd frozen in time released and made contact.

"Oh god, no. Ellis?" Dani caught me as I wavered, dropping the gun to skitter across the floor.

My lungs crackled and spots formed in my peripheral vision.

"That sound—the bullet hit your lung, didn't it? Can't you heal it?"

"Can't turn my own time back." Inhaling deeply, I leaned on her for balance.

Michael scrambled behind me, and I turned in time to see him—laptop back in his possession—grab the gun. Another loud crack, and pain exploded through my knee.

I crumpled. Dani tried holding me up, but he shot again. My upper arm.

"No!" she screamed, the sound growing distant as I hit the floor.

Again. My shoulder.

I ground my teeth against the strain of each breath, the sticky pool around me expanding with each pump of my pathetic little human heart. With all my strength, I pushed onto my side to see her move as the world faded.

She flung herself at him, and I tried slowing him, freezing him, but the room was too hazy. He was going to take her. Her last moments of mortality would be the cruelest of all.

And there was nothing I could do for her.

He shoved her out of the way, and she smashed into the piano, making a dramatic crescendo as she hit half the keys, head bouncing off the lid.

He shot again.

Square in my chest. Through my heart. It had to be my heart, didn't it? Piercing it before it could break when she died.

I should have taken her to Paris all along. Shouldn't have brought her back from the island. Alex had warned me, hadn't he?

Michael took a step backward, trembling, extending the gun toward my head. "Why aren't you dead yet? What are you?"

"He's the Grim fucking Reaper, you asshole!" Dani had recovered, blood streaming down the side of her face from a cut on her head where she'd collided with the piano. She hauled the laptop from under his arm and smashed him across the face with it.

His head whipped to the side, and he stumbled briefly, but snapped back to focus on her. This was it. He held the gun toward her, and she grabbed for it.

My eyes slid closed, and I tried hard—so hard—not to breathe. In Reaper form, breathing was habit, not necessity. But in this fragile human costume, it was critical.

"Dani—" I croaked the name out, to tell her to stop, to just let him go. Let us hold each other and say our good-byes.

The crack of the gun sounded again, and my eyes shot open. They separated, both with blood on themselves, both falling to their knees in stunned silence.

Dani! It was the third time in two weeks she was covered in blood. Had I really given her a second chance that night in the cellar? Or had I simply doomed her to repeat this cycle over and over? Maybe this *was* my punishment, watching the woman I loved die three times.

Michael dropped the laptop and the gun. The death wave was muted while I was on vacation, but he was so close, a weak ripple passed through me as he slumped forward against her.

"I'm so sorry, Uncle Mike." She eased him down, her shoulders heaving with one tremendous sob. "It didn't have to be this way."

Then she collapsed next to him. Facing him, not me.

My heart fell.

Her two weeks were up.

And we hadn't said good-bye.

Chapter 42

Ellis

"Were you looking for this contract?" Warmth spread through my back and lung as Reg's skeletal form coalesced in front of me and he healed the damage. A yellowed parchment with letters flashing in golden ink floated above his hand.

The name at the top: *Michael Gregory Edmonds*.

The word at the bottom: *Damned*.

"This human really messed you up, old friend, didn't she?"

Once the healing was complete, all the blood back inside my mortal husk, I attempted to move, to be with her. But Reg anchored my form to the floor. "Reg, she's dying. Let me—"

"You revealed yourself to him." The skull provided little indication of emotion, but his tone, deep and rasping, was clear. I was in trouble. Big trouble. "So, you're going to have to watch while someone else deals with her."

Ice splintered through my spine. "No! No! I promised her!" The one thing I'd sworn to her the night of the accident—and so many times after that. It was my guarantee. "We Bonded, Reg. Please?"

"Yes. That was interesting." Reg's bony fingers dug into my arm, hauling me up to standing. "But there are rules."

Her body lay beside Michael's, his blood soaking into the pale-green carpet of the parlor. I'd sat at the piano and played for her several times. Her in the living room reading, in the dining room on her laptop, or sitting on the floor—where she now lay—playing with Byte.

Her life force was draining away, pulling me toward her, but Reg's grip was too strong. Darkness swirled around their bodies as Reg called forth the Pit. The room glowed red, filled with the wails of the damned, shadowy hands clawing up from the depths. Sirens blared from the street, the police cars' lights alternating red and blue against the front windows.

They wouldn't see any of what Reg did, and when they arrived at the scene, they would simply discover two dead bodies. I'd be a Reaper once more, invisible, uncaring, and capable of nothing more than watching them take her shell away.

"Stay." The flame in his eyes flared as he commanded me. Stretching to his nine-foot height under the tall ceilings, he strode the few steps toward them and swept his hand into Michael. "Stop hiding from me, worm."

Michael's soul separated from his body, eyes as wide as they'd been when I'd shown my nature.

"Michael Edmonds, I am here to deliver you to the afterlife. Your judgment has not been a favorable one." His voice boomed through the house, louder than mine had been, and he gestured toward the Pit with his scythe. "You are a thief, a liar, a covetous wretch. You plotted the death of your brother, sister-in-law, and their children. And tonight, you attempted two murders and stole a fortune from someone you called a friend. Be grateful we have more important work to do here, or you would have suffered before being cast into damnation."

The soul hovered, his arms and legs moving as though he were still substantial, trying to escape. "Please, no! I didn't mean to—"

Reg waved his hand, and Michael's soul flew into the Pit screaming, the cacophony of voices and howls growing louder, reaching a fever pitch that drowned out the sirens. But this time, they didn't call for Danielle to follow him. She was out. Her soul was safe, and my heart rose in thanks. Reg returned to me, to my height, and the Pit vanished, leaving behind the stench of sulfur and decay.

"Reg, you need to end my vacation. Please, let me take her."

He folded his arms, the bones clattering together, and shook his head.

The flashing lights and sirens outside slowed until we were bathed in blue alone, and the sound paused. The room was still. Quiet. Other than the grunt Reg made. "Behave yourself."

Tiny motes of light formed in the parlor, more and more winking into being until the room glittered like the heavens. They pushed aside the lingering smells of the Pit, replacing it with lavender and vanilla, sea breezes and new-fallen snow. The Archangel of Death coalesced out of the light and knelt next to my fallen lover.

The tightness in my chest gave way to a peace so overwhelming I smiled. I tried to contain it—it was an insult to Danielle's death—but Azrael's presence was too great.

Tall and slender, she wore ivory robes shot with gold under gleaming silver scale armor. Her brilliant-white wings matched her hair, contrasting with her skin, which was as dark as midnight. She flapped the wings once, sending the motes circling around the room, and stretched out to occupy the space.

"Ellis." Her voice—laced with bells and whispers and sighs—floated on the air, so beautiful it made my skin prickle. I'd never seen her while I was on vacation, and it was awe-inspiring. "Her contract."

I took deep breaths, trying to fight her influence over me, but I wasn't strong enough. I pulled Danielle's contract from the ether, its golden script flashing across the page as though inked by a flaming pen.

"And your permission."

Her contract still belonged to me, and no one else could take her. If I refused, she'd be doomed to walk the Earth, lost and searching for a home for eternity. As much as I didn't want to let another take her, I couldn't condemn her to that. I swallowed hard and whispered, "Be good to her. Take her soul for me."

The parchment appeared above Azrael's hand, and she leaned down to whisper to what remained of the woman I loved. But Danielle wasn't dead yet. Her life force flowed through me, like a loose thread hanging off a shirt I could tug at—barely there, but I could still sense it. I tried to step forward, but Reg's hand shot out to block me.

"We Bonded," I whispered.

"I know." His voice was as quiet as mine, with a hint of... regret? Pity? As much as Reapers didn't experience emotions, Reg was often on the brink. As one of the first of our kind, he'd reaped for millennia before learning that control.

Azrael's whispers filled the space. No distinct words, but a gentle hum wrapping me up, trying to weave the loose thread back in. Her wings moved, blocking my view of Danielle.

Let me see her. Maybe she'd look for me. Would her soul remember?

The white door appeared, flung open, the Stairs beyond.

I gasped and fell to my knees, heart leaping so strongly in my chest I could feel its pulse through my entire body. *Thank you, thank you, thank you!* In two short weeks, we'd lifted her up from damnation to paradise. To paradise! And all it took was—was—but she was still alive.

"Please, Reg. Let me go?"

"No."

I cleared the tears from my eyes. Tears of sorrow for losing her mingled with tears of joy for this wondrous moment. The love of my life had been blessed by the Archangel of Death herself!

Maybe I wouldn't lose her. I could retire and go up the Stairs with her. I could, couldn't I? Would they allow that after a mortal Bonded with an immortal?

Azrael nodded twice, and the contract disintegrated. Blew away into nothing. What was going on? She stood and tucked her wings along her spine as a streak of white and gold slammed into the floor next to Danielle.

What was he doing here?

Raguel straightened, the corner of his mouth already curled. He shot me a cursory glance before looking at the bodies. His golden wings spread wide, nudging Danielle's fallen form. "She's ready?"

Ready? Ready for what?

I clung to Reg's cloak, rising slowly. "Reg? What's happening?"

The door vanished.

No! They were going to call the Gray Hallway. Leave her to wait.

"Azra—"

Reg clamped a hand over my mouth. "Quiet."

"There's been a change of plans, Raguel." Azrael's musical voice held no apology in it, just a fact. "The Fates have canceled her death contract."

What?

"No. She's mine!" Raguel's wings ruffled, as they had when I'd challenged his authority in the Becketts' house. "They wrote her contract! Her mortal life is supposed to be over."

"I understand this, but sometimes they change their—"

"You have thousands of Reapers! My Furies have diminished every century! I need her!"

Fury? I surged forward, but Reg hauled me back. Danielle was a Fury? She was an immortal?

"It is not her time." Was Azrael saying Danielle would live? "She Bonded with one of my Reapers—"

"Let me guess!" Raguel's wings shot out as he spun to face me, jostling the shimmering in the air, sending it swirling about the room. "Couldn't keep your little scythe to yourself, could you?"

"She's my—" Before I said another word, Raguel was a foot away from me, wingtip at my throat.

"You don't deserve her," he growled.

But for once, I knew he was wrong. I *did* deserve her, the happiness, and the Bond. "She's my soulmate."

"Let him go." Azrael's voice switched from harps and bells to a deep, rattling bass, as she wove her wing around Raguel's. The comfort she inspired vanished, replaced by an aura which raised the hairs on my neck. Reg remained still, even his cloak calm. If these two fought, Reg and I would be nothing more than collateral damage.

"You had to insert your little self into the equation, collector, didn't you? Your pathetic warning almost ruined everything. I've been cleaning up your messes for the last two weeks!" His sickly sweet scent came over me as he leaned closer. "You make a mockery of Order."

"Raguel, leave him be!" Azrael nudged him back, stepping between us.

"She was supposed to be asleep upstairs when they broke in. Called Alexander in a panic, then found the room, the check, and the signature with him. Despite your interference, she passed every test we put in front of her." He turned to look at the fallen bodies. "She was supposed to start her new job today."

This whole time, Raguel hadn't been after me. He told her about the drive inside the knight, ensured I knew about Chris Beckett and Hayden Younge so I could tell her, stopped me before I could take the revenge. It all made sense. He was after *her*. Alex was testing *her*.

"The Fates have chosen, Raguel. We must abide." Azrael raised her arms. The glittering light which had preceded her—which Raguel had been stirring up with his rage—traveled toward Danielle's form, bearing her limp body into the air. Her loose clothes whipped about her, hair flailing all around, blood still marring her cheek and shirt.

"Instead of the greatness she could have achieved..." Raguel stepped back, pointing at me and folding his wings along his spine. "She'll waste her choice on you."

Then it dawned on me. Each new Fury was given the same choice a Reaper was at death: take on the mantle or pass to the afterlife. Calling the private investigators, searching for the source of the strange money and the signature. Raguel had been influencing her, testing her, but everything had been her choice.

Just as I'd told her happiness was her choice.

The light grew, extending toward me, tugging at me, pulling me into the parlor. Her floating body straightened, and her eyes opened. My heart fluttered, seeing her face again. Maybe I hadn't lost her.

She reached for me, and I took her hand, peace and strength flowing between the two of us. Love. Adoration. Eternity.

"Ellis." Azrael's musical voice surrounded me like the light, everything else falling away into nothing. "For over seven hundred years, I've watched you devote yourself to saving souls who were destined for the Gray Hallway. Your training time has lifted up countless more. I'm proud of the work you've done with Danielle, reminding her of the goodness inside of her, despite the other elements working against it."

I could have been wrong, but that almost sounded like a criticism of Raguel's actions. I whispered, "It was the best assignment I've ever had."

Danielle smiled, the light shimmering across her skin and through her hair. She was the ten most wonderful things in the world, but more importantly, she was my truth—I wasn't a monster.

"The Fates have never chosen to Bond two immortals of different types before." Azrael wrapped her wings around us. "Neither has the Bond ever sparked as completely as yours while one of the two was still alive. I can feel the energy flowing between the two of you, which it shouldn't be able to."

"And her death contract?"

"I simply weigh souls. Those who choose when to snip the thread of life have changed their minds." Azrael gestured to Danielle. "Your turn, child."

Dani's hand pulled back slightly, and her gaze fell. The light set her down on the ground, so she stood before me. "Ellis, I've been given another extension to my life, and I don't want to spend it alone."

"Due to these strange circumstances, I have an offer for you, Ellis." A soft smile spread across Azrael's face. "Your kind used to reap while under the influence of human needs and emotions. I can let you attempt that, if you wish."

Raguel's wings flew out, whipping the air around us. "What?"

My free hand flew to my chest, and I swallowed hard. "End my vacation, but keep the emotions?"

Danielle nodded, speaking hesitantly. "I know it's a lot to ask, but I'm really hoping—"

"Yes!" I grabbed her and pulled her body to me, wrapping her up in my arms. "A million times over, yes!"

She laughed, a shiver running the length of her, and I pulled back to gaze upon my soulmate. My living, breathing soulmate.

"Danielle Edmonds, I would live a thousand vacations to be with you."

A flash of gold neared me, the wingtip heading for my throat again, but it stopped short. As one, still in our embrace, Danielle and I turned to face the Archangel of Justice.

"My choice"—her voice was firm—"is Ellis."

Raguel's face flushed red. "You have a duty, girl."

She held me tighter, warmth emanating from her. For a human, she was surprisingly in control while facing an archangel, even more so than I would have been. Two weeks since she learned about my world, and now she stood in front of him with confidence.

His wingtip slowly receded as his eyes widened, locked on Danielle's. Then he smiled. "Good."

Suddenly, he crouched, and with a tremendous flap of his wings, shot away in a blur.

"Good?" I asked.

Danielle met my surely confused gaze. "To talking more about it later."

No one had said that. What just happened?

"Now that we've settled everything..." Azrael tucked her wings behind herself and joined us. "Reg will help you transition, Ellis, as he worked with the emotions for a long time before we changed the rules. I'll visit occasionally to evaluate your condition, and I expect you'll see a great deal of Raguel. Hopefully, we'll figure this out within the next decade or so."

The light fell away from Danielle, and she was again the beautiful young woman I'd been with on the beach. Wearing her little T-shirt and shorts, her chestnut hair windswept and only slightly matted from the blood. But now she was more. Not just my Pair, but we knew she was an immortal—at least, would be once she died for real.

We would have time together. No cold, no lingering death, no fear for her life. Us. Together.

Azrael flapped her powerful wings, which took up more space than the parlor had available, and vanished. The glimmering motes blanketing the room faded, and it was just the three of us. Plus, Michael's body.

With the archangels gone, the lights outside resumed their alternating blue and red, and the sirens wailed. Voices could be heard, officers, people, barking dogs.

Reg stalked toward us, still carrying his scythe. The white pinpricks in his eyes flared to red flame as he faced Danielle. "Be good to him, or you'll answer to me, human."

"I will." She tucked an arm around him. "And I didn't get a chance to thank you for healing me last weekend. So, thanks."

His shoulders sagged. "You're not afraid of me?"

"Reg, I've seen all of Ellis's memories of you. You're a good friend." She leaned her head against his cloak. "And you taught him to bake. I really appreciate that one."

Had he been human—or, knowing Reg, had he worn a face at that moment—he would have scowled at her. Instead, he vanished in a whirlwind of darkness.

"Time to deal with the police again." I moved outside to retrieve Byte, who whimpered when I picked him up. Back inside, he resumed growling at Michael's body.

But Danielle stood frozen, staring at the corpse and the blood soaking the carpet. Without Azrael's calming presence, the gravity of the moment must have been sinking in. She touched the wound on her head, shuddered, and gripped the blood-splattered shirt she wore. "Oh my god, Ellis. Ellis?"

"Focus on me, Danielle." I tucked Byte against my shoulder with one hand and lifted her face to mine. Not a flinch from the cold, thank the powers that be.

"He was my uncle." She trembled, clutching my hand. "He didn't want anyone dead, he said. All the stuff I did..."

I pulled her close, lowering my voice to a whisper. "Chris tried to kill you twice, Dani. Neil did something to your father's car, planning to kill him. And Michael just tried to kill us both. Remember what I said about intentions?"

She blinked at her tears and kept her eyes on mine.

"We need a cover story for the police."

The longer we remained in contact, looking at each other, the more her breath and body steadied. The Bond was still fresh, but it carried an unmistakable power. She nodded slowly, picking up speed, then finally broke from me to kneel on the floor by the laptop. It had tumbled far enough away from Michael's body that she could keep her back to him.

She started it and handed me the miniature drive. "You hide that, and I'll get rid of any trace I ran it on this machine."

I tossed the drive into the air, tucking it into my invisible pocket. "We'll tell them he snuck in with the gun. Considering someone else did the same two weeks ago, that should work."

"I wrestled for the gun with him and accidentally shot him." She worked frantically on the keyboard, pausing to take a long breath and touch the cut on her head. "Self-defense. Not a lie."

"And then, as long as Chris stays in jail..." I knelt in front of her as she closed the laptop, sharing her warm air, leaning my forehead against hers. Byte licked both our faces. "Sweetheart, you're safe."

"We. We're safe." She kissed me, holding her lips against mine, and we breathed. "And together."

CHAPTER 43

DANIELLE

Tuesday morning, I moved the French toast around the pan, impatient for it to brown. How much longer would this take? After all the waiting and doing nothing for two years, it was like I was finally awake. Ready to act. Do something.

Instead, all I could do was wait.

The floorboards creaked, and I spun to see a rumpled Reaper.

"Hey, sleepyhead!" I'd been warned to go slowly with him at first, so instead of running and jumping into his arms, I dipped another piece of bread in the egg mixture. "You're finally up."

Ellis ran his fingers through his hair, as though he didn't have infinite control over his appearance. He let out a long yawn and shook his head. "I... I slept?"

"Yeah." I leaned against the counter, giving him whatever time and space he needed. "For a day and a half. Less time than I needed after Reg healed me."

He yawned again and stretched his arms, showing off his remarkable body. All the muscle, the smooth skin, and the low-slung pajama pants. Far yummier than the French toast would be. "I shouldn't have needed healing though."

"Azrael said the circumstances were strange." I shrugged, waving the spatula toward the front of his pants. "Very human morning reaction you've got there though."

He glanced down, swiping a hand over his tented pants. "Interesting."

"Very." I chuckled and took the finished toast from the pan and put fresh slices in. "You're not actually human now, are you?"

"I'm still hungry, like one." He winked at me, resuming his trek into the kitchen. His eyes glittered with golden flames, and he extended his hand to the side, an ancient scythe forming in a swirl of black smoke. "But definitely still a Reaper."

I swallowed hard and adjusted my stance, heat flashing between my legs.

"Still breathing." The scythe vanished, and he wrapped his arms around me. "And my heart is still pounding every time I see you."

The electric jolt from his touch crackled over my skin, bringing every cell to life. "I don't think I'll ever tire of that feeling."

"Me either."

My lips lifted to his and we kissed for the first time as a Bonded Pair—the ones while I was in shock or after he finished yawning through our police statements didn't count. This time, it held all the promise of whatever future the Fates had given us.

"Do we need to finish breakfast first?"

"Patience. We have time."

"Did you add cinnamon to the eggs?" He stepped behind me, pressing his chest against my back and grinding his hard cock against my ass.

"I did."

He plucked the spatula from my hand and nestled his head over my shoulder, prodding at the bread. "Did I miss anything while I was out?"

I swayed against him, my hands running down the sides of his thighs. This was so much better than when he was cold. "A lot. I had a nice chat with Raguel."

"Nice chat?" He snorted. "I wouldn't have thought him capable of that."

"Did you know Alex was a Fury?"

"I did." He kissed the side of my head before flipping the toast. "And now that we know you are, I'm surprised I didn't recognize the signs. The way crooked things bother you, how skilled you are at chess and programming—both very logical and strategic. Or how you just *knew* something else had happened with the crash and couldn't rest until justice was done—although I suspect Raguel and Alex had a hand in that."

"It was an interview, apparently. Alex's job was to punish Chris, Neil, and Mike for their roles in the crash, and they figured it was the perfect opportunity to test me." I pulled his free hand around my waist. "You said the spark of immortality is like a genetic mutation? How far in advance do they know someone's a candidate?"

He shook his head. "I don't know. I'm only aware once the contract comes to me. If someone's destined for the Pit, they won't receive the job offer, but otherwise, their contract will say Reaper or Fury or what have you, rather than Blessed or Undetermined."

I twisted so I could see the side of his face. "But you showed me my contract. It said Undetermined, not Fury."

"Good point." He frowned at me before moving the cooked toast to the serving plate and shutting off the burner. "I have a feeling no one's going to share the full story with us, either. Not yet, at least."

"Maybe I can get it out of Alex."

"Alex?" His lip curled. Was he still jealous?

"He's going to be training me."

Ellis stepped back and spun me to face him. "While you're still human?"

"Apparently."

His gaze wandered off toward the parlor, where our lives had gotten even more confusing than they'd already been. "I would have followed you up the Stairs, you know."

"Azrael didn't make that sound like an option."

His brows pinched and he turned to look at me. "She wouldn't have let me retire?"

"It was more that she strongly encouraged me to choose life." I gave a little shrug, just as lost over the decisions and offers of angels as he seemed.

Ellis stared down the long series of rooms from the kitchen. The parlor's blood-stained rug was gone, as were the remnants of the dining table he'd shattered. Was he reliving that night? Reviewing every second, every choice, every moment where things could have gone differently?

Each time the memories had crept in while he was sleeping, I'd gone upstairs, crawled into the bed next to him, and just breathed. Even asleep, he'd been my strength.

Time to do the same for him.

I skimmed my hands up his chest, settling them over his heart. "Abby came over to check on me yesterday. Chris has been charged with the break-and-enter and a bunch of other things. He and Wanda had been having marital problems for several years, and Abby thinks her mom's considering it almost a blessing they finally found out about his second life."

"Good." Ellis nodded absently. "How are your memories doing?"

"Settling down." Although that was only comparatively. It was difficult sifting through which were mine and which were Ellis's sometimes. "Anya and Katrina stopped by to help me with some exercises. They said they experienced the same confusion when they Bonded, but since they were both immortal, it hadn't been as overwhelming. It's helped."

"Your father loved you very much, you know?"

"Yeah." I put my knuckles under his jaw to return his focus to me. "I went searching through memories of his reaping to find out if he'd given any hints about what happened."

"I would have told you if he had."

"I know." I rubbed my thumb across the scar by his eye. "But I managed to zero in on the moment he told you he chose the Pit."

"It was out of love." A sad smile crossed his face, and he brushed his fingers through my hair. "He spoke of how much he cared for all of you and said he'd rather spend fifty years in Hell to ensure his soul was ready to accept that all over again, rather than risking that one year in Heaven wouldn't."

"That decision kinda earns the White Stairs all on its own, doesn't it?"

"The soul knows what it needs." He separated from me and pulled my hands to his lips. "Just as our souls knew even more deeply than the Fates or the angels did."

"The soul remembers," I said, quoting his favorite line from *The Count of Monte Cristo*. "I love you, Ellis Grimm."

"And I love you, too, Danielle Edmonds." He kissed my forehead and flashed a devilish grin at me. "Now, can we take care of this ridiculous human condition I have going on?"

I stepped closer and wrapped his arms around me, so we could travel together. "Let's skip the stairs."

Epilogue

ALEX

The crowd flowed around my little table, hundreds of people descending on the small market. Fruits and vegetables to my left, meats and poultry to my right, jewelers, bakers, leather workers, and dozens of other farmers and artisans filled the space.

I gripped the coffee cup in front of me, keeping up the ruse that I was nothing but a customer. Meanwhile, I reached out with my mind, prodding at the souls surrounding me. Throw down the coffee, he slips, his apples fall, two other people jostle out of the way, four are distracted, sixteen end up five to ten minutes late leaving.

Go deeper. I stretched, feeling for the bigger ripples. For the man who'd miss his bus and his job interview. He'd suffer for a few weeks before landing the better job. That was his reward for volunteering at the children's hospital for five years.

I tipped my coffee onto the floor. "Sorry!"

The man passing me slipped on it. Apples went flying, but they slowed too quickly, one rising in its bounce and hanging in the air. The rest of the shoppers, the sales staff, and a man doing magic tricks for the kids upstairs all stopped. The voices and music quieted.

Bad timing.

I looked up.

The white and gold streak slammed to the ground next to me. Had Raguel been solid, he would have crushed three of the apples.

"Morning, boss."

He frowned deeply. "What are you doing?"

"Those apples." I gestured around his feet. "They're supposed to cause the next ripple, but right now they're—"

"I didn't mean literally." He pulled out the chair across from me, nudging one of the time-frozen humans back a foot, and sat. "It's been a month since Neil McEwan's death already. I need you back in New York City."

"Braiden has it covered." Was that his name? Or was it Caiden?

"His name is Aiden." Raguel plucked one of the apples from the floor, raising it a foot. Of course. It would bounce farther that way. "He's supposed to be working here, not covering for your little pity party. He's too new to handle all the variables there."

Him and me, both.

I pointed to the apple he'd moved. "I can't even get that right."

"Get over it. You work in probabilities, not certainties."

"A man died because of a ripple I didn't see coming. I didn't even see it as a possibility. You said I could have time in a smaller population to recoup and realign my powers."

"A man died because the Fates drew up his contract. The only reason Danielle Edmonds wound up in the equation—which is what you're really feeling bad about—was because her little Reaper manipulated things. Immortal disturbances are near impossible to navigate."

"Maybe involving her in an assignment that was so personal was a mistake."

He glowered at me. Of course. Archangels didn't make mistakes. "This is why I need you back in the city. She needs a mentor, in case she manifests too many powers without learning how to remain impartial."

"Why does she need a mentor? Last I heard, she was still human."

"She is. The Fates stepped in and canceled her contract before her thread could be cut." He leaned closer, lowering his immense voice. That was a first. "I think Fortuna and her Fates are up to something. Danielle and her pet Reaper formed a Bond. That's never happened between two different types of immortals before."

The Fates and their leader were more powerful than the rest of us. If they had grander plans, didn't that mean it was the way things were supposed to be? I reached out, trying to feel for the rightness in his words. It was always more difficult when an angel was present, since I wasn't attuned to the speed of their existence.

Nothing.

I scanned the room visually, knowing full well if a Fate was listening in, I couldn't see them. At least Raguel could, so hopefully, there was no one eavesdropping. "You remember that night in Times Square, when she was stabbed?"

"Yes."

"Something was off in the Balance. I felt the wrongness in the air, but I was too focused on another job to follow it."

"You think someone else was involved?" His eyes narrowed. "Someone's pulling strings I'm not aware of?"

"And then there was her contract. Ellis showed it to me, but it said she was Damned instead of saying she was a Fury." I'd almost revealed everything to Ellis at that moment. Impartiality was one of a Fury's most important skills, but not with each other. We protected and watched out for our kind, and I'd started doing that with Danielle too early. "She was angry when I met her, but it didn't warrant that. And any of the work she did for us should have received a pass, so that's not it."

"I never saw her contract. It had already been destroyed when I arrived. Azrael said the Fates did it." His gaze rose to the ceiling and back to me. "How long are you going to be here?"

I swiveled in my chair and pointed to a woman standing behind a display case full of cakes, chocolates, and confections. She wore a black chef's jacket with a high collar and had tied her light-brown hair with auburn highlights up in a knot. "The chocolatier, the man in the booth next to her, and"—I shifted to point behind Raguel—"the man working the crepe cart over there. One will have a reward, and the other two will have punishments. I'm working out the details on how and I'll be back after that."

"Don't be long. Danielle's already exhibiting powers." He stood and pushed the chair in. "She sent me a message telepathically just after Azrael promised her more life."

My head jerked back, and the same wrongness invaded my cells as at Times Square that night. "Telepathy isn't a Fury power."

His frown returned. "I know."

THE END

BONUS EPILOGUE: Soon after the adventures of this book, Danielle and Ellis will tie the knot in a special ceremony. Where do you think they'll hold it? Who'll be there? Big ceremony or small one? Best man? Maid of Honor? Visit the link below to find out!

Join Janet's author newsletter and get
Dani & Ellis's wedding, behind-the-scenes details,
and updates on the next Reaper's Grace books at
https://janetoppedisano.com/newsletter_reaper/

Acknowledgements

Writing this book has been an intensely personal journey for me. I'll spare you the long tales of my journey through depression and how I arrived at a place of joy, but suffice to say, there's a lot of me in several aspects of both Danielle's and Ellis's personalities.

To my husband and son, thank you. For excusing me from hockey duties while I was under deadline, for making sure every game is streamed, and for being so understanding of the time I spend in the writing cave.

To my beta readers: Paula, Pat, Bethany, Liv, both Kates, Rose, Kim, and Sera. Thank you for all the comments you gave, your insights, and for harassing me for two years to publish the book!

Thanks to the Georgia Romance Writers, who selected this as their Best Paranormal Romance of 2021 in the Prepublished category!

Many thanks to my editors: To Miranda Darrow for pushing me to dig down deep and build up my Reaperverse; and to Brandi Aquino for ensuring the words were polished.

And finally, I'd like to thank you, my dear reader. I hope you enjoyed the roller coaster, the ups and downs, and I can't wait to share more of this story universe with you.

About Author

Janet Oppedisano hails from Canada's East Coast and has lived in five provinces, from the Maritimes to the Prairies. Growing up with a Mountie for a father and marrying a Navy diver, it's no surprise she writes romance with a hint of danger and mystery in it. Not to mention strong heroes and equally strong heroines.

Prior to publishing her debut novel, she won awards for two of her unpublished works, including the Romance Writers of America's 2021 Vivian Award for Most Anticipated Romance, for *Burning Caine*.

When not writing, you can find her... thinking about writing. And indulging in her favorite pastimes, like baking, traveling, hiking, playing with her dog, and watching her hockey goalie son on the ice.

Oh, and it's pronounced oh-ped-ih-SAH-no. Exactly the way it's spelled. Honest!

You can find Janet and all her social media profiles at:
https://janetoppedisano.com

www.ingramcontent.com/pod-product-compliance
Lightning Source LLC
Chambersburg PA
CBHW051314190726
48290CB00001B/143